The Green Lama:
UNBOUND

by: Adam Lance Garcia

The Green Lama:
Unbound
by: Adam Lance Garcia

First printing 2015
ISBN: 978-1-936814-89-3

Cover Art: Mike Fyles

Edited by: Tommy Hancock

Prepress: Lewis Chapman

Published by Moonstone Entertainment Publishing, Inc.
1128 S. State Street, Lockport, IL 60441

Published by Moonstone, 1128 S. State Street, Lockport, IL 60441.

The Green Lama:
UNBOUND

UNBOUND by Adam Lance Garcia

For Ilena George.
For every way she made this book better, she made me better.
And for that, I will always be grateful.

PART 1: THE MADNESS FROM THE SEA

Chapter 1
FAR AND AWAY

1923

*W*hy have you come?" *the Tulku whispered, his accent heavy, the long white wisps of his beard flowing over his green robes, his bald head gleaming.*

"The King Regent, sent me here—I came... searching for—for... purpose," the young American said, his teeth chattering. He shivered on the temple floor, his lips blue, his furs still coated with snow.

The boy was so young, the Tulku thought, but then again, despite appearances to the contrary, the Tulku had grown quite old over the last few centuries. He tilted his head as he regarded the young man in the golden light of a thousand candles. "Purpose? I have come to understand that Americans have no need of such things."

The young man bowed his head. "I have no want of money, fame, or excess. But of purpose, I am impoverished. My father had only one vision: wealth. He wanted me to work toward that end, to fulfill the destiny he had prescribed for me. But I want more... More than money could ever give me... I want purpose. I want to know my destiny."

"Destiny?" The Tulku raised an eyebrow, toying with the six-color braided ring on his right middle finger. "There is no destiny except for the karma you have created for yourself, with body, speech, and mind. Om! We are here to strive for enlightenment, for the benefit of all sentient beings. We are not here to hand out destinies to wayward Americans."

The young man nodded in sober understanding. A clump of melting snow fell off his head onto the temple floor: "Please, Tulku, I have traveled so far and endured so much..."

The Tulku stood, pulled his green robe tighter around his body and walked past the other lamas, silent in meditation, to the kneeling American. "What is your name, young one?"

"Jethro. Jethro Dumont."

The Tulku raised his chin. "Son of John Pierre Dumont, yes?"

Dumont nodded. "Yes, Tulku."

The Tulku pulled at his beard in consideration. "I am Geshe Tsarong, Khenpo of the Temple of the Clouds, as you well know. Mr. Dumont, I do not doubt your intent, but we must meditate on your request for admission. Come back in three days' time and we will tell you our decision," he said as he turned away.

Tears began to pool in Dumont's eyes. Desperate, he grabbed at the Tulku's right hand. "Please…"

There was a burst of emerald light as the Tulku's rainbow-colored ring suddenly unraveled, ripping open his skin, and shot through the air. "Om! Ma-ni Pad-me Hum!" the Tulku screamed in pain as blood poured from the wound, spilling onto the floor. The other lamas jumped to their feet, murmuring mantras as they watched in amazement.

"Oh God! Oh God! What—What is happening?" Jethro shouted as the ring wound itself around his finger, glowing green.

"It seems, Mr. Dumont…" Tsarong breathed, cradling his arm, "that Destiny has found you."

1939

Tsarong raced down the hall, ignoring the throbbing arthritic pain that radiated from his joints. The moon was high, sending streams of blue light through the windows to pool on the floor. Despite the chill of the night, sweat dripped down his forehead and into his eyes. He had seen and experienced terrible things in his many years that even Jethro Dumont, the Green Lama, could never begin to fathom. But now, for the first time, he felt the cold grip of terror seize at his throat. He had prayed that this day would never come, but ever since that day in the Temple of the Clouds sixteen years ago, he knew the prophecies were true.

The sunken city was rising.

Rounding a corner, he made his way into the apartment's massive study to find Jethro still awake at his desk, half hidden behind a mountain of books. It had been weeks since Jethro had slept, or so it seemed. Since his battle with Nazi Field Marshal von Kultz atop the Brooklyn Bridge, Tsarong had watched helplessly as Jethro worked without pause in a vain attempt to translate the second Jade Tablet. Tsarong wanted to believe Jethro's obsession was solely due to his desire to understand the artifact, but Tsarong knew his friend better than that. Jethro wasn't trying to learn—he was trying to forget, to ignore the absence of the woman named Jean Farrell.

However, all that was about to change.

"Tulku," Tsarong said, breathing heavily.

Jethro, sensing Tsarong's urgency, pulled himself away from his books. Deep pockets sat below his bloodshot and glassy eyes, his skin unnaturally pale.

Tsarong hesitated, shocked by his friend's deterioration. "The Tablet," he said finally. "Tulku... Something's happening."

Jethro threw open the doors to one of the many hidden rooms in his sprawling Park Avenue apartment. Every cell in his body, already pushed beyond the limits of exhaustion, shook with anticipation. The room was small, little more than a walk-in closet, lined with ornate silk tangkas Jethro had kept from his time at the Temple of the Clouds. The second Jade Tablet sat on a short stanchion in the center. Covered in ancient, almost alien hieroglyphics, the Tablet appeared to be at most an insignificant archeological relic, the sort one would find in a poorly lit corner of the Natural History Museum. But beneath that simple carved exterior lay power that Jethro was only now beginning to comprehend. Its power radiated out in a cold green light, thrumming like a heartbeat, threatening to explode. He could feel it even now, a sensation reminding him of that horrible day aboard the *Bartlett* and the demons he faced.

"I heard the sound only moments ago," Tsarong said. "I thought it might have been a trapped bird, until I saw—"

"Something triggered it," Jethro said quietly as he approached the glowing stone.

Whereas the original Tablet—the braided ring of rainbow-colored hair Jethro wore on his right middle finger—had only given him the ingredients to his radioactive salts, this new Tablet had not only breathed life into the inert, but had also granted its previous owner a horrifying glimpse of the future. But until now, it had refused to reveal any of its powers to Jethro.

Extending his hand, Jethro let it be engulfed by the emerald light. The hairs on his arm stood on end and he could feel the air crackle with electricity, flowing through his skin and into his veins, as intoxicating as it was painful. He found himself drawn forward, closing his eyes as he was completely enveloped by the light. For an instant, he felt as though he were underwater, floating away with the tide.

And then it all came rushing down upon him.

"*Tayata om muni muni maha munaye soha,*" he whispered as his eyes shot open, glowing green.

Blurry and muddled visions filled his mind. The past, present, and future, he saw it all at once but could not discern one from the other; weapons beyond measure, creatures of unimaginable horror, incalculable death. He saw the heavens ripped asunder, old enemies reborn, and a lost world recovered. He met a man with black eyes and a crimson scar, felt a jade bullet pierce his heart, and took an odyssey of redemption. He watched the sky aflame, the world at war and a new century turn.

He saw Jean, the only woman to ever come close to holding his heart.

He heard the gunshot, like thunder.

He felt the bullet rip through her leg as if it was his own.

He screamed, as she had not.

He whispered: "*Nyarlathotep Ul'pra! Iä! Iä! Nroac shrnek! Ph'nglui mglw'nafh Cthulhu R'lyeh wgah'nagl fhtagn!*"

Jethro shut his eyes and crumpled to the ground, the light from the Tablet suddenly diminished, the world once again falling into silence. Smoke wafted off his shoulders, his head pounding.

Tsarong ran up beside him. "Tulku!"

His eyes still shut, Jethro gripped Tsarong's sleeve.

"*Om!*" Jethro rasped, his voice hoarse. "Jean… *Om! Tare Tuttare Ture Soha* … Jean's in trouble."

Jean Farrell was on the run.

Mud caked her high boots and khakis; her fiery red hair hung wet and limp across her face. Shivering in the shadows of a dilapidated house, she clutched her shiv—a narrow shard of glass with an improvised handle of wrapped twine—like a crucifix. She could hear the dogs in the distance, knowing without a doubt that she was their quarry. Lightning shattered the sky, an instance of daylight. Thunder rolled and the downpour grew heavier, bullets of water shooting from the sky.

She had been in Greece only three days before everything had gone straight to hell. *Murder.* How in the blue blazes could she have been accused of murder? She wasn't even certain why she had traveled all the way here in the first place. She had told Ken she needed time away after their experiences with the golem, the creatures from the *Bartlett*, and that whole mess atop the Brooklyn Bridge. Privately, she argued she was trying to ignore her growing, and ever-confusing, feelings for Jethro Dumont, but even then she knew she was lying. It was a calling, like a buzzing in the back of her head, drawing her here, to the small port town of Kamariotissa on the island of Samothrace. Of course, had she known that she would be framed for killing the mayor with an axe to the head, she would have ignored the feeling outright and gone somewhere less dangerous… like a mob den.

Lord, how she missed the Green Lama.

A warm hand pressed against her shoulder, startling her. She bit back a scream, but couldn't stop herself from swinging her shiv at her apparent assailant.

"Easy there," Aïas Prometeo breathed as he caught Jean's arm. "It's just me." A full head taller than she, he was bigger than even Lieutenant Caraway. His accent was slight but noticeable, though Jean couldn't place it. He wasn't American, and despite the name she could tell he definitely wasn't Greek. Like Jean, he was soaked, his matte black hair bunched into wet clumps. His unshaven visage was brutish but handsome; his eyes the deepest black, constantly moving, never focusing on anything in front of him. Jean doubted she could trust him, but had it not been for him, she would still be in jail, condemned to the gallows.

"Don't ever sneak up on me," she whispered, pulling her arm free. "I could have killed you."

Aïas chuckled silently. "Unlikely."

"There's confidence. Don't forget that I am accused of killing your mayor. Most boys would consider that impressive."

"Even if that were the case, that is no axe," he said, indicating her shiv before gesturing out into the storm. "There is an abandoned station house over the hill. It does not look like anyone has been there for a long time, so we might be able to hide there for the night."

"This place isn't up to snuff?" she asked, indicating the ramshackle building beside them.

Aïas shook his head. "There's barely a roof. We will probably drown in there with all the rain. Plus, you said you needed to get in touch with your friends back in New York, yes? There might be a phone, or at least a telegraph."

Jean sucked her teeth. He had a point; things had gone belly up and the sooner she could get in touch with the Green Lama—or at a minimum, that rich playboy Jethro Dumont—the better. But something about this plan didn't sit right with her. "And what about our four-legged friends and their buddies with the guns? They'll definitely catch a glimpse of us running off into the horizon."

"You really think they are going to keep searching in this?" he waved his hand to the sky. "They can barely see two steps in front them and the rain will cover our scent. Come," he said, turning to leave. "Before they get any closer."

"Remind me again why I should trust you?"

He looked back and shrugged. "You shouldn't, but then again… They haven't caught us yet, have they?" he asked, before disappearing back into the rain.

Jean hesitated, wondering, not for the first time, why Aïas had been arrested. A man that big could do some serious damage and for all the skills Jean possessed, she wouldn't be able to fight him off easily. Not that she wouldn't make him hurt. If he had any special plans when they got to the station house, he had another thing coming.

As she stepped forward, there was a sudden crack of thunder and Jean felt a sharp pain in her right leg. Glancing down, she saw blood seeping out of a small wound in her calf, mixing with the rain.

Oh, she thought, collapsing into the mud. She reached down to touch the wound, her leg throbbing. The bullet had gone straight through the muscle and out the other side, missing the bone. But that didn't stop the pain, or the blood. Beneath the din of the pouring rain, she heard a dog's bark and a policeman's cries as they ran toward her, their footfalls splashing against the muck.

"Aïas!" she shouted as she ripped off the edge of her sleeve to fashion an impromptu tourniquet, no longer concerned that the police would hear her. "Dammit! Aïas!"

Click!

Jean looked up behind her to find a pistol barrel staring down at her. "Βάλτε τα χέρια σας στο κεφάλι σας!" the Greek policeman yelled, while the leashed dog growled ferociously.

"Aw, hell," she said through gritted teeth, quickly slipping the shiv beneath her remaining sleeve, and cupping her hand to keep it in place.

"Βάλτε τα χέρια σας στο κεφάλι σας!" the policeman shouted, pontificating each word with a thrust of his pistol.

"I don't understand a lick of what you're saying, buddy, but I can probably guess."

The policeman grabbed her by the collar and harshly pulled her off the ground, yelling, "Ηλίθια αμερικανική πόρνη!"

"Yeah, yeah. Like I said…" With subtle grace she cocked her wrist, loosing the shiv in her palm. She grabbed the policeman's arm with her free hand, squeezing down and quickly twisting the gun away while she stabbed him in the shoulder with her handcrafted blade. The officer hollered in pain, releasing Jean and falling back as he tried to remove the shiv, dragging the dog with him. Despite her injury, Jean dove to the ground, grabbed the pistol and smacked it across the officer's head, knocking him unconscious. "I can't understand you."

"Jean!" Aïas shouted as he ran back over to her. "I heard a gunshot, are you—" His eyes went wide at the scene before him. "—okay?"

"Yeah, fine. Thanks for the help," she added sardonically.

"You're bleeding."

"This? Buddy, I've fought monsters and mobsters. This—this is nothing…" she trailed off as she fainted to the ground.

Lieutenant John Caraway awoke to a ringing phone and a splitting headache. *Too much wine*, he thought, gripping his temples. *Far too much wine.*

Francesca shifted beside him. After so many months apart, he was still unaccustomed to waking and finding her lying next to him, but he wasn't complaining. She had grown older and softer over the years but he still loved her shape. He ran his hands over hips that would break a younger man's heart and allowed himself a crooked, self-satisfied smile. She had shown up so suddenly, walking into his office after she had sworn she'd never speak to him again. Things had moved quickly from there. That was their cycle, off and on, round and round, a carousel made for two. Maybe this time—

She pulled the blanket over her head and grumbled, "If that's the office, tell them it's your anniversary and your wife is going to kill you. And I will, too."

Caraway glanced at the clock as he swung his feet off the bed. It wasn't even four in the morning, which must be some sort of record. His lower back popped as he stood, reminding Caraway that his days as a beat cop were a long way behind him. "Technically, sweetheart, our anniversary was months ago," he said as he stumbled toward the unremitting phone, the icy floor biting at his feet. "You remember, fifteenth of June, nineteen thirty? You wore a white dress as a joke."

Francesca buried her head beneath the pillow. "Just answer the damn phone!" she shouted, her voice muffled.

Rubbing his eyes, he picked up the receiver and muttered, "This better be good."

"*Om! Ma-ni Pad-me Hum!*" the strong yet soft-spoken voice echoed through the phone line.

Caraway sighed. "Jesus. Do you sleep, Lama? I mean, ever?" Normally, he wouldn't mind hearing from the Green Lama, but then again, Francesca wasn't normally sleeping in his bed and he wasn't normally this hung over. "And how in the hell did you get my home number?"

"I beg your pardon for waking you, Lieutenant, but your assistance is needed."

"Who is it?" Francesca murmured through the pillow.

"Just the Green Lama, sweetness. Go back to sleep," Caraway said over his shoulder. "You're gonna get me killed here, Lama."

"Again, my apologies," the Green Lama said, sounding less than sincere, "but time is of the essence."

Caraway glanced mournfully over to Francesca. They never got a break, did they? "What is it this time? Did someone take out the Italian consulate now?"

"Please meet me at Three-fifty Fifth Avenue, hundred-and-second floor, in one hour. I would recommend bringing some travel clothes," the Green Lama said without responding to Caraway's question.

"Three-fifty Fifth Avenue," Caraway repeated as he jotted down the address on a piece of scrap paper. It wasn't until he read it over that he realized where he was going. "Wait. You want me to go where and bring what?"

The Green Lama's reply was the audible *click* of the phone disengaging.

Caraway took another sip of coffee, watching the numbers increase as he rode the elevator up to the 102nd floor of the Empire State Building. His arm was still smarting from the bruise Francesca had given him as he left the apartment. She didn't scream. Hell, she didn't even speak. Just socked him on the shoulder and gave him the "you're-in-trouble" look, which he found more frightening than the rampaging golem he had faced several months back.

The elevator bell rang and the doors slid open. Shifting the small duffel over his shoulder, he walked out onto the 102nd floor, the wind howling and dawn light hinting morning on the horizon. It had been a little over four years since he last set foot in this building, a hundred story firefight against the terrorist group known as the Medusa Council. His knees ached at the memory.

A lone man stood waiting on the observation deck, nursing a cup of coffee as he watched the sunrise. He had a handsome face, blond hair and a chiseled chin. He was the sort they painted on movie posters with titles like *His Lady Luck* or *Distant Dreamers*. The women swooned and the men rolled their eyes, but there was no denying the fact that he was the kind of man that would forever have his name in lights. His wrinkled suit matched the black pockets and red rims around his movie-star blue eyes, the smell of alcohol floating around him like a cloud. Wherever he had come from, it had been a lot of fun.

"Morning, Ken."

Ken Clayton raised his cup as Caraway approached. "John. Let me guess," he said, his words slightly slurred. "Green Lama?"

Caraway shrugged, as if there were any other answer. "He call you too?"

"Something like that." Ken shrugged. "I was at this amazing party until I found a little note at the bottom of my drink telling me to get here," he said, swirling his finger over the cardboard cup. "Told me to pack a bag too, but I... uh... I forgot." He gave Caraway a sheepish smile. "I'm not even sure how the hell he did that, putting the note at the bottom of my drink. How do you think he did that?"

Caraway sighed. "Wish I knew, buddy. I've known the guy a few years now.... Well, as best as one can know a 'masked vigilante' and I'm not sure how he does half the crap I've seen him do."

"Radioactive salts," Ken said matter-of-factly, topping it off with an affirmative nod. He held one hand over his cup, moving his fingers as if he were sprinkling sugar into his coffee. "He puts it in his water and drinks it. Makes him strong. He's even got a special batch that can make him fly."

"Heal people too," Caraway added, tapping his chest with the knuckle of his thumb.

Ken gave Caraway a sideways glance. "Oh, yeah, I remember that, the golem almost killed you."

"Thanks for the reminder. You know, I was there, right?"

Ken shrugged. "I'm so hung over right now, let's just be impressed I'm standing up, okay?"

Caraway grunted a laugh. "Hell, I'm pretty sure I would've died a dozen times if it weren't for that Buddhist bastard. Every time I think I'm done, he appears out of the shadows. *Lama ex Machina.*" He sipped thoughtfully at his coffee. "Aren't you supposed to be in the army?"

Ken looked out toward the sunrise, his inebriated grin shrinking. He looked thinner than Caraway remembered, his eyes a bit more guarded, sadder. "Honorably discharged," he admitted after a moment.

"Couldn't keep up?" Caraway chided.

"Wasn't meant to be," Ken replied mournfully with a distant look Caraway recognized as heartbreak. "Time to step back into the real world." He waved his hand at the horizon. "If you could call this reality. So it's back to the stage." He paused to clear his throat. "Just landed the lead role in the new Broadway show *On Your Toes*."

"Can I ask you something that's been bugging me for a few years now?" Caraway asked after a period of weighted silence. "No offense or nothing, but why does the Green Lama have an actor working with him?"

Ken shrugged. "Hell if I know. Jean and I met the guy on a ship from Los Angeles and for whatever reason we just jumped at the chance to help him. Hell, the first time I ever spoke to him, he was hiding in a baggage room. Who in their right mind would listen to a guy hiding in a baggage room?" Ken sighed as he rubbed his eyes. "What time is it?"

Caraway checked his watch. "Five minutes to five in the morning."

"Christ on a cross!" he exclaimed, massaging his eyes. "I wonder if Gary and Evangl ever had to deal with this sort of crap too."

"*Om! Ma-ni Pad-me Hum!*"

"Speak of the devil," Caraway murmured as they turned to find the Green Lama standing solemnly behind them. For all they knew he could have been there for several minutes, listening to their whole conversation, which, Caraway silently admitted, wasn't all that surprising.

"Lieutenant Caraway, Mr. Clayton," the Green Lama said in greeting, his voice strained and hoarse. Caraway couldn't help but notice that the Green Lama's face, though shadowed by his large hood, appeared almost Native American, noticeably different from his more Caucasian appearance several weeks prior, which itself was a change from the Asian man he had seen a few days before that. Most striking, however, were the deep pockets seated beneath the Green Lama's blazing eyes.

Ken raised his coffee in a mock toast. "Lama."

"Thank you both for coming here on such short notice and at such an early hour."

"Could we get right to the point?" Caraway said testily. "I've got a wife at my apartment seriously considering a return to single life, so can we get this over with quickly?"

The Green Lama gave him a terse nod in acknowledgment. "Mr. Clayton, you will recall at the conclusion of our recent exploits with the golem the discovery of a second Jade Tablet."

"How could I forget?" Ken sighed.

"As of two hours ago, the Tablet, just as it did for Rabbi Brickman, revealed to me a glimpse of the future. And while these visions were unclear…" the Green Lama grimaced. He closed his eyes, as if he were trying to replay the visions in his mind. "I believe that the delicate order of this realm has indeed been thrown off balance and that we are at the forefront of a great upheaval, somehow tied directly to the entity known as Cthulhu."

"Aw, great," Caraway grumbled. "You're getting us involved in some apocalypse-type business aren't you? "

The Green Lama tilted his head and considered Caraway. "No," he said after a moment. "Not if we stop it."

Ken took a sip of his coffee. "There's a non-committal answer if I ever heard one."

Caraway ran his hand over his face. "If you were another man, Lama, I would tell you to shove it where the sun don't shine."

The Green Lama gave him a small nod and smiled. "Thank you, Lieutenant."

"And where will this apocalypse be going down? New Jersey?" Caraway asked.

The Green Lama hesitated before simply saying, "Greece."

As if on cue, Caraway heard the roar of a propeller engine approaching. Looking out over the cityscape, he saw a massive dirigible heading toward the Empire State Building. It had been years since anyone attempted to use the building as a mooring mast, but leave it to the Green Lama to disregard safety and logic.

"I have arranged transport for you," the Green Lama said over the wind and motors. "Mr. Masters is an excellent pilot and he will ensure you arrive quickly and safely."

"You're not goin' with us?" Caraway hollered as a mechanized gangway extended from the dirigible.

"I have business to attend to here before I can make the journey. Our mutual acquaintance Jethro Dumont will accompany you in my stead."

Caraway spun around to face the Green Lama. "You roped *Jethro* into this? Shouldn't he be sipping cocktails at the Stork Club?"

"You have got to be kidding me!" Ken shouted, exasperated. "You know, I am the lead in *On Your Toes*, and while I can't speak for the Lieutenant here, I can't just go gallivanting around country-to-country like some whip cracking pulp hero! I helped you out during that whole to-do

Tsarong retorted. "I will guide him through his journey, show him the path, but I will never reveal to him his destination. That he must find on his own, if he is truly destined to..." he trailed off as he turned to an image of a lone hooded figure standing before a horrific squid-faced chimera. Tsarong shivered as he regarded the long asleep creature.

"If we are blessed, he will be this age's savior," Magga said. "Its Bodhisattva."

"And if we are not?" Tsarong asked.

"Then darkness will fall."

"Good morning," Aïas said as he noisily spooned soup out of a wooden bowl.

Jean's eyes struggled to open, the sunlight blinding. She was lying on a rock-hard cot, a thin, coarse blanket wrapped tightly around her body. "God, what time is it?"

Aïas squinted as he glanced out the window. "Maybe two or three in the afternoon. There is no clock here. But you... You have slept like the dead."

"I feel like someone took a steam shovel to my head," she grumbled, rubbing her temple with the heels of her hand as she sat up. "How long have I been out?"

"Two days."

Jean pulled off the blanket and found her right leg wrapped in a neat bandage. There were small spots of deep crimson on either end despite binding. She flexed her foot, feeling the muscles throb in sync with her head. "Two days?" she reiterated.

"You slept like a rock," he said while he ate, gesticulating with his spoon, yet never meeting her gaze. "Do not worry about your leg. It should heal well, I think, though it might scar. Lucky for you the police here are terrible shots. If this was Athens you would be dead. Sparta is worse. They shoot to kill. You should see what they did to me down by Olympus."

Jean pushed herself off her bed, testing her leg, grimacing at the sharp pain that shot up to her lower back. She moaned through gritted teeth as she limped over to the table and eased herself into the chair.

"See?" he said. "Back on your feet already."

Jean cocked a skeptical eyebrow at him. "What are you eating?"

"Chicken soup… Well, chicken in hot water. There were a few wandering around outside. Still have plenty more if you are hungry," Aïas said, sliding over a small wooden bowl and spoon.

Jean grabbed the bowl and hobbled to the small stove in the corner of the room. She ladled a few scoops of grey liquid from the old dented pot into her bowl and tried not to grimace at the smell. "Mm," she said. "Definitely not a cook, huh?"

"Not at all," Aïas shrugged. "Been in and out of jail for most of my life. This is the best you are going to get from me."

"Career criminal, huh?"

"Just petty thievery. I am kind of like, what is it you call him? Robs from the rich, gives to the poor?"

"Robin Hood," Jean said, trying not to gag as she forced down some of the stew.

Aïas, however, had no trouble swallowing another spoonful. "Right. Him." He leaned back and gazed up at the ceiling. "You, though, are far more impressive," Aïas said. "Killing the mayor is not something to sneeze at. That is the saying, yes?"

Jean pushed her bowl away, unable to finish. "Sorry to burst your bubble, but the only thing I had to do with Mayor Astrapios was turning down his idea of a 'private party.' So, despite what they might have said, I didn't kill him."

Aïas chuckled and shrugged. "And I did not steal his most precious possession. See? We are both innocent."

Jean cocked an eyebrow, unconsciously recalling the large cracked crystal egg in Astrapios's bedroom. "So, that's what you were in for? Stole the mayor's 'most precious possession'?"

Aïas gave her a quizzical look. "I am pretty certain I just said that I *did not*."

Jean laughed. She wasn't certain if she liked this guy or wanted to kill him. Either way, he was no Green Lama. "So… what's the plan, Stan?"

"Run. Hide." He shrugged, returning to his stew. "Do not get caught."

"Where are we going?"

"We?" He squinted his eyebrows. "That is a little… what is the word? Presumptuous. I stayed around to make sure you did not die. Owed you that much. Now you are on your own."

Jean shrugged. "Fine by me, buddy. Much as I appreciate the bandages, you are totally useless in a fight. Guy your size should be throwing people around, not running away."

"They had guns."

"Please. What kind of criminal are you?"

Aïas thumped his chest. "The living kind."

Jean leaned forward, proudly indicating herself with her thumb. "I ran into a room full of heavily armed mobsters with only a pistol and a guy who likes to dress up in green robes. I didn't blink."

"You Americans have such strange interests."

"We're a unique breed." Jean shrugged. "Speaking of breeds, where's that accent from? Based on the way you don't use contractions, English is definitely not your first language."

Aïas smiled. "It is a very old accent." He lifted up his bowl and slurped up the last of his soup. "You say you are innocent of killing Astrapios, yes?"

Jean raised an impatient eyebrow in reply.

"I will make you a deal," he said, tapping the table. "There is an item I have hidden. It is very dear to me and now that I am free I would very much like to have it again. But I cannot get to it alone. If you were to, say, help me retrieve it, I would help you find Astrapios's killer."

Jean pursed her lips. "As long as you promise it wasn't you," she said, crossing her arms. It had already occurred to her that there was a chance that Aïas was involved in Astrapios's murder, and while she didn't trust him, she knew if it weren't for him she would be at the gallows by now.

Aïas shrugged. "Even if I did, would you believe me?"

The corner of Jean's lips curled. He had a point. "Probably not."

Aïas stared at her for a moment before he reached into his pocket and placed the policeman's pistol on the table. "Then there is no debate, is it not so?" he asked, sliding the gun over to her.

Jean easily caught the pistol, her forefinger instinctually slipping next to the trigger. She glanced down at the chamber and saw five bullets remaining. Her eyebrows cocked. "Guess not. It's not like I have many options at this point, do I?"

"It will not be easy," he warned.

"Never is, but if you can clear my name, I'll take the chance." She extended a hand. "Partners?"

Aïas gave her a broad smile and shook her hand. "Partners."

Jethro walked through the airship. Outside the wind howled, an unearthly tone that sounded like whispers, the floor moving ever so slightly with each step. Caraway had found the swaying relaxing, a reminder of the days when he flew against the Kaiser, while Ken had locked himself in the bathroom for most of the flight. And though his mind was elsewhere, Jethro had taken the opportunity to spend some time talking with Caraway, whom he had considered a friend long before he became the Green Lama. But there was still a distance, an unspoken demarcation, between them. As the Green Lama, he and Caraway had shared many adventures and had gained a tremendous amount of mutual respect. But Caraway would always look at Jethro with a suspicious eye, a distrust that pervaded every conversation, as if Caraway were waiting for Jethro to confess a truth they both knew was sitting right in front of them.

That was perhaps the hardest part about the path Jethro had chosen. No matter how close Jethro felt to his companions—especially Jean—he could never truly be himself around any of them. He would always be set apart, an island in the ocean.

Which was why he decided make this visit to the pilot's cabin.

"Hello, Rick," he said as he entered.

Rick Masters half-turned back to face Jethro, but didn't take his focus off the airship controls. Rick was a well-built man in his late thirties, only now beginning to go soft. The slight bump in his gut hinted an increasing reliance on alcohol, and the half bottle of whiskey stashed below the controls confirmed it. "Hey, Jethro. If that's what you're callin' yourself today."

Jethro had met Rick before his return to America, shortly before he had decided to keep his identity as the Green Lama a secret, making him one of the very few people to know the truth.

"Just Jethro today."

Rick nodded as he worked the controls. "We should be in Kamariotissa soon. Have to admit, buddy, wasn't really expecting to hear from you ever again. It's been what… five years since that whole mess in Tibet?"

"Six," Jethro said as he sat down in the co-pilot chair.

"You mind tellin' me what your plans are all the way out on this side of the pond? Not that it's really any of my concern, mind you, but based on the last time you used my services—"

"To help a friend," Jethro said, refusing to elaborate.

Rick grunted in understanding. "Good thing you don't have to deal with that psychopath…" Rick searched for the name in the recesses of his memory before it finally made its way to his tongue, "Hayden ever again."

"Heydrich," Jethro corrected, closing his eyes, remembering the insane Nazi sorcerer and his quest for the Jade Tablet, feeling the mad life he had taken all those years ago weigh down upon him. "Your business seems to be doing well. Are you still working with Twin Eagle?"

"Yup. He would've come along but he's out west dealing with his own stuff. Family, I think. He wouldn't say. You look like crap," he added.

Jethro smiled ruefully at that. "I feel like it, too."

"Well, at least you're self aware," Rick said. He then glanced over at Jethro for a moment. "Some of those adventurer-types, I've seen them run halfway across the world, talking big and getting themselves and their friends killed without batting an eye. Kinda like how you were back in the day. Though you don't seem as tightly strung as I remember."

"I've been through a lot," Jethro replied simply.

"Yeah, I've read a little about you over the years," Rick said as he turned away. "Seems like you've been busy. You and that guy who lives in the Empire State Building. Now, *he's* wound *really* tight."

Jethro chuckled. "I know what you mean. I was his root guru for a time while he was studying in Tibet. His heart is in the right place, though I don't agree with some of his tactics."

"Buddy, I generally don't agree with any tactic that can get me killed."

Jethro leaned back into the chair, unsure how to respond, his mind once again drifting back to Jean. They had known each other for over two years, but she had only come to know Jethro Dumont recently. To her, Jethro was just another face from the tabloids, drunk off his family's wealth, giving nothing to the world beyond celebrity gossip. She didn't look at him the way she looked at the Green Lama, a fact that made him impossibly jealous of *himself.* It was partially why he had chosen to keep that persona in America for the time being.

He watched the clouds drift outside, like waves on the ocean and, out in the distance, a dark wall in the sky.

Jethro leaned forward. "What's that?"

Rick peered through the window. "Looks like a storm, but there wasn't anything on the meteorological charts. Not to worry, it's pretty far from us so we'll be able to get around it."

As Rick turned the wheel to guide the dirigible away from the storm, Jethro watched as the massive cloud began to shift toward them.

Jethro stood out of his chair. "It's moving," he said. He could feel electricity pulse through his system, as though the radioactive salts in his body were reacting to something in the air. He watched in horror as tentacles seemed to grow from the cloud wall, extending out and reaching toward the airship.

Rick's eyes went wide. "Okay, that's not supposed to happen."

Jethro Dumont, a thousand voices whispered, resonating from the back of Jethro's skull, *we see you*. He gripped his head and stumbled back, grabbing onto the back of a chair to regain his footing. He *knew* that voice, but from where?

"Something has been thrown off balance…" Jethro breathed.

"You're not kiddin'," Rick said, oblivious to the voice. He picked up a small headset and turned on the loudspeaker. "Hey everyone, this is your captain speaking. We're about to hit a pretty big, uh, storm, so if you can find something to strap yourself in with, that might be a good idea." He hung up the speaker and turned to Jethro, panic visible in his eyes. "Okay, I'm not gonna lie to you, this might be bad."

They watched the cloud tendril enveloped them, the cabin shuddering from the sudden gust of wind. Large droplets of rain began smattering against the windshield, lightning arched across the sky.

The door to the cabin burst open as Caraway stormed in. "Are we going to explode? I don't want to explode."

"No, no, no… Well…" Rick frowned. "If lightning hits the hydrogen, then yeah, we could go Hindenburg."

"Goddammit," Caraway grumbled. "See, Jethro, this is the kind of stuff I was bitchin' about."

"How close are we to Kamariotissa?" Jethro asked Rick.

"Technically speaking? We're practically on top of it."

"Can we land?" Caraway asked.

"Land?" Rick scoffed. "Lemme put it this way. I'm focusing on trying to keep her *off* the ground."

"We have to get down there, Rick," Jethro said.

"I'm gonna be honest with you, Jethro. I haven't exactly finished paying this airship off. I'm not going to risk trying navigating it through a storm like this. I'm sorry, but right now the only way you guys are getting down there is if one of you could fly."

Jethro felt his eyebrow shoot up.

"I'm going to go on record by saying this is a bad, bad, very bad idea," Caraway shouted over the roar of the wind as they climbed down into the cargo hold. They ran toward the far end where, hooked into the ceiling over an empty expanse of air, was Rick's modified bi-plane, the name *M. Lawrence* emblazoned on the side.

Jethro pulled three parachutes off the side of the hold and tossed one each to Ken and Caraway. "Not the time for doubt, John," Jethro said as he fastened on his own chute.

"Guys, guys… listen," Ken said, clutching his chute, his face a sickly green. "I'm—I'm with Caraway on this. I think—think we should just stay on the airship."

Jethro shook his head. "The Green Lama was explicit," he said, reflecting on how accustomed he had become to referring to himself in the third person. "Jean's in trouble and we need to get to her as quickly as possible. We may already be too late. Rick should be able to make it out of the storm safely, but if we don't go now, we might not be able to get to Kamariotissa for another day, maybe more."

"Not that I love the idea of weathering the storm up here, but how do we even know that's where she is?" Caraway hollered.

Thunder cracked outside and lightning flashed, illuminating the cargo hold for an instant.

"The Green Lama told us that's where she would be," Jethro replied.

"And the Lama's never wrong?" Caraway asked incredulously. Jethro silently turned to *M. Lawrence*, knowing Caraway had a point. But Caraway wasn't finished. "Listen, Dumont, you're still new to this adventuring stuff," he said, stepping in front of Jethro, "so let me bring you up to speed. It's *already* been two days since the Lama sent us out. That's two days' worth of running, two days' worth of hiding. For all we know Jean's miles away from here, sunning herself on a beach in Italy."

There was another flash of lightning, followed by a deafening explosion that rocked the airship and threw the trio off their feet.

"Lightning just took out our left propeller," Rick said over the loudspeaker. "If you're gonna get going, you'd better do it now."

"Well," Caraway said, resigned. "That settled that argument. Out of the way, rich boy. Of the three of us, I'm the only one who flew with Eddie Rickenbacker."

Jethro picked up the hold's transceiver and called up to the pilot's cabin. "Rick, are you sure you'll be all right?"

"Been through a lot worse than this, buddy," Rick responded via intercom. "I'll be fine, just promise me you'll pay me back for all this."

"Promise," Jethro said as he hung up the transmitter. Climbing into the modified biplane, Jethro allowed himself some regret at having rescued only one vial of his radioactive salts, leaving his enhanced radioactive salts onboard. "Come on, Ken, we haven't much time."

Ken gave him a weak nod, but his feet remained nailed to the floor.

Jethro gingerly touched Ken's shoulder. "Mr. Clayton…"

"I know," he said hurriedly, careful not to look Jethro in the eye. "I just… Help me up there, would you?"

"Of course," Jethro said calmly. As he helped Ken climb up, Jethro suddenly realized that while Ken had fearlessly fought against crooks, had even faced down the supernatural, of all things, he was afraid of flying.

"I'm not gonna lie to you fellas," Caraway said as he strapped himself into the pilot's seat, "it's been a few years since I've flown."

"We're not worried about the flying, right now, John. Just the landing," Jethro said, climbing into his seat.

"Oh, we are going to die," Ken whispered behind them.

The engine began to rattle and the propeller spun into a circular blur. Lightning flashed and thunder roared. Jethro noticed the airship was beginning to turn listlessly to the left. Caraway paused as he reached up to the latch that would disconnect the plane from the airship.

"Hey, Jethro," Caraway said, swallowing the lump in his throat.
"Yes?"

He glanced back over his shoulder at Jethro. "You Buddhists, you believe in God, right?"

Jethro nodded sideways. "Tricky question."

"Okay," Caraway nodded slowly, visibly discomforted by Jethro's response.

"Why do you ask?"

"'Cause I would start praying really hard right about now," Caraway said as he snapped open the latch, sending the plane into free fall.

They spun into the darkness, rain hitting them from all directions, soaking them instantly. The world around them had grown black, the sun a distant memory while lightning flashed about them. Above them, save for the flaming propeller, Rick's airship was completely lost in the black cloud, like Jonah within the whale. Jethro felt the pit of his stomach shift upward; his body was on fire, energy bursting through every pore. Clutching the handholds on the sides of his seat, he closed his eyes and whispered, "*Om! Ma-ni Pad-me Hum!*"

"OH GOD!" Ken hollered, covering his eyes.

"Hold on!" Caraway shouted through gritted teeth.

"We have to get out of this storm!" Jethro shouted to Caraway.

"No shit!" Caraway bellowed as he struggled with the controls.

They barreled downwards, the wind and rain rushing past in the darkness, flashes of lightning giving fleeting glimpses of the tempest surrounding them. The plane was thrown wildly by the turbulence, threatening to catapult them from their seats. Just when it seemed there would be no end to the nightmare, they suddenly burst through the cloud cover into clear blue skies. They could still see the mass of dark cloud above them, but, impossibly, not a drop of rain fell upon them.

"We're dead," Ken whimpered in the seat behind them. "Oh, God. We're dead, aren't we?"

"Tell that boy to shut the hell up!" Caraway called back as he steadied the plane.

Below them the island of Samothrace looked like a malachite crystal, shimmering in the pyrite sea. A small diamond of red and white buildings sat along the western coast, glinting in the sunlight. Kamariotissa.

Jethro turned in his seat to look up at the storm, the cloud pulsating like a giant black worm in the sky. Rick's airship was still hidden within; only the faint orange glow of the flaming propeller could be seen.

"I think there's a clearing over there where we might able to land," Caraway said, indicating a flat section of land near the port town. "It'll be bumpy, but we should get there in relatively one piece… I think."

Jethro felt his heart jump into his throat as he watched the cloud suddenly pull away from the airship, and impossibly, began turning toward them. The airship was heavily damaged, but still flying; Jethro could see Rick in the cockpit, working the controls. As the cloud extended toward them, Jethro once again heard the otherworldly voice echo out from the back of his skull.

We see you, Jethro Dumont, the voices said, laughing. *We see you, Green Lama.*

Fighting back panic, Jethro spun around and tapped Caraway on the shoulder. "Fly faster, John!"

Ken lifted his head up and ventured a glance back behind them. His eyes went wide and whatever color he had left drained from his face. "Oh no, no, no!" He shook his head violently as he watched the cloud speed toward them.

"What is he yammering about?" Caraway said.

"Don't look, just fly!" Jethro screamed.

Ignoring Jethro's plea, Caraway craned his head around, his jaw dropping at the sight. He unconsciously stiffened his arms, throwing the wheel forward and sending the bi-plane into a nosedive. "The storm is chasing us!" he cried. "Why is the storm chasing us?"

"Pull up! Pull up!" Jethro shouted, falling into his seat when Caraway complied.

"How in God's name are we going to outrun a goddamn storm?" Caraway shouted.

"It wants me…" Jethro whispered as he watched the smoky mass snake after them. He knew they couldn't outrun it for long, and there was no assurance that if they landed it wouldn't follow them down. There had to be a way to stop it, he was certain. But how?

"You boys have any ideas back there?" Caraway demanded as he swung the plane into a sharp turn. "'Cause I'm open to suggestions!"

Jethro suddenly remembered the airship's propeller. "John, how far up are we?"

Caraway looked over the dashboard. "Uh, about three thousand feet."

"Good. I need your gun!"

"My gun?" Caraway grumbled as he pulled his pistol out of its holster and handed it back to Jethro. "You'd better have a damn good plan, Dumont!"

"Just trust me on this," Jethro said as he climbed out of his seat and onto the wings.

"Jethro, what are you doing?" Ken shrilled.

Gripping onto one of the struts, Jethro positioned himself by the fuselage, the propeller roaring beside him. "Do you have your parachutes on?" he shouted to the others.

"Yes," Caraway said.

"Uh… Maybe," Ken murmured.

"I need you to jump," Jethro said matter-of-factly, ignoring their dumbstruck looks. "Once you're clear I'm going to blow up the plane."

Caraway slammed his palm against the wheel. "I *knew* this was a bad idea!" He glanced back at the chasing storm, deciding Jethro's was the best idea they would get. "Dammit. Fine. What about you?"

Jethro shook his head. "Don't worry about me. I'll jump clear before it blows. Quickly! We don't have much time."

Ken whimpered under his breath, but couldn't pry himself loose from his seat.

"Ken, you need to jump!" Jethro yelled. "Jump now!"

Fighting every fiber in his being, Ken slowly swung his legs over the edge of the plane and tightly shut his eyes. "I'm beginning to hate adventures." He took a deep breath, but failed to take the leap.

"No time for cold feet, kid," Caraway said as he shoved Ken off into the air, the young man screaming as he fell to Earth.

"Don't worry, he'll open the chute in time. The plane should stay aloft for a few moments before it starts going down. Don't wait too long, Dumont," Caraway said as he climbed out of his seat. He glanced back at the storm one last time. "Remind me to sock the Lama in the face when we get home."

"You might get the chance sooner than you think," Jethro said pleasantly, as if they were chatting over a couple of drinks.

Caraway allowed himself a sardonic grin. "Here's hoping. See ya soon, Dumont," he said before leaping out of the plane.

Jethro watched as his friends fell clear and opened their parachutes. Thankfully, the living storm failed to follow them, which meant his suspicions were confirmed. It wanted him. Without Caraway in the pilot's seat the plane began to slow and tip toward the ground, giving Jethro the sense of free fall. He waited until the storm was upon him, rain and lightning shooting from all angles. He kicked off the cap, gasoline spilling out into the air in long tendrils. *"Om! Ma-ni Pad-me Hum!"* he chanted as he pressed the pistol against the fuselage.

We see you, Green Lama, the voices echoed around him, a cacophony of sound. A tremor echoed inside Jethro's mind, at last recognizing the voices. They were the creatures from the *Bartlett,* who had killed so many in their hunt to kidnap Jean, their "Keystone." And here they were, once again unfettered upon the world.

"See this," Jethro growled as he fired, the heat of the blast singeing the edges of his suit as the *M. Lawrence* exploded around him.

Chapter 3
THE DIPLOMATS

*Y*ou're not wearing your green robes anymore, Tulku," Dumont said as Tsarong entered his room. The American was seated cross-legged on the floor, nearly unrecognizable in his red and orange robes. His shaved pate shone in the cold mountain light.

"They are no longer mine to wear," Tsarong said with a slight nod, tugging his blue vestment closer to his body. "It is chilly in here, no?" he asked.

Dumont glanced at the open window overlooking the jagged white and purple expanse of the Himalayas. "I've never seen anything like it before. They remind me how small I really am."

Tsarong knelt down beside Dumont and the two men stared out into the distance in silence. It was almost an hour before Dumont spoke again.

"We are but pebbles on the shore," Dumont sighed.

"Hm?"

"Oh. It's just—We'd been sitting here awhile… Thought someone should say something that sounded profound."

Tsarong chuckled. "Pebbles on the shore. Ah, yes, I must remember that."

"Have you ever been to New York City, Tulku?"

"No. And I doubt I ever will," Tsarong said.

Dumont slowly nodded in consideration before he continued. "It's an awful city. Full of so much decadence; one can become lost in his own hubris. You see, back home, in the mountains of brick I was a giant, magical and mysterious, almost a god if I wanted to be. But here, looking out onto these mountains, I truly know where I stand. I am a man, nothing more, simple and solid all the way through."

Tsarong hoped his face did not betray him. How little the young man understood of his destiny, of what he really was. "The Buddha said that the *joys and sorrows of beings all come from their actions, their past lives; from their karma. Your karma brought you your wealth just as it brought you here. You are more than flesh, Jethro, far from simple and solid. You are the accumulation of dozens, maybe even hundreds of lives," he said.*

Dumont raised his eyebrows in approval. "Yeah, that was sufficiently profound."

Tsarong smiled before he noticed Dumont idly playing with the Jade Tablet. "Any discomfort?" he asked.

Dumont glanced down at his hands, once again consciously aware of the rainbow ring of hair tied into his right middle finger. "No," he said quietly. "Just not used to it. I gave up trying to get rid of it."

"Yes, I heard there was quite a bit of blood."

A rueful smile cracked Dumont's face. "Yes. Quite a bit. There are symbols on it, in the fibers. Did you ever notice that?"

Tsarong nodded. "Would you like to learn how you remove it?" he asked in response.

"Yes."

"Then there is more blood to spill."

Pain echoed through Jean's leg, each step more excruciating than the last. As far she could tell they had been running for six hours straight. Aïas wouldn't let them stop moving for more than a few minutes at a time, pushing them further out into the wilderness where the only lights were the pinpricks of starlight in the sky.

"I need to slow up a bit," Jean shouted to Aïas a few yards ahead of her.

"No time," Aïas said, refusing to look back.

"I gotta wonder if you're leading me into a trap," Jean said, pointedly drawing her pistol. "Hate to burst your bubble, buddy, but I'm a good Montana girl and I *don't* go down that easily."

"Do you normally pull guns on men you are working with?" he asked without looking back.

Jean cocked the pistol's hammer. "Only men I don't trust. What's your game, mister?"

Aïas shook his head. "No game. We made a deal. Keep your end and I will keep mine." He gestured at the gun and added, "If you do not kill me first. Come, we need to get over this ridge before the moon gets too high. Hurry up."

"Tell that to my leg," Jean said with a grimace as she pocketed her gun. Something tickled her nose, a strange smell she couldn't identify.

"The slower we go the more likely we are to get caught. Samothrace is a small island, with very little in the way of forest and caves. Not many places to hide. Learn to walk or stay behind," Aïas said. "I will take care of it when we stop."

"Which will be when?"

"Later."

"You could at least *pretend* to care," Jean grumbled under her breath as she climbed over a half-rotted tree. Her foot got caught on a branch, twisting her leg and tossing her to the muddy ground, ripping open the wound. She screamed as blood began to spill.

Aïas sighed as he slowly turned to face Jean. "What is it now?" he asked sharply.

"I—I think I, oh God, I think I br—broke it," she whimpered, keeping her eyes shut, unable to look at her leg.

Aïas walked over and carefully lifted her free of the muck. Carrying her over to a small clearing, he unraveled the bloody wrapping and cautiously examined her leg.

"How—How bad?" Jean asked, trying to ignore the overpowering pain as Aïas silently redressed the wound.

"We make camp here," he said as he finished dressing her leg. He stood up and began collecting wood for the fire.

"Here's a joke," Dimitri said as he locked the glass cabinet behind the counter.

"Oh, here we go," Andonis said, burying his face in his hands. He had hired Dimitri several months ago more out of pity than his skill as a salesman—and definitely not for his sense of humor.

"No, listen," Dimitri said earnestly. "This is a good one. Really."

Andonis kept his face buried and groaned in response.

Dimitri held his hands up, setting the scene. "Three men walk into a store—"

"Stop," Andonis said as he uncovered his face and pointed a stern finger at his employee. "You're not telling that joke. Everyone tells that kind of joke. Sometimes it's three men, sometimes it's a horse, but no matter who walks into that bar it's lazy and it isn't funny."

"I heard it the other day from Teodoros," Dimitri whimpered.

"And how does that make it good?"

Dimitri gave Andonis a wide-eyed expression. "It's Teodoros."

Andonis sighed and massaged his eyes. "Will you just go close up the cellar, *please*? I want to get home before the sun rises—or before Anthe kills me, which is much more likely."

"Fine, fine!" Dimitri said as he threw his arms in the air, grumbling to himself as he climbed the stairs down to the cellar. "Man wouldn't know comedy if it bit him in the ass."

"Idiot," Andonis sighed. It had been days since they had made any sort of sale. The economy wasn't as bad as it was in the rest of the world—most people said that was thanks to General Metaxas—but that hadn't stopped Andonis's business from slowly falling into failure. He doubted he could last until the end of the year, let alone the month. But he kept opening the door, hoping for some sort of miracle to walk through so that maybe one night Anthe wouldn't greet him with one of those reproachful looks.

He walked over to the counter and reached for the bottle of ouzo hidden beneath the register when the front door slammed opened, jolting Andonis from his thoughts. Andonis jumped up as three men marched in. He recognized the man in front, but couldn't remember from where. From the way he walked Andonis was certain he was American. He was dressed in an elegant suit, singed at the edges, the shoulders smoldering as though he had just walked through a fire. The other two men looked as if they had just finished riding a tornado. The smaller one in particular looked as though he had been painted green, whereas the taller one seemed to favor his right leg.

"Excuse me, sir," the lead man said in perfect Greek. "I don't mean to impose at such an hour, but perhaps you can help us. My friends and I are traveling and were in a—" he paused, glancing back at his compatriots, who both shrugged noncommittally. "My friends and I were in an accident and have lost our luggage. We would like to purchase some clothing if at all possible."

Andonis idly scratched behind his ear. "Well, I'm sorry, sir, but we're closed for the evening. Perhaps if you come back early tomorrow morning we could—"

The lead man reached into his jacket pocket and brought out a long, slightly burned book and a pen. "Do you take checks?" he asked.

"Excuse me?"

"Checks," the man repeated. "You take checks, of course? These are from my account in Athens…"

"Oh, ah… " Andonis furrowed his brow, considering. "Yes, I suppose."

"Good," the man said, quickly jotting down a number onto the check. He spun it around so Andonis could read it. "Will this cover your overtime and all of our potential purchases?"

Andonis's eyes widened and he felt his jaw slacken. "Yes, sir. Whatever you need."

"Excellent!" the man said, signing the check, tearing it off and handing it to Andonis. "Please get these two men anything they ask for. I will take four of your finest suits, we can get them tailored later, and shoes to match."

"Right away, sir!" Andonis exclaimed, holding the check gingerly as he read the printed name below the signature. "Wait. You're—Wow! You're—"

Jethro Dumont allowed a small smile to crease the corner of his lips. "Yes. I am," he nodded.

"I saw you in a newsreel! You dated—Oh, I forget her name!" Andonis snapped his fingers in frustration. "Bette Davis, right?!"

"Briefly, yes."

"Tell me," Andonis raised an eyebrow. "How was she in the… you know?"

"I try not to dwell on past relationships," Dumont said with a noticeable frown. "I'm sorry, I don't mean to be rude, but if you could take care of my friends, please."

"Oh! Oh! Yes, of course! Dimitri! Dimitri!" he called down the cellar. "Come back up here, we have customers!"

"Pull the other one!" Dimitri shouted.

"Get up here, you idiot!" Andonis barked.

"And, um, sir, can I ask you a few questions?" Dumont quietly said, placing a hand on Andonis's shoulder as he leaned in.

"Oh, of course, sir!"

"Well, firstly, do you have any green hooded robes?"

They had arrived on the docks one night several months ago during one of the worst storms Kamariotissa had seen in over a decade. It was still vivid in Vasili's mind, the black clouds that seemed to soak up the sun and the sky, the rain and the lightning that came at all angles. No one had seen their boat arrive, their clothes soaking wet as if they had walked out of the sea. They hid their faces beneath coral masks; the eyeholes covered in black glass, shaped like a nightmarish idea of what a human should look like. It wasn't just the masks, though. It was the way they walked, as if they were still learning to use their legs, swaying arrhythmically like a broken metronome; and how they talked, or rather didn't, only ever speaking in whispers, breathing their words in long gasps of air. He wasn't even sure if they had names; they were simply known as the Twins.

Whatever you called them, Vasili didn't trust them and were it not for his boss, Alexei—who had been more than happy to work with the Twins from day one—he would have avoided them like the plague. Right now, they stood in the shadows at the front of the meeting house, looking over the gathered mass of townspeople, whispering to each other in their warbling native tongue.

"So, what do you think, Vasili?" Petros asked, slapping Vasili hard on the back. Petros was at least a head shorter than Vasili, his body ropy from years working the docks. He was also deadly fast, able to move in and out of the shadows without a sound. There were at least a dozen unsolved murders that Vasili knew could be attributed to Petros. "You look like crap. Late night, eh? Knocking boots with Sotiria again?" Petros asked as he scratched at his unshaven jaw.

"Bad dreams," Vasili replied.

Petros sucked his teeth, disappointed he was denied any racy details. "Pretty big crowd, eh?"

Vasili looked over the people shifting in their seats and milling in the aisles. Alexei had stationed him and Petros by the front doors, just in case. That was, in effect, Vasili's job; he was always there "*just in case.*" He guessed there were about one hundred, maybe a hundred and fifty people filling up the space by now, a dull roar of conversation echoing up to the rafters. There were familiar faces scattered amongst the seats, but only one stood out: Sotiria, whose amber gaze Vasili could feel raking over his body.

"You know what I think?" Petros said, aggressively tapping his bony fingers against Vasili's arm. "I think they got Astrapios's killer. Yup. They got her. It's gonna be a whole big announcement. You'll see. They'll be hanging her by morning. Swing, swing."

"You actually think the American girl did it, huh?" Vasili asked with a sideways glance.

"Aw, yeah. I mean everyone saw her leaving the place."

"I dunno, Petros, she seemed all right to me."

Petros waved a dismissive hand at Vasili. "Everyone seems 'all right' to you. A Turk could walk in here with a rifle in one hand, a dead Greek baby in the other, and you'd go over to try and shake his hand."

Vasili ignored this. "Still, I doubt, of all things, Alexei would call a meeting to announce an arrest. You know how he felt about Astrapios. Hell, Alexei was practically dancing on the man's grave."

Petros shrugged in concession. "True, true… Wait, you're not saying, that you killed…?" he began, aiming a finger at Vasili.

"And here I thought Alexei made you do it." Vasili smiled bitterly. "Old man probably did it himself and framed the girl, just like he did with that judge back in '34."

"Except I was the one who did the killing and it was the mistress we framed," Petros corrected. Laughing, he nudged Vasili with his elbow. "Though I did get to go a couple of rounds with her before she got the rope."

Vasili bit back a venomous response. Disgusted as he was, ultimately, who was he to judge? Had it not been for Alexei taking him under his wing as a boy, he would've been working the docks, struggling to keep his belly full.

"It's probably about that storm we had this morning, then," Petros ruminated, returning to the topic at hand. "Did you see it? Black as night it was."

Vasili nodded. "We've seen worse," he said. "Speaking of which, your two favorite people are here tonight," he added, indicating the Twins.

"They smell like week-old fish," Petros said, sucking his teeth.

"I figured you'd be used to that by now," Vasili commented.

"They smell like *month*-old fish. Month-old fish that's been sitting out in the sun," he corrected.

Vasili chuckled at that. He didn't like Petros, but he did make him laugh.

A door at the front of the hall burst open, throwing the house into silence. Vasili noticed that even the Twins—twitchy as they were—had ceased their discussion. There was a smattering of unenthusiastic applause as Alexei walked onto the stage, his smile as false as his masked friends' faces. He wore a simple outfit, as he almost always did, his white hair slicked back. He was tall, slim, tanned and well built for his age, his outwardly joyous manner a veil for a violent temper. As sheriff, Alexei was the most powerful man in the small port city after the now deceased mayor, and as corrupt as Alexei was it had always been debatable as to who really ran the show. Vasili had long ago settled that debate for himself.

"My friends, thank you so much for coming on such short notice. It means quite a bit," he said with mock humility. "Now I'm certain you're all wondering why it is I called for this meeting tonight…" He let the word trail into silence. Vasili rolled his eyes. Alexei was forever the showman. "Unfortunately, we have not yet captured our dearly departed mayor's killer, but as our friend Oretis here can attest to, she is not such easy prey." Alexei indicated the wounded policeman in the audience, his shoulder bandaged from his encounter with the American woman. There were a few uncomfortable chuckles around the room. Very few had taken the death of mayor Elefterios Astrapios lightly, but they knew better than to show Alexei otherwise.

"Yes, do not worry, we shall find her soon, mark my word," he said, finger aimed at the heavens. "But that is not why we are here tonight, my friends. No, tonight I am here to tell you of a wonderful opportunity for the citizens of Kamariotissa in these unsure times. As many of you may have noticed, there has been some very unsettling news coming from up north. There's been talk of war; another Great War, in fact. While I can't speak for the rest of Greece, I can say to you now, should war ever come to this continent, it will not find itself at *our* doorstep."

"That's a pretty tall promise," someone shouted from the audience.

Alexei smiled warmly and clasped his hands together. "Indeed it is. Allow me to show you how I intend to keep it." He gestured toward Vasili and Petros. "Gentlemen," he said, "if you would."

Vasili and Petros eyed each other as they turned to open the doors, mystified as to Alexei's plans. Looking out into the dark of night he heard the crowd audibly turn in their seats as twenty men, all of them dressed in matching grey uniforms, marched in tight formation behind a black-collared man in dark grey regalia, a pencil thin mustache lining his upper lip. The black-collared man walked into the meeting hall, arched his back, clapped his booted heels together and shot his right arm forward, palm down.

"Heil Hitler."

Chapter 4
BLOODLETTING

*A*RGGGH!" *Dumont screamed as the blade cut across him, leaving a thin line of blood across his chest.*

Tsarong placed his sword into its sheath as he stepped back. "What did you do wrong?"

"What did I—? You cut me with a goddamn *sword!" Dumont yelled, indicating the chest wound.*

"You attacked in anger, leaving yourself exposed," Tsarong lectured, ignoring Dumont's protests. "When the fire of anger touches you, do not grasp it. Release it like a burning coal lest it burn you. You must let go of your anger."

Dumont grimaced as he sheathed his sword. "I mean no offense, Tulku, but you are not helping your case right now," he said in a huff.

"Buddhism is the middle way," Tsarong said calmly. "We follow a moderate path, avoiding extremes such as asceticism or indulgence, eternalism or nihilism. We must find the balance within ourselves, and burn away the evil inside us that obscures our basic goodness if we are to even the scale."

"'Even the scale?' 'Burn away evil?'" Dumont asked incredulously. "I didn't come here to burn—let alone fight—'evil,' Tulku. I came here to find purpose, to understand my destiny. I came here for peace and all I've found is madness. First, I get bonded to a scary magic ring," he said, waving his ringed right hand, "and now, swordfights! Shouldn't we be sitting around, cross-legged and humming 'Om! Manny padmay hoom'— or whatever it is you're always muttering—instead of slicing me in half? I thought Buddhists are supposed to be peaceful!"

Tsarong placed his hands behind his back as he paced around the edge of the circle. "There is no peace in your heart, Jethro Dumont. You are at war with yourself, with what you are and what you will become. Do not dwell in the past, do not dwell in the future, concentrate the mind on the present moment. You must find equanimity inside yourself if you are to attain enlightenment."

"And how is slicing me open going to achieve that?!"

Tsarong paused and turned to Dumont. "You said you came seeking purpose, did you not?" he asked simply.

"I didn't expect it to be this painful," Dumont replied, visibly deflated.

"Rebirth can often be painful. Close your eyes and calm yourself, find the place of serenity in your mind."

"You promise not cut me again?"

"I promise you will not be harmed," Tsarong replied with a slight nod.

"Okay," Dumont sighed as he closed his eyes.

"Breathe deep. Calm yourself," Tsarong said softly as he began to pace around Dumont.

Dumont exhaled. "I'm calm. I'm calm. I'm calming myself down."

"Breathe in… Breathe out… You will find your windhorse."

"Windhorse? That sounds ridiculous."

"Most people do when they speak English."

"Ha. Ha."

"Find your center. The rest will come."

"You could have just called it 'my point of Zen.'"

"I would, but last I checked, we are not in Japan."

"Pain in my ass…" Jethro grumbled with a crooked gin. He closed his eyes and continued to breathe deeply.

After several minutes of silence, Tsarong said: "How do you feel?"

Dumont breathed deeply. "Calm."

"Good."

There was the soft whistle of steel slicing through the air followed by the clang! of metal striking metal. Dumont opened his eyes to discover he had—in an instant and without thought—unsheathed his blade and deftly blocked Tsarong's sword. Dumont's mouth fell open as his eyes moved back and forth between the blades and the smiling Tulku.

"Holy moley."

"I'll tell you what I think," Vasili said as he slammed his stein down, splattering beer onto the table. "This is bad. This is big time bad. Nazis," he added, spitting to the ground. The bar was filled to the brim with the usual late night clientele, though there was a sense, despite all their merriment, they were trying their best to ignore the assembly at the back of the establishment.

"That's some pretty big talk there, Vasili boy," Petros said, propping his feet up onto the table. "What ya gonna do about it?"

Vasili shrugged, starring at Alexei, the Twins and their goose-stepping compatriots at the other side of the bar. Only four uniformed officials sat at Alexei's table, the rest of the regiment had been sent back to their makeshift camp outside of town. Alexei sat at the center of the inexplicable gathering, acting as both host and jester. To Alexei's right was the man with the pencil thin mustache Vasili had learned was Obergruppenführer Albrecht Gottschalk. Seated besides Gottschalk were his subordinates, none of whose names Vasili had been able to learn: one had hollow cheeks, dented with horrible acne scarring; the second had black balls for eyes and picked at his Van Dyke incessantly as though he was unaccustomed to its presence; the third was a balding man with a terrible scar that stretched from his scalp to his right cheek. The Twins sat silently to Alexei's left, enjoying the spectacle.

"What *can* I do?" Vasili grimaced as he took another swig. "Shut my mouth. Doesn't mean I have to like it."

Petros took a long drag from his cigarette. "Nazis... eh. What's the big deal? All they want is elbow room," he said, flapping his arms like stunted wings. "More room to breathe. Nothing wrong with that."

Vasili shot Petros a withering look. "You remember what happened the last time the Germans got all hot and bothered."

"Please," Petros said, pressing a hand to his chest, wounded. "I'm not *that* old."

"You're not that *young* either."

Petros raised his glass in concession. "And you're too young to worry yourself, Vasili. Do you see Sotiria over there, all alone? She's waiting for you, my friend. Life is too short to let hurt hearts stop you from getting a good fu—"

"Thank you, Petros," Vasili interrupted, fighting the urge to glance over at the fisherwoman. "But I will keep my own council on the matters of my heart and bed."

"Suit yourself," he said, taking another swig of his beer. "Me, I would've let her take a ride a long time ago."

The front door slammed open.

"Bartender! Bartender!" Andonis Needa shouted as he flew in, one arm wrapped around his employee, Dimitri. Both men wore wild grins. Vasili hadn't seen them at the meeting earlier, but that didn't explain their uncharacteristic high spirits.

"We would like a bottle—no!" Dimitri exclaimed as they stumbled up to the bar. "*Two* bottles of your finest, eh… finest…"

"Ouzo!" Andonis interjected. "We would like *two* bottles of your finest ouzo!"

Dmitri's smile broadened. "Two bottles of your finest ouzo."

Andonis tossed twenty drachmas onto the counter. "And make it fast, sir. We are men on a schedule."

The bartender, a bearded brute of a man, huffed as he swiped the coins into his hands, waddling toward the bottles on the other side of the bar before either man had the chance to change his mind.

"Andonis, aren't you supposed be home with Anthe, your tail between your legs?" Petros shouted to the shopkeeper.

"There's only one thing between my legs," Andonis called back, "and I'll tell you what my wife can do with it!"

"Since when did you grow a pair?" Petros said, letting out a sound that was half chuckle and half phlegm-riddled cough.

"Since Jethro Dumont *himself* came into my store!" Andonis announced, slamming his palm proudly against the counter.

Vasili noticed that everyone in the bar, even Alexei, perked up their ears at the mention of one of the world's most scandalous men.

"Jethro Dumont? *The* Jethro Dumont," Petros asked, eyebrow raised in disbelief.

"Yup!" Dmitri interjected. "Not just *any* Jethro Dumont, but the man *himself!* Though I doubt there are many men in this world with a name that ridiculous."

"I heard he was seein' that American actress," Petros said to Andonis and Vasili alike, hoping one would give him the name.

Vasili shrugged. While almost fluent in English, thanks in part to the frequent British travelers that passed through the port, he knew little to nothing of American culture. There was the theater that played old American films—usually two-year-old serials like *Undersea Kingdom*—but Vasili never had any interest in anything from across the Atlantic. He cared about Samothrace and Samothrace alone.

"Bette Davis," Andonis said after a massive swig of ouzo, grimacing as the fiery liquid ran to his stomach, his face red. He let out a wet cough. "Yeah—'scuse me—he says she wasn't worth the trouble."

"Pity," Petros sighed a yellow cloud, aggressively grabbing at his crotch. "'Cause I'll tell you what I'd do with her, yes sir."

Vasili saw Alexei watching them. The old man kept his body turned toward his guests, nodding ever so slightly in Andonis's direction. Vasili frowned in understanding, finishing off his last finger of beer before walking over to the bar.

"How's the store, Andonis?" Vasili said as he sat down, genially patting the shopkeeper on the shoulder.

"Didn't you hear?" Andonis exclaimed, his eyes bright. "Best one-day sale we ever had!"

Vasili nodded slowly. "Yup, I heard. Iapetos," he said the bartender, "another round for me, please? So, Andonis, Jethro Dumont, eh? *The* Jethro Dumont. Who hasn't heard of Jethro Dumont? In our town, no less? That is big, big news."

"Yes, indeed!"

The bartender slid a stein across the bar counter, which Vasili caught with practiced ease. There was no reason to pay, though; he was with Alexei.

"He didn't tell you where he was staying, did he?"

Andonis scratched his cheek as he thought. "Well, I can't say for certain it's where he's staying, you know, but he's havin' me ship all his stuff to that big hotel they built down by the shore. You know the one, Aiolos or something."

"Yeah, I know the place," Vasili said. "Did he say anything else to you?"

Andonis scrunched his face in thought as he swallowed another massive gulp of ouzo. "Mm. Not that I recall. No, he just seemed to be interested in seein' the ruins," he said with a shrug.

"Anything else, Andonis?" Vasili asked pointedly.

Andonis frowned. "No. Just needed clothing, I guess," he added with a shrug. "He needed a green hooded robe. Ain't that wild? What would a rich man like Dumont need with a green robe? Americans…"

Vasili patted Andonis on the back. "Thank you, my friend."

"Except," Andonis said as Vasili turned away.

Vasili stopped short. "Except what?"

Andonis tapped at his forehead, like he was trying to shake something loose. "Except, he *did* ask me if any other Americans had come through recently."

"Really?"

"Yeah, I just told him about girl that killed Astrapios."

"Jean Farrell?"

Andonis nodded. "Yeah! He even recognized her name. Apparently, she's an actress over there or something. Small world, eh?" He took another swig of his ouzo. "You think they were ever an item?"

"Probably," Vasili answered absently. He could see Alexei beckoning him over. Allowing himself one last sip of beer, he pushed his way over to his employer's table. He leaned down between Alexei and Gottschalk, excusing himself before turning his attention to the old man.

"So?" Alexei asked, twisting his interlaced fingers.

Vasili summed up what Andonis had told him. Alexei nodded slowly as he listened, hissing at the mention of Jean Farrell. Vasili noticed that even the balding Nazi raised an eyebrow upon hearing the woman's name; perhaps she was more famous than Vasili had assumed.

The old man tapped his nails against the wooden table. "Jethro Dumont, eh?" he said in a long breath, the Twins twittering beside him. One leaned over and whispered in Alexei's ear. The old man nodded in understanding, his eyes cold.

"The American millionaire?" Gottschalk asked in broken Greek. "Yes, we know of him. We had hoped he would have been *sympathetic* to our efforts, much in the way of Lindbergh, but unfortunately our efforts were derailed due to extenuating circumstances, *nicht wahr,* Herr Oberführer?" Gottschalk said to the balding officer.

"*Jawohl,* Herr Obergruppenführer," the officer said simply, adjusting his uniform. "*Ich habe aber immer noch ein ungutes Gefühl,* Herr Obergruppenführer."

"*Bekannt,* Herr Oberführer," the Obergruppenführer replied, waving away the comment.

Alexei smiled broadly. "Well, it seems as though the stars have come right for us all! This American has something we each want. This will be our chance to bring Dumont over to our mutual efforts, gentlemen. And perhaps," he turned to the Twins, "even yours, my friends..."

Vasili found himself staring at the Twins' pale white hands. They were gnarled and bony, the joints knotted and arthritic, pushing out against the white flesh. Their nails were claw-like, extending out to sharp points that seemed capable of easily ripping into flesh. Their palms were covered in deep scars, like cigarette burns pushed into the very meat of their hands, reminding Vasili of a dead squid.

Gottschalk allowed himself a small smirk and raised his glass to the Twins across the table. "Indeed, this mission may turn out to be more successful than even the Führer himself had anticipated!"

The Twins bowed the heads in unison, croaking softly as they did.

Vasili moved to leave when Alexei grabbed him by the arm. "Let's arrange for our friends to meet this Mr. Dumont. Then we'll find out what he knows of the American girl."

Vasili nodded quickly, understanding Alexei's implication. "Yes, sir."

"There's a good boy," Alexei said, squeezing Vasili's arm as he walked away.

Like it or not, eventually, Vasili would have to kill Jethro Dumont.

"Do we even have a plan? I mean... at all?" Ken said, pacing up and down the presidential suite. They had only just arrived, and despite the lateness of the hour, all three were wide awake.

"I think whatever plan the Lama had for us went out the window when we were attacked by a *living storm*," Caraway commented from the balcony, finishing a cigarette. A cool breeze came in off the shore, the Mediterranean air salty. The night sky was clear, pinpricked with white stars. Even Caraway had trouble believing that, mere hours before, the horizon had been painted a deadly ink black.

"You don't see many living storms in New York, that's for sure," Ken added.

"Just rampaging golems, Nazi madmen, and the occasional demon,"

Caraway said, his voice cracking. He paused to clear his throat and took a long drag of his cigarette. "But yeah, a livin' storm is new."

Ken massaged his eyes, more out of frustration than exhaustion. "Of all the shit we've had to deal with over the years, now we have cognizant meteorological occurrences."

"Big words there, buddy," Caraway said, flicking the remains of his cigarette toward the shore. "You startin' to feel more like yourself?"

"Now that I'm on solid ground, yeah."

"'Fraid of heights, eh? You were doin' pretty well back at the Empire State Building."

"Once again, *solid ground*. I don't mind tall buildings you can leap in a single bound, but once you remove the ground, then…" He took a deep, stuttering breath. "Then I start losing my lunch."

"Yeah, I noticed," Caraway remarked. "What do you think about this whole mess, Jethro?" he said to the seated millionaire. "The Lama let you in on anything before we left?"

Dumont stared at his steepled fingers, his face unreadable as he shook his head. "I believe the Tulku had only a glimmer of the dangers we might face here," he said, his voice hollow. So far, Caraway had been impressed with his friend's courage, but it was possible the pressure had already overtaken him. "Had he known the extent of the darkness we would be facing, I doubt he would have sent us out alone."

"So, we're basically up shit's creek without a paddle," Caraway said. "Fantastic."

"He said this might all have had to do with Kuhchooloo," Ken ventured.

"Kookookachoo?" Caraway struggled. "Do either of you know what that means? The Lama wasn't all that forthcoming."

"Cthulhu," Dumont corrected.

"Well, however the hell you pronounce it, it's bad news," Ken said. "Hands down. Trouble with a capital 'Kuhchoo.'"

"According to the Green Lama, whatever Cthulhu is," Dumont began as he got out of his chair, thoughtfully placing his hands behind his back as he paced the room, "its power was somehow tied directly to the golem creature the Green Lama recently defeated."

"That *Jean* defeated," Ken corrected.

"And that *I* shot in the eye," Caraway added.

Dumont nodded in concession. "I also have reason to believe the creatures we faced aboard the *Bartlett* are somehow connected, though I cannot be certain."

Caraway's gaze briefly dropped to the floor. While he claimed to have no memory of his possession, there were still nights when he awoke to the sensation of nails scraping against his spine, his mind filled with visions of the evil that had briefly taken hold of him only a few months prior.

"Either way," Dumont added, "there is no doubt that it is something much more terrifying than anything we have ever faced before."

Caraway snorted. Maybe it was just his imagination, but it was as if Dumont were trying to sound like the Green Lama. "No offense Jethro, *everything* we're dealing with is more terrifying than *you've* faced before… unless you count Bette Davis. Look, I know you're into that whole Buddhist thing like the Lama, but you,"—he stifled a chuckle—"are *not* the Lama."

Dumont risked a smile, but otherwise disregarded Caraway's comment. "From what we've witnessed it's reasonable to assume that this town sits at the center of its power. And that power is growing." Dumont paused and whispered quietly: "'*Ph'nglui mglw'nafh Cthulhu R'lyeh wgah'nagl fhtagn.*'"

"Speaking Tibetan over there, Jethro?" Caraway asked.

Dumont shook his head as though trying to clear the cobwebs from his mind. "It was something the Tulku heard… Though he failed to translate it, I think he believed that it portends the…" Dumont paused and shut his eyes, as if in pain. "That it's an omen of the coming of Cthulhu."

"So, what do you think we should do?" Ken inquired. "Go around and ask everyone we meet: 'Hey, what's with all this Kuhchooloo jazz?'" he cordially asked a potted plant. "'And while you're at it, have you seen our friend Jean? Actress… redhead… carries a gun, accused of killing your mayor?'"

Caraway shrugged, playing with his mustache. "Dumb as it sounds, that's not quite the worst idea."

Ken raised a forefinger. "One problem, though: only *one* of us here speaks Greek," he said, pointing his raised finger to Dumont. "And you saw how the shop owner got when he found out you were *you*." Ken paused, his face falling. "Do you think she did it? Jean, I mean. You think she really killed the mayor like the shop owner said?"

Dumont furrowed his brow. "If she did, I'm certain it was not without cause."

Caraway snorted. "*That* was diplomatic. But you're right, Clayton, if we're gonna start doing any sort of detective work, going incognito ain't an option for Jethro. There's no way he can be anyone *but* Jethro Dumont."

"That's an assumption," Dumont said quietly. With his back turned, his associates failed to notice the smile touching the corner of his lips.

"But, maybe we can use that," Caraway said. "Jethro, you'll be more use to us in the public eye, meeting with local officials and keeping everyone's attention on you while Clayton and I work undercover in the town's underbelly."

Ken held up both hands defensively. "Once again," he said, now gesticulating heavily for effect, "we no speaka da Greek."

Dumont raised an eyebrow. "That will actually be to your benefit."

Ken massaged his temples. "Oh, I don't like where this is going…"

Jean's body shook uncontrollably despite the heat of the campfire, no longer able to ignore the excruciating pain and the worsening smell wafting from the bullet wound. Something buzzed in the back of her head, like a wasp trapped in a jar.

"Goddammit, why is it so cold?" she shivered.

"Try to sleep, Jean," Aïas calmly said as he fed the fire.

"Not—Not tired," she said, blinking heavily. "Besides, I've got the gun. If I fall asleep, who—who's gonna pro—protect you from the lions and tigers and bears?" she asked with a weak smile. "I'll be fine. Told ya. I've been—been through worse than this. I once had to kiss Harpo."

"You are weak, Jean. The fall tore open the wound and made it worse. You need to rest."

"Don't worry about me. I've never felt better. I—I—" a flash of green burst behind her eyes, erupting in pain. "Oh God, my head!" she screamed. She squeezed her eyes shut as images flew across her mind's eye.

Aïas rushed to her side. "Jean, are you all right?"

She grabbed at his sleeve, twisting it in her fist. "There's—There's a man," she said through gritted teeth as she writhed on the ground.

Aïas's face froze. "What?"

"No. He's—He's not a man. A walking nightmare. There's a silhouette glowing in jade. An undead prophet of a false god," she sputtered. "He's done something terrible. But—But, there's something worse. *Iä Iä Cthulhu fhtagn!* Crystal blade. Time, out of time. Blood dripping down into the void. The stars align. The sunken city rises. Three scions. Fire. Colors. Stone. *Iä Iä Cthulhu fhtagn!* The savior must die before he is risen. *Iä Iä Cthulhu fhtagn!* Dead, he waits dreaming."

Aïas's went wide. He grabbed Jean by the shoulders. "What did you say?"

Jean shook her head furiously, her face contorted as tears flowed down her cheeks. "I—I don't know. Gah! I don't know. There are these images and voices. Like the world is breaking and I'm at the center."

"You are sick, you have lost too much blood," he said as he began to unwind the bandage. "Let me check your—"

A putrid odor filled Jean's nostrils. Prying her eyes open she looked down at the gangrene wound. With that she broke down, sobbing with her face in her hands. "Oh, no," she whimpered.

Aïas closed his eyes in thought, realizing there was no other option. "Βλασφημία," he growled. He pressed his hands against the rotting flesh. Jean let out a soft whimper as his hands began to glow, warmth spreading through her body. Aïas opened his eyes, the formerly black irises now a blazing jade, and looked directly at Jean.

"Jean," he said calmly but firmly. His voice took on a resonance that echoed through the air; even the ground itself seemed to vibrate with every word. The world around them shifted out of focus, and the shadows grew darker. Every molecule, every atom, everything around them was Aïas's voice. "Listen to me. You will be calm and you will listen."

Jean lifted her head and faced Aïas. Her eyes were glassy, her face slack. "I will listen," she said in monotone.

Aïas grimaced, a bitter taste in his mouth. "All will be explained, but you still have a long road ahead of you. I need you to be calm. Do you understand?"

"Yes," she whispered.

"We need to keep moving," he said.

"We need to keep moving," Jean repeated softly.

Aïas nodded then closed his eyes. The air buzzed, a low pitch hum that moved through and around them. Beneath his hands the blood on Jean's bandages evaporated as the wrappings fell free and the gangrenous flesh knitted itself close, as if she had never been injured at all.

"Better?" he asked.

"Yes. Better."

"Good. Now, Forget," he said.

Jean furrowed her brow and shook her head. "No."

Aïas's narrowed. That was unexpected. "Forget," he reiterated with force.

Her face relaxed, her shoulders slumped. "Forget," she whispered.

Aïas frowned at Jean, dissatisfied with himself. "Good, now wake up," he commanded, his voice beginning to lose its resonance. He blinked and the world quickly regained it focus and substance.

Jean's face relaxed and she woke from her daze. She absently wiped away the remaining tears from her cheeks and looked sternly up at Aïas. "Who told you could get so close?" she said, pushing him away, once again sounding like herself.

Aïas chuckled lightheartedly. "Sorry. You fell asleep. We need to get moving before the sun rises, we have still got a long trip ahead of us."

"Great. More walking," she groaned.

As she followed after Aïas, Jean felt a small tingling moving around in the back of her mind, like an itch she couldn't scratch, but every time she tried to pinpoint it and nail it down, all she could think about was how good her leg felt, as if it had never been injured at all.

Chapter 5
INCOGNITO

*T*here is no night at the top of the world, just stars and the bitter, unrelenting cold; the latter of which Jethro Dumont was suffering firsthand.

"'Endurance is one of the most difficult disciplines, but the final victory comes to the one who endures,'" Tsarong had said before shutting the doors to the Temple of the Clouds, leaving the half-naked Dumont alone to the elements. A storm had passed through during the day, dropping a foot-thick white blanket across the world. But while the snowfall had stopped, the wind refused to die down, howling ferociously through the mountains.

"'I'll go to Tibet to find clarity. I'll discover my purpose there.' Jesus Christ, Jethro, you're an idiot. Second only to dating Lillian Gish, this is the worst idea you've ever had," he grumbled to himself, his teeth chattering as he stumbled through the snow, hugging himself to retain what little warmth he could. "Goddamn, it's cold."

He could feel his toes begin to freeze; it was only a matter of time before they started to fall off. How long could he survive out here, he wondered? Three hours? Two? Hell, it would be a miracle if he could make it past one. He needed to find shelter.

After several minutes of wandering he came upon a small cliff. Though his joints were almost frozen, he was able to pull himself over the bluff and onto the plateau, where he fell face first into the snow. Pushing himself up, he could hear the harsh roar of the wind relentlessly flowing over the mountain, forcing the air out of his lungs. Gasping, he didn't hear the soft footsteps and low growl of the snow leopard, and it wasn't until the beast's claws dug into his skin that Jethro realized what was happening.

"I have a bad feeling about this, sir," the Oberführer repeated as they entered their impromptu headquarters outside the city. The tent walls were covered in maps and charts, pinpricked with small flags and written over with arrows and numbers. A long table sat at one end, while smaller ones lined the temporary structure, each laden with radios, typewriters, and other tools.

"As you've mentioned, Herr Oberführer," Gottschalk said with little effort to mask his annoyance as he moved toward a chair at the far end. "It has been noted."

"Though I am loathe to admit it," Sturmbannführer Hirsch said, picking at his acne scars as he followed the others in, "I must agree with the Oberführer. This is a fool's errand."

The Oberführer gave Hirsch an appreciative—albeit cursory—nod. "We have aligned ourselves with a petty thug, a petty *Greek* thug, and for what purpose?" He waved his hands in frustration. "We should be focusing our attentions on the upcoming—"

Gottschalk raised a cautionary finger. "The Führer has ordered us here and we shall do as he commands. Besides, it is not for this 'petty thug' that we are here, but rather his two associates." He crossed his legs, then laced his fingers together. "If they can achieve what they have promised, perhaps we can finally overcome the Toht, Vogel, and von Kultz embarrassments and maybe we will have the tools we need to return glory to the Fatherland."

The Oberführer snorted. "Magic. Mysticism. Supernatural foolishness, if you ask me. I do not question the Führer on anything else, but his obsession with the occult is worrisome. Arks… Holy Grails… Even the 'Spear of Destiny.' How many men have died in vain for these 'sacred' items? I suppose the next thing we will learn is that those masked individuals are really little green men from Mars."

"Coincidentally, Herr Oberführer, you are not that far off."

The Nazi officials turned to find their bearded compatriot entering the tent.

"Herr Doktor Hammond," Gottschalk said with a slight bow of his head.

"Herr Obergruppenführer," the doctor replied as he walked over to a small dry bar in the back corner of the tent. He gave a perfunctory salute. "Heil Hitler."

"Everything go well?" Gottschalk asked.

Hammond nodded with muted satisfaction. The Oberführer made note of the ornate scabbard hooked to the doctor's belt; he had not been wearing it earlier.

"Come, now," Hirsch said with a chuckle. "You're not saying that those masked twins are spacemen, are you?"

"Oh, I never said anything of the sort!" the doctor exclaimed as he poured himself a glass of whiskey.

"Then what are you getting at, Herr Doktor?" the Oberführer asked. "From what I understand it was you who arranged this little excursion."

"Indeed," the doctor said, a smile beneath his Van Dyke. He took a sip of the drink, hissing as the liquor burned its way down. "Do any of you recall hearing of an expedition to Tibet several years ago?"

"Ah yes... the one lead by Kannenberg and that maniac Karl Heydrich," Hirsch said thoughtfully. "I read the reports. Terrible mess that was."

The doctor cleared his throat. "Yes, but while the expedition was... less than successful, our mission here is directly tied to Heydrich's failed efforts."

"And how is that?" the Oberführer inquired as he paced the tent with his hands behind his back.

"They were looking for an artifact, a tablet of sorts," Gottschalk interjected.

The Oberführer raised an inquisitive eyebrow. "What sort of 'tablet'?"

"The Jade Tablet, to be precise," the doctor said as he took a seat. "Heydrich believed the Tablet would give us the ingredients to create our very own supersoldiers, and while that may have been possible, Heydrich was mistaken about several things."

"Such as?" Hirsch asked.

"Firstly, Heydrich, understandably, believed that the Jade Tablet was a literal tablet made of jade, when it is in fact something of a misnomer. The Jade Tablet he sought was a ring of rainbow fiber. Secondly, he believed there was only one Tablet." Hammond paused and held up two fingers and a thumb. "There are, however, *three*."

The Oberführer stopped short as though he had been punched in the stomach.

"The First, the one Heydrich was after, is... lost to us for the time being. The Second is believed to have been destroyed sometime in the first century by the Ancient Jews."

Hirsch snorted. "The Jews ruin everything, don't they?"

The others chuckled briefly, and the doctor continued.

"The Third… The Third Tablet is *here*, somewhere on this island."

"Let us pretend for a moment that these Jade Tablets really do exist," the Oberführer postulated. "If one is here, why do we not just reach out and take it? All these theatrics, dealing with thugs and masked men, moving around in the night like criminals; a waste! And if we were to obtain it, do we even know what it does? You said that Heydrich believed the first one would give us 'supersoldiers.'"

Hammond sighed, exasperated. "It is believed that each Tablet, though tied to the same power source, has a unique attribute. The Tibetan Tablet, also known as the 'Sacred Colors,' is said to alter human life. The Middle Eastern Tablet, sometimes called the 'Tablet of Abraham,' can give life. The Greek Tablet, the one we seek, also known as the 'Fire from Olympus,' is said to have the *power of the gods*."

Hirsch snorted. "'Power of the gods.' Herr Doktor, you have been listening to too many fairy tales," he said, laughing. "Herr Obergruppenführer, surely you do not believe this foolishness?"

Gottschalk hesitated before saying, "The Führer believes it, and that is good enough for me, as should it be for you, Herr Sturmbannführer. As to the Oberführer's concerns, these are delicate times. We dare not risk playing our hand too soon. For the Führer's plans to work, we must move under the flag of diplomacy, lest we draw unwanted attention from the Greek government, let alone the world at large. Alexei Polyxena, criminal that he is, has facilitated our entrance into the country, and given us access to the 'masked twins.' Strange as they are, they claim to know the location of this Third Jade Tablet and, perhaps most importantly, know how to activate it and bring about the power we need to permanently tip the scales in our favor."

"How do we even know we can trust them?" the Oberführer asked pointedly.

"Because," Hammond began as he reach into his scabbard, "they gave us this."

The tent erupted with green light, glowing in the night.

Jethro opened his eyes, and all was jade.

He was standing in a massive room overlooking a chasm, a rattling wind flowing from up from the shadows. The walls were made of coral, extending out in curves, intersecting at right angles. He was bound to an altar at the center of the room. His right hand was pressed against a stone, fingers splayed, the Jade Tablet wrapped around his middle finger, glowing green. He was the sacrifice. He heard the echo of chanting: maddening, croaking, braying, inhuman sounds. They were all around him, the believers, chanting over and over again, "Iä Iä Cthulhu fhtagn!"

Jethro looked out into the darkness before him. The shadows moved and broke open and two red, green, and yellow slits began to form. Tentacles like clouds moved out into the light, twisting and undulating around him.

Someone gripped him by the hair and pulled his head back, turning his face to the ceiling.

He looked into the face of a murderer. Karl Heydrich lived. His eyes burned with madness, grinning wildly, his teeth cracked and jagged. He held a glowing green phurba *– no, it was a crystal shard – in his hand.*

Heydrich leaned in close, breath like brimstone as he whispered, "Cthulhu rises."

He plunged the phurba *into Jethro's throat and all was pain.*

Jethro screamed as he lurched out of bed, dripping with sweat. He gripped at his neck, searching for the wound but finding none.

"*Om! Tare Tuttare Ture Soha!*" he whispered, hoping the mantra would arouse his own inner strength. There was part of him that wanted it to be nothing more than a terrible nightmare, but he knew better than that. It had been prophecy, a portent of events to come, much more lucid than the ones he had experienced before.

But… it couldn't be the future, he decided. Heydrich had been dead for over five years. There was no question; he had seen Heydrich die.

Hadn't he?

Jethro stumbled over and threw open the window. He shivered; the cold ocean breeze ice against his skin. He could still hear the chanting; still feel those massive eyes staring down on him. Cthulhu. It was like a darkness encroaching on his mind. Somehow everything he had done since those terrible days at the Temple of the Clouds all those years ago was connected to this creature. Jethro shuddered. What had he done? How many lives had he now put at risk? Caraway's, Ken's, and most of all Jean's. Deep down in the pit of his stomach he knew she was at the center of this, the knot at whose center all these strings were tied.

The Keystone. They had called her the Keystone.

And if what he saw was indeed the future, could he change it? Rabbi Brickman had seen the coming holocaust of his people and had done all he could, creating a golem in hopes of altering the path of history, and even then he was unable to stop the tide.

Gazing out into the sky, Jethro couldn't help but think how green the moon looked.

He frowned. He would not be sleeping tonight.

The Green Lama jumped down into the alleyway. Having only saved a single vial of his radioactive salts during his escape from Rick Master's airship, he was mindful not to expend his energy too quickly. He had left his enhanced salts onboard the airship in an unconscious effort to prove to himself—and to Jean—that Jethro Dumont was as much a hero as the Green Lama. But old habits die hard, and Jethro once again found his face hidden beneath a viridian hood. And while his new robes fit him well, he found the lack of furred cuffs and the more monastic cut slightly uncomfortable. For now he kept to the shadows, moving silently toward the town's police station. While he had complete faith in Ken and Caraway, he hoped to aid their efforts by learning all he could about Jean's alleged homicide.

What he knew so far was scant. According to the shopkeeper, Jean was seen running from the mayor's official residence shortly before his body was found with an axe blade to the head. She was arrested less than an hour later in her hotel room across town. She broke free shortly after and had been on the run ever since.

Jethro didn't need to be a superpowered detective to know something didn't add up. Someone was framing her, he was certain, but who and for what purpose? Hopefully, he could find some clues tonight. His first stop would be the local police station, where he expected to learn more of the "official" version of the crime.

Sneaking in through an opened window, Jethro walked silently past several dozing policemen toward the record room. The door was locked, but with a quick twist of his wrist, the lock broke in two.

He found the file easily, a thin manila folder simply marked "Astrapios." Inside were the standard forms filled out by the investigating— and clearly inept—detectives, detailing the crime scene. Beyond the revelation that the murder weapon hadn't been found, there was nothing in them that he didn't already know; it was the photos, however, that took him by surprise.

There were ten of them, showing Astrapios's corpse at a variety of angles, each more gruesome than the last. Jethro had seen some terrible things since he had taken up the mantle of the Green Lama, but he was still sickened by what he saw. Astrapios's body lay sprawled out, naked on his bed, his bearded face split in two. Blood and brain matter was splattered against the headboard and wall. Jethro's stomach turned as his mind attempted to imagine the sequence of events leading up to Astrapios's demise, moments of passion and intimacy climaxing with murder. He could not decide which disturbed him more: the thought of Jean murdering a lover or of her having a lover at all.

He grimaced; of all things, was he jealous?

Jethro shook his head. No, Jean couldn't be the killer. And if Astrapios had been her lover, then…

He moved to another photo, this one of the adjacent wall. There was a noticeable egg-shaped absence of blood splatter above a small empty table. Jethro raised an eyebrow; something had been stolen, but what? Nothing else in the room seemed to be out of place. If this was indeed a robbery, the killer—or killers—seemed to know exactly what they wanted.

Then something else caught his eye. He thought it could be a trick of light, but he began looking over the images once more, finding it in every picture. Though lost in the blood splatter to the untrained eye, Jethro had no doubt about what he saw.

Bloody footprints, walking up the wall.

Astrapios's residence was, appropriately, a tomb. Even Jethro's own hushed footsteps seemed to echo throughout the estate. The building, massive compared with the relatively modest homes in town, was modeled after ancient Greek architecture and sat atop a small hill overlooking the city. Subtle Astrapios was not. As Jethro made his way toward the mayor's bedchambers, he passed no fewer than seventeen portraits and statues of the man, each more gaudy and self-aggrandizing than the last. The bedroom, twice the size of Jethro's, had been cleaned of blood, the bed replaced, though Jethro could see, just barely visible in the glints of the moonlight, the bloodstains that had seeped into the wooden walls. Walking over to the far wall, he found the bloodless egg-shaped "shadow" he had seen in the photographs. It was possibly the size of an ostrich egg, though as he gazed closer he could see a small divot in the blood spray, which meant the egg— or whatever had been there—had been cracked or missing a shard. Jethro frowned; there was nothing more he could learn here. Turning around, he moved closer to the bed, and was able to find the foot-shaped stains climbing up the wall to the ceiling and back across the room.

Impossible wasn't an adjective Jethro used anymore, but he was tempted to bring it back into his lexicon as he followed the footsteps to their abrupt end against the opposite wall, the footprint cut off mid-step. Curious, he walked through the doorway to the adjacent room and found, improbably, the other half of the footprint on the ceiling. The prints continued on toward the other side of the room, where they were once again bisected by the wall.

"Walked through the walls…" Jethro breathed in disbelief.

Something clattered in the library down the hall. Jethro instinctually dove for the shadows, pulling the front of his hood down. He heard glass shatter and wood snap, heavy breathing and garbled words that seemed foreign even to his trained ears. Peeking around the doorway, he watched as someone tore through the library. The man—at least Jethro assumed it was a man—moved through the room in quick, hopping motions, as though he were unaccustomed to walking. He was completely nude, his hairless skin pale white, glistening in the moonlight. The man ripped apart books, scratched at the back wall, sifting through the remains like a mad archaeologist. He croaked, futilely cursing under his breath. Knobby joints pushed out against his oily flesh, his spine a column of pronounced ridges, the skin cracked and scaly. Three long scars traced the side of his neck. His fingers were long, the nails pointed and serrated. Jethro could only see the outline of the man's face, his eyes massive and bulging out.

Jethro inched into the room, keeping to the shadows, as his hands unconsciously curled into fists. He suspected whatever this man was looking for had something to do with Astrapios's murder, but there was only one way to find out...

"*Om! Ma-ni Pad-me Hum!*"

The man jumped back, dropping two halves of a book to the floor, cursing again in his guttural tongue. As Jethro stepped into the moonlight, he watched with growing horror as the man slowly turned to face him. The ridges of the man's spine extended out to form a prodigious fin that ran up the length of his back and neck, ending at the top of his head. The scars on the sides of his neck began flapping, gills struggling in the open air. His eyes were massive unblinking black orbs.

"*Om Ah Hum!*" Jethro whispered. "What are you?"

The fish-man bared its teeth, hissing as it launched at Jethro. It let out a high-pitched warble, the ugly sound echoing off the rafters, sending a chill down Jethro's spine. The creature swiped its claws at Jethro's stomach, slashing his robes, narrowly missing flesh as he subtly shifted his weight to the left. But the creature was quicker than Jethro had anticipated, spinning on its heels and chomping its massive jaw down onto Jethro's right arm. Jethro hollered in pain. He tried to pull away, succeeding only in driving the creature's blade-like teeth into his muscles. Jethro sent a large blast of green electricity through his right arm and the fish-man's jaw shot open, releasing Jethro's arm from its vise-like grip. The pale creature flew across the study, smacking against the wall with a loud *thunk!*

Jethro gripped his arm. The fish-man's teeth had broken through his skin, causing blood to seep into his robes. Examining the wound, he watched in horror as black veins began to spread across his arm. The creature's bite was poisoned.

Across the room the creature held its head as it stumbled to his feet, cursing in its inhuman tongue. The electric blast had cost him a precious amount of energy from his radioactive salts, but Jethro had to attack now or lose the upper hand. Whispering "*Om! Ma-ni Pad-me Hum!*" Jethro tapped into his remaining reservoir of energy and ran forward, striking at the creature's pale midsection with a roundhouse kick. But the fish-man was too fast, catching Jethro's leg mid-kick and throwing him to the floor. Jethro landed hard on his back, smacking his head, stars shooting past his eyes. The fish-man shoved a knobby knee onto Jethro's chest and gripped Jethro's face with its clawed hands, covering his mouth, digging its nails into his skin. As it picked Jethro's head off the ground, the creature leaned its horrible face forward, its unnatural lips brushing against his ear.

"*Nyarlathotep che'fhgag tehona. Ht'chu drada gr'od'ins ri's,*" it hissed, its breath smelling like putrid seawater. Jethro thought he recognized one of the monster's words—*Nyarlathotep*—but before he could place it, his head was slammed down to the floor. Fighting back unconsciousness, Jethro tried to open his eyes, but everything was black and white spots.

"*Narrett'e ht'chutu*, Green Lama," the creature breathed. "*Narrett'e ht'chutu*, Dumont."

A pit formed in Jethro's stomach. His eyes met the creature's unblinking black pools. It smiled and before Jethro could react it slammed his head down to the ground and the world once again exploded into pain. The creature lifted Jethro's head again but before the monster could slam it back down, Jethro swung his arms up, wrapping his palms around the fish-man's wet, bulbous eyes and unleashed every last ounce of his radioactive energy. The creature screamed in agony as electricity coursed through its body. It scraped and clawed at Jethro's hands, slicing into his skin. Jethro could feel the monster's eyes melt beneath his hands. Putrid black goo oozed out through his fingers, flowing down his arms, stinging as it seeped into his wounds. Jethro grimaced, but held on until the creature's arms went limp. Its body slackened and it crumpled to the ground, freeing Jethro.

Grabbing on to a nearby chair, Jethro pulled himself off the ground. His head throbbed a thunderstorm, echoing through his body. Beneath the pounding, he thought he could hear the monster's struggling breaths, but that easily could have been his own. His vision was fogged, the world blurred beyond recognition, leaving only shapes and shadows. He spit out a wad of blood, wiping his mouth clean with the sleeve of his robe. His injured arm felt stiff. He flexed his fingers as he unsuccessfully attempted to regain feeling. Stumbling away, Jethro heard a tremendous crash behind him. Racing back, he saw, beneath the haze of injuries, that one of the mansion's windows had been smashed open, glass littering the floor.

The creature was nowhere to be found.

Chapter 6
THE SHARD

*J*ethro screamed as the leopard's claws dug into his skin, ripping into muscle. Without thinking, he thrust his elbow up in the beast's chest, audibly cracking a rib. The leopard howled, loosening its grip. Rolling out from beneath the animal—the snow stinging his wounds— Jethro forced himself onto unsteady legs. His heart was thumping as sweat trickled down his body despite the frigid temperature.

"Easy there, kitty," Jethro breathed as they began to circle one another. "I don't want you to eat me and you don't want to eat me. I've been living off a lean Buddhist diet for a couple of months now—lots of vegetables— so there's not much meat left on me for you to snack on. How about we call it a night and go our separate ways?"

The leopard growled in response, stalking closer.

"Yeah, that's what I figured..." Jethro sighed just before the leopard barreled toward him. Sidestepping into a tight roll, Jethro evaded another strike from the beast's claws by mere centimeters. Wheeling into a crouch, Jethro saw the leopard spin around and dive toward him. With his body nearly frozen, the wounds in his back ringing with pain and the blood spilling down, his options were limited. As the snow leopard launch forward, he instinctively pinched his eyes shut and shouted, "Om! Ma-ni Pad-me Hum!"

When death didn't come, Jethro forced open his eyes to discover that the beast had come to a sudden halt, stopping just short of Jethro's palms. Wide-eyed, Jethro shifted his gaze back and forth between the leopard—idly licking its lips—and the braided ring that seemed to glow an unearthly jade.

"I feel like an idiot," Caraway grumbled as he rowed to shore the next morning.

"Please, you should've seen what they made us wear in *Hamlet*. Frills everywhere," Ken said, wiggling his fingers at his neck as though he were wearing Shakespearean garb rather than a simple dark sweater and pants, a wool cap atop his head. "Besides, it was your idea."

"Uh huh," Caraway murmured, fiddling with the patch over his right eye. "If my wife could see me, she would probably die laughing."

Ken tilted his head quizzically. "I didn't know you were married."

"Technically speaking, neither did I." Caraway considered this, then said, "Well, I *did*, but until recently I thought she was 'gone with the wind.'"

Ken squinted at Caraway, measuring him up. "Yeah, I guess you could play Rhett. They're making that into a movie soon. I heard Neville Sinclair was in the running until, y'know… *ka-boom!*" Ken expanded his arms out, mimicking an explosion.

"Ever spend any time undercover?" he asked after a moment.

Caraway shook his head. "I'm usually more the grab-your-gun-and-head-straight-in kinda cop."

"Hm," Ken sighed thoughtfully. "All right, then you should probably follow my lead. I'm a master at this. I was once Dr. Pali, y'know," he added proudly, puffing out his chest.

"Really?" Caraway asked with a cocked eyebrow, trying to imagine this young Caucasian as a middle-aged Tibetan priest. "And how'd that go?"

Ken's smile fell. "Oh, it was horrible."

"Fantastic," Caraway commented. "Looks like we're here."

Ken look over his shoulder toward the dock. "All right, like I said, let me do the talking," he said as he stood up.

There were several men on the dock, all working to pull crates off a small fishing vessel, except for one bare-chested fellow who simply sat smoking on one of the pillars. He was short with a ropy build, a squid tattoo on his chest. A brown bowler sat atop his head, covering long hairs of grey and black, reminding Ken of a feral dog. Swallowing a lump in his throat, Ken tried to steady himself. He had had enough experience over the years to know a killer when he saw one.

The man on the dock spotted Ken and Caraway, jumped off his pillar, and shouted at them in Greek.

"Uh, yes, 'ello there!" Ken shouted back in a convincing British accent.

"Sorry to be a bother, but my friend and I recently parted ways with our employer under less than pleasant circumstances and we were hoping to come ashore with the intent on finding more gainful employment."

"You sound *way* too intelligent for a sailor," Caraway growled under his breath.

"Oh, shut up," Ken whispered back. "So yes, may we… uh, may we dock here… Um… sir?" he yelled to the man on the pier, who took a drag of his cigarette in reply. Undeterred, Ken asked: "Do you, um, speak English, sir?"

"I do," the man said as the boat drifted up to the dock. He took a long drag of his hand rolled cigarette, squinting one eye while he measured up the two new arrivals. "What ship were you sailing with?"

"The, ah, *Jade Tulku*."

The tattooed man shrugged. "Never heard of it."

"Yes, well, you're better off for it, sir. It's Tibetan. Savages, if you ask me."

The tattooed man chewed this over. "Isn't Tibet landlocked?"

Ken opened and closed his mouth. "They have rivers. To the ocean. One assumes."

"What's your name, Brit?" the tattooed man eventually asked.

Ken's eyes widened for an instant, struggling to think of a name. "William!" he said quickly. "William…. Um… Shakespeare," he said, hoping the man didn't see him cringe.

Caraway buried his face in his hands.

The tattooed man considered Ken, with a puff of his cigarette. "Like the writer?"

"Yes! Exactly!" Ken said excitedly. "Just like the writer. My parents were… uh, big fans. Very big fans. Met at a play, if would you believe it! But my mates call me 'Shakes.'"

The tattooed man indicated Caraway with his cigarette. "And this one of your 'mates'?" he asked, a cloud of smoke billowing out of his mouth.

Ken scratched the back of his neck, squinting from the sun. "Yes, this is… uh, John… John Caraway."

Caraway shot Ken a look that said, "What the hell are you doing?"

Ken replied with a wide-eyed nervous smile and whispered, "I have no idea."

"Not much of a talker, is he?" the tattooed man commented.

"Oh, no, sir, strong silent type," Ken said. "He keeps his comments monosyllabic."

"Yar…" Caraway growled with a slight nod to the tattooed man.

"So, ah, yes," Ken said to the bare-chested man. "Might we dock here?"

"You looking for work, you say?"

"Yes, sir."

The tattooed man took a drag of cigarette and then extended a hand to Ken, who tossed him their rope. "Petros," the man said, indicating himself as he tied the rope to a pillar. "You want to work these docks, there is only one man you can talk to. Come, I will take you to him."

Vasili's night had been plagued by nightmares, visions of horrors he couldn't comprehend. All he could remember were blurred images and the inhuman chanting echoing over and over in the back of his mind. He had seen a city beneath the sea filled with…? Not humans—they were something *Other*. They were chasing him because he had stolen something important. He tried to remember what it was, but no matter how hard he tried, all he could see was the color green. There was a monk, dressed in jade. And then there was that *thing* calling out to him, playing him like a puppet. *Nyarlathotep*. He remembered that. Its name was Nyarlathotep.

A shudder ran down his spine. He felt cold, as if he had been left drifting in the ocean for hours.

"Late night, my boy?" Alexei asked, bringing Vasili out his horrific reverie. Vasili jumped a little, instantly reaching for his sidearm. "Calm down, son," the old man said. "It's only me."

"Sorry, sir. Didn't see you come in."

Alexei noticed the dark pits under Vasili's eyes and gave him a knowing smirk. "Heh, well, I didn't see you leave the bar last night. Didn't take anyone home, did you? Sotiria's been eyeing you for some time now."

"Just bad dreams," Vasili replied.

Alexei clicked his tongue. "Pity."

Vasili indicated the destruction in front of them, eager to change the subject. "Do you know what happened, sir?"

Alexei's smile morphed into a grimace as he moved into Astrapios's study. Placing his hands behind his back, he moved thoughtfully over the wreckage. The place was a disaster, far worse than when they had found the mayor's face split in two. "My boy," Alexei began as he kicked aside a broken vase, "if I knew, don't you think I would have told you already?" He slowly spun himself around as he looked over the study, humming softly as he did. The old man then closed his eyes and began to run his fingers over the walls, the broken chairs and tables, as if he were reading Braille. Vasili had seen Alexei do this several times before, and it still made him uncomfortable, as though he were watching something unholy.

Alexei stopped short and knelt to pick up something off the floor. It was a small strip of green fabric, partially soaked in blood. He turned it over, brought it up to his nose, and sniffed it. "Looks like someone had a rougher night than you, son," he said holding it up to Vasili. Alexei folded the fabric and slid it into his pocket. He began to stand when something caught his eye. Vasili followed his gaze to a small pool of black sludge. Dipping two fingers into the puddle, Alexei scooped up the ooze and placed in it his mouth, tasting it. Grimacing, he stood up and began to walk toward the exit. "I have to talk to the Twins."

Jethro's body was on fire, shivering despite the furnace within. He blindly stumbled into his hotel's bathroom, flipped on the faucet, and tentatively sipped water from his palms. Black bile singed the back of his throat, an aftereffect of several hours' worth of sickness. Coughing, Jethro wiped the back of his sleeve across his mouth and sank to the floor. The bite wounds on his arm pulsed rhythmically, wrist to shoulder growing increasingly stiff. He cautiously pulled back his impromptu bandages, cancerous black veins spreading over his arm like a spider's web. He couldn't tell if he had days, hours, perhaps even minutes left before he would succumb to the venom.

Reaching into his pocket, he retrieved his remaining radioactive salts, the vial only three-quarters full. While he had used the salts to heal minor injuries in the past, there was no assurance it would work now, but he was rapidly running out of options. He bit down on the cork and yanked it free, pouring half of its contents onto his injured arm. His arm ignited as salt met the wound, the black and green pus foaming white. Fighting back a scream, he swallowed the remaining salts, the crystals lancing his throat. Seconds passed before he felt the first burst of energy tear through his body, like knives stabbing him from within as the salts went to war. He convulsed to the floor, foam sputtering from his lips. His eyes rolled back in his head, but instead of the blissful blackness of oblivion he found the unblinking eyes of Cthulhu.

Jethro screamed in horror, praying for release.

The Oberführer chewed the inside of his cheeks as he watched the doctor examine the glowing green artifact beneath a microscope. Gottschalk stood by, watching with childlike curiosity, while Hirsch paced the other side of the tent, nervously hugging his body, reminding the Oberführer of a schoolboy fearfully awaiting his marks.

The artifact, which the doctor called the Shard, was a fascinating archeological find. To the naked eye it appeared to be nothing more than a serrated piece of shattered green crystal long ago attached to an ornate golden hilt, turning it into an archaic blade. Dried blood could be seen within the crystal's crevices, giving it a maroon hue. What was perhaps most disquieting was the low thrum and the unearthly glow emanating from the crystal's opaque center, as if it were moments away from detonation.

"Yes… Yes… Here they are…" Hammond murmured.

Gottschalk leaned closer. "Have you found them?" he asked excitedly.

The doctor grimaced, but didn't remove himself from the microscope. "Shh… Herr Obergruppenführer… It's distracting."

Gottschalk took several steps back until he was standing next to the Oberführer.

"What is he looking for, sir?" the Oberführer asked.

Gottschalk responded in a hushed voice. "The blade is covered in microscopic writing; nearly every centimeter, from base to tip. Apparently, there is some sort of 'incantation' inscribed somewhere on the blade."

"How is that even possible?" the Oberführer asked in disbelief.

"Skill," the doctor replied, his eyes glued to the microscope as he scribbled on a pad with his right hand. "Amazing, amazing skill, or perhaps technology not seen on this planet for a millennia."

"Again with the 'little green men,'" the Oberführer huffed.

"And once again, Herr Oberführer, I never said anything about 'little green men,'" the doctor said as he turned to his compatriots. "And unfortunately, Herr Obergruppenführer, what I found is not an incantation, rather it is something much more..." he stroked the tuft of hair on his chin. "...valuable."

Gottschalk's eyebrows shot up with genuine interest.

The doctor smiled. "Would you like to take a look yourself, Herr Obergruppenführer?" he said, gesturing to the microscope.

"Thank you, Herr Doktor," Gottschalk said with a slight bow of his head before walking over to the microscope.

Hammond turned to face the Oberführer as Gottschalk peered into the lens, a cold smile on his scarred lips. "Do you see them, Herr Obergruppenführer?" the doctor asked.

Gottschalk frowned in uncertainty. "Yes... What are they?"

"Numbers," the doctor replied, while keeping his eyes locked on the Oberführer. "Or at the very least, an archaic representation of numbers. Each number is indicated by the position of dots in a specific quadrant of a cross, moving counter clockwise. A single dot in the right hand quadrant equals one, a dot in all four quadrants equals ten." He lifted his pad and showed the Oberführer and Hirsch the string of "numbers" he had copied from the crystalline blade.

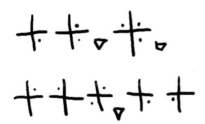

"Sounds complicated," Hirsch said, speaking up for the first time in hours.

Hammond shrugged. "I never said it was simple, now did I?"

Gottschalk looked up from the microscope. "That's all very well and good, Fredrick, but what do these numbers mean?"

The doctor cleared his throat. "Have any of you heard the phrase:

Ph'nglui mglw'nafh Cthulhu R'lyeh wgah'nagl fhtagn?"

The Oberführer shivered, but remained silent. He had heard the phrase before.

Gottschalk absently scratched his cheek. "Sounds like that gibberish those Twins were mumbling the other night."

"Almost. Theirs is a crude bastardized version of the language, spoiled over time," the doctor said as he paced the tent. "No, this is a pure example, uncorrupted. Written before the world was divided and savage."

"What does it mean?" Gottschalk asked.

"'In his house at R'lyeh, dead Cthulhu waits dreaming.'"

"And, what does that mean?" Hirsch asked.

"'Prophecy' is one word, but... 'promise' would be more appropriate."

The three Nazi officials stared at Hammond in silent bewilderment until the Oberführer audibly cleared his throat. "I'm afraid, Herr Doktor," he began, "that you have us at a loss."

The doctor placed his hands behind his back and gave them a wry smile. "The Twins, as you call them, are members of a very ancient cult that worships beings known as the 'the Great Old Ones,' who, they believe, came out of the sky centuries before man walked the Earth."

"Little green men?" the Oberführer said again, raising a skeptical eyebrow.

Hammond let out a sinister laugh. "According to myth, the Great Old Ones were massive cosmic creatures from outside our..." the doctor waved his hand as he searched for the word, "...'reality.' There are differing accounts as to what exactly the Old Ones looked like, but one thing that is consistent is that the very sight of them would drive a man to insanity."

"Sounds like a lovely bunch of gods, Herr Doktor," Gottschalk commented. "Personally, I prefer mine with a flowing white beard and toga, but once again you fail to enlighten us. What does this all have to do with the Shard?"

"The story goes that at some point before the rise of man, the Old Ones were imprisoned deep inside the earth; but being cosmic entities, they never really died. The cult believes," the doctor continued, "that the greatest of the Old Ones, Cthulhu, is locked away in the lost city R'lyeh, waiting for the stars to align so he can awake and free the other gods to reign over this realm once again.

"There are differing accounts as to how or why the Old Ones were sequestered from this world. Some say it was done by the Elder Gods, while others contend it was beings known as the *Outer* Gods. Most believe it was the Old Ones who chose to seal themselves off from our reality for reasons we cannot comprehend. However, I believe it was the power manifested by the Jade Tablets that defeated them. This Shard," he said, indicating the glowing blade, "is the key to R'lyeh and a piece of the final Jade Tablet, once thought lost to the ages…"

The Oberführer's stomach dropped as he listened silently.

"It is the key to giving Germany the power of the gods!" Hammond continued with growing excitement. "I am certain that the numbers I found are the ancient coordinates to R'lyeh, which, if my calculations are correct—and they are correct—translates to: south forty-seven degrees, nine minutes, by west one hundred twenty-six degrees, forty-three minutes."

The Oberführer forced a laugh. "South forty-seven degrees, nine minutes, by west one hundred twenty-six degrees, forty-three minutes?" he repeated. "That's the middle of the ocean."

"Just north of the Antarctic!" Hammond said with a manic smile, his voice rising with every word. "And yes, you are correct, Herr Oberführer! You could tread water there for days and not see anything beyond the darkness of the sea. But, in a few days' time the stars will align and the lost city will rise from the ocean depths. And once we have the Third Jade Tablet we can gain entrance into R'lyeh and we will be able to mold the world as we see fit!"

The German officials fell into a brief silence as they considered the doctor.

"This all sounds like the ravings of a madman!" the Oberführer finally exclaimed. "First the 'Jade Tablets' and now you speak of ancient alien gods and lost cities? This isn't some young boy's adventure story, Herr Doktor! I cannot deny the blade's craftsmanship nor can I ignore its improbable luminescence, but what you are saying is insane!" He looked to Gottschalk for another voice of reason but found only silence—the Obergruppenführer would not speak against the Führer's orders.

Hirsch softly cleared his throat. "Herr Doktor, do you have any proof of these claims?"

The doctor gave Hirsch a warm smile. "Yes, Herr Sturmbannführer. I do." He lifted the Shard off the microscope, the crystal ringing as it moved through the air. He whispered three words, *"Na'petta R'lyeh fm'ta,"* and stabbed the blade forward. The sound of tearing flesh echoed around them as they watched the blade cut a three-dimensional hole in the air. Hammond reached over, curled his thin fingers around the ragged edges of reality, and tugged open the walls of existence like a torn curtain, revealing the terrifying world beyond.

Hirsch let out a whimper as he stumbled back, his skin pale. *"Mein Gott,"* he breathed in horror.

"That's a mountain," Jean observed.

"Nothing gets past you," Aïas said dryly.

The pair stood at the base, gazing up at the snow-capped peak. Under normal circumstances this sight would mean little to a girl with Montana running through her veins, but Jean knew they weren't just taking in the scenery. She ran an exasperated hand through her hair. "You're gonna ask me to climb a mountain. You never said anything about climbing a mountain! Why would you hide something on top of a mountain?"

Aïas furrowed his brow. "Thought that would be obvious."

"Try me."

"Because no one can get up there."

Jean nodded her head sideways, conceding the point. She looked up at the mountain and tried to calculate the height. She thought she could see something at the summit, almost like a building with glowing white pillars, but before she could get a better look, a cloud moved past and it was gone.

"How far up?"

"Top."

"I hate you," she grumbled as she stormed off.

"No. No, you don't," he said under his breath. "Not yet."

"So, where is this chap you wanted us to meet, my good man?" Ken asked.

Petros gulped down a shot of whiskey and shrugged. "Probably out doing whatever it is he is doing, so help yourself to a drink."

Ken looked over at Caraway. "What do you think, old boy?"

"Yar," Caraway said, an aggravated smile plastered on his face.

"Two scotches, my friend," Ken called to the bartender, who responded with a quizzical eyebrow.

Petros shouted in Greek and the bartender quickly obliged, sliding them two glasses across the bar. Ken caught his easily, but Caraway succeeded only in batting it over with his fingers, spilling most of the liquor.

"Your friend seems to be having a little trouble there," Petros commented.

"Uh… yes," Ken began. "Lost his eye recently, I'm sad to say. Seagull, you see. Just came down and plopped it out," he said, miming a bird's beak attacking his right eye, ending with a demonstrative *pop!* He turned to Caraway. "Isn't that right, old boy?"

"Yar…" Caraway grumbled. He missed New York, but more than anything, he found himself, not for the first time, missing Francesca. He had so long ago given up on their marriage, that there was the promise of a new future together was exhilarating. To be dragged halfway across the world so soon after their renewed commitment just felt unfair. But he hadn't been dragged… Not really. He could have told the Lama no, turned on his heel, and headed straight back home. But he didn't. Sure, he had groused and complained, but he had climbed aboard that airship all the same. He hadn't even hesitated a step when the gangplank came down. Maybe it was just a side effect of working with the Lama, or maybe it was just the badge, but had he been given the same option a hundred times, he knew he would have made the same decision a hundred times over. He sighed. Francesca was definitely going to kill him.

But not before he killed Ken first. Watching the actor work undercover was a grating experience at best. For all his bluster the boy was clearly over his head, but here they were, dressed up like a couple of dime store pirates so they could… do what, exactly? Find out what happened to Jean? See if anyone knew about this 'Kookookachoo' monster? Caraway shook his head. All this supernatural hocus-pocus mumbo-jumbo was beginning to get to him, and if this was really tied to Brickman's golem and the creatures from the *Bartlett*… What he wouldn't give for a simple fistfight right now.

"American, yes?" a woman said behind him.

Caraway turned begrudgingly on his barstool to find himself face-to-face with one of the most beautiful women he had ever seen. She was slender, dressed in a simple yet attractive dress that showed off her figure while revealing nothing. Her raven hair was pulled back into a ponytail, a thin strand hanging over her left eye. She took a slow drag of her cigarette before she reiterated: "American, yes?"

"Yes," Caraway replied, unintentionally dropping his cover. "How could you tell?"

"The slouch. Americans always slouch when they drink, like they are lifting heavy weights."

Caraway ran his eye up and down her arched back. "And I take it you're not American?"

"Is my accent that bad?"

"It's pretty noticeable," he said with a crooked smile.

"Pity. You would think with all the Limeys and Yankees passing through here I would have at least picked up the accent." She eyed Caraway as she took another drag of her cigarette. "So, are you going to offer me a drink or am I going to have to ask myself?"

"You're on your own, sweetheart. I don't speak a lick of Greek and the bartender over there doesn't seem to understand a drop of English."

"Ιαπετος, μπορεί εσείς να δώσει σε ένα κορίτσι ένα ποτό?" the woman called. The bartender rolled his eyes as he poured her a glass of whiskey and slid it over. Deftly catching the glass, she gulped down the amber liquid in a single swig. Caraway had to admit he was impressed. "So, you are with the Limey?" she asked indicating Ken with wave of her cigarette.

"Billy Shakespeare over there?" Caraway said with a frustrated smile. "Yeah, I'm with him. Not that I have much choice."

She frowned, considering Ken as he chatted endlessly with Petros. "He likes to talk."

Caraway laughed. "You noticed that too, eh? Loves the sound of his own voice."

Her lips subtly curled at the corners. "What is your name, American?" she asked with a cloud of smoke.

"John," Caraway said, raising his glass.

"Pleasure to meet you, John. Sotiria," she said with a nod. "What brings you to the beautiful rock of Samothrace?"

"Work, as in lack of and searching for."

Sotiria tilted her head. "Bad time to be looking for work, no?"

Caraway shrugged. "Not like we have much choice."

Sotiria breathed in smoke. "No, I suppose we do not," she said quietly.

"Pretty crowded for this time of day, isn't it?"

Sotiria looked over the mass of people crowding the bar. "Yes, it should be slower, but then again, we all have something in common."

"And what's that?"

"Work, as in lack of and searching for."

"Don't tell me you worked the docks like these creeps," he said indicating the riffraff behind him.

Sotiria raised an eyebrow at him. "I think I should take some offense at that, John."

"I didn't mean to imply—"

"None of these men are creeps. Except for those over there," she said, indicating a particularly rancid group of men. "They are disgusting."

Caraway allowed himself a smile. He liked this bird, maybe because she reminded him so much of Francesca. Or probably because she didn't.

"But yes," she continued, "I work the docks. Not in the way you think. I saw the way your eye moved, John. My father was a fisherman, and when my mother died, he brought me aboard. When he passed, the boat became mine and I survived on our—on my own, at least until the storms… I still have my boat, but the fish are gone…"

A man appeared at Sotiria's side. He was short but built, a man who had dedicated his life to the sea. With a drink sloshing around in his right hand, the man wrapped his left arm around Sotiria's shoulder and smiled a broad, yellowed grin. Caraway crinkled his nose at the man's overwhelming odor.

"Sotiria, χορός με με," the drunk said.

"Αύριο, Nikolaos," she calmly replied, carefully peeling off Nicholaos's arm.

The drunk stumbled, closing his eyes as he tried to think of a response. "Ah…" he slowly began, "αυτός είναι αυτό που είπατε εμένα-ειπωμένος με χθες. Αυτός είναι αυτό που είπατε."

Sotiria gave the man a thin, unwelcoming smile. "Και θα πω το ίδιο πράγμα αύριο," she said. "Παρακαλώ, Nikolaos, κουβεντιάζω με το φίλο μου."

Nicholaos's tan and bearded face twisted into a scowl. "Είπα, χορός με με τώρα!" he barked, violently grabbing her arm.

Caraway jumped off his stool, grabbed the drunk by the collar, and pulled him over. "Hey, bucko, the lady said no!" he paused and then looked to Sotiria, quizzically. "That is what you said, right?"

Sotiria nodded quickly, her eyes wide.

Caraway looked back at Nicholaos. "She said no," he reiterated, "so why don't you take a long walk off a short pier? I bet there are plenty of 'em around here, so take your pick. Or else we're gonna have to get nasty, and you don't want that." He nodded to Sotiria. "Now, say that to him in Greek."

The drunk smashed his bottle against the bar in response, and aimed it at Caraway's face. "Piss off, American," he said in passable English.

"All right, that's how it's gonna work?" Caraway said with an eager grin. Without hesitation, he twisted Nicholaos's arm in the wrong direction. The drunk howled in pain as the broken bottle crashed to the floor. Caraway then quickly grabbed his own glass and smashed it hard onto the drunkard's head. Nicholaos stumbled backwards into a crowded table, throwing drinks and food into the air. The bar fell silent as more than twenty men shot out of their chairs.

"Aw, hell…" Caraway grumbled.

Sotiria jumped behind the bar as a bear of a man ran screaming toward Caraway. Without thinking, Caraway grabbed his barstool and swung at the man's face. Wood splintered and the man crumpled to the floor as two bruisers charged forward, ready for a pounding. Caraway braced himself from impact when the two hulks' legs suddenly flew out from under them, slamming to the ground. Before Caraway could react, Ken appeared beside him, brandishing a pair of barstool legs as impromptu billy clubs. They instinctually moved back to back as an increasing mass of angry, drunken sailors encircled them.

"What the hell did you do!?" Ken hissed.

"I was talking to a girl," Caraway said with a sardonic smile.

"Aren't you married?"

"What can I say? Women love me." Caraway shrugged. "Besides, we were just talkin'."

"See, it's because of guys like you that I'm still single," Ken grumbled.

"Yeah. That's the reason," Caraway said.

"So we gonna do this? Beat everyone up?"

"Yup."

"*Om! Ma-ni Pad-me Hum!* Eh?" Ken said with a smirk.

"*Om! Ma-ni Pad-me Hum!* Indeed."

Petros lit a cigarette, watching the fight escalate with a thin smirk. He liked these boys.

"Might I have a word?" Hirsch asked from the entryway of the Oberführer's private tent.

"Of course, Herr Sturmbannführer," the Oberführer said as he finished writing a letter at his desk, offhandedly gesturing to the chair opposite him. "I'll only be a moment."

Hirsch sat down, watching the Oberführer scratch out the remainder of his letter. "A note to your wife or your mistress?" he asked with a smarmy grin as he picked at his cheek.

"A dear friend, if you must know," he said, signing his name. He folded the correspondence and sealed it inside an envelope. "Johann!" the Oberführer called.

Johann ran in. Hirsch was quietly startled by his appearance. The young soldier's skin was ghostly pale, his hair an unnatural grey bordering on white, looking as though he had aged in an instant. His eyes were glass, wavering left and right in case the shadows came alive. "Sir?"

"See that this is delivered," the Oberführer said, handing the envelope to the *Soldat*.

The boy read the address listed and nodded in understanding. "Yes, sir."

"Skittish little fellow, isn't he?" Hirsch commented as he watched the boy run out.

"Poor boy's been through a lot recently," the Oberführer stated.

Hirsch noticed a recently pressed suit hanging in the corner. "Planning a night out?"

"Being that Jethro Dumont and I are acquainted, Gottschalk requested I pay a visit to his hotel tomorrow." The Oberführer impatiently tapped his pen against his desk. "What is on your mind, Herr Sturmbannführer?"

Hirsch laced his fingers together and gazed at his navel. "I want to get your perspective."

"On the dagger the doctor showed us last night, I assume," the Oberführer said without question. "What he claimed to be a piece of this supposed Third Jade Tablet."

"The Shard," Hirsch said, nervously cracking his knuckles. He cleared his throat. "I understand you've recently had some dealing with the supernatural."

The Oberführer shifted uncomfortably in his chair, unconsciously running a finger over the long scar on his forehead. "I am hesitant to call what I experienced in New York 'supernatural.'"

"As you stated in your report," Hirsch said, refusing to look the Oberführer in the eye. "However, I also remember reading that the local authorities were far more superstitious. They claimed it was a giant clay monster—a golem—that attacked our embassy."

The Oberführer shrugged. "Americans. Their country is full of men and women dressing up in audacious costumes, gallivanting about, claiming to have," he waved a hand in frustration as he searched for the word, "…'superpowers.' Gullible imbeciles. A whole nation willing to believe the slightest suggestion of the fantastic to distract them from their pitiful existence. I am absolutely certain that whatever—whoever—attacked the consulate was, despite the opinions of my American counterparts, nothing more than a very disturbed man in an impressive costume."

Hirsch considered this. "Then what is your take on the Shard?"

"Do you want my opinion as an officer or as a German citizen? As an officer, my superiors believe that this item will help bring about our victory, and I will do all in my power to ensure that it does."

Hirsch finally looked directly at the Oberführer. "And as a German?"

"It is nothing more than a trinket that belongs in a museum or, at most, used as a night light," the Oberführer said.

Hirsch sat silently for a moment. "It cut through the air, Herr Oberführer. We saw it slice right through reality, and what we saw on the other side… Explain that."

"Well, that, Herr Sturmbannführer, I cannot explain."

Hirsch massaged his forehead as he spoke. "I do not tell many people this, Herr Oberführer, but I am not a man of faith. I believe in the Führer, I believe in Germany. I have never, not for one second, believed in angels, demons, or for that matter, God. I believe in what I can touch," he said, tapping his chest with his fingers, then waved his hand in front of him, "what I can see. But, what we saw last night…" he trailed off, replaying the events of last night in his mind once more. He licked his lips. "That kind of *power*."

The Oberführer remained silent.

"I believe, Herr Oberführer," Hirsch said conspiratorially. "For the first time ever, I *believe*. This Third Jade Tablet, the 'Fire from Olympus.' It is the power of the gods and is more formidable than anything we could possibly imagine."

The Oberführer rested his elbows on his desk, folded his hands, and leaned forward. "If that is the case," he began skeptically, "then what do you think we should do with it?"

Hirsch moved closer and lowered his voice until it was almost inaudible. "We should destroy it."

The Twins' "home"—if it could be called that—was situated in a small cave about a mile outside town, overlooking the sea. Vasili had heard of the cave from Alexei and gossip around town, but nothing could have prepared him for what they found. Covering his mouth and nose with cuff of his jacket, Vasili tried to fight back the overpowering stench of rotted fish and seawater that permeated the space, the bile rising in his stomach. It was all he could do to keep it down.

"Pretty foul, eh?" Alexei said, laughing at Vasili's reaction. If he was at all affected by the stench, he didn't show it.

"Yes, sir," Vasili coughed as they moved through the entrance. "God, what is that?"

Alexei ducked his head as he walked through a low overhang. "They don't cook their fish," he said. "Raw, festering; that's how they like it. They leave it out to rot for days before they eat it."

As his eyes adjusted to the darkness Vasili could see piles of fish carcasses in varying states of decay, squelching beneath his boots with each hesitant step. But Alexei kept moving deeper and deeper into the cavern with unshakable purpose, while the entryway dropped down to a clouded pinprick in the darkness. And even though the sea fell further and further into the distance, the crashing of waves grew louder with each minute. Despite the torches set up intermittently throughout the cave, Vasili struggled to see more than a few steps in front of him, while Alexei seemed to walk through every turn and over every divot with practiced grace.

"You come here often, sir?" Vasili asked.

"Too often, my dear boy. Far too often," Alexei replied without looking back. He stopped short at a small opening in the cave and grumbled. "Where are they…? Ke'ta! *Narreta nu?*" he shouted in the Twins' bubbling tongue, his voice echoing.

There was no reply.

Alexei glanced back to Vasili. "Do you have your pistol, son?"

"Of course," he replied, feeling the weight against his side.

"Give it to me," Alexei instructed. Vasili placed the weapon is the old man's extended hand, knowing better than to question him. "Thank you. Ke'ta!" Alexei shouted into the darkness again. "Ke'ta!!! *Narreta nu, b'eheh soui tu'kanar'ren en!*"

The words were lost on Vasili, but he understood their intent: Alexei was angry.

A moment passed before one of the Twins' voice echoed through the cave. To Vasili's ears he sounded reluctant, maybe even scared. Alexei gave Vasili a mirthless smile, beckoning him forward. "This way," he said indicating a turn in the passage.

They moved down into the gradually darkening passageway, the sound of water—rushing, crashing, dripping—growing louder. Vasili glanced back to find the entrance had now completely disappeared, and wondered, not for the first time, if he could find his way back alone.

They squeezed through a small opening at the end the path and stepped onto a small jetty overlooking a massive subterranean sea. Light poured in through a small hole in the ceiling, casting everything in a pale blue glow. The Twins stood side by side, waist deep in the water, the bottom of their robes floating with the tide while the tops clung to their bony frames. Water dripped from their masks and headdresses. They had been swimming, Vasili realized, hoping his face didn't betray his surprise. One Twin stood up straight, almost regal, while his compatriot was hunched over in pain.

"Welcome," the regal Twin gurgled, bowing slightly.

"Ke'ta, what happened to Roe'qua?" Alexei asked, indicating the hunched Twin.

Vasili glanced back and forth between the two as the regal Twin—Ke'ta—babbled a response while the hunched Twin—Roe'qua—swayed back and forth, threatening to collapse. Up until now Vasili would have never been able to tell them apart, how Alexei could was beyond him.

Alexei held up a disciplinary hand, cutting short the Twin's rambling. "Ke'ta, please say it in Greek so Vasili will understand. Now, you were telling me about last night..." Alexei lead.

Ke'ta's head bowed in thought. "Yyyesss... As I say to you, I had gave Germans Shard, you ask as I do," Ke'ta croaked in awkward grammar. "Bearded One, D—Doctor. He, I gave to. Understood Shard's importance."

"Very good, but that doesn't explain Roe'qua," Alexei said with a tight smile. He looked over to the swaying Twin. "Tell me, Roe'qua, why were you at Astrapios's last night?"

Vasili's eyebrows shot up. How could Alexei know that? Even the Twins seemed surprised, their bodies stiffening.

Alexei stepped into the freezing water, unaffected by the cold. Standing in front of Roe'qua, Alexei placed his hands behind his back and slowly asked the question again. Roe'qua shook his head slowly, mumbling in his unusual tongue. Alexei tilted his head as he listened, but Vasili could see the old man's face begin to turn red. Even Ke'ta sensed Alexei's growing anger, slowly moving away as Roe'qua rambled on.

"Answer my question!" Alexei shrieked, his voice echoing throughout the waterlogged grotto. Ke'ta jumped back in surprise while Roe'qua curled into himself. The old man's face was blood red, the veins on his neck and forehead bulging, his eyes pushing out from his skull. Vasili had been witness to Alexei's rages before, but he had never seen him like this.

Roe'qua whispered a response, which only succeeding in angering Alexei more.

"What does he mean, you don't know where the Tablet is?!" Alexei screamed at Ke'ta, spit flying from his mouth like venom.

"Tablet you had gave forgery!" Ke'ta protested. "Not real! Not source of Shard!"

Alexei gritted his teeth. "Then who has it?"

"No know. Send Roe'qua look for it, thought hidden in secret. But then—"

Roe'qua croaked, interrupting Ke'ta with a long string of sounds. Vasili thought he heard something that sounded like "jade monk," but it could have easily been his imagination.

Alexei's eyes went wide. "He was there?" he whispered, stepping over to Roe'qua.

The Twin nodded affirmatively.

"Why?"

The Twin shook his head. He didn't know.

Alexei, though unsatisfied, knew he wouldn't get a better answer. "And what happened?"

Roe'qua gurgled a sad reply.

Alexei's face was a dark maroon—nearing black, but his voice was calm when he instructed Vasili to step outside.

"Sir?"

Alexei refused to meet Vasili's gaze. "Just next to the opening. Stay there unless I call for you."

Vasili nodded, knowing better than to protest. As he walked away, he could see Alexei rubbing his thumb along the gun handle. Vasili knew what was coming next.

"Don't look back," Alexei said over his shoulder.

Vasili ducked back through the hole. He walked a few steps away from the opening before shifting over to the side, out of view of Alexei and the others, but still within earshot.

"Show me, Roe'qua," he heard Alexei say, the old man's voice hoarse yet firm.

Vasili tried to fight the urge to look back inside. No one knew what the Twins looked like, but if Alexei saw him… But even then, Alexei was so inflamed, so focused, he probably wouldn't notice, would he? No longer able to hold himself back, Vasili pressed against the wall and leaned over just enough to peer inside to see Alexei standing over Roe'qua. He could see the Twin's pale white hand appear from beneath his cloak and reach up to remove his mask. Black slime dripped down scaly white flesh, pooling at the crook of his neck, but before Vasili could see any more, Alexei shifted his stance, blocking Vasili's view.

"Dammit," Vasili breathed. He watched as the three of them spoke in soft, croaking whispers, an unintelligible conversation that sounded like a confession.

"You did what?!" Alexei screamed.

Vasili flinched, almost losing his footing, his stomach twisting into knots, as if Alexei's anger was radiating out, affecting the world around him.

Ke'ta stepped into view, holding his pale hands up, pleading. "Please. He act on instinct! You see what happened. No choice. Poison work fast, nothing we could do."

Vasili watched as Alexei silently aimed the pistol at Roe'qua's head and fired. The gunshot echoed through the grotto as the Twin limply splashed into the water. Quickly turning away, Vasili stuffed his hands into his pockets and stared at the ground. Alexei walked through the opening moments later, wiping a thin layer of sweat from his brow with the back of one hand, while casually handing Vasili the warm gun with the other.

"Let's go," the old man said, his eyes bloodshot, his face lined with hair thin cracks that visibly healed as he marched off. "We're done here."

Vasili followed after, hesitating momentarily to glance back into the grotto. Tenderly cradling Roe'qua's lifeless body, Ke'ta solemnly replaced his brother's mask before carrying him out into the cave's deeper, blacker waters. A small pit had formed inside Vasili's stomach, growing deeper with each passing second. It wasn't the fact that Vasili had just seen Alexei kill one of the Twins; it was that they were answering to him as if he was their *master*. Nothing Vasili had seen up until then would have ever led him to believe that the Twins were beholden to Alexei, something he found extremely unsettling, though he couldn't pinpoint why.

"Take me back to town," Alexei said to Vasili as he caught up to the old man. "I need to find something."

Vasili cleared his throat. Alexei's cold heart didn't surprise him, but it didn't comfort him either. "Do you still want to meet with Dumont?" Vasili asked hesitantly.

Alexei paused for a moment and sighed, massaging his eyes in frustration.

"Jethro Dumont is dead."

Chapter 7
SECRET ALLIANCES

*H*e's dead, Tulku," Dorje said, placing a sympathetic hand on
Tsarong's shoulder.

*Tsarong brushed away the fat lama's hand as he walked deeper into the
snow-covered expanse. It had been nearly five days since he had sent
Dumont into the frozen wilderness. Five days of constant vigilance, prayer,
and waiting. The other monks had given up on the American three days
ago, believing him lost to the ice and mountains—but despite the protests
of his students, Tsarong refused to lose faith, sitting by the entrance of the
Temple of the Clouds from sunrise to sunset. On the fifth day, Tsarong finally
stood, opened the great and massive doors, and stepped out onto the
mountains. Dorje alone had followed, if for no other reason than to try and
bring his ancient master in from the cold. They had been marching through
the frozen land for several hours now, finding nothing more than rocks and
snow, but Tsarong kept moving, kept searching.*

"Do you remember, Dorje, when I went out into the frost for ten days?"

*"Yes, but Tulku, even if the Jade Tablet has chosen the American, he
does not have your skill—your training. He has only been with us a few
short months. You cannot expect him to survive such conditions!"*

"If I did not expect it, Dorje, I would have not sent him out."

*"Even you have said the prophecy was vague, open to interpretation.
How can we be sure we understood it? That we understood its true
meaning? Maybe he was brought to us to remove the Tablet from human
hands. By dying—by taking the Tablet from us—he has brought balance to
Dharma once again."*

*Tsarong waved this away. "Were that even a consideration, do you not
think I would have done so myself when the Tablet was mine?"*

Dorje swallowed his protest.

"There is a cave not too far from here," Tsarong said, indicating a small black speck several yards away. *"He might have sought shelter there."*

"Om! Lama kyeno!" Dorje sighed three times before following after his master.

It was nearly an hour before they made it to the cave. Tsarong knocked away the loose snow from above the entrance with his walking stick, revealing the opening to be only large enough to fit a thin man crouching on his knees. He glanced back at Dorje. *"I suppose you will have to wait outside,"* he said with the slightest hint of a smile before crouching down and climbing inside.

There was little light to be found, though the air was noticeably warmer than outside. Lifting his hand above his head, Tsarong discovered the roof of the cave rose quickly and was able to stand after only a few steps. He reached into his furs, bringing out the small cigarette lighter he had found amongst Dumont's personal effects, the letters JPD engraved on one side. Clumsily lighting the flint he was able to make out scant details around him. There were bones scattered around the ground, most were of local fauna, but some Tsarong recognized as distinctly human. He continued to move deeper until he came upon a snow leopard and her two cubs. Blood coated their muzzles, their eyes staring intently at Tsarong's minimal frame.

"Om! Tare Tuttare Ture Soha!" Tsarong whispered. *"Please, no!"*

"You have nothing to fear, Tulku," Jethro Dumont said as he stepped into the light. Dumont was bare chested, unaffected by the cold. *"The old girl won't hurt you. Sorry, I didn't come back sooner, but her cubs were sick and I thought it best I stay behind and take care of them."*

"Are you injured?" Tsarong asked.

Dumont unconsciously touched the black bruise on his side. *"Only a little. We had a misunderstanding before, but I'm fine now."*

"Come back with me to the Temple of the Clouds, we have been quite concerned."

Dumont looked wistfully at the snow leopard. *"*Tayata Om Muni Muni Maha Munaye Soha,*"* he recited. *"Yes. I suppose I should."*

"Dorje has some extra furs for you."

"That was thoughtful. Thank you. But, Tulku..."

"Yes?"

"When we return to the Temple, I think its about time you start

explaining what exactly this is," he said, holding up his right hand, the rainbow ring glowing in jade.

The sun had arched past it apex and was making its way beneath the horizon when Jean and Aïas finally made camp beneath a small overhang roughly a quarter of the way up the mountain. They had been climbing for most of the day, and while hunger and exhaustion never found them, Jean couldn't shake the sense that something was wrong. His gaze kept falling to her leg, though she never knew why. It didn't hurt, it wasn't even sore, but a part of her, a buzzing in the back of her mind knew it should be. She pinched her eyes shut and leaned her head back against the rocky wall.

"You all right, Jean?" Aïas asked as he kindled the campfire.

Jean rubbed her eyes. "Just this damn headache. I dunno, maybe its 'cause the air's thin, but it's getting worse."

"What's it feel like?"

Jean closed her eyes. "Like a jar full of bees and someone decided to shake it."

"Probably just the altitude," he said after a moment.

"Mm," she sounded, furrowing her brow in a vain effort to fight back the sensation. "You ever hear of the Green Lama?" she asked after a moment.

Aïas nodded. "I have, and some of the others. Men and women dressing up in costumes…" He chuckled. "You Americans certainly have flair."

Jean smiled weakly. "I once guessed his secret identity."

"Did you, now?" Aïas said with a subtle arch of his eyebrow. "How did he take it?"

"Oddly nonplussed," she admitted with a frown. "I thought he was Jethro Dumont. You ever hear of him?"

"Everyone has heard of Jethro Dumont, Jean." He poked at the fire. "Why did you think they were the same person?"

She shrugged. "I always had my suspicions, it just made too much sense to be otherwise. Most people seem to think the Lama's alter ego is Dr. Pali, but Pali's clearly just theatrical greasepaint and a halfway decent accent. Not many people notice that. But I did. Maybe because I work in movies and the theater or maybe I'm just that impressive," she said with mock arrogance. "It wasn't until I saw Dumont stand up against these... demons a few months ago that I was certain. So, one night after one of our adventures—I can never remember which, they all blur together—I followed the Lama to one of his hideouts and Dumont walked out shortly after. I never said anything. Why would I? It was too much fun to have a secret, to simply know something no one else did. At least until that Nazi von Kultz came to town and I had a chance to rub it in his face. I was so damn proud of myself, too. He just shrugged it off, like I was telling him the weather, because... I was wrong. The next day both the Green Lama and Jethro Dumont showed up at my apartment together. I was sure it was a trick, just another way to keep me on my toes, but then I saw them both fighting atop the Brooklyn Bridge. And... that was that. The thing is Dumont's as much a hero as the Lama. Heck, more so, really."

"How? Because he has slept with every woman in Hollywood?"

"No." Jean shifted uncomfortably. "No. I mean... I know that's what everyone thinks of him—I've seen the newsreels—but there's something more to him. Deeper. There's a spark to him; this caring for everyone he comes in contact with, and me—Maybe it's his Buddhism, maybe he's just a decent man, but for all the gossip they like to sling around, Dumont is the most grounded man I have ever met. And when he talks to you, it's almost like you're the first person he's spoken to in years." She tucked a strand of hair behind her ear. "Not that long ago we were kidnapped by these demons—or something like that—and Dumont, the man the tabloids treat like a mindless Casanova, risked his life to save mine... Perhaps I just wanted Dumont to be the Green Lama. There was always just something about him—Dumont, I mean—something that made me feel—" She caught herself.

"Made you feel?"

She shook her head and ignored the question. "It's just that when I learned Dumont and the Green Lama were different people, it felt like someone had cut something out of my memory, as if everything I thought I knew was wrong." She curled her legs to her chest and wrapped her arms around her knees. There was something on the edge of her memory, something she had said, a word she could almost remember. Something so simple and powerful... "I feel like that again, only worse."

Aïas looked up from the fire. "How so?"

"It feels like missing time, as if the world around me was changed without my knowing. At least with the Green Lama and Dumont, I *saw* them together. It was real and right in front of me. But now… I keep trying to remember something, but all I can see is a big white blank."

Aïas regarded her for several moments before he tentatively asked, "And how long have you been feeling like this?"

Jean shrugged. "Day? Day and half?" She ran her hands up and down her legs in an effort to warm her limbs when her finger caught a small hole in her right boot. She glanced and saw the bullet hole torn through the leather. When had that happened? Shifting her body, she glanced at the inside of her leg, finding another hole directly across from the first. The buzzing in her head suddenly worsened. She pressed the heels of her hands against her temples, trying to fight back the pain. She screamed in agony as images flashed past her eyelids and she began to remember.

"I was shot," she mumbled, then saying it louder. "I was shot! Wasn't I?"

Aïas stiffened, his eyes wide.

"My leg. They shot me in the leg." More memories burst to life in terrifying, painful clarity. "And then—Oh, God."

Aïas stood up and looked directly at Jean, his black irises once again a blazing jade. His voice shook the world around them. "You can't remember that."

Jean gritted her teeth. "What did you do to me?"

"Jean, calm down," Aïas commanded, the ground cracking beneath him. Jean's heart skipped a beat when she realized he wasn't casting a shadow.

Jean jumped to her feet and drew her gun. Tears streamed down her face, but she kept the pistol level, her sights on Aïas's glowing eyes. "What did you do to me?" she screamed.

"You don't understand the role you have yet to play," he said as he stepped through the fire, his voice resonating from the mountain.

Jean pulled down on the trigger, firing every last bullet at his chest. The shots echoed out into the night as the bullets passed harmlessly through him. Aïas glanced down at his unwounded chest and then back at Jean, his eyes ablaze.

Suddenly, the world was enveloped in light. A howling wind came down upon them and beneath it Jean could hear voices, ancient, inhuman but somehow familiar.

Then, all was silent.

Caraway adjusted the slab of frozen meat over his black eye, grimacing as the pain radiated into his skull. Lying down across the bar, left arm wrapped behind his head, he glanced at the deserted war zone that was once a pub, a no-man's land of spilt liquor, broken glass, smashed wood, and a fair share of blood.

Sotiria appeared from behind the bar, a half broken bottle of whiskey in one hand and a shot glass in the other.

"Pretty brave, huh?" Caraway said proudly, a small grin curling the corner of his lips.

"Stupid is another word for brave, no?" Sotiria asked as she poured herself whiskey, picking out the glass shards with her fingers.

"Yeah… Stupid is another word for brave," Ken interjected from a table nearby, heavily resting his head on his hands.

Sotiria threw back her shot and quickly poured herself another. "You did not think," she said between drinks, "that maybe I might have been able to handle him on my own?"

Caraway removed the slab of meat and shifted up onto his elbows so he could face the raven-haired woman. "Sweetheart, the look you gave me didn't exactly say 'Step back while I take care of this guy.'"

Sotiria raised an eyebrow. "Nicholaos Adrian is a hothead, a drunk, and a very, very *brave* man," she said pointedly to Caraway, eliciting a chuckle from Ken. "Had you given me a moment, I would have distracted him with a simple math equation."

Caraway rolled his eyes and smirked, at once enchanted and exasperated. "Listen, dame, if you—"

"No!" Sotiria exclaimed as she slapped him hard, intentionally hitting a massive welt on the back of his head. Caraway grunted in pain. "You do *not* call me 'dame.' My name is Sotiria, and if you call me 'dame' again I will shove this bottle into a place you would not enjoy," she said, raising the broken bottle to pontificate her statement.

"Jeez, woman," Caraway grumbled as he rubbed the wound. "I just fought a whole friggin' bar of really big, really violent men for you and you're hittin' *me*."

"Hey, I fought them, too," Ken added meekly.

Sotiria leaned her face inches away from Caraway's. "And you were both very *brave*. And what did you get out of it?"

Ken showed off a large wound on his right arm. "I think someone shot me."

"I am not impressed," Sotiria said to Caraway.

"I think someone shot me with a *gun*," Ken added.

"Well, you boys impressed me," Petros said from within a cloud of smoke at the other side of the establishment, nursing a bottle of ouzo. "Once the boss gets back, he will be hearing how well you two fight."

"It's only a graze, but it still hurts."

Petros raised his glass. "Welcome to the club, limey."

Caraway swung his legs over the bar and sat upright. "Fantastic, does that mean we got ourselves a job?" he asked, no longer satisfied with being monosyllabic.

Petros shrugged noncommittally.

The front door burst open as a tower of a man walked in, all muscle and height; followed shortly by an older, slender man. Call it policeman's intuition, but Caraway knew instantly the old man was in charge, probably the local Al Capone; the tower was a bruiser, probably the old man's second-in-command or at the very least his bodyguard. These were the guys they needed to meet, and from the way the old man was eyeing him, Caraway oddly felt as if this audience had been expected.

The bruiser's jaw fell open at the sight of the destroyed tavern while the old man seemed unfazed—or possibly, too preoccupied to care. The bruiser looked over at Petros and asked him a single question in Greek, which Caraway rightfully assumed was, "What the hell happened?"

Petros pointed a thumb over at Caraway and Ken.

The bruiser turned to them and repeated the question in Greek. Caraway and Ken shared a mystified look, but before they could respond Sotiria spoke up, arguing their case—or at least Caraway *hoped* she was. The bruiser listened for a moment before glancing over to the old man who simply nodded. Looking back at the Americans, the bruiser began to speak before Petros quickly interrupted him.

"English," he said, tapping his ear.

The bruiser grimaced while he translated in his head. "Who are you?" he eventually asked with a significant accent.

"William Shakespeare," Ken said in his own strained British accent.

"John Caraway," he said with a slight wave. "And as to what happened, I figured Sotiria already covered that. Not that I understood any of it, but it sounded like an explanation."

The bruiser glanced over at Sotiria. Caraway caught a familiar glint in the other man's eyes—it was the same way he looked at Francesca. "She only said you were very *brave*."

A soft smirk curled the corner of Sotiria's lips.

"Oh, Lord," Ken groaned, burying his face in his hands.

"We were just defending the dame's honor," Caraway replied, a soft smirk curling the corner of his lips as Sotiria's expression quickly soured.

"Took on a good thirty or more on their own," Petros said in English for Ken and Caraway's benefit. "I have not seen fighting like that since the War."

The bruiser's eyes shot between Ken and Caraway. "And you two just came to my town looking for fights?"

"Work," Caraway said, and then gestured to Petros. "He said you could probably give us some."

"I can't give you anything," the bruiser replied.

Caraway nodded to the old man. "What about Al Capone over there? Can he give us anything? He looks like the type of guy who can."

The old man measured the two foreigners and licked his dry lips. He leaned over and whispered something to the bruiser in Greek.

The bruiser shrugged and began walking toward the other end of the tavern. "All right, come with us," he said with a beckoning wave. He opened the door at the back, letting the old man step through with Petros following after.

Caraway jumped off the bar, wincing slightly as his various bruises all throbbed at once. "You comin' with?" he asked Sotiria, tossing a thumb toward the door.

She shook her head. "No, you enjoy your boys' club. I'll work on finishing this," she said, jingling her glass.

"What do you think he'll have us do?" Ken whispered to Caraway as they walked toward the other room.

"As long as they don't make me wear anything frilly I think I'll be fine, Shakespeare," Caraway whispered through the side of his mouth.

Ken squinted at his compatriot. "Oh, shut up."

Vasili didn't like the way Sotiria looked at the American, but then he didn't like the way Sotiria looked at anyone. Ultimately it didn't matter once Alexei gave the newcomers the okay, and after today Vasili was not going to start questioning the old man's judgment. Alexei sat down behind his desk and laced his fingers together, eyeing the two foreigners.

"So, you boys are good in a fight?" Alexei said in Greek to the two foreigners, which Vasili quickly translated. Alexei was fluent in German, Turkish, Egyptian, even Italian, but knew only a little English, so it was up to Vasili to act as translator.

"Yeah, we're not so bad," the mustached man named Caraway said with a self-satisfied shrug.

"Good, as it happens I am in need of some help," Alexei said through Vasili. "If you are as good as Petros says you are, then you may be of some use to me."

The little one calling himself Shakespeare smiled broadly. "Well, that's what we're here for, old chap."

Alexei nodded thoughtfully, his gaze piercing. "There is a book I need," he said eventually.

Caraway snorted. "Doesn't this island have a library?"

Alexei ignored the comment. "Its contents and why I need it are none of your concern."

"Not a problem," the American said. "Despite the name, Billy Shakespeare here can't read a word."

"Vasili will take the lead, Petros will assist you as well. Normally, I would go through… *different* channels, but unfortunately time is not a luxury I am currently afforded. You will begin tomorrow morning."

All of this surprised Vasili as he translated. He couldn't remember the last time Alexei had picked up a newspaper, let alone read a book. And based on the old man's tone, Vasili knew that this wasn't going to be a simple pick up or smash-and-grab. But why would he ask these men when he could easily pick from the hundreds of men they knew could be trusted?

"If you are not up to the task," Alexei said, "I can always find someone else. I assure you that no one else in this town will pay you a quarter of what I would pay you, let alone offer you a job."

The American puckered his lips as if he had bit down on something sour. "Fine…" he said at last. "Count us in."

"Excellent." Alexei knocked on his desk quickly. "I will supply you with all the details shortly. For now get some rest, you will need it. Vasili will arrange a room for you. That is all," he said with a wave toward the door.

"Yeah, yeah," Caraway said. "One more thing. Before we go riskin' our necks, you mind telling us the *name* of this book we're gonna risk life and limb for?"

Vasili translated Caraway's question, admittedly curious as well. Alexei considered both Caraway and Vasili for a moment before he simply replied, "*Necronomicon.*"

"Oh, please, let this be another dream… Another weird, really realistic, scary dream…" Jean murmured as she awoke. "Please just let me wake up in bed, in a beautiful villa overlooking the Mediterranean. And room service... Room service would be really nice right about now." She risked one eye open to discover a pure white ceiling above her. Opening the other, she found herself on a king-sized bed in the middle of a massive suite opening out to a veranda overlooking the Mediterranean. The sun was shining and the birds were chirping. A cool, comfortable sea breeze flowed in, the pure white drapes billowing in lazy waves. She was still dressed in her clothing; her boots laid neatly to the side of the bed, her stolen pistol placed on a small nightstand. Instinctually grabbing the gun, she slipped it into the back of her belt, climbed out of bed, pulled on her boots, and walked over to the veranda. The sea was a glistening blue-green; the breeze rustled through her hair, masking the heat of the sun, tasting of salt and water.

"Okay," Jean breathed. "Amazing as this is, I *really* need to stop waking up in strange places," she said. "What would my mother think?"

But something was off; she could feel it buzzing in the back of her head. The last thing she remembered, she was sitting by the fire with Aïas when she felt the bullet hole in her boot and then—

"All right, Aïas!" she shouted. "I know this isn't real, so you might as well get whatever the hell this is over with."

In an instant, the horizon and the suite evaporated, leaving the world a seamless white. Light came from all angles, but there were no shadows. There was no floor, no ceiling, no walls; there was nothing but white for as far as her eyes could see.

"You know, Jean," Aïas said, a few steps behind her, "most people don't figure that one out until at least the end of the first week."

Jean turned to face him, keeping her hand placed on the butt of her pistol. He was clean-shaven and dressed in the one of the blackest suits she had ever seen, a void in the light. He walked differently, almost as if he was floating with each step. He seemed taller, broader, and, impossibly, younger. Even his accent was gone.

"I'm talented like that," she shrugged nonchalantly, hoping her growing fear wasn't breaking through her façade. "So, are you going to tell me who—or what—you really are, or am I just going to have to guess?"

Aïas raised an eyebrow and smiled. "Like you said, you're talented, so why don't you take a guess?"

Jean bit her lip and hesitated. "Well, you're not human."

Aïas tilted his head to the side, clearly amused.

"Okay, to be honest," Jean blurted. "I was sort of hoping you were just going to come out and tell me, Aïas, because I'm a little lost in the woods here."

Aïas chuckled. "No, I'm not human. Technically speaking. I'm something a bit... older. And they don't call Aïas. Not up here. Here, I'm known as Prometheus."

"I cannot believe I'm doing this..." Caraway said, fiddling with his eye patch as he paced the dock hours before dawn. Water lapped up against the pier's wooden pillars, the sea breathing in long salty sighs. At the far end of the pier a ratty old fishing boat swayed with the tide. They were both dressed in all black attire, wool caps on their heads. Caraway had flipped up his pea coat's collar to fight off the cold of the night, while Ken, seated atop a wooden pillar, tackled this problem with a growing pile of scorched cigarette butts.

"Jeez, are you this bad when you work with the Lama?" Ken said as he lit another cigarette.

"I'm not typically *robbing people* when I'm with the Lama," Caraway shot back.

"Yeah, well, y'know… first time for everything," Ken mused as he breathed out a cloud of smoke.

"I'm so glad you're taking this in stride."

Ken shrugged. "We're stealing a book. A book no one's ever heard of. Cripes, you're acting like we're about to steal the friggin' *Mona Lisa*."

"At this rate…" Caraway growled in frustration. "This whole thing is getting out of hand, dammit. We're not getting any closer to finding Jean or figuring out this whole Kookookachoo business. 'Go undercover.' What does Jethro Dumont know about detective work?"

"We're stealing a *book*," Ken reiterated, unconsciously massaging the gunshot wound on his arm.

"It's all the same to me," Caraway said, firmly. "I'm a cop, first and foremost."

"No, you're *annoying*, first and foremost," Ken said, losing his patience. He jumped off his perch and marched over to Caraway with an accusatory finger. "We both know this isn't exactly what either of us had planned, but my *best friend* is out there somewhere, probably in a whole lot of trouble if not dead already. If this is what we have to do in order to find her, then so be it. Last thing we need is you getting all high and mighty right now especially when this was your goddamn idea!"

"Don't point at me, Clayton," Caraway said hotly, pushing Ken's hand away.

"Don't push me, jack off!" Ken shouted as he shoved Caraway.

Caraway raised a fist. "Back off *now* if you don't want what's coming to ya."

"Come on!" Ken clapped his hands against his chest, urging Caraway on. "Let's see it! Let's what ya got, ya jerk!"

Caraway launched forward, grabbing Ken by the collar.

"Whoa there, boys!" Sotiria shouted as she dove in between them, pushing them apart. "I do not mean to step into your lovers' squabble," she huffed, "but last I heard you two are going to be robbing someone tonight."

"It ain't nothing," Caraway muttered as he adjusted his wool cap. "Just a difference of opinion is all. Ain't that right, Shakes?"

"Aye," Ken said in his faux British accent, eyes locked on Caraway. "Just a difference of opinion." He turned to Sotiria. "But if you don't mind me asking, young lady, what in the bloody hell are you doing out here so late?"

"My boat," she said indicating the old trawler.

"Little late for a fishing trip, isn't it?" Ken asked.

"Fishing?" Sotiria laughed. "I'm your transport."

Caraway placed his hands on his belt. "Bullshit."

"How did you think you were getting there? Car? Train? This is not America, boys." She snorted as she walked past them. "Fastest way to get anywhere around here is by water. And besides, there are not many people you could trust with this kind of job."

"No offense, Sotiria," Caraway said as he followed after her, "you don't really seem like the criminal type."

She paused and glanced back over her shoulder, eyebrow arched seductively. "I'm not. Do you not remember our conversation yesterday? I am the 'looking for work' type. Besides, you cannot always judge someone by his or her appearance. Take Alexei for example, you would never know that he was the town sheriff."

Caraway's jaw fell open. "He's the what?"

Sotiria laughed. "Did you not know?"

Caraway tapped his temple, playing away his shock. "You have to remember I've been knocked around a little bit recently."

"That is true," she chuckled as she climbed up the short gangway onto her boat. "Besides, Vasili owes me a few."

Butterflies danced around Caraway's stomach. "Oh yeah…? What's the story with you two?"

"No story to tell," Vasili said as he and Petros appeared out of the darkness. Like Ken and Caraway they were dressed in all black, though Caraway couldn't help but notice the knives holstered to Petros's hips.

"Well, I would not say that," Sotiria said with a touch of sorrow.

Vasili cleared his throat. "Sotiria, please get the boat started."

"Would you mind telling me where we will be heading?" she asked.

Vasili reached into his coat pocket and took out a folded piece of paper.

He read over it quickly before placing it back in his pocket, his hands shaking. "South. That's all you need to know for now."

"South is a very vague direction," she retorted.

"Start the boat. Now, Sotiria," Vasili commanded.

Pursing her lips, Sotiria showed Vasili an open palm and headed toward the cabin, indignantly stomping her feet. Caraway caught a small, sad smile break Vasili's face before he turned his attention back the others. "Shall we?" he said, gesturing to the boat.

"You got nothing to worry about, boys," Petros said, placing his hands on Caraway and Ken's shoulders. "Me and Vasili, we have been through much worse than what we got in store tonight. No?"

"Hope you boys have your sea legs," Sotiria called from the cabin.

"As long as we don't have to *fly* anywhere," Ken commented, "I'm just dandy."

The Oberführer steepled his fingers as he gazed out the window. "You understand, of course, there are those who would consider what you are proposing treason," he said to Hirsch. They rode in the back of their Volkswagen, dressed in civilian clothes in hopes of avoiding any unnecessary attention from the locals as they made their way to the Aiolos Hotel. The Oberführer noticed Hirsch's nervous glance over at their driver. "You need not worry about Johann, Herr Sturmbannführer," he said, answering Hirsch's unspoken question, "he is one of the few people you can trust."

Hirsch nodded slowly, though not fully satisfied. "If I were suggesting," he began hesitantly, "that we go against Germany, then yes, you would be correct. But I want to save Germany, Herr Oberführer. Protect it from this... *evil*. The Führer has brought us to the cusp of a brave new world; so close within our reach I can feel it at the tips of my fingers. I do not want to fail that dream." He paused, considering his declaration. "Do you consider that treason, Herr Oberführer?"

The Oberführer regarded Hirsch. "No, Herr Sturmbannführer," he said after a moment. "I do not."

Hirsch dropped his head and let out a long sigh. "Thank you."

The Oberführer leaned back in his seat and pressed his thumb to his lips in thought. "It will not be easy," he said after a moment.

Hirsch closed his eyes as if in pain. "I know, sir."

The Oberführer nodded. "It will take some planning, though time is not a commodity we can waste. Appearances and secrecy, above all else, will be the keys to our success."

"So, you will help?"

"Where I can, Herr Sturmbannführer. Where I can." The Oberführer leaned forward and tapped the driver on the shoulder and pointed to the large building to their left. "The hotel is over there, Johann."

"*Ja, Herr Oberführer,*" the young soldier said, pulling the car up to the Hotel's main entrance.

"Herr Sturmbannführer," the Oberführer said as the car came to a stop, "you can stay here for the time being. There is no reason for both of us to waste our time if the American isn't here."

"Yes, sir," Hirsch said with a nod.

The Oberführer stepped out of the car and walked into the hotel lobby, bypassing the receptionist and making his way toward the elevator. There was no point in asking for assistance; he already knew where he was going. Exiting the elevator at the penthouse level, he walked over to the presidential suite. He knocked at the door but there was no answer. He tested the doorknob, finding it locked. Undeterred, he reached into his pocket and retrieved a small metallic pick. Inserting it into the keyhole he twisted and turned it until he undid the lock and swung open the door.

Stepping inside, he found the suite to be in utter disarray, a pungent order wafting out from the other side of the flat. He covered his mouth and nose. He moved toward the bedroom and bath where the smell was most pervasive. Sliding open the double doors he found a man in torn green robe unconscious on the ground. Rancid black bile covered the floor.

"*Verdammt nochmal!*" the Oberführer growled as he raced forward. He pressed his hands to the man's throat, shocked by the clamminess and the near freezing temperature of the other's skin. He could feel a pulse, soft and weak. The man was barely alive. Running over to the bathroom, the Oberführer filled a small glass with water and brought it over to the unconscious man. Doubting it would work, he tossed the water on the man's face in hopes of reviving him.

Miraculously, the man sputtered and coughed, regaining consciousness.

He feebly lifted up his head as his eyes fluttered open. He gazed up at the Oberführer for a moment before a weak smile broke his bruised face.

"Good to see you again, Herr Oberst Gan," he said feebly.

"It's Oberführer Gan now, and it's good to see you too, Herr Dumont."

Chapter 8
MYTHS & LEGENDS

*N*o one knows the true origins of the Jade Tablet," Tsarong said as he lit the butter candles of the antechamber. Dumont paced the room, once again dressed in his orange and red robes. He remained unshaven from his days out in the mountains, a thin fuzz outlining his features. "We only know that it was and always has been," Tsarong continued, carefully choosing his words. "It has been passed down for countless generations—there are some who believe that even Buddha himself once bore the Tablet."

"It's not exactly a jade tablet, is it?" Dumont wondered aloud. "Rainbow Hair Ring would probably have been more appropriate."

Tsarong turned to his pupil. "The name Jade Tablet is only a rough translation of its original name, much in the same way 'Om! Ma-ni Pad-me Hum!' only appears to mean 'Hail, the jewel in the lotus flower.' Neither truly reveals the meaning—the power—within."

"Is that what this thing is? Power?"

"Unlike anything else this world has ever seen," Tsarong said quietly. "Power to fight the darkness and keep all realms in balance."

"The sword fighting, sending me out into the cold. You're training me, not just to be a lama, but to be… something more."

"Yes."

Dumont rotated his hand as he examined the ring before clenching his fist. "I didn't come here for power, Tulku. I came for enlightenment. I wanted to find peace in the Dharma so that I may bring it back to my countrymen."

Tsarong nodded in understanding, pleased to hear this. "And you will find it. You see, though you are not aware of it you are on the path of a Bodhisattva, a journey that will lead all sentient beings out of the darkness. Bearing the Jade Tablet is, for you, but one aspect of that journey, albeit a painful one."

"You're not kidding," Dumont laughed sardonically.

"No one knows the full extent of the Tablet's powers or its true purpose. Even during the time I wore it, I had only experienced a fraction of its abilities..."

Dumont turned to face Tsarong. *"You're telling me that in the thousands of years this thing has been passed down, no one has been able to figure what it really is?"*

"Yes."

Dumont scrutinized Tsarong for a moment. *"You don't know how to get it off, do you?"*

Tsarong's shoulders fell in defeat. *"No, I do not, but it is said that there will be one who will be able to remove it and learn its secrets."*

Dumont's eyes drifted away. *"I didn't want this. Any of this,"* he said softly. *"Why did the Tablet choose me?"*

Tsarong placed his hands behind his back and sighed. He would not lie to Dumont, but could not tell him the truth, at least not the whole truth. *"Because, Jethro Dumont, you are* the Green Lama.*"*

"So, Herr Dumont... Or should I call you the *Green Lama?*" Oberführer Gan asked as he poured himself a drink from the suite's bar. Like Rick Masters, Gan, a member of the Jewish Underground, was one the few people who knew that Jethro Dumont, Dr. Charles Pali, and the Green Lama were all one and the same. After the destruction of the golem, Jethro chose to reveal his identity to both Rabbi Brickman and Gan in hopes of making amends.

Even then it was a tenuous relationship.

"Call me Jethro, please, Herr Oberführer," Jethro said with a slight bow of his head. He had changed out of his robe and cleaned himself off. Miraculously, the wound on his arm had healed considerably since he had blacked out, thought he still felt woozy and weak. He guessed he had been unconscious for nearly a day, possibly longer.

"No, Herr Dumont will suffice," Gan said as he gulped down his drink and poured himself another. "So strange to find you here. I am not sure if you noticed, but we are a long way away from New York City."

"I was about to ask you the same question," Jethro hoarsely replied.

"*Ach was!* Herr Dumont. I was making an observation," Gan said with a wag of his finger.

"I'm looking for my friend Jean Farrell. She was framed for the murder of a local politician and has gone missing."

"The redhead who destroyed Rabbi Brickman's golem? And she seemed so *nice*," he said, dripping with sarcasm.

Jethro choice to ignore Gan's slight. "I'm afraid the mystery goes far beyond a simple murder. While investigating the crime scene I was attacked by... a creature," he said. He related his encounter at Astrapios's and his narrow survival. "I don't know what it was searching for, but I'm almost certain it is tied to... *other* dark forces I have faced..."

"Dark forces..." Gan gazed down at his glass. "How do you mean...?"

Jethro told Gan of the demons aboard the *Bartlett*, the living storm, the voices, and his vision of the dark ceremony. He chose not to tell him of Ken or Caraway in hopes of aiding their undercover efforts. "I believe, Herr Oberführer, it is now your turn to tell me why you're in Kamariotissa."

Gan cleared his throat. "You are no doubt aware of Hitler's obsession with the occult. Your little adventure in Tibet all those years ago was only one part of his crusade to claim any and all mystical artifacts in hopes of aiding his efforts of world conquest... Yes, I know all about your encounter with Heydrich," he said, responding to Jethro's reaction. "I understand you killed him. Pulled the life out of him to save a young boy... Suffice to say it is because of your efforts there that I have been brought here."

Jethro grimaced, knowing all too well what the Oberführer was hinting at. "The Jade Tablet," he said mournfully.

Gan nodded. "The Third and final."

"*Gate Gate Paragate Parasamgate Bodhi Svaha*," Jethro breathed. He looked up at Gan. "A *third* Tablet... Here? Have you seen it? Do the Nazis have it?"

Gan shook his head. "Not yet. At least, not completely. Those we have aligned ourselves with have given us a *piece* of the Final Tablet. They call it the Shard, and amongst other things, it is the key to the lost city of R'lyeh."

"*Ph'nglui mglw'nafh Cthulhu R'lyeh wgah'nagl fhtagn*," Jethro said from memory.

Gan raised an eyebrow. "What do you know, Herr Dumont?"

Jethro shook his head. "Very little. Mostly flashes of images and moments. Signs and portents from—"

"Brickman's Tablet…?" Gan gasped.

Jethro nodded. "It revealed aspects of the future to me. From what I saw, someone is going to try to raise something called Cthulhu."

"It's a god," Gan hesitantly began. "An evil god of horrors you can't—" His voice caught in his throat. "Brickman told me he had seen flashes of Cthulhu while using the Second Jade Tablet but… I never thought…" Gan trailed off and took a large gulp of his drink, his hands shaking. "I saw it. Cthulhu. I looked into its eyes." He stuttered as he told Jethro how the Shard had sliced open reality. Jethro remained silent, the room growing colder as Gan described the horrors he had witnessed.

"They believe they can control it," Gan said as he finished his tale, "use it to defeat their enemies. Madmen. There is one, however, who doubts this, and wants to see the Shard and the Jade Tablets destroyed before the others can give rise to this monster."

Jethro raised an eyebrow. "You're saying we have an ally in the Nazi military?"

"To a degree."

After a moment's consideration, Jethro asked, "You said Brickman had seen flashes of Cthulhu, just as he had seen signs of the coming holocaust. Did he give any specifics?"

"He was unclear as to whether the Nazi's efforts will succeed at raising the creature. Even if they do, no one can control Cthulhu. It wants nothing more than the destruction of our world, of all worlds… There was one thing Brickman was certain of, though." He looked away, distastefully rolling the words over in his mouth. "No matter what happens, Herr Dumont, you will die."

Sotiria manned the helm while the others nodded off below deck. Vasili stood at the bow toying with his worry beads, rereading the instructions Alexei had given him, gooseflesh running down his back. They had been sailing for hours now, the sun breaking through the darkness, as they headed toward the city of Aghios Panteleimon. That much didn't concern him; he had made several trips like this before. But, it was the prayer Alexei had instructed him to say before they removed the book that caused Vasili's skin to crawl.

"Nyarlathotep klaatu barada nikto. Ph'nglui mglw'nafh Cthulhu R'lyeh wgah'nagl fhtagn."

The doctor tugged the tuft of hair on his chin as he leafed through his notes. While he had long since grown accustomed to the itch, he still found its necessary presence cumbersome, but such are the sacrifices one makes for a dream.

Scribbling down a brief annotation, he saw the shadows shift in the corner of his eyes. He put down his pen and delicately closed his journal. A wraithlike laugh filled the tent, a thousand voices all speaking at once, but the doctor was unmoved, patiently folding his hands as he stared into the shadows.

"The scare tactics notwithstanding, there's no use in hiding. I know you're there," he said to the emptiness.

"You always were so perceptive," Alexei said as he appeared from the shadows.

The doctor grimaced. "I may not be fluent in Greek, but I can detect sarcasm when I hear it, and it is not appreciated, even from the likes of... well, whatever you are."

Alexei laughed as he sat down on the doctor's desk. "Oh, I miss the old you. You were so much more... vibrant! Volatile! So much we lose in death."

Hammond unconsciously picked at his beard. "I do not consider what happened to me 'death.' Not in the most literal sense of the term, at least."

Alexei scoffed. "Please, when I found you in Tibet, you were barely a dry husk of flesh—a pile of bones frozen in the mountains. You may not consider what happened to you death, but I can assure you that you're not technically *alive* either."

The doctor stood up and cleared his throat, ignoring Alexei's comments. "The Shard is as you promised," he said as he paced the tent.

"Did you have any doubts?"

Hammond paused. "Some."

"Tsk! I am heartbroken. Stab me through the heart and leave me to the wolves," Alexei mimed.

"When will you give us the Third Tablet?" Hammond asked, not amused. "By my estimations we are only days away from the alignment."

Alexei's smile waned. "It has been safely stored away. I have sent my men to retrieve the Book in the interim. We will need it for the ceremony."

The doctor nodded in consideration. "Dumont will make the perfect sacrifice," he said with an echo of a smile. "I owe him that much."

"Which brings us to why I am here," Alexei sighed. "Forget Dumont."

Hammond's beard hid his scowl. "Why? You promised."

Alexei idly waved this away. "In time. Dumont is too *public* a figure right now. His death would bring us too much unwanted attention before we have finished. Besides, I have a perfect lamb in mind; she will give us the blood we need to find R'lyeh. Her life will not be missed."

"We will still need Dumont's Tablet, the 'Sacred Colors,' to raise Cthulhu, no?"

Alexei crossed his arms thoughtfully. "Not necessarily. The prophecy is vague, at best. No need to worry your scarred little face," Alexei said, patting the doctor on the cheek. "All will go as planned and soon you will have the power of Cthulhu behind you," he said, pronouncing the ancient god's name with a guttural *k't'hoo'lhoo*.

"And what a glorious day for the Reich that will be," Hammond said.

"Yes, glorious indeed," Alexei said with a cryptic smile. "Your time is near, Karl."

Fredrick Hammond's eyes drifted to the ground. "That's not my name anymore."

Alexei laughed as he disappeared into the darkness. "Call yourself whatever you want, you'll always be Karl Heydrich to me."

"Okay, okay," Jean said tentatively, holding up her hands as she tried to process it all. "Let's say for one second I believe you, that you're the Greek god Prometheus."

"Titan," Prometheus corrected.

Jean rolled her eyes. "Whatever floats your boat. So, you're this all-powerful 'titan' who can make hotel rooms appear and disappear, walk through fire, and do Lord knows what else."

"Healed your leg," he said, pointing to the holes in her boot.

She pursed her lips. "I surmised as much... and thank you."

A smile curled the corner of Prometheus's mouth. "You're quite welcome."

Jean began pacing, her footsteps silent in the white void. "You can do all those things, bend reality to your will... Then why the hell did you let yourself get arrested, thrown in jail, and chased half way across an island when you could just snap your fingers and turn everyone into popsicle sticks?"

"I had to find you," he replied. "And who said anyone else even knew I existed? Far as anyone else knows, you escaped all on your own. I'm kind of like an imaginary friend, except I'm not imaginary and only vaguely a friend."

Jean crossed her arms and walked over to Prometheus. "Still, there had to have been a much easier way to go about that."

"True," Prometheus concurred. "But then again, my powers are a shadow of what they once were." He turned and began walking toward the infinite distance. Jean followed after him. As they walked a marble floor began to appear beneath their feet, while a massive painted ceiling manifested above. Stone pillars grew out from the ground, while idols of Greek gods seemed to fade into existence. The lights dimmed until almost everything was in shadow save for the small pockets of candlelight. Before Jean knew it, they were inside an ancient temple.

"That still doesn't explain why I'm here," she ventured.

Prometheus uncomfortably cleared his throat. "I was getting to that. Put simply, you are here because of that," he said, pointing behind Jean.

A muculent, leathery sound slithered in her ears, undulating and writhing. She hesitantly looked over her shoulder and felt the madness creep into her mind. In the darkness above her, amidst the green, vile spawn of the stars, were two yellow, unwavering eyes staring down.

"Cthulhu," Prometheus said quietly.

"Please tell me you're doing this," Jean whimpered.

Prometheus regarded Jean before he continued. "As old as I am, my existence is but a blink of an eye for the Elder Things... For the Great Old Ones. They are older than the Earth, older than the galaxy, nearly as old as the Universe itself. They ruled our world and all others until... they didn't. They scattered themselves across the worlds, sleeping, waiting for their time to return. '*Ph'nglui mglw'nafh Cthulhu R'lyeh wgah'nagl fhtagn!*' They awoke only once before… because of my...” He turned his gaze down, blinking away tears. “The world was burning… We were strong then, but even then we weren't strong enough by ourselves. We can't stop it, Jean,” Prometheus said, his eyes glowing green. “Not anymore. *That* is why *you* are here.”

“What do you want from me?” she moaned as tears streamed down her cheeks, unable to look away from the horror floating above her. She gripped Prometheus's collar, begging, “Just tell me what you want and make it go away, please. Please, just make it go away.”

Prometheus looked at her mournfully. “Jean, I need you to listen to me… The stars are aligning. Its time is approaching—”

Jean scrunched her eyes shut, her face gleaming red. “What? What are you…? Please, just stop it, make it go away.”

“Every generation has its heroes. You are the *key* to stopping the rise of Cthulhu,” he said, grabbing her by the shoulders.

She shook her head, unable or unwilling to open her eyes. “I'm not a god; I'm not a hero… I'm not Foster Fade, Richard Knight, or even the Black fuckin' Bat. I'm Jean Farrell of Montana. I can't—you can't ask me to…”

“I'm not *asking* you, Jean. I'm *telling* you,” he said, genuine sorrow filling his voice. “You are the Keystone, one part of three. Without you this world—*all* worlds—are doomed.”

“Why?!” she sobbed, her body shaking. “I don't want this. I never asked for this.”

“I'm sorry, Jean.” Prometheus looked away. “All will be revealed in time.”

She screamed as the creature's tentacles wrapped around her legs, arms, and waist, and began pulling her toward its horrific maw. “Oh, God. No, please. Help…” she whimpered, trying to grab hold of Prometheus's hand.

Frowning, he let his hand slip through hers as she slid away and was lifted off the ground. “I'm sorry, Jean. I can't help you. You need to face it.”

“Please…”

Prometheus closed his eyes and turned away. In her panic Jean thought she could see a glimmer in the corner of his eye as he walked away, disappearing into the darkness.

"No! Prometheus! Come back! Don't leave me!!!" she screamed, but her pleas echoed unanswered into the void.

PART 2: THE UNKNOWN KADATH

Chapter 9
THE DREAM-QUEST OF JEAN FARRELL

Jean's lungs were burning. Her eyes fluttered open to find the world overlaid with shades of grey like a motion picture. She was in the middle of a forest, possibly late winter, the trees bare and twisted. Ground to branches was coated in a foot of grey, powdery snow. It reminded her of Montana in December, just as winter began to take its stranglehold, but the trees were too thin, too deformed, as if they had never seen the sun. Sitting up, she ran her hands through the snow-covered grass, finding it strangely warm and dry. Was she dreaming, she wondered? She didn't remember entering a forest, nor could she recall falling asleep. Standing up, she idly brushed the snow off her clothes. She was dressed in her khakis and tall boots—a bullet hole in the right shin—a light brown leather jacket, and a gun on her side. She had been wearing this before. She remembered that.

She could smell the distant echo of smoke, like rancid meat cooking on a skewer. Her eyes burned as she staggered through the forest, her legs weak and head heavy. She glanced up at the sky, trying to determine the time of day, but the clouds blanketed the world, hiding the sun beneath an opaque grey screen

They weren't clouds. They were too dark, too ashen, to be natural. She could make out two long streaks flowing down toward the horizon. Using them as her guide, she made her way through the forest, the trees gradually thinning until she found her way to the edge of the woods. There she found the dark tendrils reaching down from the sky into two tall massive smoke stacks.

It wasn't snow…

It was ash.

She wouldn't risk getting too close to the factory—if that's what it was—keeping herself to the weeds and brush surrounding the complex. She hadn't found any sign of people beyond the occasional footprints. Whoever was operating the factory didn't leave it too frequently, and right now that was fine by her. She needed to figure out where the hell she was before she started chatting it up with the locals. A fence lined the building but there were no signs—warning or identifying—as if the building's mere existence was enough to drive people away.

As she made her way toward the corner of the enclosure she came upon a small piece of yellow fabric half buried in the dirt and ash. Picking it up, she discovered it was a six-pointed star, the word *Jude* printed in the center.

By Jean's guess, the procession stretched out for nearly half a mile, a black parade of ruined humanity. Men, women, and, worst of all, children huddled together, vainly trying to fight back the biting wind. They were dressed in rags—no, not even that—they were dressed in remnants; strings of fabric wrapped together. Their bodies were nothing more than desiccated sacks of bones, their skin ashen no matter their race. This was Death displayed before her. The Rabbi's prophecy had come true, a holocaust.

She could see two guards by the entryway, dressed in what she recognized from the newsreels as Nazi stormtrooper uniforms. They watched the procession with disinterest, and while the crowd cowered in their presence, neither seemed to be carrying a gun. This was good—probably the only good thing Jean had seen so far. From this distance it looked like both guards were wearing strange white leather masks with bulbous black goggles, a twisted version of the hangman's hood.

She checked her gun, fully loaded. This was a really bad idea, but she had been hanging around the Lama too long to just sit back and watch. All she needed was two quick shots at the guards and to get the people into the forest. Her plan ended there, but at least she had one, which was admittedly a change from the usual. Lying on her stomach, she wormed her way through the weeds until she was a few yards away from the entrance.

Only then did she get a good look at the guards.

She forced her hand over her mouth; it was everything she could do not to scream. The Nazis weren't wearing masks at all. The pale white leather was their skin and the goggles their eyes. A long fin ran up their necks to the tops of their heads, their spine and joints a collection of knots.

Whatever they were, they weren't human.

Jean shook her head clear. It didn't matter what they were, she wasn't going to let them kill these people. Shifting to a crouch, she readied herself. She pulled the pistol's hammer back and began to move forward when—

"Get down!" someone hissed, pulling her back down to the ground.

"Get your hands off me!" Jean cried as she tried to kick her assailant away, but he was too quick, too strong. He pinned her down, knocking her pistol out of her hands. A thick beard of grey and dirty blond covered his gaunt, sunburned face, wrinkled like old leather. He looked half-alive.

"You tryin' to get yourself killed?!" the bearded man whispered harshly, his breath reeking. "If those Deep Ones had seen you, you would've been dead in a second!"

"What the hell are those?" she asked, struggling against the old man's feral grip. It wasn't until she saw his pale blue eyes that she recognized him. But it couldn't be, that wasn't possible—"Oh dear God. Ken?"

The old man's maw of a mouth creaked open. "Jean?" he breathed, a familiar twinkle growing in his pale blue eyes as he looked over her face. But then his gaze went cold and in a blur, he snatched up Jean's gun and pressed it against her skull. "I'm not going be playing any more of your games, Karl!" he growled, cocking back the hammer.

"Ken! KEN! Oh, God—God! It's me Jean!" she pleaded, tears streaming down her cheeks. "Jesus Christ, Ken, it's Jean! Don't kill me, Ken! It's me!"

Doubt laced Ken's haggard face. "Prove it."

"Look at me, Ken! It's—"

"Prove it! How did we meet?"

Jean furrowed her brow. "Wha—?" she stuttered as Ken shoved the gun harder against her temple. "We were extras! *A Night at the Opera*. We had to sit next to each other for six hours and I thought—I thought you were cute! And I—I asked you out to drinks!"

"And when you asked me home, what did I say?"

"Ken, I…" She looked him in the eyes. "Ken, you made me promise not to say."

Tears welled up Ken's eyes as he removed the gun barrel from Jean's head. "Oh, God. Jean!" he sighed as he wrapped his arms around her.

"Jesus Christ, Ken, what happened to you?" she asked once the factory was out of sight.

"What happened to me? Jean, you've..." he hesitated. "There was a war, the one they were all worried about. The one Rabbi Brickman warned us about."

"A Second Great War? It happened? But I..." she trailed off, her head buzzing. She pinched the bridge of her nose. There was something she wanted to say, something about where she had come from, but she couldn't connect the dots. The harder she tried, the worse the sensation became.

"There was nothing *great* about it," Ken said bitterly, pulling her out of her reverie. "It was worse than anything we could have—The Nazis, they had something on their side; they didn't even *need* allies. They just tore through us like paper dolls."

"Wait. When did all this happen?"

He studied her in disbelief. "Jesus, you really don't remember any of this."

"Ken, I don't even know how I got here, much less where I was... The last thing I can remember it was nineteen thirty-nine, right after that whole business with von Kultz and the beardless corpse, and I..." she trailed off again, the buzzing in her head growing.

"Nineteen thirty-nine? The last thing you remember was nineteen thirty-nine," he reiterated, a statement rather than a question.

Jean furrowed her brow as she nodded. "Yeah."

Ken took a step toward her, facing the ground as he laced and unlaced his fingers, trying to find the best way to break the truth to her. He took a long breath and looked her in the eyes. "Jean... It's nineteen fifty-nine."

"Nineteen fifty-nine?" she gasped, holding her head as she stumbled back.

"Jean?" Ken exclaimed as he rushed toward her, catching her before she fell.

She gripped at his ragged collar, desperate for something to ground her.

She struggled, a flood of questions pouring through her mind. "Where are we?" she finally managed.

"Where…? Babe, this was Central Park. We're in New York."

"Oh God," Jean croaked as she fell to her knees and curled over herself, one hand still gripping onto Ken's collar. It wasn't possible; none of this could be real. Not this nightmare, not this horror. She looked up at him, her eyes pleading. "What about the Green Lama?"

Ken's lips formed a narrow line and Jean could feel her stomach begin to drop, already knowing the answer. "Jean… The Green Lama's dead."

The bombed-out remains of the New York Public Library sat silent beneath the ashen sky, the twin lions that once bordered the steps long ago shattered to pieces. She could still remember the first time she had seen it only two— no, *twenty two*—years ago, not long after she stepped off the *S.S. Cathay.* It had seemed so monolithic then, glistening white, and now the remains crunched beneath her boots. Leaving the island, Ken told her, wasn't an option. "The Deep Ones control the waters." It had taken them nearly four hours to traverse the rubble of the city, keeping to the shadows of ruined buildings and abandoned subways, sometimes stopping for minutes at a time while Ken listened for movement above. Along the way, he had given her a short history of the last twenty years, though he was unable—or more likely unwilling—to give her any real details.

The War started in the early months of '39, shortly after Jean had gone missing. The Green Lama had sent Ken, Lieutenant Caraway, and Jethro Dumont looking for her, but things had gone to hell quickly and by the time Ken limped back home both the Lama and Caraway were dead and Dumont was missing.

"How did it happen? The Lama, how did he die?" Jean asked, her throat tightening, unable to contemplate her life without him.

Ken shook his head. "Not well. There was this ritual… Karl used the Lama to summon this," he said, waving his hands over the destruction.

"You mentioned him before. Who's Karl?"

Ken let out sardonic laugh. "Karl Heydrich. *Amerikas Führer.* If you wanted to blame anyone, it would be him."

The War in Europe had lasted less than six months, the German army spreading like a cancer; first Paris, then Moscow, and then finally London, before Asia and Africa were consumed. By 1940 all but America had been conquered, but even then it was only a matter of time.

Jean placed a hand on his arm. "What about Gary and Evangl? What about your... Benn?" she asked quietly.

Ken gave her an empty smile. "They took out the best of us. Those that didn't submit were killed. Most that survived didn't last long. They started rounding us up. First it was the Jews—just like the Rabbi warned us. But it didn't stop there... They started grabbing anyone they deemed 'impure,' anyone that didn't fit into their Master Race."

"You mean the Deep Ones. Those bug-eyed things."

"They're only *part* of the problem," he said as he knocked on the door to the library.

"Who's there?" a voice sounded from within. Jean could see a pair of eyes moving behind a small slit.

"It's me, Evan," Ken said, exasperated. "Open up."

The eyes glanced at Jean, then back at Ken. "You got a girl with you."

"Glad to know your vision still works. Let us in."

Jean heard whispering through the door before Evan spoke again. "Password."

"Evan," Ken sighed, massaging his eyes.

"It's your rules, boss," Evan replied. Jean thought she could even *hear* him shrug.

She glanced toward Ken and mouthed with a smile: "Boss?"

Ken gave her a half-cocked grin that reminded her of the man she once knew. "Which means I can break 'em," he said to Evan.

"Rules are rules. Even for you," Evan said.

"Yeah, rules are rules." Ken said, enjoying the repartee. "Muh em-dap in-am mo."

"Thanks, boss," Evan said from within as Jean heard bolts and bars removed from the door. "You get what you needed?"

"Yeah, in a minute. Jean, you no doubt remember Evan Wayland, formerly Sergeant of New York City's Special Crime Squad."

"Holy Cow!" she exclaimed when she caught sight of the muscular man, recalling the massively obese policeman she once knew. "Moses in a hand basket, Sergeant, you look... You look amazing."

"Man's pushing sixty," Ken added. "We like to say you can tell how many years he's been fighting by the size of his biceps. And this," he said, indicating a shrimpy middle-aged man, "is David Heidelberger, also a former member of the Special Crime Squad."

Heidelberger smiled, thrusting a friendly hand forward. "How do you do?"

Wayland was less charitable, crossing his arms over his powerful chest. "Who's the broad?" he asked.

"Jean Farrell," Ken replied. "Adventurer, part time actress, all around hero."

Wayland pursed his lips and raised a skeptical eyebrow. "Thought she was supposed to be dead."

"Yeah," Ken said with an ironic laugh. "So did I."

"Well, I'm just happy to be here," Jean said with a small wave.

"Hmph," Wayland grumbled. "You'd be the first."

"I bet," Jean said.

Ken took her by the arm. "Come inside. I'll show you around and introduce you to everyone else. Don't expect anything fancy though," he said as they moved into the ruins. "We don't exactly sit still too long."

"So, she's supposed to have been dead fer twenty years?" Heidelberger asked Wayland once the others were out of earshot.

Wayland shrugged. "Apparently."

"Boss's takin' it pretty well."

"After all we've seen?" Wayland said as he locked up the door. "Dead broad comin' back to life ain't that big a thing."

The interior of the Library had fared little better than the exterior. Stone rubble and the charred remains of countless books filled the Rose Main Reading Room; the golden ceiling cracked open, letting in angled pillars of light that cut across the small encampments littering the once majestic space.

"How many of you are there?" Jean asked as they moved through the rubble. She could feel the survivors' eyes on her, their dull expressions hiding distrust, anger, and resignation.

"Thirty. We were forty," Ken whispered, as if the space were still used for its function. "Lot of us are broken families. Parents without children, children without parents. Tom lost most of his family back in the early days of the war," he said indicating a young Hispanic man cleaning his gun.

"Grew up fighting, the poor kid. He and his brother Joe, they're probably our two best fighters. Saw him once kill a Deep One with his bare hands."

"You keep talking about the Deep Ones, but you still haven't told me what they *are*."

Ken stopped short and firmed his lips. After a moment he faced Jean and said: "I should probably take you to Valco."

"I'm afraid there isn't much I can really tell…" Doctor Harrison Valco began as he cleaned his glasses with a grimy rag. Like Ken and Jean, Valco had worked with the Green Lama back in the day, and was by far the oldest person in the encampment, probably pushing seventy by her guess. And though he seemed worn down by the world, he still retained a small glimmer of hope in the back of his eyes, as if he was waiting for someone to jump down from the rafters and make it all go away.

"Humor me, Doc," Jean said, crossing her arms as she leaned up against the rotted wooden table in Valco's makeshift lab. "I've been away for a while."

Valco hesitated. He glanced at Ken, who nodded in reassurance. Satisfied, Valco continued. "Well, for starters despite their bipedal anatomy they are not in any sense of the word 'human.'"

"I've seen 'em up close. I figured as much."

Valco turned to Ken, a small smirk pulling at his cheeks. "She's snippier than I remember."

"That's why we loved—" Ken cut himself short and turned to Jean. "Excuse me. That's why we *love* her."

Jean gave Ken a nod and a sad smile.

Valco cleared his throat. "Far as we can tell, from the few specimens we've been able to examine, they evolved from fish—or some distant relative thereof—but have more in common with frogs or other amphibians. Their bite is toxic thanks to poison in their saliva; it can kill a grown man within hours of injection. Their bulbous eyes, while generally poor in the air are vastly superior underwater and can cover well over a hundred-and-eighty-degrees of sight. Much like frogs, they mate—"

"Yeah. Thanks," Jean cut in. "Really don't need to know about their mating habits. What I want to know is why the hell they're out there dressed like Nazis."

"She really doesn't know?" Valco asked Ken.

"She really doesn't know."

"All right, look, guys," Jean cut in, "all the enigmatic statements and looks were cute for about a minute. Just tell me what happened and what we're gonna do about it."

Ken held up a finger. "One word," he said before raising two more, "three syllables."

"Why do I get the sense I already know the answer to this one...?" Jean sighed.

"Cthulhu."

Ken shifted uncomfortably in his seat as he began. "It's been a while since I've talked about this with anyone, so you'll have to bear with me."

"Take your time, I've got nowhere else to go."

"Ain't that the truth?" Ken said with a sardonic laugh. He scratched at his bearded cheek. "You remember what the Rabbi told us when he found the Second Jade Tablet? The statue grown like coral, 'Cthulhu waits'?"

Jean nodded. "Like it was only a few months ago."

"Well, what we didn't know at the time was that Cthulhu wasn't going to be waiting around much longer. See, what no one knew then was that these stars were aligning and when they did, they raised the sunken city R'lyeh down in the South Pacific, just north of Antarctica. Honestly it still sounds like a whole lot of hocus pocus mumbo jumbo, if I hadn't seen it all myself... Anyways, while we were looking for you, Karl and his Nazi buddies were looking for the *Third* Jade Tablet."

"Aw, crap," Jean groaned, massaging her eyes, "there are three of them?"

"Oh, it gets better. Karl was in league with the Deep Ones. Together they found the Third Tablet and this blade-thing the Lama called a *phurba*. The Germans called it the Shard. They used these to open the gates of R'lyeh, sacrificing good people to do so—including Caraway." Ken let out a painful sigh. "Stupid bastard. He tried to save the girl and he just... They drained him like a cow in a slaughterhouse. God, I can still remember the sound of his blood, like a broken faucet." He wiped the tears off his cheeks.

"Me and the Green Lama followed the Nazis to R'lyeh. The Lama thought—well, he hoped we could stop them before they raised Cthulhu. What we didn't know then—*Goddammit, we were idiots!*" he cursed, slamming his hand against the table. "There was so much we could've *done* if only we had known what the hell was going on."

Jean shook her head. She needed a drink, but the barrels had gone dry twenty years ago. "Shoulda, coulda, woulda."

"We thought they were going to basically, y'know, open the doors for the bastard, let him out, go *Sieg Heil* and let him go wild, but we didn't—" Ken cut himself short. "They *wanted* us to follow them. They had everything except the *key* to awakening Cthulhu, and that was the Green Lama.

"The city was full of Nazis, Deep Ones, and these horrors… The Lama thought we could fight our way through, but there was no way. The Tulku, he put up a damn good fight, but they overpowered him, dragged him up to the altar, and—"

Jean held up her hand, cutting Ken short. "That's enough. I don't need to hear anymore," she breathed.

They sat in silence until Jean cleared her throat and asked, "So, what do you guys have planned for the factory?"

Valco's eyebrow shot up. "How did you—?"

"I'm not stupid, Doc. Coincidental as it was, I know Ken wasn't hanging around the death factory looking for yours truly, and he definitely wasn't sightseeing. He was scouting for something, and whatever that something is, I want in."

Ken bit back a smile, realizing, not for the first time, how much he had missed his best friend. "Besides blowing it up?"

Jean nodded. "Besides blowing it up," she said with a smirk.

"Show her the map," Ken said to Valco with a beckoning gesture.

Valco reached into a small cupboard and brought out a large rolled fabric. "Apologies for the crudity," he said as he unrolled the map on the table, "it's been nearly nineteen years since they produced paper."

Drawn in charcoal, the layout of the factory was surprisingly detailed, showing the number of entrances, the breakdown of the rooms and floors, as well as guard and "prisoner" in-take schedules.

"Looks like you've been planning this for a while."

"Too long, if you ask me," Ken replied, eyeing Valco.

"The Lama never went in without a solid plan," Valco said as he looked over the map, feeling Ken's stare.

"That's a lie and you know it," Jean commented.

Ken cleared his throat. "Either way, we know the factory is primarily used as a, um…" he hesitated, stealing a glance at Jean before continuing. "As a *crematorium*, but we have reason to believe that Nazi officials use it as a base from time to time and we think Karl is there with the Third Tablet."

"You're telling me the Third Tablet is *here*?" Jean asked, tapping the map. "Now?"

"We *think* so," Valco said, nodding hesitantly. "The troop buildup in recent weeks, the abnormal climate, the subtle changes in the city's ambient magnetics. It *must* be here."

"*If* we can break in and *if* we can grab it"—Ken licked his chapped lips—"we can use it to turn the tide."

"It's a long shot at best," Valco said with a skeptical shrug.

Jean cracked a sardonic smirk. "Long shot's all we ever get, Doc."

Valco and Ken laid out their plan, which was as simple as it was suicidal.

"So," she summarized, "we're going to bust in through the back door, shoot everything that moves until we get what we need, and try and make our way out."

"Essentially, yes," Valco replied.

Jean looked over the maps once again. "It's really just a one way trip, isn't it?" she said after a moment.

Ken crossed his arms. "Either we win this or it ends here," he said, keeping his gaze locked on the map.

"Guess we gotta win it, then," Jean mused.

"Guess we do."

There were ten of them, the best of what was left. Ken and Jean took the lead, heading through the South entrance and closest to where they believed Heydrich would be. Wayland and Heidelberger's team took the North entrance; Tom and Joe's, the West; both teams creating diversions for Jean and Ken. Valco and the rest stood ready as reinforcements in the East near the main gate.

"Jean," Ken whispered as they moved through the ashen brush toward the factory's electrified fence. He laced wrinkled, leathery fingers with hers. "I need to—I never told you I went back to the Rabbi after that whole mess with the golem."

Jean silently eyed her compatriot, unsure how to respond.

"I felt guilty about the whole, you know, dooming a whole race of people to genocide. So, I went back to apologize, I guess. Learn more about the Jewish culture, a sprinkling of Hebrew, that sorta stuff."

"Not that this is the best time for this kinda conversation," Jean whispered, "but how'd it go?"

Ken shrugged. He stared at the dark pillars billowing from the smokestacks. "Pretty well, for the most part. Only really got to learn the basics before everything went wrong," he said, subtly waving his hand at the world before him. "After I returned to New York—after Cthulhu had risen—Brickman *did* tell me one thing that was really important. He told me all *this* was going to happen."

Jean's stomach began to twist. "What do you mean?" she asked.

"The war, you coming back twenty years later, us here now going after the Third Tablet. Everything. Truth was I *was* looking for you, have been almost every day. Still doesn't mean it isn't surprising to bump in to your long dead friend." He ran his hand through his hair. His shoulders fell as tears flooded his eyes. "I didn't believe him. But now, here at the end— how can there be any doubt?"

Jean struggled to breathe, as if something were pressing against her chest. "What else did he say?"

Ken cleared his throat. "That the only way to prevent this all from happening was to make sure we got you to the Tablet in time."

"In time for what?"

"In time to get you *back*."

"Back where?"

Ken looked her in the eyes. "Back *home*."

Bullets rang around them, a symphony of gunfire.

Making it into the complex, Jean and Ken found themselves quickly surrounded, Deep Ones pouring in from every corridor and stairwell. They weren't too difficult to kill—a shot to the head or midsection took them down quick—but they kept coming without pause, rapidly exhausting Jean and Ken's limited ammo.

"Jesus!" Jean exclaimed as she ducked behind a wall to reload her pistol. "Where the hell are these guys coming from?"

"They hatch from a massive clumps of eggs, dozens at time," Ken shouted as he fired off several shots into the oncoming throng of fish men. "One female can produce over thirty living offspring at a time, over a thousand in her lifetime. You would know this if you had let Valco finish his lecture!"

"And I don't need one now! Dammit, we can't keep this up," Jean shouted. "Where the hell is our goddamn distraction?!"

As if on cue, a deafening *Ba-THOOM* resonated through the building, rattling the walls and raining down small pieces of paint and cement. The attacking Deep Ones came to an abrupt halt, their massive, inhuman heads swiveling madly. Croaking in unison, they spun on their heels and raced out of the building, leaving the dead and injured behind.

Jean looked over at Ken and smiled. "Well, *that* was good timing."

"Tell me about it," Ken said as walked into the vacated hallway. "Never doubt the Special Crime Squad, eh?"

"Not for a—" Her eyes went wide and the color drained from her cheeks as one of the injured Deep Ones jumped up. "Ken, watch out!!!"

Ken drew his pistol and spun around, but it was too late. The Deep One's powerful jaw clamped down on Ken's neck, its serrated teeth piercing deep into his flesh, black venom dripping down.

"KEN!!!" Jean screamed as she shot the Deep One in the head. The creature's jaw flew open. Its limp body crumpled to the ground.

"Hell." Ken touched his wound, eyed the black bile that now coated his fingers, and fell to his knees. "Damn, damn, *damn*."

Jean ran over, catching him in her arms. "Oh, God, Ken. I'm so sorry."

"Don't—Don't apologize," he rasped, coughing up blood. Vein-like black growths began to extend out from the wound, like wildfire in a California summer. He smiled painfully. "We both knew this was gonna be a one-way."

"Come on, Ken. We've gotten outta worse," she said bravely as tears streamed down her cheeks, lying to herself more than anything else. Ken couldn't—wouldn't die, she told herself. They were the big damn heroes, part of the Green Lama's inner circle. They had gotten out of everything before; they would get out this. He would be fine. He had to be.

Ken shook his head, coughing violently. "There's not much—much worse than this, Jean. Trust me, I kn—know how this works." He let out a string of terrible bloody coughs as five black veins extended across his face like a hand. His breaths grew more jagged and pained as he forced himself to breathe. "Stop—Stop worryin' 'bout me, you got a job to finish. Listen— I—if this works, if you can fix this… you… You make—make sure… make…"

His eyes rolled up and his head lopped back as if he was staring up to the sky.

"Ken… Please…"

Everything had gone wrong, but Jean was done crying, done being the little girl lost. The future might be a Nazi apocalypse, but she was going to do something about it. Taking Ken's pistol and remaining ammo, she ran up the stairs toward the top floor where they believed Heydrich's inner sanctum was housed. With the Deep Ones distracted by the attacks to the North and West, she faced little to no resistance, killing what few creatures she came upon with indiscriminate ferocity.

There was no door at the top of the stairs, just an entryway opening out to a massive room. Stepping forward, she began to feel a familiar buzzing echo out from the back of her mind. The room was empty, save for a single egg-shaped crystal sitting atop a short stanchion, bathed in a single column of light in the center of the room, a sizable crack running down its side.

It was the Third Jade Tablet; she knew it without needing to be told.

"Hello, Fräulein Farrell," a voice said from the darkness, its accent thickly German. "I've been *dying* to meet you."

"That's sweet," she said, eyeing the shadows. "Why don't you come on out and we can chat about it?"

A silhouette formed behind the Tablet, the shape of a man, dented and twisted like a forgotten doll.

"I'm gonna guess you're Karl Heydrich," she said.

"What is left of him, yes." The silhouette tilted its malformed head as it studied Jean. "Hm, I forgot. We did not meet in this timeline."

"Lucky me."

"Oh, *Liebchen*, luck had nothing to do with it," Heydrich said as he stepped into the light. Jean let out a small gasp at the sight of the man's distorted visage. Wrapped in a tattered, bloodstained green robe, Heydrich's face was a deformed, decaying mass, pieces of flesh hanging off his black, brittle bones. His red, lidless eyes were unwavering. There was a small rainbow ring of hair on his right hand. He gurgled a laugh at Jean's expression. "Being *undead* for so many years does have its side effects."

"No offense, but Freddy Dmytryk's Mayan Mummy looked better than you."

Heydrich smiled and bowed his rotting head. "None taken. Normally, I suppose you and I would spend some time bantering back and forth. But like our dearly departed Green Lama, you and I have reached the end of our journeys, so let us—how does one say—cut to the chase?"

"Sounds good to me," she replied as she shot Heydrich in the head.

Black liquid splattered out from the back of his head as the undead Nazi mystic tumbled back into the shadows. Jean ran toward the Tablet, coming within inches when a blast of green electricity shot out from the darkness, knocking her clear across the room and smashing her hard against the wall.

"It has taken me twenty years and two lives to find the Third Tablet and secure Cthulhu's reign!" Heydrich screamed as he hobbled over to Jean, his hands crackling with green energy. "Did you *really* think it would be that simple?!"

"It would've been nice if it were," Jean said through gritted teeth, pushing herself off the ground, pain radiating throughout her body. Something inside her had broken, but she fought through the agony and stood. She fired three quick shots at Heydrich, but they weren't enough, and the mad monk was instantly upon her, wrapping his skeletal right hand around her throat and lifting her off the ground.

"Nyarlathotep gave you too much credit, girl," Heydrich mused as he squeezed down on Jean's windpipe. "We have all three Tablets, the Power of the Ages is ours, and with Dumont and Vasili out of the way, and now you, all three Scions will be dead and Cthulhu's reign will be eternal!"

"Don't... bet... on... it...!" Jean said through agonizing gasps. Raising her pistol to Heydrich's hand, she fired off a single shot, shattering Heydrich's already decomposed wrist. Heydrich's skeletal hand broke off from his arm and dropped her to the ground.

Heydrich screamed as electricity and black ooze poured out of the wound.

Pulling Heydrich's disembodied hand off her throat, Jean scrambled back toward the Tablet. Falling forward, her fingers laced around the cracked crystalline egg, tracing the ornate etchings that covered it. She could feel the world around her begin to slip away. The buzzing in her head grew louder, deafening her from within. For an instant the room was enveloped in a familiar green hue. A howling wind came down upon her as if she were suddenly sucked into the vortex of a hurricane. Beneath it Jean could hear eerily familiar voices, but couldn't make out the words.

Chapter 10
BOOK OF THE DEAD

*D*o you ever miss New York?" the big man asked as they approached the massive steel airplane idling outside the Temple of the Clouds.

"...There are times, yes..." the lama said, with a protracted nod.

The big man chuckled. "I'm not gonna lie, Tulku... I can't wait to get back to the Empire State. The last year here has been an eye opener, but I miss my concrete jungle."

The Tulku smiled and placed a friendly hand on the American's shoulder. "And you will be missed here."

"I'll be sure to write you when I get back. I cannot wait to share everything I learned with my team. And I'm sure my cousin could learn a thing or two..." The muscular man gave the Tulku a broad smile. He bowed his head. "Thank you again, Tulku." He climbed up the gangway to the airplane before stopping short at the hatchway and looking back at his teacher. "And if you ever need anything," he said as the propeller engines came to life, "I and my friends would be happy to help! All of them are top men, the best in their fields!"

The Tulku smiled and bowed deeply in gratitude as his student closed the airplane door. The propellers turned to face the sky, pulling the ship up into the air before it rocketed out toward the horizon. The Tulku imagined there wouldn't be another such craft in decades.

"I confess, Tulku," the old priest said as the Tulku re-entered the Temple of the Clouds, "I expected you to journey home with your student."

"And leave the Temple of the Clouds? No, Tsarong, my place is here," Jethro Dumont said, placing a hand on the old man's bony shoulder. He had finally begun to show his age, Jethro noticed with a slight twang of regret, as if his former Khenpo's rapid aging had been his fault.

But, then again... Wasn't it? Were it not for Jethro, Tsarong would still be the bearer of the Jade Tablet and would still be granted its regenerative powers. By merely coming to the Temple of the Clouds nine years ago, Jethro had effectively shortened his friend's life. But that was simply his Western thinking, that life ended with death. Jethro knew Tsarong would face the next rebirth with vigor, all part of the path of Dharma.

"You look sad, Tulku," Tsarong said softly.

Jethro glanced at his former Khenpo, torn from his reverie. "Hm? Oh... No, Tsarong... Just thinking of what an odd coincidence it is that today is the ninth anniversary of my arrival."

The old man's face was unreadable. "Yes, I had not forgotten."

They walked on in silence, Jethro quietly debating how he was going to tell Tsarong that the Jade Tablet had begun to unravel.

Jethro had long ago accepted the inevitability of his own demise as part of the cycle of life, death, and rebirth in *samsara*, though he hesitated to say he looked forward to entering some otherworldly Nirvana anytime soon. To have it prophesized was another matter altogether.

"Did he say how?" he quietly asked Gan as they rode the elevator down to the lobby.

Gan shook his head. "That much was unclear."

"Well, that's helpful," Jethro commented sarcastically as he adjusted his tie, once again looking the part of a millionaire playboy on holiday. "At least if I knew *how* it was going to happen, I could find a way to avoid it."

"Even if you did, you more than anyone know it is impossible to fight the tide of history."

"This is still only prophecy, not history," Jethro snapped back. "Not yet."

"And in my experience I have learned the two are one and the same," Gan replied coldly.

They rode the remaining floors in silence.

"I suppose I do not need to tell you that it is vital we keep our true identities a secret," Gan said as they made their way to the exit.

"I'm not sure if you noticed, Herr Oberführer, but I *am* a costumed adventurer by trade."

Gan regarded him with a raised eyebrow. "Is that supposed to impress me, Herr Dumont? Correct me if I am wrong, but did I not just find you in a puddle of your own vomit?"

Jethro sighed. "It's going to be a long day."

"Well, that can't be good," Caraway commented as Ken raced toward them. He glanced over to Vasili with a rueful smile. "Here's my guess: Guns. Lots of guns."

"Did you expect no security?" Vasili asked as he crossed his arms.

"Expected? No," Caraway said with a shrug. "Hoped for? Yes."

They had been in town for a few hours; the sun was high overhead, short shadows and a cool breeze. Sotiria had stayed behind with the boat, engines ready, while the four of them made a beeline through the narrow cobblestone streets toward the destination. Vasili had sent Ken ahead to take a reconnaissance of a small, squat building, while they hid inside a small alleyway a few blocks away. Small beads of sweat formed along Caraway's brow, more from his nerves than the sun. He wiped them away with the cuff of his sleeve, careful to keep his face expressionless. Something in his gut told him it was all about to go belly up, thought he couldn't tell why. Maybe he just didn't like being on the other side of the law.

"Hey—Hey… hey guys," Ken gasped as he ran up, his feet flapping against the dirt road.

"You okay, Shakes?" Petros asked, a cigarette hanging from the corner of his lips.

"Me?" Ken wheezed. "Oh—Oh, yeah. Just, uh, a little—" He bent forward, resting his hands on his knees. "Whew! Just a little out a breath is all…"

Caraway rolled his eyes. "What's it look like in there, Shakespeare?"

"Um…" Ken said with a thoughtful frown. "Like there's a really old guy asleep in his parlor."

Vasili's stern face twisted with chagrin. "Parlor?"

"Yeah, it's just some guy's apartment," Ken said as he stood back up. "I have to stop smoking so much."

Caraway turned to Vasili. "You're certain this is the right place."

Vasili turned the folded piece of paper over in his hand, but didn't risk a glance. "Yes," he said with finality. He looked to Ken. "Did you see the book?"

Ken shrugged. "Which? It's practically a library in there."

"I'm just going to come out and say this," Caraway groaned, massaging his eyes in frustration. "Something doesn't add up."

Vasili rubbed his chin in thought. "Much as I hate to admit it, and I *do* hate to admit it… I think you are right," he said to Caraway. He looked to Petros with an inquisitive frown.

Petros placed a hand on his sheathed blade. "Boss says that is the place, then that is the place."

Vasili nodded. "Okay, let's figure out our plan then. Get in there after dark, make it quick and get back home before sunrise. And Petros, try to keep it clean, I don't want another bloodbath like we had in Athens."

"Bloodbath?" Ken squeaked under his breath.

Caraway grimaced. "I've got a bad feeling about this…"

"*Gratuliere, Herr Oberführer! Wie ich sehe, haben Sie den mysteriösen Jethro Dumont gefunden!*" a German officer with a pencil thin mustache exclaimed as Jethro, Gan, and Hirsch exited the car into the makeshift base. He was dressed in a sharp, dark grey uniform, an iron cross hanging between the black points of his collar. Another official walked in tandem, noticeable burn scars beneath his Van Dyke, a short sword in a leather scabbard attached to his belt. They were followed by a small contingent of armed guards, more for effect than any real threat. "Sir, it is a pleasure to meet you, I am Obergruppenführer Albrecht Gottschalk," the black-collared official said, extending his hand.

"*Ich bin nicht wirklich so schwer zu finden, Herr Obergruppenführer, hatte gerade ein zu viele lange Nächte,*" Jethro said as he shook Gottschalk's hand. "*Es ist ein Vergnügen, Sie kennenzulernen; Die Herren Oberführer Gan und Sturnbannführer Hirsch haben von Ihnen gesprochen.*"

"*Sie sprechen ja Deutsch! Und Ihr Akzent ist perfekt!*" Gottschalk replied with a smile. "But please, Herr Dumont, you are our guest! There is no need to pander to us. Besides I believe it is best for me to practice my English, *ja?*"

"Whatever you prefer, Herr Obergruppenführer. I for one would not want to upset the German army!" Jethro said with a boisterous laugh.

"You have nothing to fear, Herr Dumont!" Gottschalk said pleasantly, clapping Jethro on the shoulder. "Your name carries too much weight. Who here has not heard of your exploits?" Gottschalk leaned in close to Jethro and lowered his voice. "Tell me, is Ginger Rogers that beautiful in real life?"

Jethro gave Gottschalk a knowing smile. "Herr Obergruppenführer, believe me when I say her dance moves are not her most thrilling skill," he said with a friendly jab of the elbow. He had never met Ginger Rogers.

Gottschalk let out a jovial laugh. "Oh, I can only imagine! Now, tell me, what brings you to the island of Samothrace, Herr Dumont?"

"Vacation. For one such as myself even New York City can become quite *boring*," Jethro moaned. "So, I decided to take in a bit of scenery. Greece! All ruins and history, though it seems this island is all just ruins… Hm. What about you, Herr Obergruppenführer? Oberführer Gan was rather elusive as to your intentions for this beautiful island."

Gottschalk risked a glance at Gan and softly cleared his throat. "Diplomacy. These are delicate times, as you know."

"Indeed," Jethro said with a solemn nod. "I remember hearing about an 'international incident' at the German consulate in New York recently. In fact, if I recall correctly, it was why the Oberführer had to cut our dinner short. I hope that was all ironed out," he said, eliciting a small echo of a smile in the corners of Gan's lips.

"Uh, yes, yes. Completely resolved," Gottschalk stuttered.

"And that madman, von Kultz, I believe that was his name… He kidnapped me."

Gottschalk's face blanched. "Ah… Yes… I—We had heard about that…"

"Oh, don't look so terrified, Herr Obergruppenführer!" Jethro said warmly, privately enjoying the Nazi's discomfort. "One bad apple doesn't spoil the bunch. I doubt Hitler would ever do anything as insane as order the murder of innocent people."

"Yes. Yes… Of course. Now, please, allow me to introduce you to the rest of our *diplomatic* staff. Oberführer Gan you already know, and Sturmbannführer Hirsch you've met, but you have not been properly acquainted to Herr Doktor—"

"Dr. Fredrick Hammond, at your service, Herr Dumont," the man with the Van Dyke said as he stepped forward and took Jethro's hand into his, shaking it firmly.

Jethro's stomach turned and his head buzzed as he stole a glance at the Doctor's blade, the ornate hilt covered in a strange, alien script that Jethro recognized. Then there was the man himself: He was tall, possibly half a head taller than Jethro, his eyes black like pits of tar. Jethro guessed his age to be forty-five, but the taut, leather-like skin around his eyes and forehead told of a more advanced age. There was something so *familiar* about him, but Jethro couldn't quite place it.

"I'm sorry," Jethro said with a sheepish smile. "Have—have we met before, Herr Doktor?"

There was a sinister twinkle in the doctor's tar eyes that Jethro *knew* he had seen before. "Perhaps in another life, Herr Dumont," Hammond said with a broad smile. He glanced down at the ring of rainbow-colored hair on Jethro's middle finger. "That is a *very* interesting ring you have there."

"This?" he said, pulling his hand out of the doctor's viselike grip, holding it up as if the Jade Tablet were nothing but a trinket.

"It is very…" Hammond said, carefully choosing his next word, "*unique.*"

"Oh, it's just a silly token from my time in Tibet. A gift from the locals. You know how they can be." Jethro fought to not let his smile waver, struggling to ignore the growing sense of vertigo. He recognized that voice, that smile, but from *where*? "You can find hundreds just like it at any bazaar."

"Oh, I very much doubt that," the doctor said softly.

"Are you certain we haven't met before?"

"I suppose I just have one of those faces, as you say," the doctor said, his smile never faltering as his hand traced the hilt of his blade. "Tell me, Herr Dumont, I always wanted to know. Do Buddhists believe in God?"

Chapter 11
EYES OF THE STORM

O m! Ma-ni Pad-me Hum!" *Jethro grimaced, not so much from the pain—which was considerable—as from the anticipation. Sitting alone in the center of his room, he hooked his thumbnail beneath the loose end of the Tablet's string, pulling it up and away, unwinding it from his middle finger. It had been nine years since the Tablet had woven itself into his flesh, and nearly eight since he had given up hope of ever removing it; as to why it had begun to unweave now was a mystery. He had chosen not to tell Tsarong—though he wasn't sure why he hadn't. He simply knew he needed to do this alone.*

Blood trickled down his hand, flowing in long red streams over to his wrist and arm before dripping into the bowl Jethro had placed on his lap. He could feel the fiber move beneath his skin as he continued to pull the ring free, the color shifting from the deepest reds to brilliant violets as he worked his way down the strand.

It took him nearly an hour before the Tablet was completely freed from his hand. Laid out on the ground before him, Jethro estimated the string was nearly the length of Ebbets Field, end-to-end. Impossibly, there were infinitesimally small symbols lining the fiber, ranging from Sanskrit and Latin to ancient Mayan and Arabic, even English, as well as some Jethro didn't recognize. There seemed to be portions of words, but there was no pattern, no sense to their organization; if there was a hidden message to this string of symbols, it was lost to Jethro. But that was impossible... If the Tablet was as old as Tsarong said, then how could there be letters, let alone words, for languages that had barely existed for a millennia?

But there had to be something. The Jade Tablet had been worn by some of humanity's greatest individuals and had powers Jethro was still decades away from understanding. There had to be a code or a hidden message.

Inching over, he found that a large section of the string had overlapped and crisscrossed itself, causing three symbols in the Devanagari script to align and form a single word that Jethro recognized: soma.

A rueful smile crossed Jethro's lips. He had his work cut out for him.

Petros kicked down the door, sending wooden shards flying into the air. "I do always love a good smash and grab," he said with a wicked smile as he unsheathed his blades, twirling them over his fingers with panache.

"Come on, boys," Vasili said to Ken and Caraway as he followed Petros in, a gun in each hand. "Quick and clean."

"No one gets killed, you got that?" Caraway whispered to Ken once Vasili went inside.

"Yup. No one," Ken said with an earnest nod. "Especially me."

Caraway sighed. "Yeah. That's exactly what I was thinking."

There was a sudden blast of gunfire as he stepped through the doorway, followed by a rain of splintered wood. Caraway dropped to the floor, clutching his pistol. It had certainly gone belly up real quick. "Aw, crap."

"Dammit!" Ken cursed as he tumbled down beside Caraway. "Why do people *always* end up shooting at us?"

"Doctor!" Gottschalk shrilled. "My apologies, Herr Dumont, I do not believe Herr Doktor Hammond intended to be so rude."

Dumont waved this away. "Nonsense, Herr Obergruppenführer, it's nothing I haven't dealt with back in the States," he said before turning back to Heydrich. "It's a complex question to answer, Herr Doktor Hammond. The invocation of deities—even demons—*is* an important part of the tantric practices of Tibet, yet the Buddha taught that there is no Creator deity like the one we Westerners call God."

"Ah," Heydrich sighed, forcing back a smile. The fool had no idea who he was! Here, standing before him, was Jethro Dumont—*the Green Lama!*—the very same man who had *killed* him five years ago, and who had no clue to the true identity of "Herr Doktor Hammond." He could slice Dumont open with the Shard and spread his innards across the ground before the fool even suspected the truth. "But, what do *you* believe, Herr Dumont?"

Dumont pressed his lips together as he considered his answer. "Well, while I was raised Christian, I…" He cleared his throat before continuing. "I believe in the inherent good—the Buddha nature—in all beings. But in my travels I have seen some amazing and terrible things done in the name of a God—or gods—*but* I have yet to meet one myself. However, when I do, you will be the first to know, Herr Doktor."

Heydrich raised an eyebrow and bit back a smile. "I have no doubt you will." He turned to Gottschalk. "Herr Obergruppenführer—Herr Dumont—though I would *love* to continue this conversation, you must excuse me. I am late for a meeting with our local associates."

Gottschalk nodded. "Then we shall not delay you any further."

"Thank you, Herr Obergruppenführer. *Auf Wiedersehen*, Herr Dumont," Heydrich said with a slight nod, hoping his face did not betray him. "I hope to see you again, soon."

"Likewise, Herr Doktor," Dumont quietly replied as Heydrich spun on his heels and marched out of the camp

Heydrich could feel his insides twisting as he tried to stem the tide of his rage. He could have killed Dumont right there, stabbed him through the heart and watched him bleed until his boots were covered in blood. If only Alexei would let him…

Heydrich stopped himself. His temperature was rising quickly; if he didn't calm down soon he ran the deadly risk of overheating and destroying his reformed body. The life of the undead was not without its caveats.

"Alexei!!!" he shouted once he was a good distance from the camp, unbuttoning his uniform in an effort to cool his body. "Alexei, I know you can hear me, you inhuman bastard! Show yourself!" He heard the muffled sound of air being displaced behind him.

"Karl, my dear boy, you sound upset," Alexei whispered in mock concern as he paced around to face Heydrich. "A little hot under the collar today?" he commented once he saw Heydrich's beet red visage. "You know how bad that is for your heart."

"Dumont is there with the Jade Tablet!" Heydrich shouted, pointing an angry finger back to the base camp.

"What?" the creature masquerading as man hissed as thin black lines began to form on his face like cracks on a frozen lake.

Heydrich took a bold step forward. "He is meeting with the others as we speak. He is right there, surrounded. The *key* to raising Cthulhu could be mine for the taking!"

"That's…" Alexei shook his head, his eyes shifting wildly. "No, that's not possible."

"What do you mean, that's not possible?" Heydrich shouted, foaming at the mouth. "I saw him with my own eyes! I felt the Sacred Colors against my skin. All I needed was to draw my blade and it would've been mine!"

"If Dumont is alive…" Alexei growled before letting loose a string of incomprehensible curses, the cracks on his face widening, splitting open his face enough for Heydrich to glimpse the horror within. "I should have known it would have taken more than a Deep One's bite to destroy the Green Lama. Fools! I will *kill* Ke'ta for this."

Were he a lesser man and had he not already stared into the face of Death, Heydrich would have succumbed to madness at the sight of Alexei's true visage; instead he grabbed Alexei's collar. "You sent one of your idiot fish men after him and didn't tell me?"

Alexei shot his gaze to Heydrich. In an instant, Heydrich flew back through the air as though he had been blasted out of a cannon, landing hard several feet away. Before he could push himself up, Alexei was pressing his boot against Heydrich's windpipe.

"You forget your place, Karl," Alexei snarled, his voice echoing through Heydrich's skull. "I brought you back to this world and I can just as easily remove you from it!" He reached down and unsheathed the Shard from Heydrich's scabbard, the crystalline blade glowing despite the sun.

"I am sorry, Master," Heydrich struggled to say.

Alexei took his foot off Heydrich's throat, wordlessly accepting the mystic's panicked apology. Heydrich could feel his heart thump against his chest as he watched the cracks on Alexei's face continue to grow and connect, revealing the putrid black flesh beneath. Alexei thrust the glowing blade above his head and chanted an ancient invocation as the sky above them darkened with ink black clouds.

"*We see you, Jethro Dumont,*" Alexei said, his voice shifting octaves with every word, a thousand voices at once. "*We see you, Green Lama…*"

"An intense fellow," Gan said to Jethro after Hammond was out of earshot.

"You need *not* concern yourself with him."

Jethro nodded, understanding Gan's insinuation. "Well, he seemed pleasant enough," he said politely, quietly relieved that the strange buzzing that had rattled his mind had dissipated.

"He is quite brilliant, but then again, with brilliance comes eccentricity… But, we digress. Herr Dumont—" Gottschalk began. He wrapped an arm around Jethro's shoulders and led him into the command tent.

"Please, call me Jethro, Herr Obergruppenführer," he said with a smile.

"Jethro," Gottschalk corrected himself with a smile. "I understand you are good friends with Herr Lindbergh."

Jethro nodded slowly. "Charles, well, we used to run in similar circles, but I—" he cleared his throat. "We lost touch when he moved to Europe."

Gottschalk shook his head in feigned regret. "Yes, it is a pity what happened to his boy, but what I wish to discuss are his *political* leanings."

"Ah, yes…" Jethro said as he peered over at Gan, who responded with a raised eyebrow.

"Now, I don't want you to misunderstand me, Jethro. I am not asking you to support National Socialism, but with all these whispers of war on both sides of the Atlantic, the world needs someone like you to help diffuse the situation. As a Buddhist you can act as a… Voice for Peace."

"Well, to be honest, Herr Obergruppenführer," he began, but stopped when he heard thunder echo in the distance, and then something else, almost like a whisper, a voice he had heard before. No, it was a thousand voices speaking in tandem. "Did you hear that?" he asked Gan, barely hiding his panic.

Hirsch shrugged. "It is rain, perhaps?" he said in broken English.

Gan looked out to the camp. "There is a storm, but it does not look— *Was zum Teufel…?*"

"What?" Gottschalk asked. "What is it, Gan?"

The whispers echoed again. *We see…* Jethro twisted himself free of Gottschalk's grasp and hurried over to the tent's entrance. *We see you…* He pulled aside the flapping canvas, and his stomach dropped at the sight of an enormous obsidian column thundering toward them. He could feel the air around him electrify, the hairs on his arms standing on end. *We see you, Green Lama!*

"*Om! Ma-ni Pad-me Hum!*" he whispered.

"Is that a tornado?" Gottschalk voiced as he walked up between Jethro and Gan.

"*Ich meinte, in bei den Griechen gebe es keine Tornados,*" Hirsch wondered aloud.

"That's no tornado," Jethro responded as the funnel cloud turned midair like a bent finger and stretched toward them.

Gan's mouth widened in shock as the spinning black tempest rushed forward. "*Mein Gott.*"

Jethro grabbed Gan by the collar. "We have to get out of here… Now!"

"This old boy is armed," Petros said as he shimmied over to where Vasili was pressed against the wall. Wood, plaster, and brick sprinkled down upon them like a powdered rain.

"How bad?" Vasili asked, checking to make sure his revolvers were loaded. They had been in tighter spots before—the bungled robbery in Chania was still fresh in his mind—but there was a strange sense of finality permeating this job. Even if they survived tonight, there would be no coming back.

Petros shook his head. "Big gun. Big *damn* gun." He angrily spit a wad of yellow phlegm to the ground. "Remind me to kill Alexei when we get back."

"Probably not the best idea you've ever had, old man," Vasili said as he snapped the chambers into place.

"But it will make me feel better."

"Please tell me there's a plan," Caraway said as he crawled over to them.

"Besides not get killed?" Vasili shook his head. "No, not really."

Caraway gave Vasili a withering look. "Pull the other one."

It was all Vasili could do not to put a bullet between the American's eyes. Then again, accidents do happen… "Wait until he runs out," he said. "My guess he's got only six rounds left."

"Oh, yeah? And how do you figure that?"

Vasili shrugged nonchalantly. "It was a guess."

After another few shots—bullets, wood, and plaster flying madly like birds from a bush—they heard the shooter shout a jumble of throaty lyrical phrases. They exchanged a collective look of bewilderment.

"You get that?" Petros asked Vasili.

Vasili shook his head and looked to Caraway. "What about you, American? You understand what our friend is shouting?"

Caraway furrowed his brow. "Don't look at me. English and Bad English, that's all I understand."

The three of them then turned to Ken, who was staring off into the distance, his head cocked to the side as he listened to the shouting gunman. His eyes went wide in realization. "Wait," he breathed. "Wait! I know what he's saying." He looked to Caraway, his mouth curled into a smile. "It's Hebrew."

Caraway furrowed his brow. "How the hell do you know Hebrew?"

"Long story," he replied, leaving it at that.

"So, he's Jewish. Fantastic. How does that help us?" Caraway asked, eyeing him suspiciously.

"It means he's one of the good guys!" Ken said excitedly.

"Yeah, but last I checked, we ain't," Caraway grumbled.

Ken's face fell. "Goddammit."

"Say something to him in Hebrew," Petros said calmly. Off Ken's expression, he added, "Humor me."

"I only know a few phrases…"

"Say something—anything—but say it loud, Shakes. Make sure our friend can hear it," Petros said with a wicked grin.

Ken cleared his throat and shouted: *"Eyfo ha-shirutim, bevakasha?"*

Silence echoed from the other room. Petros flashed Ken a gracious smile before he whipped around and hurled his knives into the other room.

Ken and Caraway cringed at the scream.

Panic. The Nazi camp had fallen into bedlam as the storm rapidly approached, a lion's roar that tore through the sky. Wind whipped dust and leaves swirled through the air, stinging eyes and skin. Gottschalk and Hirsch had run out in hopes of regaining some order and organize a hasty evacuation, giving Jethro and Gan the chance to break away.

"Dumont, what is that thing?!" Gan hissed, forcibly grabbing Jethro by the arm.

Jethro nervously kept his gaze on the approaching storm. "You remember the living storm I was telling you about?"

Gan pinched his eyes shut. *"Verflucht."*

"Haste is the operative word, Herr Oberführer," Jethro said with a quick nod. "I was able to stop it before, but I don't know if I can do it again."

"How did you stop it before?"

"I blew up a plane."

"Du Lusche!, Du bist schlimmer als Caraway!" Gan cursed through his teeth. "Come with me," he said, leading Jethro toward his Volkswagen. The air crackled with electricity, emerald bolts of lightning bursting in the distance. "Let's get you out of the camp. Hopefully we'll figure something out that doesn't involve blowing up our only means of transportation."

Jethro glanced back at the Obergruppenführer's tent. He was foolish to even consider this, but what better time than now—with the Nazi regiment thrown into disarray? "What about the Shard?" he shouted over the wind.

"Now is not the time, Herr Dumont!"

"But if what you said is true, perhaps we can use it to stop the storm!" And hopefully prevent the prophecy from coming true, he didn't say.

"We will just have to take our chances," Gan said as they approached the vehicle. His driver, the white haired boy Jethro recognized from the attack on the consulate in New York, stared up at the sky, slackjawed, eyes brimming with tears. "Johann! Johann!"

"Es will mich abholen..." the boy whispered.

"Johann! *Fahren wir los!"* When the soldier failed to reply, Gan grabbed him by the collar. *"Mach schnell, Johann! Sofort!"*

Brought out of his stupor, Johann faced his superior, nodded briskly, and climbed into the driver's seat.

"Das ist 'n braver Junge," Gan said as he and Jethro climbed into the passenger seats.

Johann started the car, revving the engine before peeling out of the camp, the back tires sending dust flying into the air. They launched down the hillside, swerving down the narrow dirt road. Johann, white knuckled, struggled to keep the speeding vehicle upright, the wind jostling them ferociously left and right.

Jethro's head throbbed as he heard the voices echo inside his skull over and over. Squeezing his eyes shut, he pressed the heels of his hands against his temples in vain effort to fight back the pain. Gritting his teeth, he prayed: *"Om! Tare Tuttare Ture Soha!*

Gan glanced through the rear window to see the funnel cloud charging toward them, blasting down the hillside. "It is following us!" he shouted. He turned to Jethro. "Why is the storm following us?!"

Jethro grimaced. "It wants me," he admitted through the pain.

Gan's jaw fell open. "Why did you not tell me this *before* I got in the car with you?" Without taking his eyes off the storm, he leaned forward and forcibly clapped Johann on the shoulder. *"Los, gib Gas, Johann!"*

"It's almost on us," Jethro said as he peered into the tenebrous tempest. He thought he could make out a shape within it, something almost human…

"I hate you, Dumont," Gan said bitterly.

"Thank you, Herr Oberführer, that is very helpful right now," Jethro replied.

The black cloud engulfed them in a blast of air. The windows shattered inward and the world plunged into darkness. Lightning flashed around them, shooting in every direction. Jethro's body burst with energy, a sensation that seemed to tear at his flesh. It was all he could do not to scream. The Jade Tablet erupted in green light, casting an unearthly hue over the car, the fibers violently constricting around his finger. Johann did his best to keep control of the car as it barreled forward in the darkness. Black mist seeped in through the windows and swirled into place besides Johann, forming the outline of a man. Jethro and Gan watched in horror as the phantom's hand instantly morphed into a blade and drove its way through Johann's skull.

"Johann!" Gan screamed as blood exploded across the dashboard. The young soldier's body crumpled forward, pressing his foot down against the gas petal. The car sped forward, blindly hurtling toward certain doom.

"You know what this book looks like?" Caraway indignantly asked Vasili as he kicked aside a pile of discarded books. They had been rifling through the small library for the last thirty minutes to no avail, tossing books haphazardly to the floor. The dry, dusty smell permeating the room reminded Caraway of his days in Sunday school, the dour white faced old men and crusty nuns that judged him with their eyes.

"Ask him," Petros replied pointing to the gagged man tied to the chair on the other side of the room. They had shoddily bandaged up the knife wound in his shoulder, the white fabric now a deep maroon turning brown. His face was pale from blood loss but remained alert, his eyes watching the robbers as they moved about the house.

Vasili looked at their captive and shook his head. "He will not talk."

Petros stepped forward and flourished his knives, the metal ringing. "I can make him talk," he said with a devilish grin.

"Hey!" Caraway shouted, stepping forward. "He doesn't know who we are, doesn't understand what we're saying… I thought we talked about this, quick and clean, right?"

"It is up to him," Petros frowned. "He tells us what we need, I will make it quick."

"We're not going to kill him!" Ken snapped, grabbing Petros's arm.

Petros dropped an indignant gaze at Ken's hand. "Listen, Shakes, I like you. I do… but you do *not* tell me what to do," Petros said with a quiet fury, aiming his knife at Ken.

Ken let go of Petros's arm and took a cautious step back, holding up his hands. "Let me try to talk to this guy, okay? Maybe if we talk—instead of stab—he might be more helpful."

"The man doesn't speak Greek too well and he clearly ain't gettin' A's in English," Caraway stated, tossing their captive a frustrated gesture.

Ken looked to Vasili, pleading. "I have an idea."

Vasili glanced at Petros, who only shrugged. Rolling his worry beads in his hand, Vasili thought about returning to Kamariotissa empty-handed. He held up two fingers and stepped back.

Ken nodded, gracious for the two minutes. He ripped out a small piece of paper from one of the books. With a pencil he found nearby, he scribbled three symbols and walked over to the old man. The man jerked back, cringing as Ken knelt down in front of him. Ken held up a placating hand. "Don't worry, I'm not going to hurt you." He showed the old man the piece of paper and the old man's eyes went wide. "*Emet*," Ken said, reading the word. "Truth."

The man looked at Ken, tilting his head quizzically. Ken nodded in response.

"Yup," Caraway sighed. "This is *real* helpful."

Ken shot Caraway a sideways glance and took a tentative step closer. "*Emet.* Truth," he reiterated, and then whispered: "*Golem.*" The man's eyes grew wider as he stared at Ken. He shifted in the chair and tried to remove the gag around his mouth.

"Don't worry. I got it," Ken said as he reached over and removed the gag.

The man opened and closed his mouth and moistened his lips with a slow roll of his tongue. He furrowed his brow. "Brickman?" he said with a hopeful breath.

A small smile cracked on Ken's face. He nodded slowly. "Yes. *Ata yakhol la'azor li?*" he asked.

The man stole a glance at his other captors and then looked back at Ken. "*Ech efshar la'azor lecha?*"

Ken firmed his lips and said, "*Necronomicon.*"

The phantom launched at Jethro, grabbing him by the throat and slamming his head against the door, stars erupting behind his eyes. Bullets whizzed by as Gan fruitlessly tried to shoot the immaterial assailant, grazing Jethro's shoulders, chest, and cheek, and puncturing holes in the side of the car.

"*Give us the Tablet!*" the phantom hissed as it snaked itself around Jethro's neck, his lungs screaming for oxygen. He struggled to pry himself free, but his left hand passed through the phantom as if nothing were there. It slammed him against the door again, the hinges breaking free and sending the door tumbling onto the road. Jethro swung out, his head falling just short of hitting the ground as he grabbed onto the inside of the car. The phantom pushed him down to the ground, the wheels tossing gravel into the air, stinging his face. Without his radioactive salts, Jethro's strength was only a fraction of what it once was, but his grip held firm.

"*Om! Ma-ni Pad-me Hum!*" Jethro choked. He clenched his right fist and swung through the haze of asphyxiation. His fist hit the phantom as if it had been made of solid matter, the shock of impact echoing down Jethro's arm. The phantom flew back; it's snakelike arm dissipating from Jethro's neck. Jethro gasped as air rushed into his lungs. Pulling himself up, he saw Gan struggling to regain control of the vehicle from Johann's bloody corpse.

"What in *Hashem*'s name is that?!" Gan screeched.

"I don't—" Jethro gasped. He glanced at his right hand where the Jade Tablet glowed and crackled with electricity, and he understood. "*Om! Vajrapani Hum!*"

Jethro swung at the phantom again, the Jade Tablet exploding with power as it met the creature's spectral frame. The phantom fell back, its body losing shape as it hit against the opposite door. Jethro could see the contours of a face appear in the shadows of the mist—something that was at once human and not. It was *smiling* at him. The phantom's arm formed into a blade once again and moved to strike. Jethro readied himself to dodge to blow when he realized its target wasn't him.

It was Gan.

"*Necronomicon?*" Ken asked again.

"*Lo! Lo!*" the man exclaimed as he shook his head furiously, unleashing a torrent of unintelligible protests.

"Calm down!" Ken said, trying unsuccessfully to placate him. "You— you have to trust us! We need it for the right reasons!"

Petros drew his blades. "My turn."

Ken caught the man feverishly glancing away. "No, wait," he breathed, jumping to his feet. Following the man's gaze, Ken walked over to a recently emptied bookcase in the corner of the room. He ran his hands over the wooden shelves, while the man continued his increasingly thunderous protestations. Ken's fingers fell over a small symbol—a single line with five shorter lines branching off—on a slightly raised wooden panel at the back of the bookcase. Tracing its edge, his nails clicking into the carvings, he could feel the soft yet distinguishable flow of air. Wordlessly pushing the panel, Ken heard the sound of gears and mechanisms echo out from the walls. He jumped back as the bookshelf broke away, revealing a small chamber. A pedestal sat in the center, a large leather bound book placed atop. The cover appeared to be made out of the flesh of a human face, stretched and twisted until it was nearly unrecognizable.

"Well, shit," Caraway swore under his breath.

Vasili nodded his approval. "Not bad, kid."

Caraway stepped toward the hidden room. "How did you know that would work with him?" he quietly asked Ken.

Ken shook his head slowly, his gaze never leaving the book. "I didn't."

"You are one lucky asshole," Caraway said, patting Ken on the shoulder.

"Tell me about it," Ken sighed.

"So, all that trouble just for this, eh?" Petros voiced as he paced around the pedestal. "Ugly little book, isn't it?" He reached for the book.

"Wait!" Vasili exclaimed, stepping between Petros and the *Necronomicon*, producing the small piece of paper from his pocket. "Alexei told me to repeat this before we removed the book."

Petros looked at Vasili incredulously. "He told you to repeat something?"

Vasili shrugged as he read over Alexei's message again. "A prayer…"

"Why didn't you say that before when we were tossing all the other books around?" Caraway asked angrily.

"I forgot, all right?" Vasili shot back. "This has not exactly been the most normal day for me either."

"What sort of prayer is it?" Ken asked.

"I do not know. I think I have heard it before…" Vasili trailed off as he firmed his lips. He looked over to Petros. "I think it sounds like something the Twins would say."

"This has to do with those fishy bastards?" Petros shouted. "Alexei told us it would be a simple smash and grab, and instead we got this idiocy. To hell with him and the Twins and their goddamn prayers," he grumbled as he lifted the book off its perch.

Suddenly, the room was filled with intangible screams, inhuman voices from the shadows. A howling wind came down upon them as if they were suddenly sucked into the vortex of a hurricane filled with air that smelled like sulfur and rot. Ken fell back against the wall, ducking his head beneath his arms. Caraway screamed, unconsciously clutching his chest, the memories of the *Bartlett* raging through his mind. Vasili silently stumbled a step back, his stomach twisting into knots, tightly gripping onto Alexei's note like a talisman.

Petros's eyes rolled back into his head. The color leached out of his skin and hair, like water flowing down a drain. Foam bubbled from his mouth. "*Iä! Iä! Cthulhu fhtagn!*" he sputtered as his knees buckled and he dropped to the floor, unconscious.

The world fell into slow motion as Jethro leapt forward to intercept the creature. He felt the incorporeal blade's edge slip across his palm, drawing blood. But it wouldn't be enough, a hollow gesture in the face of death. The blade came within millimeters from Gan's skull when the phantom let out a violent disembodied scream. *"THE BOOK!"* it shouted as it instantly dissipated like a pall of cigarette smoke out the window. The black cloud blanketing the car suddenly lifted, turning the world into a blur of motion. Ahead the road came to an abrupt, sharp end, the Mediterranean extending beyond.

"Stop the car, Gan!!!" Jethro shouted as they barreled toward the cliff, bracing himself against the back of the seat.

"*Scheiße!* I cannot!" Gan cried. "Johann's foot is stuck!"

Gan tried to steer the car away but it was too late. The car's wheels spun out, launching the vehicle over the cliff, toward the frigid waters below. As certain death rushed toward them, all of Jethro's thoughts were of Jean Farrell.

Chapter 12
REUNIONS

*T*sarong knocked tentatively at Dumont's door. It had been nearly a fortnight since the Bodhisattva abruptly locked himself in his quarters, refusing all visitors, and often neglecting the small meals left outside his chamber. Whispers and the frequent sound of feet pacing against the stone floor were often reported by those curious enough to press their ears against the door. A growing concern for Dumont's wellbeing had spread across the Temple of the Clouds, with many secretly believing the Jade Tablet had driven the American insane—a concern Tsarong was ashamed to admit he shared.

"Come in, Tsarong," Dumont called from within.

Tsarong pushed open the door hesitantly. Dumont was kneeling in the center of the room, his back toward the door, a large rainbow-colored rug laid out on the floor before him. He looked back at Tsarong and smiled. His skin was pale, his face haggard from what Tsarong guessed was blood loss and lack of food, but his grey eyes remained vibrant, almost glowing. "There's something I want to show you."

Tsarong sat down carefully beside Dumont. He furrowed his brow as he looked over the rug. "What is this, Tulku?"

Dumont smiled. "It is the Jade Tablet."

Tsarong's eyes went wide, his heart racing as his stomach fluttered. His skin prickled and the thinning hair on his head began to stand on end. It was a sensation almost like arousal, yet deeper and somehow more divine. "Om! Ma-ni Pad-me Hum! *Tulku...* How is this possible? How did you remove it?"

"I don't know." Dumont's smile faded and he somberly shook his head before continuing. "There are words etched into the Tablet, Tsarong. Not just Tibetan, but from every language on Earth, everything from cuneiform to English and some I don't..." He trailed off, his mouth moving silently *before he could once again find his voice. "And that only scratches the surface… There is a* code *hidden in the strand. It took me days to figure out the pattern, several more to piece together the letters and phrases."*

"A code? A code for what?"

Jethro frowned in thought, unable to wrench his gaze off the Tablet. "I can't be certain—it's been so long since I ended my studies at the university—but I think *it's the chemical ingredients for a new kind of* salt.*"*

Jean blinked back tears and shivered despite the warmth. Smoke wafted off her shoulders. She was lying in a fetal position on a marble floor, the stone cold against her cheek. Looking up, she found herself once again in the center of the temple. White columns pierced the darkness, bordering small enclaves with statues lit by shallow firelight. The buzzing in the back of her head drifted into silence and the cloud that had settled over her mind slowly began to clear. Cupped in her hands was the Third and Final Jade Tablet, gripped so tightly she had impressed hundreds of ancient runes into her palms. Turning it over, she realized it was identical to the large cracked crystal egg she had seen in Astrapios's bedroom.

"Welcome back, Jean," Prometheus said, standing over her. Twelve figures were hidden in the shadows behind him, their faces hidden. Jean knew who they were without asking—the gods of Olympus. "We're very proud of you."

"You son of a bitch," she hissed. "Everything I just went through. All that destruction and death… Ken… All of it!" she screamed, shaking with rage. She had been played, like a pawn in a game of chess, moved around the board by a sadistic god. "That was all some kind of goddamn test, wasn't it? Wasn't it?!"

"Yes and no. Where you went, everything you saw and did, was *real*, as it has, will, and *could* have happened, if you had failed."

"Failed at what? Getting this?" she asked holding up the Third Jade Tablet. "You sent me to the apocalypse to get a *broken crystal egg*?"

"This is the *Fire from Olympus*, Jean," Prometheus said. "What I gave man at the dawn of existence. It is the—"

"I don't care!" She shook the Tablet angrily. "If this was so goddamn important, then why was it sitting in Astrapios's bedroom, collecting dust?"

Prometheus shook his head. "That was a fake, meant to mislead our adversaries. With R'lyeh rising so soon, we couldn't take the chance. So, we *moved* it into another time, another *reality*."

"Another reality?" she huffed incredulously. "There was nothing real about that world, it couldn't be!"

"You think of time as a single thread; it isn't. There are thousands, millions of different worlds, mirrors and refractions of one another overlapping and coexisting. The one you visited was a possibility, a counterfactual. The damage there had already been done, so we hid the Tablet there for safekeeping."

"Safekeeping," she reiterated. "Buddy, you have no idea what that means. You're a *god*, why not just hold on to it?"

"Jean, if only it were as simple as that. Had I not moved the Tablet when I did, it would have already been in the hands of the Cult of Cthulhu. The forces at play are more powerful than you can even begin to comprehend. They have spent years, decades, even millennia planning for this day. Even framing you for the murder of Astrapios was part of their plan."

Jean rolled the Tablet back and forth between her hands, trying to make sense of it all. Alternate worlds, ancient cults, sleeping gods; it all seemed like the stuff out of those pulp magazines the kids were reading. But after everything she had seen, everything she had done, what was not possible? The candlelight refracted through the crystal, turning her hands an unearthly green. Runes lined the lower two thirds of the egg, while the top third depicted three robed figures standing before a massive creature, each holding an item defiantly above its head; a ring, a stone, and an egg. The creature was a twisted chimera, a tentacled head atop a grotesque dragon's body, enormous batwings extending out.

"Heydrich mentioned three scions," she said quietly, more to herself than the others. "Me, someone named Vasili, and Dumont… But, Ken said Dumont had gone missing—" A smile creased her lips as she connected the dots. She had been right all along. "You tricky bastard."

"The three bearers of the Jade Tablets," Prometheus said, ignoring her revelation. "Only you three can prevent the rise of Cthulhu."

"You're the reason I decided to come to Samothrace," Jean said. "How long have you been playing me, the Green Lama, all of us, like this?"

"We've had our influence over you and the Green Lama for some time now," one of the male figures said, his voice like thunder.

A woman spoke up next, her voice somber and intelligent. "Though Vasili is currently beyond our grasp."

"When I transported to Coney Island and met Rabbi Brickman, that was you," she said pointing an accusatory finger at Prometheus and the other gods. "Some kinda *deus ex machina* crap."

Prometheus furrowed his brow and turned to his fellow Olympians. No one replied, but Jean got the sense they *were* communicating. He looked back to her, his face downcast. "No, that wasn't us," he confessed reluctantly.

"Well, that's not very comforting," she said, clearing her throat. "Let me guess what's next. I have to go and complete some ancient prophecy and defeat Cthulhu. If I don't, the reality—the future I went to—"

"Will become *your* future," another woman said, her voice sultry. "And there will be no reset."

Jean nodded in understanding. "Dumont and the others are here, aren't they? Looking for me, just like Ken—the other Ken—said. That's where the points diverge, in that world they never found me."

"It's a bit more complicated than that, paradoxes and so forth, but you grasp the basics," Prometheus said with a smile.

"I was there a few days, maybe a week." She furrowed her brow. Or had she been there longer? Or less? It was like trying to remember a dream. "Do we have enough time?"

Prometheus nodded. "Time moves faster in the counterfactual. Relatively speaking, you've only been gone an hour."

"Then take me to them, Dumont and the others. Let's get this show on the road before it's too late."

He considered the request and nodded.

"But after this, that's it," she said sharply, trying not to think of the absurdity of scolding the gods. "I don't want any of you messing with my life ever again."

"Oh, don't worry, Jean," Prometheus said as a howling wind began to fill the temple. "After this, you're on your own."

The monster screamed, a sound like flesh being torn apart. The black clouds sank back into the Shard, leaving the sky a rich blue. Heydrich forced himself to his feet. Finding his knees weak, he grabbed onto a small branch and watched as the black wormlike head shrank down and reformed into Alexei's face.

"*Pih qob xowz vczr o aob og qzsjsf og tozghott? W kcbrsf!*" Alexei whispered through a Cheshire grin, his eyes black. The world around him seemed to waver with every syllable, bending reality until it threatened to snap. "*Ewetwjk gx lzw uomt—ywl slgesf! Al'k lzw yjwslwkl esysrafw af ugeak.*"

"Master," Heydrich choked, loosening his collar. His lungs were on fire, his ears bleeding. He could feel his mind begin to boil as Alexei's rant continued. Man was not made to hear these words. "Master. Stop. You're— You're using the Old Tongue."

Alexei paused to consider Heydrich, and the world quickly regained its form. Heydrich gasped as he once again collapsed to the ground, this time in relief. Alexei's ebony eyes faded to ivory as he sheathed the Shard and handed it back to Heydrich.

"What of Dumont?" Heydrich asked.

"Get your people to the Sanctuary of the Great Gods after the setting of the sun," he said in response. "The time for sacrifice is at hand."

"Mother of God, what happened to him?" Sotiria shrilled as they dragged Petros's chalk-white body onboard. His body was frozen, his back arched in an unnatural angle, his face contorted in terror. His eyelids were at half-mast, busted veins turning the orbs underneath into black and crimson balls. A book was clutched between his hands, rigor mortis fingers pressing into the ancient leather. Sotiria shivered at the sight, as though someone had walked over her grave. To Vasili, she asked, "τι συνέβη στον Πέτρος;"

"Δεν ξέρω, Sotiria, να αποκτάται ακριβώς από εδώ!" Vasili snapped as they carefully placed Petros on a table in the galley.

"Μοιάζει με αυτός είναι νεκρός!"

"Μας πάρτε πίσω σε Kamariotissa τώρα, Sotiria!" he shouted, eyes blazing.

Sotiria nodded nervously and ran toward the cabin, leaving the three men to stand over Petros in silence. The boat rumbled to life beneath their feet, the sound of propellers churning water audible through the walls. They stared down at Petros's corpse expectantly, as if he would grant them some solution, but despite his mouth frozen open mid scream, he remained mute and cooling on the table.

"What do we do now?" Caraway asked softly after they had cleared the docks.

"We get the book off him," Vasili replied.

Ken held up his hands and took a theatric step back. "I helped you find it, but I'm not ending up like the Mayan Mummy here."

"You have the magic words," Caraway said to Vasili. "Make it happen."

Vasili silently shot Caraway a contentious look and carefully unfolded the small scrap of paper, his hands shaking. It was simple, he told himself, he just needed to say the words and take the book. Simple. He ran a shaking hand over his mouth. He glanced at Petros's body and felt a sense of unbecoming, as if he were stepping outside himself. Petros. Vasili had never liked Petros, had once believed they would one day end up at each other's throat, but here he was dead on a table, murdered by a book. Just simple words—strange, foreign, alien words. Vasili licked his chapped lips and began reciting Alexei's prayer. "*Nyarlathotep klaatu barada nikto. Ph'nglui mglw'nafh Cthulhu R'lyeh wgah'nagl fhtagn.*"

Ken and Caraway watched in muted horror as Vasili's eyes began to glow green and then rumbled with thunder. Pulling the book free of Petros's icy grip, Vasili turned it over and stared into the vacant eyes of the book's inhuman face, feeling as though something inside him had shifted. Simple words. He silently glanced at Ken and Caraway, and then walked out of the galley.

"Did you see that?" Ken asked once Vasili was out of earshot.

"Yeah," Caraway replied quietly. "I saw it. This whole mess got a lot more complicated."

"He was protecting it," Ken said after a moment.

"Excuse me?"

Ken slid his hands into his pockets and slowly walked toward the aft of the boat. "The man we stole the book from—the Rabbi. He wasn't hiding it, he was protecting it." He looked back at Caraway. "From us."

"Gan! Gan!" Jethro sputtered, trying to keep his ringing head above the surface. Water was rapidly filling the car, pulling them down toward the depths of the Mediterranean. Gan sat motionless in the front seat, his face covered in blood, either killed or knocked unconscious by their fall. Wading forward, Jethro placed his hand on Gan's neck, feeling the soft echo of a pulse. Lacing an arm around Gan's body, Jethro pulled the German free, kicked open the door, and dragged him out of the sinking vehicle. They were only a few feet from the rocky cliff, but Jethro could already feel the tug of the sea current pulling them away. With Gan's limp form weighing him down and without his radioactive salts to strengthen him, Jethro knew he only had moments to get them back to shore before exhaustion took hold. Swimming toward the rocky precipice, Jethro struggled to keep his and Gan's head above water. "Come on, Gan—I need you to wake up," Jethro gasped. "Can't do this without you." He heard Gan groan. "Heinrich! Heinrich, can you hear me?"

"*Ja*, Herr Dumont," Gan said, his voice weak, his eyes half open. "I am right next to you."

"Can you swim?"

"*Ja. Ja*, I think so," Gan replied after a moment, nodding his head. He grimaced. "But I cannot do it on my own."

"Just hold on to me and make for that outcrop," Jethro instructed as they swam toward the cliff face, keeping one arm wrapped around Gan's chest. While Gan's efforts took some weight off him, it was Jethro who was pulling them forward.

Minutes seemed liked hours as they inched closer to the cliff, fighting against the tide. At first Jethro's fingers only brushed against the wet rock, pulled away by the waves. It took three more attempts before they were able to grab on, digging their fingers into the slippery crevasses.

Jethro looked up toward the top of the cliff. "It's about a hundred feet straight up. You think you can climb it?" Jethro asked.

"I do not think I have a choice, Herr Dumont."

Jethro's muscles burned with exhaustion as he struggled to climb, the gash on his palm stinging against the rocks while the saltwater burned into the lacerations covering his body. It had been years since he had suffered from such minor wounds, his radioactive salts quickly healing his body long before it registered inconsequential trauma such as gunshots, stabbings, and burns as pain. It was limiting, the injuries, the bone breaking exhaustion, an invisible border that prevented him from achieving what needed to be done. He could feel the salt's absence in his veins, like a word hanging off the tip of his tongue. Gan wasn't doing any better. While he had pulled himself free of the water, Jethro could see the German was only using his left leg to climb.

"Your leg," Jethro said over the crash of waves.

Gan shook his head, his face red. "Broken or twisted. I do not know."

Jethro secured his footing and extended his hand. With considerable effort Gan pushed himself up and grabbed Jethro's hand, using it as leverage as they made their way up, with Jethro frequently having to pull Gan upward. As they inched closer to the top Jethro could feel Gan's weight pulling on him more.

"Dumont," Gan struggled as they neared the summit, his voice hoarse. "Dumont, I do not think I can—I can do this much longer."

"We're almost there, Heinrich! Hold on!"

"I—" Gan wheezed. His eyes rolled back in his head as his injuries took hold and stole his footing. Jethro tightened his grip as the Oberführer began to fall away, but the added weight tore at Jethro's anchor and his bloody fingers began to slip free. He couldn't hold on much longer.

"Give me your hand!" a woman shouted, extending her hand over the cliff edge. Without any other option, Jethro let go of the wall and grabbed onto the woman's hand. With her help Jethro pulled himself and Gan onto land.

His lungs and muscles burning, Jethro crawled forward and looked up at their savior. "Ne-tso-hbum!" he whispered as he gazed into her sparkling emerald eyes, forgetting himself.

"Good to see you too, Jethro Dumont," Jean Farrell said with a knowing smile. She was kneeling over him, a satchel strung across her shoulders.

"Jean!" Jethro jumped up and grasped her by the arms. His heart hammered in his throat, his body trembling as much from shock as exhaustion. She was here, alive, miraculously, wonderfully, alive. She seemed somehow more real, more vibrant than ever. Her scarlet hair shimmered, her skin glistened, and her smile shone like the sun. He wrapped his arms around her and pulled her body close as her arms wrapped around his. He felt her fingers dig into his back, and their chins hooked into the crooks of their necks.

"I was so worried about you," he breathed. He felt their cheeks touch for the first time and suddenly became conscious of the way her body fit against his. He heard a sound like thunder echo nearby and noticed thirteen figures standing off in the shadows. Suddenly feeling like the Lothario the gossip rags always purported him to be, Jethro reluctantly disentangled himself away from her and looked to the figures. Only one was completely visible, a tall man dressed completely in black. "Who are they?"

Jean rolled her eyes, her cheeks ruddy. "Pains in my ass. Trust me, you wouldn't believe me if I told you."

"Try me."

"Gods."

Jethro's eyes went wide. "I don't believe you."

Jean smiled. "Told you."

Jethro glanced at the man in black, who nodded in greeting. Jethro weakly waved his hand in response. The man in black turned toward his shadowed compatriots but not before giving Jean one last somber look. Jean nodded her farewells, her face unreadable. There was a flash of light followed by the sound of a rushing vortex. Jethro shielded his eyes as the thirteen figures walked into the light, and in an instant, were gone.

"Is that Oberst Gan?" Jean asked before Jethro could process it all.

"Oberführer," Gan corrected, his voice strained. He propped himself up. "Hello, Fräulein Farrell. I see you are doing well."

Jean knelt beside him, smiling. "And how's my favorite Jewish undercover agent doing?"

Gan furrowed his brow. "I am sorry, Fräulein, did we start liking each other all of a sudden?"

Jean pursed her lips. "Guess not."

Gan sat up and, looking out into the sea, began to chant in haunting tones: *"Yisgaddal ve-yiskaddash sh'meh rabba be-alma di vra chiruseh…"*

At last he concluded: *"Auf Wiedersehen, junger Johann."*

She followed Gan's gaze to a dark shadow in the water, then turned to Jethro. "We lost someone, didn't we?" she asked.

"Johann Adler," Gan said. "The only survivor of the Rabbi's attack on the consulate. I had taken him under my wing."

Jethro knelt down beside Gan and bowed his head. *"Om! Amitabha Hri."*

Gan gave Jethro a small nod of thanks but kept his eyes focused on the sea.

Jean looked over to Jethro and their eyes met. Her cheeks warmed. She had looked into those blue-grey eyes so many times, but it was the first time she ever felt them truly looking back. It was the first time she ever knew what was sitting behind them. She at once felt captivated by him and repulsed. He was two men and one, both whom she had respected, had even found herself drawn to, but neither of whom had ever told her the truth. For all the justice they—he—claimed to be fighting for, never once was veracity considered to play a role for those who would fight alongside him. Her face fell and she shook her head, there were more pressing issues. "We're all in trouble, Dumont. Everyone and everything." She reached into her satchel and brought out the Third Jade Tablet, glowing with green light.

"Mein Gott, that is it," Gan breathed, his eyes wide, his skin sickly in the emerald fluorescence. He struggled not to reach out and grab the cracked crystal egg in front of him. "That is the final Tablet."

"Yup, number Three." There was no mistaking the capital she placed in front of the word.

Jethro tried to control his breathing. He could feel the Third Tablet's power radiate through the air, buzzing in his head, a sensation at once familiar and foreign. "Jean, where did you find this?"

"A park, for all that matters," she said quietly. With a short nod toward Jethro's hand, she added: "Your ring's glowing." Risking a glance, Jethro felt his stomach drop in realization. He looked hesitantly over to Jean, who gave him a knowing eyebrow. The corner of her lips curled. "What do ya say, Tulku? Want to go and save the world?"

Chapter 13
WRAITH

*I*t's a little anticlimactic," Jethro confessed to Tsarong. He turned over the vial of salt, watching the plain white grains tumble over one another like in an hourglass, spilling away the days. He had half expected—hoped—that they would have substantiated in a multitude of colors or, at the very least, a vibrant green. "Thousands of years for food seasoning."

"Do not base decisions on appearances," Tsarong said, tugging at his beard, appreciating the irony in his statement. It was not so long ago that he had written the Bodhisattva off as a wayward American hedonist. Over the past few weeks Tsarong had watched in awe as Dumont created the salts from scratch, piecing together its chemical properties from the Jade Tablet's cryptic directions. He was becoming more and more certain that Dumont was indeed the scion of prophecy, a realization that at once excited and terrified him. Dumont's accession meant the time of reckoning was close at hand.

Turning over the vial again, Dumont watched the granules pour over each other. "There has to be something more to these. That the ingredients were kept secret for so long..."

"I confess," Tsarong said as he read over Dumont's copious notes, books filled with graphs, translations, and chemical formulas, "my understanding of chemistry is limited, yet I wonder, how different are these from what we put in our food?"

"Chemically speaking, they are completely unique," Dumont said as Tsarong handed him his notebook, turning to the diagram of the salt's molecular structure. "Honestly, if I hadn't created them myself, I wouldn't believe they existed. These molecular bonds have never been documented, let alone imagined, they're incredibly complex. In fact, I—" he cut himself off, his eyes darting over the diagram. His eyes narrowed as he tapped the page. "'Do not base decisions on appearances,'" he repeated. "The *molecular bonds. If they were rearranged, it could release…" He looked to Tsarong excitedly. "There's something I want to try."*

Vasili paced the deck, holding the book to his chest, feeling his heart jangle through the pages. He tried to ignore the pain echoing out from his skull, threatening to explode. Visions and sounds rolled through his head like a broken strip of film, skipping and blurred.

"He has you," he said aloud. Tears streamed down his cheeks. He stared down into the rushing waters, watching the inhuman shadows swim beneath—people, fish, both—following the boat. "Close. Keeps you close and you don't even realize you're being played. A chess piece moved off the board. Insignificant yet so important. One to rise. Three to sleep. One is lost. One in time. One to die. Nyarlathotep has you."

"You okay?"

"What?" Vasili wiped his eyes with the back of his sleeve.

"Just me," Ken said, holding his hands up defensively, a cigarette hanging from the corner of his mouth. "Needed to get away from our stiff."

Vasili laughed manically. "This accent you have is not fooling anyone, 'Shakes.'"

Ken swallowed the lump in his throat. "Vasili, I don't understand," he asked.

"Εσείς ηλίθιοι λίγο άτομο!" Vasili shouted, gesticulating wildly. "I *know* you are not British. I *know* your friend has two eyes. I *know* you are here because of the American girl."

"I—" Ken stuttered, nervously removing the cigarette from his mouth. His hands were shaking.

"Ken Clayton," Vasili said, his eyes sealed shut. "That is your real name, is it not? Kenneth Andrew Clayton. Born and raised in San Jose, California. Third child. Two older sisters, Karen and Darcy. God's gift to autograph hounds. The only man who will admit he looks like Robert Taylor, but wants to be Paul Muni. And how is Benn, by the way?"

"How could you—?"

"Have you two spoken since you parted ways?"

Ken shuddered as gooseflesh ran across his arms and neck. He could feel his heart slam into ribs. "N—no… We haven't…" he whispered. "We thought it best—Safer that way."

A manic grin spread across Vasili's face. "Your father knew. He always knew. And you always knew he did; you saw it in his eyes. How it must have killed you…"

"Stop it," Ken whispered, dropping his faux British accent.

"He gets all your checks." Vasili fluttered his fingers like bits of paper in the wind. "The ones you sent to help him along. He gets every single one. And you know what he does with them? He puts them in a drawer just left of the kitchen and lets them pile up, one by one, until he can't pull it open anymore. Now he just tosses them in the trash and he never says your name."

"Stop it!" Ken shouted. Tears poured down his cheeks, his eyes bloodshot. "Just stop it! You have no idea what it's like!"

Vasili blinked, looking at Ken as if he had seen him for the time. He shook his head. "I do not—I cannot understand how I know these things, but I do," he gasped. "They are true, yes?"

Ken took a half step back, eyeing Vasili and the book suspiciously. He had curled his hands into fists, crushing his cigarette between his fingers. He opened his hands and let the flecks of tobacco tumble away. "Yes. They are," he croaked after a moment. He cleared his throat and ran the back of his hand across his nose. He took a tentative step forward. "Vasili, listen, I think I know—"

"Do not come any closer," Vasili hissed, hugging the book closer to his chest.

"I think—I think I know what might be happening to you. You're getting flashes of images in your head. Stuff you recognize, and stuff you don't? Hearing voices like they're talking from the back of your head."

Vasili nodded furiously, his face red. "How could you know that?"

"I spend most of my time around some very interesting people," Ken said hoarsely, taking another step forward. "But I bet you five American dollars that the answers you need are in that book you got there."

Vasili glanced down at the *Necronomicon*. "Yes," he breathed like a man repenting. "Yes, they are." He looked Ken in the eye. "That is what is so terrifying."

"Herr Oberführer! Sir, are you down there?" Hirsch called as he and a contingent of soldiers made their way down the hill. Hours had passed since the storm ripped through the base, leaving it in ruins. The injuries were numerous, and though there were thankfully no fatalities, neither the Oberführer nor the American Jethro Dumont had yet to reappear. Fearing the worst, Gottschalk had sent out search parties in all directions, with no success. "Herr Oberführer Gan! Are you here?"

"*Ja. Ja*, I am here," Gan called back weakly.

"*Gott sei Dank!*" Hirsch exclaimed, feeling the knot in his stomach unwind. He ran down the hill toward the cliff edge, where he found Gan nursing his ankle. "We thought we had lost you. Are you injured?"

Gan nodded. "My ankle."

"Where is Dumont and Johann?"

Gan's gaze fell and he shook his head. "Our car fell off the cliff during the storm. They died on impact," he said as two solders lifted him off the ground. "How is the camp?"

"Demolished," Hirsch replied, walking close to Gan. "We were lucky none of ours were killed." He then added, under his breath, "Herr Doktor Hammond returned. He is unhurt."

"That is… unfortunate."

"He says we are ready for the next step needed to obtain the Jade Tablet."

Gan raised an eyebrow and Hirsch thought he saw a hit of a smile. "Did he, now?"

"Some sort of ritual," Hirsch said, picking at his cheek, "tonight, out by the ruins."

"A ritual," Gan reiterated.

"Yes, sir." Hirsch lowered his voice, "I don't like the sound of it."

"No, Herr Sturmbannführer," Gan said, glancing over his shoulder into the brush. "I don't like the sound of it either."

"So," Jean said once she and Jethro were well out of earshot. They had snuck into the brush and left Gan alone at the cliffside in order to create Jethro's cover story—an untimely death. She could only imagine what the newsreels would say. "Looks like you've been having a lot of fun since I last saw you,"

"'Fun' is a *relative* term, Miss Farrell."

"'Miss Farrell'!" she exclaimed in mock surprise. "Aren't we *proper* today? Crazy as it sounds, Tulku, I'd much prefer you call me Jean, or at the very least, Ne-tso-hbum."

Jethro paused. "How long have you known?" he asked without facing her.

"That Jethro Dumont is the Green Lama? Well, if you discount the first time I figured it out, technically over twenty years from now, but in reality, only about an hour."

"Jean," he said as he turned to face her, but unable to look her in the eye. "I *wanted* to tell you."

Jean let out a harsh laugh. "That's a load if I ever heard one, *Smug*. If you wanted to tell me, you would have. Instead, you just pranced around pretending to be several different people, making me and everyone else who cared about you look like a whole bunch of idiots. Tell me something, who was that who visited my apartment, who fought atop the Brooklyn Bridge? Was it your little buddy Tsarong or was it Magga? Silly as it sounds, but I'm putting my money on Magga."

"I—That was never my intention," he said, finding himself unusually nervous. "Keeping my identity a mystery allows me to work outside the system, beyond corruption, to be where others cannot. And if my enemies were to ever discover, the people I—"

"You think we couldn't handle it?" Jean asked sharply. "It's not like you never put us into dangerous situations every other day! How many times have I been shot at? Kidnapped? Least you could have done is been *honest* with us. Besides, you wear a goddamn hood. Hate to break it to ya, buddy, but that doesn't exactly cover your face—no matter how much you disguise it." She stormed off.

Jethro sighed. She was right. "What do you want me to say?" he asked timidly, his heart pounding against his chest, his stomach twisting.

"Honestly?" she said over her shoulder. "Nothing."

Jethro grimaced, running a hand through his hair. "And what about you and me?" he asked, barely a whisper.

Jean spun back around, steaming. "Look, Dumont, 'you and me,' in the grand scheme of things, *we* don't really matter. Right now, you and I need to do everything we can to stop them or else—" Jean choked as tears formed in her eyes. "Or else everything and everyone we ever *loved* will be destroyed. So, the only thing I want us to talk about is how we're going to make sure that doesn't happen, okay?"

Jethro looked her in the eyes and nodded. "Okay."

"So, you gonna tell me the story of you and our boy Vasili?" Caraway asked as he walked into the cockpit, lighting a cigarette. Sotiria jumped and unconsciously placed her hand on her chest in surprise. "Sorry, didn't mean to startle ya."

Sotiria cleared her throat, turning back to the helm. "You did not startle me, John," she lied. "I am just worried about Petros. Do you think he will be all right?"

Caraway took a drag. "Do you want me to lie to you?"

"No. I suppose not," she said softly.

"He's dead," Caraway stated.

"I thought as much," Sotiria said without emotion, her eyes on the dark waters ahead.

"You know," Caraway said after several minutes of silence, "you didn't answer my question."

She frowned. "What do you mean?"

"I might not be from around here, but I can tell when two people got a history."

Sotiria glanced back at Caraway. "Are you going to proposition me, John?"

Caraway looked her in the eyes while he took another drag of his cigarette but didn't reply.

"Vasili, he…" she hesitated. "He is my husband. I am sorry. I mean to say he is my former husband."

Caraway let out a chuckle. "Ah, figured as much."

"Are you married, John?"

He cleared his throat and shifted uncomfortably. "I suppose you could say I am, though honestly it really depends on the day. And after all this, who knows? Might have found the straw that broke the camel's back, and if she's not there when I get home it will hurt like hell but, well, I guess I won't be surprised."

Sotiria nodded, though Caraway wasn't sure she was really listening. "I never thought anything of all the other men, the things I did behind his back. Life is too short, too brief to let these things weigh you down. That is what I thought at least," she said, as a tear appeared in the corner of her eye. "The problem was not that I did not love Vasili, it is just that... I suppose I did not realize it until it was too late, after I had made too many mistakes. And now, even after we have been separated for so long, it feels like I have been unfaithful to him everyday."

Caraway eyed the growing ash at the end of his cigarette. "Me and the missus, we were nothing but kids when we got hitched. Right before I went into the service, before the Krauts decided to get all frisky with the rest of the Continent and mustard gas the hell out of everyone. We both had a past, but who doesn't? I just guess we both thought that they would never catch up with us, never weigh us down. But kids like to dream, until the day they learn that dreams don't come true. Love. They like to spread it across billboards to sell tickets, two people looking each other in the eye as if they were made for each other. As if it were ever that simple."

He looked up to find Sotiria standing in front of him, her bloodshot eyes staring into him. She placed a hand on his cheek and leaned forward, her lips centimeters from his, waiting for their embrace.

"I'm sorry," he said, swallowing the lump in his throat, feeling her breath against his skin. "I can't."

Sotiria pressed her eyes closed, tears pouring down her cheeks. "Yes," she whispered. "I know. I just wanted to pretend for a moment."

"He loves you, still does. Saw it in his—saw it in the way he looked at you."

Sotiria nodded and then moved back to the helm. "That is why it hurts so much."

There was a soft knock on the window. They looked over and saw Ken beckoning Caraway outside. Caraway took a long drag of his cigarette and walked toward the exit. Stopping at the door, he looked back to Sotiria. "I just want you to know, if things were different—"

"Go, John," she cut him off.

Caraway followed Ken out onto the deck, the cool wind a shock to his skin. In the pale blue moonlight, Caraway could see that Ken's eyes were red raw; dried rivulets glistened on the other man's cheeks. "Jesus, is there a reason everyone is crying on this boat?" he grumbled.

Ken sniffed audibly and self-consciously wiped his face with his sleeve. "You should take a look at this," he said in lieu of a response. He led Caraway into the galley, where they found Vasili huddled, shivering in the corner. A harsh whisper echoed from the shadows, as if the book were screaming.

"Something wrong with the Big Guy?" Caraway asked.

"Vasili," Ken called, deadpan, still looking at Caraway. "Show John what you showed me."

Caraway raised an eyebrow at Ken's accent. "I take it he knows you're not British."

Ken let out a sardonic laugh. "Buddy, you don't know the half of it."

"I have not been sleeping," Vasili confessed as he opened the book, delicately turning the pages. Like Ken, his eyes were bloodshot, tearstains covering his cheeks. "My nights are filled with nightmares. Horrors I would have never thought possible..." His voice trailed off as he leafed through the book's illuminated manuscript. "It seems," he said as he showed the book to Caraway, "that these were more than just dreams."

"Aw, hell," Caraway grumbled as he looked over the illustration, goose bumps running down his neck. "That is what I think it is, isn't it?"

"Yup. That one's Vasili, that one looks like the Green Lama and that's *definitely* Jean," Ken said, indicating three screaming figures wrapped in the creature's tentacles. He then pointed at the bottom of the page. "And those two corpses—"

"You and me," Caraway sighed.

Ken nodded. "And that girl strung up like a pig at the county fair..."

"Sotiria," Vasili said, his voice shaking. He then tapped his finger against a horrific creature with a head like a black tongue. "This is Nyarlathotep. People whisper his name in awe of his horrors and wonders, the crawling chaos, the swarthy man. He is both and neither. The Old One who walks. I have seen him before."

"When?" Caraway asked.

Tears began to stream down Vasili's face. He closed the book and wiped his eyes with the back of his hand. "If I knew, American, I would tell you."

Caraway could feel beads of sweat forming on his brow. "And I'm guessing that big monster with the tentacles and the wings that was tearing us all apart is—"

"Cthulhu," Vasili said, the name hitting Caraway hard in the stomach.

"Goddammit," Caraway growled. "We're dead."

"Yup," Ken nodded. He looked to Caraway. "What do we do?"

"We'll see what our good Sheriff of Kamariotissa can tell us."

"Karl Heydrich," Jethro breathed in disbelief when Jean concluded her story. "You are *certain* what happened to you was real?"

"Buddy, it doesn't get any more real than that," Jean replied as she took another drink of water, finding herself impossibly famished once they had returned to the hotel. "I take it you know Heydrich."

"I killed him," he said numbly. "Five years ago in Tibet."

"Killed?" Jean asked, genuinely taken aback. "That doesn't sound like you."

"I was very young," he replied with a sad smile as he began pacing the room. "He and a small contingent of Nazi storm troopers invaded the Temple of the Clouds hunting for the Jade Tablet. He murdered a young boy, a student of mine. Brutally. In my rage, I stole Heydrich's life and gave it to the boy… I suppose as someone so familiar with the supernatural I shouldn't view your story with any skepticism, but… The creatures you encountered, what did you call them?"

"Deep Ones."

Jethro nodded thoughtfully. "I may have encountered one myself. I barely survived. It took all my remaining radioactive salts to fight off the creature's venom…" he drifted off, and shook his head. "*Heydrich*. It's not possible. Even if you *did* skip forward in time, Heydrich is dead. There's no way he could have lived."

"Oh, it's possible. I can still feel his rotted hand against my neck," she said unconsciously rubbing her throat.

Jethro shook his head. "No, Jean, you don't understand. When I drained the life out of Heydrich and gave it to Ravi, there was nothing left. He was *beyond* death. He couldn't have lived, not now or twenty years from now. Whatever—whoever—you saw was not—"

"Jethro, I know what I saw!" she shouted, slamming her fist on the table. "That thing called himself Karl Heydrich, told me he had been undead for over twenty years and according to Ken—the other Ken—he's the guy behind everything. Cthulhu, the Tablets, everything is tied to him. Like it or not, Dumont, Karl Heydrich is our big bad."

Jethro collapsed into his seat, covering his face in despair. "*Thiru neela kantam! Om! Tare Tuttare Ture Soha!* This is all my fault."

"Don't flatter yourself, Dumont. We're just a bunch of cogs in a big, millennium-sized wheel, and the motor's been running long before you and I came onto the scene."

"Just a rich boy playing the games of gods," Jethro said under his breath. He looked to Jean. "What can we do?" he asked aloud.

"We got ourselves one big advantage. Me."

Jethro bit back an amused smile. "Don't flatter yourself, either, Farrell."

Jean ignored Jethro's retort. "I know all their decisions, all our mistakes. No matter what Heydrich and his friends know, I'm twenty years ahead of them. As long as we're not stupid, we can probably stop this thing."

Jethro raised an eyebrow. "Probably?"

"Well," she said with a shrug, "I gotta hedge my bets."

Alexei was waiting for them. Standing at the edge of the dock, he watched the shadows shift beneath the waves, thinking back to the time when darkness consumed the world. So many centuries, walking while the Others slept, toying with the apes, so convinced of their importance, ignorant to their insignificance. How he relished it; how little he would miss it. The city was rising, breaking through the waves. He could feel the stars aligning, singing in the void, pulling toward each other in their millennial dance. The great priest was waiting, sleeping, dreaming. All that was missing, all that they needed, was a Jade Tablet. Just one. One to rise, three to sleep.

It had all seemed so simple when he took this shell; how had it grown so complicated? He, more than any creature, living or otherwise, knew that all prophecy was open to interpretation, but in the millennia he had traveled this rock he was more certain than ever the time of awakening was at hand. He had been so meticulous, and now, one by one, everything had begun to fall apart. With only hours left until the stars' alignment, he was forced to find answers in the *Necronomicon*. But he was not without his tricks.

Tonight's sacrifice would at least assure the city's ascension and from there he would draw them in.

"Ευπρόσδεκτη πλάτη," he said to the one called Caraway as Sotiria's boat pulled up to the dock.

The American raised a suspicious eyebrow and nodded a greeting.

"Πού είναι Vasili και ο Πέτρος?" Alexei asked in Greek, knowing how it unnerved the American. In truth, Alexei was fluent in every human language, but for the sake of appearances, and more for his enjoyment, he would continue the charade.

Caraway glanced pleadingly over to Sotiria as she tied the boat to the dock. "He wants to know where Vasili and Petros are," she told him before responding to Alexei's question. "Είναι στην αποθήκη. Οδηγίες αναγκών του Πέτρος."

Alexei nodded, knowing full well what had happened. He had felt it echo through reality. He stepped onto the boat and walked toward the galley, watching the shadows in the water begin to converge. Stepping inside, he found Petros covered with a small blanket, his body frozen, skin white.

"Tsk, tsk, Petros… You just *had* to pick it up…" Alexei sighed. He looked in to the shadows. "How are you feeling, Vasili?"

Vasili stepped out of the darkness, clutching the book close to his body, looking more like a boy than a man. "There's something bad coming, sir," he stuttered. "Something really, really bad."

Alexei furrowed his brow in faux concern. "Is that so?"

Vasili nodded. "We have to stop it. Somehow, we have to stop it."

"It'll be all right, Vasili," he said, extending a hand. "Give me the book and it will be all right."

Vasili glanced at Alexei's hand and began shaking his head. "No, I—I don't think I should, sir."

Alexei smiled warmly as he stepped closer. "Vasili. Shh!" He pressed a forefinger to his lips and then touched Vasili's forehead. Vasili's eyes rolled back and his head lopped to the side, unconscious but still standing. "There's a good boy," Alexei said as he pulled the book free.

Click! The sweet sensation of cold metal pressed against the back of Alexei's head.

"Okay, buddy," Caraway barked. "I don't know what you just did but you're gonna have to put the book down and your hands in the air."

Sotiria appeared at the other end of the galley, visibly shocked. "John, what are you doing?" she whispered.

"Ain't gonna repeat myself, bucko," Caraway said, ignoring her as he tore off his eye patch.

"John, your eye!" she exclaimed.

Caraway grimaced but kept his eyes on Alexei. "I'll explain later; after our good *sheriff* starts explaining the book."

Alexei turned around to face him. "You were always so *impetuous*, Mr. Caraway," he said in English, relishing Caraway and Sotiria's surprise.

"Yeah, but we still love the big lummox, don't we," Ken said as he entered from the other side of the galley, pistol in hand.

"Ah, and Mr. Clayton, I was wondering when you'd be joining us," Alexei said, his eyes locked on Caraway.

"Yeah, I'm like a bad penny," Ken said. "Since when could he speak English?"

"Does it matter?" Caraway snapped, then to Alexei: "We want answers, slim, so start talking."

An ugly Cheshire grin spread across Alexei's face, showing the seams in his shell. "Oh no, John," he growled, his voice shattering windows. "We're done talking."

"John!!" Sotiria screamed as a naked Ke'ta jumped onto the boat and grabbed her, digging his nails into her flesh. Seawater pooled at his feet.

Caraway spun around. "Sotiria!" he shouted, aiming his gun at the Deep One.

Alexei waved a finger and Caraway's pistol evaporated. Then with a flick of his wrist, he lifted Caraway into the air. Caraway writhed in pain, his face blood red as if someone were pressing down on his lungs. Such fragile things, humans; cut off their air, and they break down. All he needed to do was twist a little more, maybe snap a few bones… Or if he wanted, he could just as easily wink the Lieutenant out of existence. It would be so much fun, but there was too much at stake, too many pieces in play.

"Put him down!" Ken shouted as he vainly fired several shots, the bullets vaporizing mid-air.

Obsidian cracks formed over Alexei's face. "Tell your friends to meet us at the Sanctuary of the Great Gods if they wish to ever see these two alive again," he said with a black tongue.

Ken shielded his eyes as the boat filled with green light. There was a gust of wind and an echo like thunder, voices in the storm. When he opened his eyes again, they were gone.

Chapter 14
RITUAL

I arrived three months later, the initials H.T.C. emblazoned across all
seven wooden crates. It took ten monks to pull them into the temple, and
six hours to open them. It would take another week until it was fully
built, a feat Dumont accomplished alone in the subterranean levels of the
temple. When it was completed it filled a six hundred square foot room, a
marvel of modern technology never before seen in that part of the world.

"I must confess, Tulku, I am almost afraid to ask what this is," Tsarong
said as he watched Dumont adjust the final settings on the machine. There
was something disquieting about it, though Tsarong was at loss to describe
what it was about the machine that discomforted him.

"I'm surprised you didn't ask sooner," Dumont replied as he fiddled
with the controls.

"I respect my Tulku's privacy."

"Have I ever told you how uncomfortable it makes me when you call
me that." Dumont paused and looked at Tsarong. "I'm your friend, Tsarong.
Nothing more."

Tsarong smiled and bowed his head in appreciation. "As long as you
are the Green Lama, Jethro, you will always by my Tulku—as well as my
friend."

Dumont smiled and returned to his work. "To answer your question, it
is a particle escalator, decades ahead of its time. Using electric fields, it
propels subatomic particles at incredibly high speeds and contains them
within a well-defined beam. Several years ago, I saw a presentation at
Columbia University where a professor inundated several different kinds of
minerals and substances with ions from a particle accelerator, effectively
rearranging their molecular structure and releasing the untapped energy
within."

Tsarong furrowed his brow as he paced around the machine. "Pardon *me, Tulku, but I must admit that sounds quite suspicious."*

"Oh, the man was a complete quack," Dumont laughed. "They arrested him three days later for fraud. But, if my theories are correct, the molecules in these salts are arranged such that a small dose of radiation will cause them to shift, potentially unleashing an incredible amount of atomic energy."

Tsarong raised an eyebrow. "I suppose I've seen stranger things happen."

"Thanks for the vote of confidence."

"What are friends for?"

Dumont poured the salts onto a glass slide in front of the machine. "Stand behind there," he said indicating the large panel of leaded glass across the room. "I don't want to dose you with radioactivity."

They moved behind the leaded glass where Dumont handed Tsarong a pair of goggles. "Can't ever be too careful," Dumont said, slipping on his own pair of goggles. "Ready?"

"Please don't blow up the temple, Tulku."

"Can't make any promises."

Dumont flicked a switch and the machine came to life, a low humming that echoed into the temple's very foundation. Lights flashed, dials spun, and the machine glowed from within.

"How are you powering this?" Tsarong asked over the increasingly deafening sound.

"Patented technology," Dumont shouted back. "It would take too long to explain. Call it magic." He flicked several more switches, causing the accelerator to thrum even louder. Reaching over to a large knob, he said, "Well, here goes nothing."

"Om! Ah Hum Vajra Guru Padme Siddhi Hum!" Tsarong whispered, instinctually covering his eyes as a beam of light shot out of the accelerator and hit the pile of salt.

"It's okay, Tsarong," Dumont said as he turned back the dials and began switching off the machine. "It's done." The lights dimmed and the room fell silent. Walking over to the machine, Dumont removed his goggles and carefully lifted up the slide of salt.

"They don't look any different," Tsarong said as he removed his goggles.

"Only way to be sure," Dumont said as he brought the slide into his mouth.

Tsarong took a cautious step forward. "Tulku, are you sure that's safe?"

"Not at all," Dumont said as he tilted the salts into his mouth and swallowed. He let out a small cough, but otherwise remained silent.

Tsarong's heart hammered in his chest. "How do you feel?"

Dumont opened his eyes and placed the vial back down. He walked over and knelt down beside the machine. He wormed his fingers under the bottom and—without visible any effort—lifted the two ton machine above his head. Smiling, he turned to Tsarong. "Powerful."

Jethro ran his fingers across the Third Tablet's surface, his nails clicking into the grooves, as he studied the multitude of symbols. His gaze fell on the three figures lined up at the top of crystalline egg and the horrifying chimera they faced.

"Can you read it?" Jean asked.

"A little," Jethro replied, furrowing his brow. "It's mostly ancient Greek. I recognize certain terms and phrases, but I confess I'm not exactly fluent in ancient Greek. Now, ancient Tibetan…"

"What about the hoedown up top?" she asked, indicating the top of the egg.

Despite the severity of the situation, a smile formed on Jethro's lips. Leave it to Jean Farrell to throw out a question like that. "Besides the obvious?" he shrugged. "I think this line," he turned the egg over and pointed at a small passage, "might relate directly to the image. 'One to rise, three to sleep.'"

"Just vague enough to keep us guessing."

Jethro rubbed his chin. "It's only a guess, but it may mean we need all three Tablets to stop Cthulhu."

"Well, we have two here," Jean said. "Where's Brickman's Tablet?"

"New York," Jethro replied sheepishly.

Jean moaned as she flopped down onto the couch. "You'd think a prophecy would be pretty clear cut. 'At this time, this will happen. Insert Tablet here.' Besides, it would have been nice if Prometheus would have given me a few specifics—"

"Jethro! Jethro, open up! They're gone!" someone shouted, pounding furiously at the front door.

Jethro ran over and threw open the door to reveal a pale, sweating Ken Clayton. "Ken?" he exclaimed as Clayton rushed into the suite. "Ken, what happened?"

Ken grabbed Jethro by the collar, his eyes full of panic. "It's Caraway. They took him. Something took him and—" He cut himself short when he saw the red headed woman walk in from the other room. "Jean!"

Jean Farrell's eyes lit up as she rushed toward him. "Ken!" she exclaimed as she took him into her arms. "Oh, Ken. Ken, Ken, Ken. Thank God, you're okay," she whispered. Tears poured down her face. She squeezed him as tight as she could, if only to prove he was really there. "I thought I'd lost you."

Smiling, Ken pulled himself free, put his hands on her cheeks, and kissed her forehead. "I thought I lost *you*, Red. We were so worried." He looked her in the eyes. "You okay? You look like you've seen a ghost."

Jean shook her head, unable to remove her eyes from Ken. "Don't worry about it. I'm fine and you're alive."

Ken furrowed his brow, confused. "Jean, what are you—?"

"Ken," Jethro interrupted, in part wanting to spare Ken the knowledge of his future death. "Tell us what happened."

"John and I were undercover, looking for you," Ken began to explain, nodding to Jean. "We were hoping to see if anyone knew anything about you, but—"

Jethro placed a hand on Ken's shoulder. "Something went wrong."

Ken nodded and related the events of the last few nights and the *Necronomicon*. "He calls himself Alexei, but I don't think that's his real name. I'm not even sure he's human. He took Caraway and Sotiria. He said if you wanted to see Caraway alive to meet him at the Sanctuary of the Great Gods."

Jethro and Jean exchanged a glance. "I think that's the ruins in the Northwest of the island. I had planned on visiting there before all this went down," she said. "It's some kind of temple complex dedicated to something called the chthonic gods, where they used to do a lot of—" Her eyes went wide in realization. "Aw, crap."

"What?" Jethro asked.

"It's where they used to practice blood sacrifice."

Caraway woke with a start, knocking the back of his head against a stone pillar, stars exploding behind his eyes. Grunting, he tried to move his arms and found them chained to the pillar. He was dangling a few feet off the ground, his legs swaying uselessly. It was night, the sky sprinkled with stars. He strained his eyes and could just make out the silhouettes of ruins surrounding him. In the distance he could see torches moving through the trees, dozens, hundreds.

"John?" Sotiria whispered from his left. "John, are you awake?"

"Barely," he groaned. He turned his head, but still could only see her in the corner of his eye. "You okay?"

"I think so," she replied, her voice shaking. "Where are we?"

"Dunno," he said, watching the procession of firelight. "But wherever we are, I've got a feeling it's going to get a lot worse real quick."

"Wait," Sotiria whispered. "Do you hear that?"

"*Brauchen wir wirklich zwei?*" someone asked in the distance.

A second voice sounded, closer. "*Das eine Mädchen wird Opfer sein, das andere soll unseren Steinbruch herausziehen.*"

"*Opfer?*" another voice asked. "*Sagen Sie mir, Doktor wollen wir jetzt mal Menschen opfern?*"

"*Warum so zimperlich, Herr Sturmbannführer?*" the second voice replied. "*Wollen wir doch Hitler's Plan für die Jüden durchführen, nicht? Hier sehe ich keinen Unterschied?*"

"What are they saying?" Sotiria hissed.

Caraway shook his head. "I don't know. It sounds like they're speaking German."

"*Hallo, da sind wir schon!*" cried a Nazi with a Van Dyke covering his scarred face, leading three other Nazi officials one of whom was—

"Gan!" Caraway shouted, unable to contain his relief. "Oh, Jesus, Gan!"

"*Kennen Sie diesen Amerikaner, Herr Oberführer?*" asked the Nazi with the pencil thin mustache.

"Yes, Herr Leutnant John Caraway," Gan replied in English as he hobbled over to Caraway. He favored his left leg, his face placid as he stared up at Caraway's desperate expression. "He is the policeman who assisted my investigation on the consulate attack in New York."

"*Und das Mädchen?*" the Nazi with the pencil thin mustache asked. Gan shook his head in response and looked back to Caraway.

"Oh God, Gan," Caraway said, laughing nervously. "I can't tell you how good it is to see you."

"My, my, my, John," Gan said with a sad smile. "Whatever brought you all the way out here?"

Caraway leaned forward as much as he could, his shoulders burning, the metal cuffs digging into his wrists. "Gan, you have to get us outta this. Something bad is coming. Something really bad."

"Oh? And what would that be?" the Nazi with the Van Dyke asked with a heavy accent.

Caraway risked a glance at the other Nazis and then whispered, "Kookookachoo."

The Van Dyke Nazi erupted in maniacal laughter, clapping and stamping his feet in glee. "Kookookachoo!"

Caraway could feel his stomach twist. He did his best to ignore the manic Nazi. "Gan, you gotta help us."

"I'm—" Gan risked a glance over his shoulder. His eyes fell to the ground and swallowed the lump in his throat. "I'm sorry, John."

Caraway gritted his teeth. "You're—you're sorry?"

Gan turned to the other Nazis and nodded. "*Lasst uns hier raus.*"

"You're sorry?!" Caraway screamed as they walked away, pulling at his chains. "Gan, you can't just leave us! You have to do something! Gan! They're gonna kill us, Gan! They're gonna kill us! You can't just walk away! Gan! GAN!"

"How are our lambs?" Alexei asked as Heydrich approached the altar. Alexei was dressed in midnight black robes, a hood covering his wrinkled visage in shadows. He carefully leafed through the *Necronomicon*, the illuminated manuscript filled with horrifying images that would drive a mortal mind insane, but Alexei just smiled. Alexei's bodyguard, the Greek behemoth Vasili, stood off in the corner, his eyes vacant, as if something had snapped inside. Torches had been lit throughout the complex as a steady stream of Nazis soldiers and hooded cultists flowed in.

"Angry, confused," Heydrich replied, unable to remove his gaze from Vasili. "As is to be expected."

Alexei laughed as he turned the page. "Good, it always helps for the blood to be boiling."

"Will we be sacrificing both?"

"No. The girl is for the city. The man is for the Lama."

"You think he will show?"

Alexei nodded, tapping an image in the book. "I *know* he will. I suppose I should have seen it, but with the μαγικός in recess I was blinded, and yet here it is, working like clockwork." He turned his head toward Heydrich. "It is not polite to stare, Karl. As to the question that has been sitting on the tip of your tongue, Vasili is not dead—at least not yet. It seems that upon touching the *Necronomicon*, Vasili's latent extrasensory perception began to take hold, flooding his mind. It's a pity, really. So many years keeping him close and in control just to see him snap before the ascension." He shrugged. "No matter. He will still play his role."

"Very good," Heydrich said as he loosened his collar and began to pace the altar.

"Something else?" Alexei asked, sensing Heydrich's anxiety.

"While I am eager to spill blood in the name of the Great Old Ones, I cannot help but feel this all just seems… superfluous."

"And why is that, Karl?" Alexei asked quietly.

Heydrich cleared his throat. "You brought the American woman here and framed her for murder to bait Dumont into following. And while it did bring him here…" He trailed off, hesitant. Though Alexei's back was turned, Heydrich could feel his master watching him, waiting to see what he would say. Heydrich cleared his throat again, feeling the heat rise within him. "You lost the woman and when you had Dumont in your hands you let him go. Added upon that you still have not given us the Third Tablet. I don't mean to misspeak or call into question your plans," he quickly added. "I know how easily a prophecy can be misread, but I must be able to show my people *something*."

Alexei turned to face Heydrich, a small smile on his lips, his eyes black. "Do not worry Herr Heydrich," he said as he closed the book. "After tonight, I will show them more than they could have ever dared dreamed."

Hirsch and Gan watched hundreds of cloaked men and women entered the complex, their heads bowed, hands held palms up as they chanted the near unpronounceable phrase "*Iä Iä Cthulhu fhtagn!*" over and over and over again.

"My God, where are they all coming from?" Gan mused, his gaze distant. The chanting was maddening, aching the back of his mind. He massaged his eyes, trying to fight back the pain.

Hirsch gripped him by the arm. "Sir, what should we do?"

"I don't know."

Hirsch shook his head. "This is wrong, sir. We cannot just sit by and do nothing."

"Can't we?" Gan snapped. "Herr Doktor Hammond is correct. Killing those two for the sake of our mission is no different than what we have planned for the Jews. Why should those two have any reprieve?"

"Sir, do not misunderstand, their lives are meaningless. It is this ritual, this next step toward the raising of that monster that I cannot abide. Heydrich and his friends could kill a hundred people, a thousand, a million and more, and I would not bat an eye if it meant saving *one* German life." He stepped closer to Gan, his voice hoarse. "Sir, if we allow this to continue it will come at the greatest cost. You know this."

"Or perhaps it is just another sacrifice, one amongst thousands we have already made in order to fulfill the wishes of our masters?" Gan spit back, his face red. "We are not even waves in the tides of history, Hirsch. If this is the direction we are pointed, who are we to try and turn away?"

"We are Germans, Herr Oberführer," Hirsch pleaded. "We are the Master Race. We do not follow the tides; we make them."

Gan's gaze dropped to the floor. "And what of the Chosen People?" Gan whispered.

"Sir, we *are* they."

Gan lifted his head and looked at Hirsch, pitying the Sturmbannführer. He placed a hand on Hirsch's shoulder and smiled weakly. "What did I tell you, Hirsch?"

Hirsch's eyes fell. "'Appearances and secrecy, above all else, will be the keys to our success,'" he repeated from memory.

"Yes," Gan said, his tone mournful, his face grey. "If we were to act now, our cause would be lost. Do you understand me, Herr Sturmbannführer?"

Hirsch nodded solemnly. "*Ja*. I understand."

"Be brave, Hirsch," Gan said, walking away. "It is all we have now."

"*Ja*, Herr Oberführer," Hirsch said as he drew his Lüger. "I will be brave."

"Jeez, where are all these people coming from?" Ken asked as they watched the steady stream of robed cultists enter the Sanctuary. They were crouched in the brush several yards away from the ancient complex, out of the sight of the oncoming mass. Stars littered the clear night sky, as if someone had punched a hole directly into space, reminding Jethro of his days at the Temple of the Clouds.

"They've been waiting for this night for millennia," Jethro solemnly replied. "They've had generations to prepare."

"Do you see Caraway or the woman?" Jean asked as she quietly reloaded her pistol, her face grim. This is when Caraway was supposed to die. If they could save him, then maybe they could save everyone else…

Jethro peered into the darkness and shook his head in frustration. "Not yet. I can see three men at the altar. One looks like he's reading a book."

"That's probably Alexei with the *Necronomicon*," Ken added. "The big guy next him is Vasili, I think. The third guy looks like—"

"A Nazi," Jethro finished. "There are about two hundred soldiers on the island, all well-armed, and at least four officers. Gan's one of them."

"Gan's here!" Ken exclaimed. A smile broke his lips. He exhaled his relief. "Oh, thank God! At least we have someone on the other side."

"Gan won't forsake his mission, just as we will not abandon ours," Jethro said. "I am certain he will do what he can to help us, but he will not compromise his cover, even if it means sacrificing John's life in the process."

Ken ran his hands through his hair, crestfallen. "Well, that's not very comforting."

Jean holstered her gun and slid beside Jethro. "What's the plan?"

He didn't have one. He looked at her, her hand still resting on her pistol handle. That was all they really had between them and an army of cultists.

He felt her eyes on him and realized that despite the incredible odds, the fact that they were facing them together made it somehow feasible. "It's a trap," he replied.

"This isn't my first dance, Dumont," she shot back smugly. "Question is: what do we do about it? Spring the trap?"

Jethro pointed out toward the throng of robed people. "See how the cultists are dispersed? More importantly, see how the Nazi soldiers *aren't*, all clumped together on the other side of the ruins? There are more of them, scattered along the brush and in the shadows, waiting for us to jump in and save the day. Even if they're expecting us—which they are—we can't let them know we're here. We need the element of surprise."

Jean raised an eyebrow and whispered, "Surprise? You can't just run out there and beat them all up?"

Jethro grimaced. "I'm out of radioactive salts," he said under his breath.

"Guys, what are you talking about?" Ken asked, straining to listen in.

Jean rolled her eyes. "You don't carry a spare on you just in case?" Jean asked. "Figured guys like you would have one in each pocket."

"Left them on the airship," Jethro replied. Then off her expression, "We were attacked by a living storm."

"Goddammit," she sighed, rubbing her forehead in frustration.

Ken tried to inch closer. "If you guys are coming up with a plan, I'd really like to hear it."

"We could go in guns blazing," Jean said, indicating her pistol. "That'll surprise 'em."

"Only for a moment," Jethro said, shaking his head. "We're outnumbered a hundred to one, and that's not counting the Nazis. They'd overtake us in seconds and there will be nothing we could do to stop them. Whatever we do, we have to remain unseen."

Ken looked out to the growing throng of hooded cultists and rubbed his unshaven chin in thought. "Well," he began with a nonchalant shrug, "we could always borrow a few robes."

Jean gave Jethro an excited smile.

"*Grenadier!*" Gan shouted.

The soldier stopped dead in his tracks and saluted. "Yes, Herr

Oberführer Gan?"

"Grenadier, have you seen Sturmbannführer Hirsch?"

"*Nein*, sir," he replied, shaking his head. "Not since we arrived at the ruins, sir."

Frowning, Gan nodded in disappointment. He rubbed the scar on his forehead and asked, "Are all the sentries in place?"

"Yes, sir," the boy nodded. "We are patrolling the forest just as the Obergruppenführer commanded."

"Good. Thank you," he said. The soldier saluted again and began to turn away. "I did not dismiss you, Grenadier."

The soldier quickly spun on his heel. "Sorry, Herr Oberführer."

"Tell me, Grenadier, did your mother dress you every day before you joined the *Heer*?" Gan asked.

The soldier risked a befuddled glance at his commanding officer. "Excuse me, sir?" he asked with a nervous smile.

Gan placed his hands behind his back. "I believe the question was very clear, Grenadier. Did your mother dress you before you joined the *Heer*?"

"I—*Nein*, sir," he stuttered, "my mother did not dress me—"

"*Lügner!*" Gan exclaimed. "Your armaments, Grenadier," he said, indicating the loosely hanging shoulder strap laced with grenades. "War is coming, boy! With sloppiness like this you will kill more of your countrymen than you will our enemy!"

"I—I am sorry, sir!" the young soldier stuttered.

"Do not apologize, Grenadier!" Gan raged. "Fix yourself or I will fix it for you!"

"Sir, I—I—!" The soldier fumbled to fix himself.

"*Dummkopf!*" Gan cursed, grabbing the Grenadier's shoulder strap and forcibly tightening it. "Here, this is how to look like a proper German soldier!"

"Yes, sir! Sorry, sir!"

"Now go! Go!" Gan repeated, angrily waving the soldier away.

The young soldier fumbled a salute and tottered off. Once out of sight, Gan considered the grenade he had lifted off the boy, wondering if he would really need to use it.

Heydrich's insides twisted with anticipation as he walked away from the main complex. For the first time since his death, he felt alive. He had heard the feeling described as "giddy as a schoolboy," but the concept was a foreign one. Heydrich had never been a schoolboy, his youth filled with beatings and worship. It wasn't until he reached puberty and was allowed to make his first sacrifice—a young boy from a local village—that he had felt anything close to being described as joy. He could still remember the warm blood spilling over his hands and the arousal it had caused. But that sensation was an echo of what he was experiencing now. After so many years and two lives of waiting and planning, here it was, the first step toward—

Click!

"Something I can do for you, Herr Sturmbannführer?" Heydrich asked as Hirsch walked out of the darkness with a Lüger in hand.

"Where is the Shard, Herr Doktor Hammond?" Hirsch whispered, pressing the barrel against Heydrich's stomach.

Heydrich glanced down at the gun with disinterest. Such a silly little thing. "Now, what would you want to do with it, Herr Sturmbannführer?"

Hirsch firmed his lips. "The Shard," he repeated. "Where is it?"

"You seem upset," Heydrich said, a smile curling his scarred lips. "Perhaps we should discuss this later when you're of clearer mind."

"Give me the Shard, dammit!" Hirsch nearly shouted.

"Oh, I'm afraid I can't do that, Hirsch," Heydrich calmly said as he stepped closer to the pock-faced Sturmbannführer, the gun barrel pushing into his stomach.

"I just want the Shard… I will—I will kill you," Hirsch stuttered as he took a half step back.

"Will you, now?" Heydrich asked incredulously. "Others have, though as you can see, they have been *less* than successful."

Hirsch's hand began to shake. "Back away, Hammond. I will shoot you."

"Please do," he said in a calm, reassuring voice. "I have been dead so long, I'm curious as to what will happen."

Hirsch's finger nervously teased at the trigger. "I'm serious…"

"So am I," Heydrich said, his smile broadening. "Please. Shoot me."

Hirsch furrowed his brow as sweat began dripping down his cheek.

"You're insane…"

"Shoot me, you *Du Schwein*!!!" Heydrich screamed, grabbing the Lüger and Hirsch's hand at once.

"Let go!" Hirsch shouted as he tried to wrench the gun free of Heydrich's hands.

There was a loud *pop!* as the gun fired point blank into Heydrich's stomach. Heydrich stumbled back, clutching his midsection in reflex more than pain. He had felt the bullet slice into his gut, but it was an echo of a sensation, a forgotten memory. He moved his hands away from the wound, expecting to see blood pouring out, but his tunic was dry, a small hole in the fabric the only indication that he had been shot. Pulling it aside, he drove his finger and thumb into the wound, searching for the bullet until he felt his nails scratch against the metal. Pulling it out with a sickening *slurp!* Heydrich held the bullet up and examined it, putrid black bile dripping off it and running down his fingers.

"Fascinating," he said with genuine interest.

Hirsch dropped his gun and stumbled backwards onto the ground. "*Gott im Himmel!*" he exclaimed. "What *are* you?!"

Heydrich shifted his gaze from the bullet to the whimpering Sturmbannführer and smiled. "Everything you feared, Herr Sturmbannführer." He was upon Hirsch in an instant, wrapping his hands around the Sturmbannführer's throat. He pressed his thumbs against Hirsch's larynx and began to squeeze.

Hirsch gripped at Heydrich's wrists, but couldn't pull them away. His legs thrashed against the ground, kicking up dust but nothing more. He tried to scream but there was no air in his lungs.

"Shh…" Heydrich comforted as Hirsch's eyes began to bulge out their sockets. His face shifted from red to purple to blue, his kicks slowed, and his grip on Heydrich's wrist weakened until there was the telltale *crack!* as Heydrich's thumbs crushed the jugular. Hirsch's body slackened, a discarded rag doll on the ground.

Heydrich climbed off Hirsch and wiped the sweat from his brow, a toothy smile cracking his scarred face.

Yes, he had not felt this alive in years.

"Is John your real name?"

Caraway glanced over at Sotiria. "Yeah, John's my real name. I'm a cop, though, back in New York."

"Ah, so you were not really looking for work, then, were you?"

Caraway shook his head. "Naw, all that—the eye patch, the thievin'— was all for show. We were looking for a friend and we thought we'd learn something by goin' undercover. It was a stupid idea by a stupid man."

"Are you scared, John?" she asked.

"Only a little," he lied, unable to even draw his gaze from the ground. His arms were burning in their sockets, his hands losing sensation.

"That bald one, the German," she said after a minute. "You knew him." This was not a question.

Caraway grunted a harsh laugh. "Thought I did. Just goes to show ya, you can't ever trust a Kraut."

"They are going to kill us, yes?"

Caraway opened and closed his mouth, unsure how or whether to tell the truth. He was no stranger to death. Since becoming head of the Special Crimes Squad he had faced mobsters and monsters and everything in between; he knew it was only a matter of time before he kicked the bucket. But for Sotiria, still young and beautiful, death was less a fact than a distant thought. "Ken went to get help," he said, finally, not sure if he believed it himself. "I'm sure of it."

"Who can help us now?" she asked weakly.

Caraway let out another sardonic chuckle. "Jethro Dumont."

Sotiria pinched her face in bewilderment. "The millionaire? I heard he once slept with—"

"Sotiria, no offense, but the last thing I want to talk about right now is my friend's sex life."

"Sorry."

"Don't apologize, it's not worth it."

"Can I ask you a question, John? If things had been different, if you were not married, I mean, would you have—?"

Caraway smiled and glanced toward her. "Sweetheart, there would've been nothing on God's green earth that would've stopped me."

Sotiria smiled at that. "Well, I suppose that is—" she cut herself short when they heard the rustle of footsteps approaching.

The Nazi with the Van Dyke entered the clearing and walked up to them, flanked by two robed men, their faces hidden in the shadows. Placing his hands behind his back, he smiled as he looked over his captives. "It is time."

The fight had been quick and silent. Jethro and Ken dragged the last of the unconscious cultists into the brush and stripped them of their robes. Pulling the hood over his head, Jethro noticed Ken's expression. "What?"

Ken blinked rapidly, failing to hide his stupefaction. "It's just… You look like—" he stuttered. "I mean, never mind."

"He kind of looks like the Green Lama," Jean commented as she threw on her hood, hiding a mischievous grin.

"Yeah," Ken said hesitantly, peaking his eyebrows. "But only from the corner of my eye. Weird."

Jethro gave Ken a shallow smile. "Come," he said as moved toward the ruins. "We have to find Caraway before its too late."

Leaving the brush, they fell into step with the line of chanting cultists. "*Iä Iä Cthulhu fhtagn!*" the cultists repeated over and over, an invocation spoken in a guttural yet lyrical voice. Entering the heart of the ruins, they could see the Nazi officials, including Gan, standing just off to the right of the altar, all visibly anxious. Vasili stood just behind the broken pillars, his jaw slack, eyes vacant. At the center was Alexei, pressing the *Necronomicon* against his body. Thin black lines covered his face; his eyes were a pair of obsidian orbs, while his wolfish grin glistened white in the firelight.

"Good God," Jean breathed, staring at Alexei's destroyed visage. "What happened to him?"

"Whatever he really is, it's starting to show," Ken whispered back.

A strange buzzing seemed to echo through the air, similar to the sensation Jethro had experienced in the living cloud. "Do you feel that?"

"Like there's a bee flying around the back of your head? Yeah," Jean replied, unconsciously lifting her hand to her head.

Ken shook his head. "I don't feel anything, except—gah!" he exclaimed, covering his ears as a tremendous *croak!* echoed through the complex.

Jethro turned toward the source, his jaw clenched in horror as he watched hundreds—if not thousands—of naked Deep Ones march out of the darkness in swaying unison behind a masked figure, stopping just short of the main altar. There was a small gasp from the Nazi officers, and Jethro could see Gottschalk covering his mouth in shock at the sight of the inhuman creatures, a dark stain forming in the crotch of his pants. For his part, Gan remained unmoved and unafraid, his hands placed behind his back as if he were under inspection. The masked figure wobbled over to Alexei and bowed deeply, pressing his masked face against Alexei's foot as if he were kissing it.

"*Iä Iä Cthulhu fhtagn!*" the masked figure rasped.

"*Iä Iä Cthulhu fhtagn, Ke'ta!*" Alexei replied in a booming voice. "I am pleased to see the Deep Ones here at the time of alignment!"

"*Iä Iä Cthulhu fhtagn!*" the Deep Ones all croaked in unison.

Ke'ta pulled off his jade mask, revealing his true nature to the Nazis. His black, bulbous eyes unreadable, he gave the German officials a stiff-armed salute and a throaty "*Heil Hitler!*" Obergruppenführer Gottschalk weakly returned the gesture.

Wide-eyed, Jean tugged at Jethro's sleeve and pointed at the ground as pockets of soil began to churn around their feet. In seconds, the complex was flowing with tentacles, littered with loathsome creatures without any clear definition beyond twisting, writhing, grey sacks of organs and appendages. At the front of the altar a gigantic mass of boneless limbs burrowed out of the ground and slithered toward Alexei. Reaching out with a long, forked tentacle, the wriggling mass touched Alexei's extended hand in a clear sign of submission.

"Shudde M'ell, god of the Chthonians," Alexei said to the beast. "We are pleased to see you and your followers here on this night."

"*Iä Iä Cthulhu fhtagn!*" Shudde M'ell gurgled. The tentacled Chthonians immediately followed suit.

"Okay, I think it's fair enough to say I'm officially scared out of my mind," Ken breathed.

"After everything we've been through," Jean said through gritted teeth as she watched a Chthonian slither by, "I guess that's saying something."

Jethro watched as the Deep Ones and Chthonians fell in place before the altar, his stomach twisting in fear. He had seen darkness in many forms since he first bore the Jade Tablet, but he had never seen horrors like this.

This sight before him was maddening, monsters that seemed to defy all theories of evolution, that were at once alien yet bound to this world. What was most frightening of all was the knowledge that this was only the first wave of atrocities they would be facing. And if Rabbi Brickman's predictions were to be believed, it would all end with his death.

Alexei threw his arms in the air, and the complex fell silent. "*Iä Iä Cthulhu fhtagn!*" he shouted.

"*Iä Iä Cthulhu fhtagn!*" the congregation called back.

"We have waited six millennia for this day!" Alexei howled, speaking in every language at once, the black lines on his face growing with each word. Holding the *Necronomicon* over his head, he continued. "'That is not dead which can eternal lie. And with strange aeons even death may die.' So are the words of Abdul Alhazred. The stars have come right! Glyyu-Uho, Celaeno, Algol, Baalbo, Ogntlach, Yifne, Arcturus, Fomalhaut and Xoth align to raise the son of Vhoorl! *Iä Iä Cthulhu fhtagn!* For the stars to align! *Iä Iä Cthulhu fhtagn!* For the city to rise! *Iä Iä Cthulhu fhtagn!* For the Great Old Ones to awaken! *Iä Iä Cthulhu fhtagn! Iä Iä Cthulhu fhtagn!*"

"*Iä Iä Cthulhu fhtagn!*" they replied.

A scream echoed out from the darkness. "Let us go, you bastards!"

"John," Jethro breathed as Caraway and a sobbing Sotiria were dragged past the Nazi officials.

"Burn in hell, you piece of shit!" Caraway growled as he spit in Gan's face.

"Oh God," Jean cried out. "It's happening just like he said." She pushed her way through the crowd. "Come on, we have to get closer before it's too late."

"Blood!" Alexei cried as they tied Caraway and Sotiria to two wooden poles. "Blood must be spilled for R'lyeh! Blood must be drawn by a Scion!" He walked over to Dr. Hammond, who placed a sheathed blade in his hand. Turning back the throng of humans and monsters, Alexei unsheathed the blade, held it above his head, and the night erupted in green light. The crowd shielded their eyes and bowed their heads in reverence. "Blood must fall on the Blade of the Elder Ones to open the gates! Blood of Adam! Blood of Eve! *Iä Iä Cthulhu fhtagn!*"

"What's that he's got in his hand?" Ken asked as the cultists began to chant louder and louder.

Jethro's eyes went wide, recognizing the crystal blade from his dream—the blade that would kill him. "It's the phurba! *Om! Tare Tuttare Ture Soha!* It's the Shard, the missing piece of the Third Tablet!"

Alexei walked over to Vasili and placed the Shard in his hands. "By the hand of a Scion must the blood run!" Despite his vacant gaze a thin, unnatural smile formed on Vasili's lips. Alexei placed a hand on Vasili's shoulder and led him over to Sotiria.

"No," Sotiria whimpered, tears pouring down her cheeks as Vasili stumbled toward her. "Please help me. Anyone, please, please help."

There was a wave of laughter from the crowd.

"I don't like where this is—" Ken said when a cultist suddenly grabbed him by the throat. His face red, Ken tried to pry himself free, but the cloaked man was too powerful.

"*Você não parará a cerimônia!*" the cultist screamed, pressing down on Ken's windpipe.

"Ken!" Jean shouted, pulling out her gun and shooting the attacker in the head.

On the altar Alexei smiled broadly as everyone turned toward the sound of the gunshot. "He's here!" he exclaimed, unable to contain his excitement.

"Jethro!" Caraway shouted, looking hopefully out into the crowd. "Don't worry, Sotiria! It's gonna be okay!"

His mouth agape, Gan stepped toward the edge of the altar. "Dumont!"

"He's alive?" Gottschalk asked in shock.

Two cultists threw themselves at Jethro. Elbowing one of his attackers in the throat, Jethro spun out and kneed the other in the groin. But before he could move, three more cultists were on him, grabbing him by the arms and throat.

"*Om Ah Ra Pa Cha Na Dhih!*" Jethro shouted as he struggled against their hold. Thrusting his head back, he crushed the nose of one of his attackers with an audible *crack!* Using this momentary surprise, Jethro quickly sidestepped and kicked out the legs of the cultist on his right. As the man's weight pulled him down, Jethro swung his left arm, throwing the other assailant on top of his compatriot, their heads colliding with a bone cracking *smash!* Freeing himself, Jethro launched forward and vaulted over a broken pillar. He caught a low hanging branch and swung into the air toward the altar.

Meanwhile, Ken weaved his way through the crowd when something caught onto his leg and pulled him back. Looking down he found a Chthonian wrapping its tentacles around his leg.

"None shall stop the rising!" the creature said in a gurgling, bubbling voice.

Screaming, Ken pounded his fist as hard as he could against the creature's pulpy grey sack of a body, sending tissue and plasma spraying into the air.

Nearing the altar, Jethro was close enough to see inside the deep crevices of Alexei's face, black ooze flowing beneath the skin. He was almost there. He could save her, could save them both. It would all be—

"Dumont!" the doctor screamed as he leaped off the altar and knocked Jethro to the ground, grabbing him by the throat. His eyes blazed, spit flew from his mouth as he screeched, "Do you remember me now, Green Lama? Do you remember me? You stupid *Amerikaner!* Look me in the eyes and tell me you remember me!"

Jethro's eyes went wide, at last recognizing the scarred face beneath the Van Dyke beard. "Heydrich!" Jethro wheezed as he fought against the madman's grip.

Heydrich laughed manically as he pressed down on Jethro's windpipe. "I want you to watch this, Green Lama. I want you to watch the birth of the world *you* helped create."

"Let the blade taste blood!" Alexei commanded as Vasili mindlessly pressed the Shard up against Sotiria's throat.

Sotiria looked into Vasili's vacant eyes. "Vasili," she begged, shaking her head. "Please, Vasili, don't."

"Vasili, stop!" Caraway shouted, struggling to break free. "It's Sotiria! Can't you see! Don't do this!"

"Please, Vasili!" Sotiria begged. "Please, it's me. Please, don't do this. I'm so sorry. Please, Vasili, I love—!"

Vasili plunged the crystalline blade into Sotiria's throat, slicing across as blood spilled out down her neck, soaking her shirt and pooling onto the ground.

"NOOO!!!" Caraway screamed.

"*Iä Iä Cthulhu fhtagn!*" the cultists screamed in unison. The ruins erupted with green light as the Shard blasted a column of energy thundering into the sky. The earth began to shake, threatening to rip apart beneath them.

"Do you see, Dumont?" Heydrich laughed, blissfully watching the energy climb into space. "Do you see the dawn of a magnificent new era?"

"Hey, jackass!" Jean shouted as she pressed her gun against Heydrich's temple. "Looks like we meet in *this* timeline!" She fired twice, black ooze erupting out of Heydrich's skull. Heydrich screamed in pain, clutching his head as he fell away, one eye hanging loose from its socket.

"That won't stop him for long," Jean said as she helped Jethro off the ground. "Trust me."

Jethro gripped her shoulder for support. "Jean, we've failed."

She touched his face and said simply, "Caraway."

Jethro's eyes steeled over as the earth shook again, cracking the ground. Taking Jean's hand, they shielded their eyes as they jumped onto the altar, blindly searching for Caraway.

"John!" Jethro shouted over the chanting and roaring beam of energy. "John, can you hear me?"

An eternity passed before they heard, "Jethro!"

Jethro turned at the sound of Caraway's voice. "John, we're coming—!" he choked as the air suddenly rushed out of his lungs. Jean fell to her knees, gripping her throat.

"Come, now," Alexei laughed, walking out of the light. His face was cracked beyond recognition to the point that he no longer appeared human. "Did you really believe I was going to let you just walk away? Ah, Jean Farrell," he said as he ran his fingers through her hair, twisted it around his fist, and pulled her head back. "You've caused quite a bit of problems since I arrested you, haven't you? I confess I was quite saddened when you didn't recognize me then. How do you think you were transported clear across New York City and just *happened* to find the bearer of the Second Tablet? But then again, I had played with your memories." Throwing her down, he sauntered over to Jethro and ran his nails down the side of Jethro's face, drawing blood. "And of course, Jethro Dumont, *the Green Lama*, how I longed for this day! You played your part so well, I thought you had rehearsed! But then again, the lamas at the Temple of the Clouds *were* training you for this for ten years." He looked over both Jean and Jethro with a warm smile. "And now here you both are, the last two Scions, all mine!"

Jethro watched through the haze of light and asphyxiation as a grenade fell at Alexei's feet. Without a moment to spare, Jethro grabbed Jean and quickly pulled her behind a broken column as the grenade went off, blasting Alexei into a thousand pieces. Jean and Jethro gasped as air rushed back into their lungs. The green light that blanketed the complex instantly disappeared. Vasili dropped to the ground unconscious, the Shard clattering against the altar's stone floor. A cacophony of screams echoed through the ruins at the sight of Alexei's dismembered remains splattered across the altar, black ooze flowing out of the chunks.

Someone grabbed Jethro by the arm. "What in the hell just happened?" Ken asked in between gasps of air. "Looked like the sky just cracked open!"

"It's worse than that, Ken," Jean said, woefully. "Good move with the grenade, though."

"I didn't throw it, Jean," Ken confessed.

"Run, Dumont! You don't have much time!" Gan whispered as he slid down beside them. He pressed a folded piece of paper into Jethro's hand. "You have to hurry to these coordinates. It is where the doctor told us the city would rise. No matter what happens you *must* get there before they wake Cthulhu."

"Not without Caraway," Jethro said.

Gan glanced behind the column, instantly measuring the horde of cultists and creatures, and nodded. "I'll buy you some time." Running up to the altar, he shouted: "*Herbei, ihr Soldaten! Feuer frei! Nichts soll am Leben bleiben!*" The complex erupted in gunfire as the Nazi soldiers hidden within the brush began mowing down anyone and anything within the ruins.

They found Caraway on the ground, still bound to the wooden pole. His face was slightly burned and bruised, but he was alive. "Sotiria... No..." he moaned.

"He's in shock, but he'll recover," Jethro said as he and Ken removed Caraway's bindings and lifted him up off the ground. "Jean, keep an eye out."

"Got it," she said, reloading her weapon. "Let's get the hell off this island."

PART 3: CALL OF CTHULHU

Chapter 15
TROUBLE ABOARD

*T*he boulder tumbled down the side of the mountain, a sound that echoed through the snowcapped world like thunder. "How many pounds was that?" Dumont asked with a broad smile as he dusted off his hands. He looked younger, more energetic, and seemed to have grown several inches taller since he had begun taking the radioactive salts. Muscles pushed against his robes; even his eyes seemed to glow in the shadows.

"Two thousand, four hundred and one pounds and—" Tsarong paused as he reread the measurement in his notebook. "—forty-two ounces. A new record, Tulku."

Dumont furrowed his brow in disbelief. "You're lying."

Tsarong turned the book toward Dumont. "Take a look yourself, Tulku."

"Om! Ma-ni Pad-me Hum! That's impossible," he jovially declared as he looked over the notebook in fascination. "I'm not even breaking a sweat! Heck, I don't even feel tired. This radioactive salt!" he exclaimed, pounding his chest with his fist. "I can feel its energy flowing through every cell in my body like an electric current, and the most amazing thing about it, Tsarong, is that I know I'm only scratching the surface."

Tsarong raised an eyebrow. "Truly? And what does one do with such power?"

Jethro rubbed his chin. "That is an excellent question, but the real question is why I was given this power?"

"Perhaps that is an answer you will discover when the time is right."

"And how will I know when that will be?"

Tsarong smiled. "You will know, Tulku. You will know."

Rick Masters woke with a start, fell out of his chair, and tumbled to the ground. His head knocked against the hangar's cement floor, his ears ringing with a wavering trill. No, it wasn't just his head… The phone. Pulling himself up to his desk, he searched through the darkness until he found the screaming devil. Yanking the receiver off its cradle he mumbled through the fog of concussion and whiskey. "Huhlo?"

"*Om! Ma-ni Pad-me Hum!*" a quiet voice breathed.

"Gaw… Hell. You're kiddin' me, right?"

"Do you regret not telling him?" the woman asked from the shadows of the Park Avenue penthouse, her voice and face ever changing, as if she were several women instead of one.

"It is not fair for him to unknowingly take on so much," Tsarong said as he carefully finished sewing over the small lump in the fur-lined cuff of the green monk's robe. "To sacrifice himself as he will."

"Was it not you who once said: 'to know one's destiny is to void it'?"

Tsarong's ears perked up. "Did I say that?" he asked with a smile. "Age has not been kind to me; my memory is not what it once was when I bore the Tablet."

"And yet you carried it, just as he has done."

"Yes, but I *knew* my role. I understood the weight of my actions. Jethro was not afforded such choice."

"He has done more than anyone before him."

"Will that be enough, to fight such a darkness as this?" Tsarong asked, gazing into the shadows, a note of fear in his tone. When the woman remained silent, he asked, "Do you know if he will succeed?"

"You, more than anyone, know that the future is uncertain."

He walked over toward the silhouetted figure. "Who are you, Magga? You are more than the *jetsunma* you have claimed to be. You were with me all those years in the Temple of the Clouds, and you've helped the Tulku for so long, yet none of us have ever known your true face or name."

"I am the Revealer of the Secret Paths," Magga said, bowing her head. "That is all you need to know, young Tsarong. And while I have been able to assist the Tulku in the past, in this instance I am unable to help him. I cannot dip my hands into the tides of fate."

Tsarong considered this as he walked over to a small golden Buddha statue at the far end of the room, moving it aside to reveal the strongbox hidden behind it. Entering in the six digit code, he unlocked the intricate locking mechanism and opened the door to unveil a small vial of salt, glowing green in the moonlight

"Yes, but I can stack the deck."

"As I knew you would," Magga smiled.

"May Buddha guide his footsteps," he said as he carefully removed the vial and placed it in a small protective box.

Magga bowed. "*Om! Vajrasattva Hum!* Dark times are ahead, Tsarong, be prepared."

Tsarong flinched as someone knocked at the front door, and when he peered back into the shadows, Magga was gone.

"It's four-in-the-morning, goddammit!" Francesca screamed as she wrapped the robe around her dressing gown and stormed across the apartment. She swung the door open and shouted, "What the hell do you want?!"

"Uh..." the man stuttered as he scratched at his unshaven jaw. "Yeah, um, hey. My name's Rick... I've got a message from y'r husband."

Francesca crossed her arms. "Far as I'm concerned, I have no husband."

The man cleared his throat. "Yeah. Well, anyway... listen, I'm kinda short on time and he told me to tell you this before I head out, so do you wanna hear it or not?"

Francesca huffed in frustration and pursed her lips. "Fine. Out with it."

"Right..." he grumbled as he brought out a folded piece of paper. He cleared his throat again as he unfolded it and read the note aloud. "'Frankie, you've got every reason to be mad at me for leavin' and not explain' why. But know it was for the right reasons. A lot of terrible things are about to happen and I want you to know that no matter what happens, I never stopped lovin' you and you'll always be my girl in white. Love, John,'" Rick finished and cleared his throat for a third time. "So, yeah, that's what he said."

Francesca was silent, visibly taken aback. A small tear formed in the corner of her eye.

"So… uh, you want me to tell him something when I see him?"

She looked up at Rick as if she was suddenly surprised by his presence. "Yes, you can give him this," she said before slapping him across the face.

Captain Gabe Harris flicked the remains of his cigarette over the side of the *S.S. Delphine*, rubbing the bristles of his beard as he watched the butt tumble through the air and disappear into the sea. They were two days out from the small port town of Kamariotissa, where they had been forced to dock after an earthquake made the sea violent. But the detour had been fortuitous, bringing on four passengers offering to pay an exorbitant price to leave the island as quickly as possible. Gabe knew better than to ask questions, and while the massive expansion of his wallet was a welcome change, he couldn't shake the feeling that he had brought on a whole lot of trouble. Walking over to the cockpit, he found his first mate Stuart manning the helm.

"Gave Cohen the night off, hope you don't mind," Stuart explained as Gabe closed the door. "Think he's coming down with something—the boy looked yellow."

Gabe nodded in understanding. "How're our passengers faring?"

Stuart shrugged. "The big guy still seems a little under the weather, but the other three seem to be doing all right."

"Good," Gabe said as he took out his rolling papers and tobacco and began rolling himself another cigarette. "With what they're payin' us I wanna make sure they get all the comforts of home. Hell, we could practically buy a fleet with what we're makin'." He licked the edge of the paper and sealed it shut. "How much longer 'til we reach our destination?"

"Few more hours, though I gotta admit I never thought we'd get asked to drop someone off in the middle of the water. You don't mind me sayin', sir, but I think all four of 'em gotta few screws loose, if ya catch my meaning. 'Specially that one that keeps praying 'oh many padded home' all the time. The dame ain't so bad, but even she seems a bit wonky, keeps looking over the side of the boat like she's expectin' something to jump out at her."

"Could've been worse," Gabe said, lighting his cigarette. "They first asked to go down near Antarctica. Money was damn good, but I wasn't gonna risk that kinda trip."

"All the better, you ask me."

"I'm gonna agree with ya there—" Gabe cut himself short when something caught the corner of his eye. "You see that?" he asked, pointing starboard.

"See what, boss?"

Gabe shook his head and rubbed his eyes. "Thought I saw something climb up the side of the ship… Probably, just my imagination. Maybe I'm going a bit wonky myself," he laughed as the scarred white creature crawled out of the sea and onto the deck.

How many days had he gone without sleep, Jethro wondered. Three days? Four? He could no longer tell, his nights filled with such nightmares that sleep was impossible. No, not nightmares, he reminded himself. Signs and portents: the terrible shape of things to come.

With rest out of the question, Jethro had instead spent the past two days alone in his cabin, repeating the vow of refuge in the Buddha, the Dharma, and the Sangha as he studied the Third Jade Tablet—the Fire from Olympus as Jean called it. Analyzing the crystal, he could tell by its peculiar shade of green, minimal opacity, and inherent luminance, that it was indeed not of this world. This realization did not so much surprise Jethro as it disturbed him. Did this mean his Jade Tablet was otherworldly as well? Were the radioactive salts, his abilities, everything he was directly tied to Cthulhu? Jethro grimaced. No, he refused to believe that. He had dedicated his life to fighting the darkness. He would not accept that he could be a part of it. Then there was the dystopia Jean had visited. Whether it was real or not was of little consequence, it was a harsh reminder that the fate of the entire world—indeed, of all six realms of samsara—now rested squarely on his shoulders. Massaging his eyes, he fought back a sob. All he had ever wanted was to find his purpose in life, and for a time, he believed he had found it as the Green Lama, as a Bodhisattva, but the path had drawn him here, and it had become too much to bear. He wasn't the world's savior, he was simply Jethro Dumont, a rich boy from Manhattan trapped playing the games of the gods.

There was a knock at the cabin door.

Jethro wiped his eyes. "Come in," he said, placing the crystalline egg back into Jean's satchel.

"Hey, just wanted to check in on you," Caraway said as he walked in. "None of us have seen ya in a while, so I figured I'd stop by."

Jethro chuckled quietly. "You've been through a lot more than I, John. You have no reason to concern yourself with me."

"Yeah, well," Caraway began, looking at his feet. "Jean and Ken, they've been messing around with the Green Lama for a while now, but you, you're still new to all this 'hero' stuff. We make it look easy, but the truth is… I just wanted to make sure you were handling it okay."

"I've been better," Jethro admitted.

Caraway nodded, but Jethro could tell his mind was somewhere else.

"Did you know the woman well, John?" he asked after a moment.

Caraway thinned his lips and shook his head. "No," he whispered in reply.

"But you cared for her."

"I'm married, Jethro," Caraway shot back, but when Jethro remained silent, he confessed, "Yeah, I cared for her. She wasn't—Hell, she didn't deserve to die like that. Not like that. I ain't saying its your fault or nothing, you did your best, but I mean… I was right there, Jethro. I was right next to her and I watched them kill her, and there was nothing I could do. And you know what's the worse part? The part that is digging through my brain like a goddamn earthworm is the feelin' that if I had never met her, she would still be alive."

"You can't know that, John."

"Can't I? Jesus, I don't even know what's up or down anymore. Those creatures and that wizard, and what they did to Vasili… What I wouldn't give for the Murder Corporation or even a reefer dealer in Brooklyn. But this—This is big, Jethro. I ain't saying that to scare ya, but truth is, I'm not sure we're getting out of this alive."

"I have considered that," Jethro said, recalling the Rabbi's divination.

"Goddamn Green Lama," Caraway cursed. "I don't think he knew what he was throwing us into. Don't think he knew how big this really was."

"I'm sure he wouldn't have sent us out here if he didn't think we could handle it, and I know that when the time comes he'll be there when we need him."

"We've been putting our faith in a man whose real name—whose real *face*—we don't even know. Sometimes I figure he's Dr. Pali, other times I'm not sure. Hell, I'm not even sure he's even one person. And don't get me wrong, I ain't saying all you Buddhists are bad guys, but how do we really know he's been playing for our side and it wasn't all just some big ruse just to get us out here?"

"In my limited interactions with the Lama," Jethro said hesitantly, "he has never given me any reason to believe he had any malicious intent."

"Maybe that's just what he wanted us to think?"

"John," Jethro said calmly. "The man saved your life. You told me yourself, if it wasn't for him you would've died."

"I—I," Caraway stuttered. "You're right. I'm sorry. I didn't mean to come in here and dump on you like that. It's just… I've been shot, stabbed, and beaten to a pulp. I've been possessed, fought my way through the Murder Corporation, gone toe-to-toe with giant clay monsters and worse, but I don't think I've ever been this terrified."

Jethro glanced at his ring. "Did I ever tell you about my time in Tibet?"

Caraway shook his head. "Just that you were there in a lamasery for ten years."

Holding up his hand, Jethro showed Caraway the Jade Tablet. "I got this while I was there. It might not look like much to you, but when it was 'given' to me it was the most terrifying experience of my life. I didn't know it then, but this was my birthright. My destiny. It has many names, some call it the Sacred Colors, but most call it the Jade Tablet. It is, in essence, one of three. This one gave me my radioactive salts. The Second Tablet gave life to the golem you fought."

"Wait, Jethro… What are you saying?"

"The Nazis were searching for the Third." Jethro reached into Jean's satchel and brought out the crystalline Tablet. "This one. In many ways it was the same reason Jean went to Samothrace."

Caraway's face slackened as he processed what Jethro was saying. His hands curled into fists.

"Had I known I never would have brought you and Ken along, but Jean was in trouble and a man in love is not a wise man. I lost sight of—"

Caraway struck Jethro hard in the jaw, sending him reeling to the floor. "John, listen I—"

"Save it. Whatever speech you got lined up I don't wanna hear it. You got me, Green Lama?" He asked angrily, pausing until Jethro gave him a hesitant nod. "The only thing I wanna know is how you plan on getting us out of this mess."

Jethro rubbed his jaw. Standing up he shook his head. "I don't have a plan. Not yet."

"Then you better get started," Caraway growled as he walked out of the cabin, slamming the door behind him.

Cohen hacked into his handkerchief. Wiping his nose, he felt as though mucus was flowing from every orifice. One month; he had been sick for one long, excruciating month, each day getting a little worse, but at every port they docked, the local doctors just shrugged and told him to get some bed rest, little good it did him. He was dying, he knew it. If it wasn't tonight, it'd be tomorrow, but the Reaper was coming, waiting for him to let his guard down and take him when he least expected it.

Shivering in his bunk, he watched the stars through the narrow porthole, his eyes trained on the unusually bright star that seemed to twinkle between red and vibrant green, almost as if it was several stars all bunched up together. He smiled weakly, remembering the old rhyme. "Twinkle li'l star, how I wunda wha' ya are? Up above da sky so high—"

There was a knock on the door.

Cohen sat up. "Who dere?"

Another knock, but no answer.

"Boss, dat you? Cap'n Harris?" Another knock, followed by the sound of nails scratching against the metal. "…Gabe?"

Climbing out of his bunk, Cohen hobbled over to the door. "Boss, if dis is about not coverin' helm tanite, Stu said he'd cover for me. I didn't wanna, but ya know how he gets," he said as he opened the door, letting death in.

It was over before he could scream.

"Jean, you need to sit down," Ken said. He unrolled the bandage on his arm and began cleaning the bullet wound.

"I'll sit down when we're on dry land again," she replied, pacing the cabin, pistol in hand, only stopping to briefly look out the porthole. "Until then, I'll keep on my feet."

"You're making me nervous, which, when one considers the fact we are most certainly heading toward our deaths, would indicate just how weird you are behaving."

"You always knew the way to a girl's heart, Ken," she said, her voice dripping with sarcasm.

"You and I both *know* that's a lie," Ken laughed as he redressed the wound.

"How are you so calm?"

He shrugged. "I'm not. Not really. I'm just a fantastic actor. Come on, sit down; let's talk about something." He kicked a chair toward her. "Can't remember the last time you and I actually had a few minutes to talk. It's starting to feel like the only way we ever meet up is if one of us is in peril. The Murder Corporation, the golem, demons, now the end of the world. We're running out of reasons to see each other."

Jean allowed a sad smile, but didn't sit down. "Yeah, it's been a while hasn't it?"

"A long time, Red," Ken nodded. "Remember the last time we were on a boat?"

"The *S.S. Cathay*," Jean said, reminiscing about the time when she and Ken had first met the Green Lama.

"Yeah," Ken chuckled as he raised an empty glass in toast. "Here's hoping this trip will be a little less exciting. I'm still surprised we haven't run into Magga yet."

"She's already here," Jean observed, waving her hand over the room, "disguised as a deck chair or, more likely, a propeller."

"I always figured she and the Green Lama were an item, y'know? They're both Buddhist; both like to put on disguises; both are mysterious and kind of creepy." Ken laughed at that. "Speaking of which, what's going on between you and Dumont?" And then off her reaction, "I'm not blind, babe."

Jean bit her lip. "It's a tad bit more complicated than—" Her voice dropped. She raised a finger to her ear. "Did you hear that?" she whispered.

"Aw, come on, Farrell," Ken laughed, rolling his eyes, "you can't get out of it that easy—"

"Shh!" she hissed, covering Ken's mouth. "Listen!"

They stood in silence for several moments, the low thrum of the ship's engines and the sound of waves crashing against the metal hull seemingly the only noises they could hear.

"I don't hear anything," Ken murmured beneath Jean's hand.

Ignoring Ken's comment, Jean tiptoed over to the door. Delicately placing her hand on the knob, she slowly turned it until it was open. Looking back at Ken, she motioned for him to stay down and get cover. Ken responded by picking up his gun and nodding as if to say: *There's no way you're going in alone.*

"Okay," Jean mouthed. "One… Two… Three!" She threw open the door, and they both whirled out and fired two quick shots each at the lone figure in the hallway.

"What the hell?!" Caraway shouted as he ducked down to the floor, the bullets barely missing him.

"Oh God!" Jean exclaimed, her heart jumping to her throat. "You okay?!"

"Why the hell were you shooting at me?!" Caraway barked.

"Why are we shooting at Caraway?!" Ken exclaimed.

"I thought he was a Deep One!" Jean cried to Ken. "You told me yourself the Deep Ones control the water. If any were left standing after the ritual, they might be coming after us."

Ken grimaced in confusion. "What are you talking about? Up until two days ago I didn't even know those things existed."

"I—No, I mean," Jean stammered. "I'm sorry," she said, dashing down the hall.

"It is a very terrifying thing, death," Heydrich said as he shoved his eye back into its socket. "It isn't anything like you might think. Your life doesn't flash before your eyes. There is no beam of light or your ancestors calling you forward. There isn't even a man in a toga looking up your name in a book, nor do you meet the great Satan himself." He paused when his jaw fell loose. He forced it up until it clicked into place. There was no point in him dressing the wounds, or even trying to hide them; the time for pretense was over. They had all seen it, watched in shock as the Farrell woman blasted two bullets into his brain, then watched him walk away, as if it were nothing but a scratch. He continued. "There is just darkness, never ending darkness. And you are alone. Alone in the darkness, for all time. Is it any wonder, then, that I would prefer this horror to the alternative?" he asked, waving at his shattered skull. "When I first died, there was still so much work to be done, so many things I had to accomplish for the Reich. I could not let *death* stand in my way." Heydrich looked over to Gottschalk, standing in the shadows across the room. "There's no reason to hide from me, Herr Obergruppenführer, I will not bite. Despite my appearance, I can assure you that you have nothing to fear from me."

Gottschalk took a hesitant step forward. "What are you?"

Heydrich frowned with what was left of his lips. "Did I not just say? I am a patriotic German, sir, like you and the Oberführer," he said, indicating Gan seated across from him.

"Are you even alive?" Gan asked.

"Somewhere in between," he said with a smile.

Gottschalk took off his hat and scratched the balding patch at the back of his head. "Herr Doktor Hammond, I must confess this is all a little too much—"

"No, no, please, Herr Obergruppenführer," Heydrich said with a wave of his hand. "Please, call me by the name my mother gave me. Karl Heydrich."

"No, but, but, I don't under— " Gottschalk stuttered. "You're Heydrich?"

"In the flesh," Heydrich said, touching a hand to his chest and bowing. "What little there is left."

"Why the deception, then?" Gan asked.

"Ask yourself, Herr Oberführer, if I had returned from Tibet after my failure, impossibly alive despite all evidence to the contrary, how do you believe that would have seemed to our commanders, to the Führer, hm? No, it was better to work incognito."

Gan leaned forward. "And what of your allegiance to that creature?"

"A means to an end," Heydrich replied. "Whatever he is, he is helping us play out a prophecy that will give us the Ultimate Power. You have seen the power held within the Shard. Imagine what lies within the Tablets, within R'lyeh!"

"But at what cost, Herr Heydrich?" Gan slammed his palm on to the table. "Hirsch is dead, and despite all the creature's—and your—promises, we have yet to obtain a single Tablet. We have been in league with demons. More and more this journey seems like a fool's errand. How do we know we are not being played as rubes to service that monster's real motives?"

"Prophecy does not play out cleanly and simply just as you would like, Herr Oberführer," Heydrich retorted. "Like any game of chess, pieces must be moved around the board, and yes, occasionally lost until the King is in check. And while I would *love* to sit here and answer every question you might have, perhaps the Obergruppenführer would like hear why it is that Jethro Dumont showed up at the sacrifice after you yourself told us he had died."

Gan sat back, keeping his eyes on Heydrich's destroyed face. "I saw him go down with the car along with Johann," he said with confidence. "How he escaped I do not know. Perhaps there is more to Dumont than we knew."

"Perhaps there is," Heydrich reiterated. He turned to Gottschalk. "Sir, you might recall the Oberführer's report from New York, which detailed, in part, his encounters with the costumed vigilante known as the Green Lama..."

Vasili screamed. Everything was pain, radiating through his body, threatening to tear him apart. Nightmares, horrific images filled his mind, ravishing his sanity. Thrashing, he found his arms and leg bound to a small bed. The room was pitch black; the sound of an engine thrumming echoed around him. He screamed again, out of fear, confusion, and madness.

"Ah, Vasili, you're awake!" Alexei said pleasantly from the shadows. "You had been asleep so long I thought you'd never wake up."

Vasili tried to turn his head but found it braced. "Sir? Are you there? Where am I? Why am I tied up?"

"You are on a U-boat, my dear boy," Alexei said with a laugh, his voice seeming to come from all directions. "One of many marvels of modern times. You are secured for your own protection. You've been having some very bad dreams, Vasili. We were afraid you were going to hurt yourself."

"How did we—?" he cut himself off, unable to finish the question, his head buzzing terribly. "Sir, are you okay? You sound hurt."

Alexei chuckled. "Nothing that won't heal. Calm down, son, you've been through quite a lot recently and you still need your rest."

"Could you loosen the bindings, please?" Vasili begged, shifting uncomfortably.

"All in good time," he said, patting the back of Vasili's hand. His skin was cold, like marble. "Tell me, Vasili, what is the last thing you remember?"

Vasili squeezed his eyes shut, working through the buzzing that rang out from the back of his skull. "Petros," he said eventually. "He was hurt."

"Yes," Alexei replied. "And your nightmares, do you remember any of them?"

"How are the others?" Vasili asked, licking his chapped lips. His memories were fragments, broken shards of glass spread across the ocean floor. "The foreigners? And Sotiria…?"

"Don't concern yourself with them," Alexei said, soothing, running a hand through Vasili's hair, a father calming his son. "Your nightmares, Vasili, tell me "

Vasili saw the flash of a green dagger in his mind's eye, followed by a torrent of blood. "Sotiria," he weakly asked. "Is she okay?"

"Your nightmares, Vasili," Alexei reiterated, his voice beginning to steam with anger.

A wave of pain rolled down his spine. Gritting his teeth, Vasili sputtered, "I saw—I was in a city."

"Good," Alexei said with muted glee. "Describe it to me."

"Why do you want to know, sir?" Vasili asked, quaking with fear. Violent images shot through his head, the sound of screams filling his ears. "Please just tell me, is Sotiria okay?"

"Tell me your visions, *now*, Vasili," he commanded, his voice resonating. He pressed an ink black finger against Vasili's forehead, causing the young man's eyes to glaze over. "Tell me what you saw."

"The ground was wet, the air pungent," Vasili began in monotone. "It hadn't tasted daylight in millennia. The walls, they turned at the wrong angles. It all looked grown… like coral. The shadows moved. We were walking together, all of us, toward a building at the center of the city. It was… It was a temple. The Temple. We went inside and it—" he paused, his voice cracking. Blinking back tears, he continued. "And there was an altar overlooking the darkness, and something beyond, something terrible."

"Yes, and tell me on the altar… Who was sacrificed?"

"Sacrificed?" Vasili's eyes regained their focus. "Wait, there was another sacrifice… I… Sotiria…" The shards began to reform in his mind and he began to remember. He gasped. "Oh God. Sotiria."

"Tell me who will be sacrificed!" Alexei screamed, leaning into the light, grabbing Vasili's face with his black claw like hand.

"Jethro," Vasili whimpered, his mind snapping as he looked into the wormlike obsidian face of the Crawling Chaos. *"Jethro Dumont."*

Jean stood at the bow of the ship, the cool sea air blowing back her hair. She clung to the railing, the ice cold metal reminding her that this, right now, was real.

"You know, we first met on a ship," Jethro said as he walked up besides her.

A small smile pierced her sour expression, but she refused to face him. "You were dressed up like Dr. Pali, so technically that doesn't *really* count, Dumont."

"No," Jethro frowned, "I suppose it doesn't."

"Nice shiner," she said, indicating the large black-and-blue welt on Jethro's face. "Where'd ya get that?"

He reached for his jaw, wincing at the throbbing bruise. "I may have *indirectly* told Caraway that I was the Green Lama," he told her reluctantly. "He was less than pleased by the revelation."

Jean gave him a terse laugh. "Have I ever mentioned how much I *agree* with his methods? Boy, I would've paid money to see that."

"You're concern for me is almost touching, Ne-tso-hbum," he said.

"You know me. All heart."

Jethro leaned on the railing and laced his fingers together. "What brought you here, on a cold night like this? That is if you don't mind me asking."

Jean pursed her lips. "Almost shot Caraway. Thought he was a Deep

One." She paused to consider this. "Boy, he's having a really rough week, isn't he?"

"And you?" Jethro asked.

Jean's gaze fell to the breaking waves below, her knuckles turning white as she tightened her grip on the railing. "I've had better. Wish I could say I've had worse. Though it feels more like a lifetime. Take it from me, Dumont, time travel is *highly* overrated."

"There's still a lot you haven't told me about what you saw."

"And there's a reason for that," she said curtly.

Jethro chewed the inside of his cheek as he contemplated his next statement. Hesitating, he said: "Gan told me that Brickman foretold my—"

"For what it's worth, Jethro," Jean cut in, "we *are* doing better than before."

"But will it be enough?" he asked.

Jean raised an eyebrow. "Worried about your karma, Dumont?"

Jethro gave her a wry look. "Always, but in this case I'm more concerned about this world than the next. No matter the cost, I will not fail."

"'No matter the cost,'" she whispered. She blinked her eyes quickly and turned her head up to the stars. "The creatures from the *Bartlett* and *Prometheus* both called me the 'Keystone.' Keystone... Like I'm at the center of it all."

"They would not be the first to believe you are the most important person in the world," Jethro said softly.

"But I'm not," she said, tears brimming in her eyes. "I'm not. I'm just a girl from Montana, good with a gun and probably too quick of a draw at that. I used to—I once thought I was supposed to be a movie star. That was the dream; the one they sold us on the silver screen, at least. Damn if I didn't go and fight for it. But then... Then I met you and now all I can ever think about is... What I can do, how many lives I can save. I'm happiest when I'm with the Green—when I'm with you. But this... This is too much. I'm not like you, Jethro, I'm not—"

He placed his hand on hers. "No. You're stronger."

Jean glanced down at their hands and bit her lip to fight back the smile. "Always keep it interesting, don't we?"

"I suppose we do," he said with a sad smile.

A tear streamed down Jean's face. Jethro reached up to brush it away and found his hand holding her cheek. Her emeralds eyes stared into his. He leaned closer.

"Dumont!" something hissed behind them. They spun to face the deck, Jean's gun instantly drawn.

"What was that?" Jean breathed.

There was a guttural roar as a scarred Deep One shot out of the darkness, brandishing its claws.

"Get down!" Jethro shouted.

"Like hell I will," Jean snarled, shooting at the attacking creature. But the Deep One was quicker than she expected, ducking a split second before she fired. Knocking the gun out of her hand, the creature grabbed her and threw her over the side of the ship.

"No!" Jethro screamed as Jean tumbled away. Before he could react the Deep One was on him, throwing him onto the deck as it sliced at his abdomen. Jethro quickly pulled his legs up to his chest and kicked the soft member hanging between the creature's ropey legs. The Deep One howled in pain and stumbled back. With little time, Jethro rushed to the railings, his heart pounding against his chest as he shouted, "Jean!"

Desperately peering over the edge he let out a small gasp of relief when he found her precariously holding on to a narrow ledge.

"Jethro, watch out!" she shrieked as the Deep One came up from behind and grabbed him by the throat.

"You kill Roe'qua!" Ke'ta growled, digging its nails into Jethro's larynx. "You make Master kill my brother!"

Choking, Jethro struck his elbow into the Deep One's massive eye. The creature growled in pain, but only tightened his grip on Jethro's neck.

"Jethro!" Jean screamed, her fingers slipping. "I can't hold on much longer!"

Stars burst behind his eyes as the Deep One continued to squeeze. A loud whirring sounded above them, filling the night as a spotlight suddenly shone down them. "Dumont!" a familiar voice boomed from the air. "Get down, now!"

Jethro kicked his legs out from beneath him and dropped to the deck, leaving Ke'ta's scarred head open. A deafening *POW!* resounded over them and Ke'ta's head exploded, showering Jethro in blood, bone and brains.

Prying himself free of Ke'ta's limp hands, Jethro stumbled back over to the railings.

"Jean!" he called, leaning over the side. "Reach for my hand!"

"I think I can," she said as she tried to pull herself up, lifting a hand toward Jethro's.

"Almost," Jethro grunted, leaning further forward, his fingers brushing against hers. "Just a little further…"

"Jethro, I can't—" Jean said, just as her hold slipped and she fell into the black waters below.

Chapter 16
A SAVAGE APPROACH

*T*here were twenty of them, armed with a variety of swords and guns, each bigger than the last. For the past month they had raided the local villages, stealing food and livestock, killing the men, raping the women, and butchering the children. Witnessing the proof of their destruction was almost too much to bear. It had taken Jethro two weeks to find the thugs' hideout, a hidden cave beneath the shadows of the mountains.

"I only ask that you leave the villagers in peace," Jethro said in Tibetan, resolute as they began to encircle him. "The lamasery can aid you in your efforts to find food and livestock. There will be no need to resort to violence anymore."

"Ah, but what if we don't want to stop, Lama?" the leader, a wiry stump of a man, asked. "What if it's just too much fun?"

"I promise there is more to life than this. We can find a peaceful way to—"

The leader laughed. "There is no peace here, Lama! Only death."

A blade flew out at Jethro. Catching it easily, he threw it back at the leader's feet, the metal wobbling as it stuck out from ground. "Violence begets violence. Please do not misinterpret my peaceful offerings, I will not allow you to harm any more people. If you strike me I will respond in kind."

"I see through your lies, Lama!"

"A lama never lies," Jethro said with a slight bow. "He only promises."

"Kill him!" the leader shouted as the cabal began to attack.

"Man overboard!" Jethro shouted as he dived after her, hitting the water without so much as a splash. Swimming through the black waters to her unconscious form, Jethro wrapped his arms around Jean and pulled her to the surface and clear of the oncoming ship. Holding up her head, he could see she wasn't breathing. "Ne-tso-hbum… Please, no."

A spotlight in the air moved onto them. Looking up into the blinding light, Jethro waved for help.

"Hang in there, Dumont!" the voice called. "I'm sendin' down a ladder! Grab on and I'll pull you up!" Seconds later a rope ladder dropped down in front of them. Paddling over, Jethro placed Jean between him and the ladder, then wrapped his arms around her, twisting the rungs around his forearms so they were secure. Tugging down against the ladder, they were swiftly lifted out of the water and swung back over onto the ship's deck where Caraway, Ken, and Captain Harris were running over toward them.

"We heard shouting," Ken said. "You guys okay?"

"Jean," Jethro gasped as he placed her on the deck. "She's not breathing."

"What in holy hell?" Captain Harris exclaimed at the sight of the decapitated Deep One. "What the hell did you bring on my ship?"

Jethro ignored Captain Harris. Tilting Jean's head back, he lifted her chin and listened for a faint indication she was breathing. When none came, he pinched her nose and placed his lips over hers and gave her two quick breaths, her chest rising. When she didn't regain consciousness he placed his hands on her sternum and began to compress. Once, twice, then again. Seconds felt like hours before Jean coughed up water.

"Oh thank God!" Ken exclaimed, clutching his chest, as if his heart was threatening to explode.

"Ne-tso-hbum," Jethro whispered, removing a wet strand of hair from Jean's face. "Hi."

"Heya, *Smug*," Jean replied, smiling weakly. "You saved me."

Jethro chuckled. "A bit of a change from the usual, I know. I'll try not to let it happen again."

"Someone mind telling me, what in God's name just happened?" Captain Harris shouted. Then, pointing to the floating spotlight above them, "And what in the hell is that?"

"That, Captain Harris," Jethro said as he looked up into the sky, watching the familiar hovering plane come alongside, the mustached pilot waving from the cockpit, "is where we get off."

"Now *this*… This is an amazing plane," Caraway commented as he and Ken walked into the gleaming cockpit.

"Wish I could say it's mine," Rick Masters said as he worked the controls. "But yeah, the Big Guy has a lot of very impressive toys."

"The Big Guy…?" Ken stuttered in disbelief. "You don't mean—?"

Rick nodded. "Yup. *The* Big Guy."

"How the hell you swing that?" Caraway asked.

"Ask Uncle Money Bags," Rick replied under his breath, pointing a thumb behind him. "He set the whole thing up."

"Heh," Caraway huffed. "Shoulda figured."

"Tell me about it," Rick said, and then murmured to himself, 'Green Sleeves' got *connections*."

Ken glanced back toward the main cabin and then looked back at Rick and Caraway quizzically. "Green Sleeves? Green Sleeves who?"

"Thank you again for your help, Captain Harris," Jethro said with a slight bow of his head. He and Jean were standing on the plane's gangway, hovering just off the side of the boat. "I am truly sorry for the loss of one of your men. Had we known the creature was on board we would have never—"

Captain Harris cut in. "I appreciate the sentiment, but I don't hold you responsible, Mr. Dumont. Cohen was a good man. He didn't deserve to die like that," he added mournfully, rubbing the wool of his Afro-textured hair. "But the fault lies with that… thing. Not with you."

"Sir, if I there's anything we can do…"

The captain shook his head. "If you're out to stop monsters like the one that murdered Cohen, all I'd ask is that you promise you're gonna make sure to kill one of 'em for me."

"We'll do our best, Captain," Jean said solemnly.

The plane's gangway began to retract as they waved goodbye and climbed aboard. Captain Harris watched as the plane rose vertically before the propellers turned forward and headed west. Taking a thoughtful drag of his cigarette, he realized it would be a lifetime before he ever saw a plane like that again.

"Have I ever mentioned that generally speaking I don't approve of killing—human or otherwise?" Jethro asked Jean as they walked through the cabin.

"Probably," Jean rebutted, with a crooked grin. "But, who said I was listening?"

"Welcome aboard, lady and gentlemen," Rick said over the loudspeaker. "If you'll all take your seats and buckle up, we'll get headin' toward our destination shortly."

Jean caught sight of the monogram stitched into all of the seat backs. She placed her hands on her hips and scrutinized Jethro. "I didn't know you had such impressive friends."

"You'd be surprised," Jethro said humbly as he sat down and buckled his safety belt. "One day I'll tell you about my old detective friend in London."

Jean raised an eyebrow as she sat down beside him. "I can't wait."

Ken and Caraway walked into the cabin. Ken's face had turned a sickly green, his arms wrapped around his stomach.

"You okay there, Clayton?" Jean asked.

Ken sighed and shook his head as he and Caraway took their seats across from them. "Ask me again when we're on solid ground."

Caraway leaned over to Jean with a smug smile. "Our matinee idol here is afraid of flying."

Jean's eyes went wide. "Shut up. Really?"

Ken nodded weakly. "Why do you think I insisted on taking a boat from Los Angeles to New York?" There was a sudden sound of motor and gears shifting overhead and Ken blanched. "Oh Lord, what now?"

Outside, the thin metal panels atop the plane slid back to reveal a complex web of mechanisms and weaponry. Cogs turned and gears shifted as a giant engine rose up on powerful steel supports until it was six feet above the fuselage, the chrome metal gleaming in the moonlight.

"Okay, everyone," Rick called over the loudspeaker. "That really loud sound you just heard was the plane's advanced propulsion moving into ready position."

"What?" Ken whimpered.

"Gonna be honest with you folks, I've never used this thing before, so it might get a little bumpy," Rick continued. "So you might wanna hang on to something."

Jean placed her hand in Jethro's as the engine came online and the horizon came rushing toward them.

"Everyone comfortable?" Rick asked as he walked through the cabin some time later, lugging a large briefcase. "Autopilot," he said simply off Ken's panicked expression, though this failed to give Ken any comfort.

"How long until we reach our destination?" Jethro asked as he unfastened himself out his chair.

"A while yet. The what's-it gave us a good boost but we still have a whole hemisphere to cross. Which leads me to ask: Where the hell are we going?"

"The sunken city of R'lyeh," Jean replied as she stood. "Home of the Great Old One, Cthulhu."

"Heydrich's returned," Jethro gravelly added.

Rick clicked his tongue and allowed himself a rueful smile. "This is End of the World type stuff, isn't it?"

"Basically," Caraway said without amusement.

"This is why I have to stop answering the phone," Rick sighed, massaging his eyes. He looked to Jethro. "I'm assuming you have a plan against whatever it is we're heading toward, right?"

Jethro meekly shook his head. "Not as of yet."

"Of course. Hopefully, you might find some answers in here. Your assistant *Sor-wrong* gave it to me. Feels like there's a rock in there," he said, handing Jethro the briefcase.

Jethro took it without correcting him. Feeling the weight in his hand, Jethro allowed a small smile to curl his lips, knowing exactly what was inside.

"Hey," Caraway said, grabbing Rick as he began to walk away. "Did you give my message to Frankie?"

Rick hesitated. "Yeah," he said with a slight nod.

"What did she say?"

Rick rubbed his cheek. "Wasn't exactly what she said, buddy, more of what she did."

Caraway's stomach dropped. "Oh, boy," he moaned, running his hand through his hair.

"Yup. We make it out of this alive, you better buy her a lot of flowers," Rick said, patting Caraway on the shoulder before walking back toward the cockpit. "A shit ton of flowers. And maybe a few diamonds."

Meanwhile, Jethro sat back down and placed the briefcase on his lap. Opening it, he found a small protective box placed atop green fabric. Peering inside the box, Jethro's smile broadened into a toothy grin. "Thank you, old friend," he whispered as he lifted the small vial of enhanced radioactive salts.

"That the special batch that makes you fly?" Caraway asked, recalling the conversation he and Ken had atop the Empire State Building.

Jethro looked to Caraway. "Yes, and much more," he said after a moment, a small weight lifting from his chest. He could tell that while Caraway didn't completely forgive him for his deception—and probably never would—their friendship was beginning to mend. Returning to the briefcase, Jethro unwrapped the vibrant green fabric and found the Second Jade Tablet, glowing softly in the dim cabin lighting. Lifting it up, Jethro looked over it solemnly. "Now we have all three."

"Which puts us a little ahead of the curve," Jean said.

"Only a little," Caraway added.

"Hopefully, that will be enough," Jethro said as he placed the Tablet beside him. Looking into the briefcase he discovered two last items: a large, dark green hooded robe and a long, deep red *kava*.

"Hey, those kinda looks like the Green Lama's," Ken observed as Jethro brought them out. "Wait a minute…" he trailed off as the truth dawned on him. "Jethro, are you the Green Lama?"

Jethro looked at Ken and smiled in response.

Ken's eyes went wide in shock. "Get outta town!"

Several hours passed before all four of them met again. They were crossing over Brazil, the lush greenery of the Amazon extending as far as the eye could see. Though exhausted, none of them had attempted sleep, adrenaline and fear keeping them awake. Caraway had spent the majority of his time in the cockpit with Rick, trading stories of women and adventures. For his part, Ken kept himself far from the windows, congregating between the bathroom and his aisle seat. Meanwhile, Jean and Jethro spent their time examining and comparing the Jade Tablets.

"We think we've made some progress," Jethro said when they reconvened. With the Second and Third Jade Tablets laid out in front of him, Jethro indicated a small section of script on the crystal egg. "'Roughly, this reads: 'One to rise, three to sleep.' If I understand it correctly, that means only *one* Tablet is needed to wake Cthulhu."

"Don't forget the 'blood sacrifice,'" Jean interjected.

"But to stop him," he continued, "we need all *three* Tablets placed in *three* specific points by the *three* 'Scions.'"

"Jethro, me, and Vasili," Jean said, pointing at the three figures at the top of the crystal.

"'The crystal on the column, the stone in the wall and the ring in the hand,'" Jethro said, pointing to another passage from the Third Tablet.

"Just vague enough to make it difficult," Caraway grumbled, stroking his mustache. "And we're missing one key element."

Jean nodded. "Vasili."

"The Nazis are no doubt on their way to R'lyeh," Jethro added. "It's safe to assume that they're bringing Vasili with them."

"He killed Sotiria," Ken said.

"He was possessed," Caraway said under his breath, his eyes downcast.

"Possessed or not, how do we even know he's on our side?" Ken asked. "Hell, how do we know he's alive?"

"We don't," Jethro admitted.

Caraway shook his head. "I saw the boy up close at the ruins. The way his eyes looked, I could tell he wasn't in control. And the way Sotiria— God rest her soul—was screaming you'd think that would've elicited some kinda response, but there was nothing. Just blank. And you remember what happened when Alexei grabbed him," he said to Ken. "I wouldn't be surprised if that monster was controlling him the entire time."

"And may still be in control now," Jethro said. "Whatever Alexei really is, he is extremely powerful. With him and the Nazis, getting to Vasili will not be easy."

Ken snapped his fingers. "Wait, why would the Nazis be heading to R'lyeh when they don't have any of the Jade Tablets?"

"Isn't it obvious?" Jean asked. "They're expecting us."

Black ooze leaked from Heydrich's eye socket, dripping down the side of his cheek like a demon's tear. Wiping it away with the back of his hand, he walked through the narrow maze of the U-Boat toward Alexei's cramped quarters.

"Do you like it?" a tall Egyptian man asked, appearing out of the shadows. He was dressed in regalia reminiscent of the Pharaohs, an obsidian and gold squid-like pendant hanging from his neck.

Heydrich fell back in surprise. "Who are you?"

"You do not recognize me, Heydrich?" the tall Egyptian laughed. "This is what I once was, back in the days when I was human, if you could have called me that. Back when I ruled the Nile. When they used to call me by my given name, Nyarlathotep."

Heydrich furrowed his brow, at last recognizing his master, no longer using the guise of Alexei. "Did your true form no longer suit you? I imagined you reveled in the looks of disgust and fear you elicited in the men."

Nyarlathotep smiled, reminiscing. "It was pleasurable, yes, watching the madness break their minds as I walked past. But if I am to see the Great Cthulhu again, I want him to see me as he remembers."

"You are confident that Dumont will come to R'lyeh?" Heydrich asked.

Nyarlathotep frowned. "Do you truly doubt me so much, Heydrich? Have I not given all that I promised you?"

Heydrich hesitated. "Gottschalk and Gan. They doubt the truth of Dumont's alter ego and his possession of the Sacred Colors. They also question your—our intentions. They feel that despite our promises they have seen few results."

"Humans. They only see as far they can reach, they are not worthy to be in the same reality as Cthulhu let alone gaze upon him. If I were to bring them the Sun, they would ask why the Earth is so hot," Nyarlathotep scoffed, waving his hand in frustration. "While the rising of the sunken city has put the fates in flux, they can rest assured, all will go as promised. Dumont will be at R'lyeh and you will have your sacrifice."

"Your boy," Heydrich began nodding a chin toward the end of the corridor. "Has he woken up yet?"

"He is awake, though I fear I might have broken his sanity," he said with the disinterest of a child breaking a forgotten toy. A devious smile curled his tanned face. "Though he has one final role to play."

Heydrich unconsciously picked at the wound in his skull. "We will still need to appease the others. I doubt I can keep them satisfied with promises and prophecies for much longer. With another week ahead of us before we reach R'lyeh, I urge you, Master, please, show them *something* to ease their doubts before they jeopardize our plans."

Nyarlathotep smiled and tilted his head sideways. "A week? Really?"

Heydrich jumped as the klaxons began to blare, red lights flashing. The entire submarine began to shake around them as a panicked voice came over the intercom, shouting: "*Auftauchen! Auftauchen!*" Heydrich covered his ears, as the pressure quickly dropped as they rose to the surface.

"What's happening?" Heydrich screamed.

"We've arrived," Nyarlathotep laughed.

"You guys might wanna come and take a look at this," Rick said over the loudspeaker several hours later.

Caraway rubbed the sleep out of his eyes as he rose from his chair. "Up and at 'em," he said as he passed by Ken, slapping him on the shoulder. Ken wiped the drool from his chin and stumbled behind Caraway toward the cockpit where they found Jean and Jethro already waiting. Outside the window, an ever growing black dot protruded from the blue expanse like a twisted nail.

"R'lyeh," Jean said as they entered.

"I've got a bad feeling about this," Caraway said, bracing himself against Jethro's seat back.

"You and me both, brother," Rick agreed as he worked the controls. "We're still a few minutes out. Once we get closer I'm gonna try and circle around, see if there's any place to land, though I'm not gonna lie to ya, that island doesn't look too friendly."

"Please tell me we don't have to jump out of another plane," Ken begged.

"Do any of you hear that?" Jean asked. "Sounds like a whistling."

"Just the wind, sweetheart," Rick said. "Don't worry."

Jethro shot Rick a scolding look and leaned forward. "I hear it too. Look! Over there." He pointed toward the faint black and red mass spiraling out of the center of the island.

"Jesus," Rick breathed. "What in God's name…?"

Caraway stepped forward. "Another living storm?"

Rick shook his head. "No, look at the way it's spiraling up like that. Reminds me of the way bats fly out of caves down in South America."

Jethro stood up, his hands clenched in fists. "It's a swarm."

"A swarm?" Ken asked, panic lacing his voice. "A swarm of what?"

"What else?" Jean asked as they watched the black and red dots form into cancer-like polyps and winged dragons. "Monsters."

"What are those things?!" Ken screamed as he, Jean and Caraway chased after Jethro.

"Your guess is as good as mine," Jethro replied as he entered the cabin. "Whatever they are, they're coming for us." He uncorked the small vial of radioactive salts, swallowed them in one swift motion, and picked up his robe and *kava*.

"Dumont, where are you going?" Caraway asked.

"Out there," Jethro responded as he pulled on his robes and tied the *kava* around his waist. He ignored the small lump that seemed to weigh down at the cuff of his right sleeve. He could feel the salts moving through his system, from cell to cell, a sensation like gripping an exposed wire.

Jean's eyes went wide. "Jethro, you can't!" she shouted, grabbing him by the sleeve. "You go out there and they'll—"

"I know the risks, Jean," he said gravely as he gently pulled his arm free. "The enhanced radioactive salts will give me flight and the strength to fight off these creatures long enough to give Rick the time to get all of you safely to R'lyeh."

"You can't be serious!" Ken exclaimed. "Jethro—I mean, Green Lama—this is insanity! Those things will eat you alive!"

"This is the only way you will be able to put the other Tablets in place in time." He turned to Jean. "Besides you said yourself you know the future, didn't you? All the mistakes we make."

"Yes…" Jean said hesitantly.

"Then you know how to correct them, don't you?"

"I—I," Jean stuttered, tears pooling her eyes. "But what if I can't?"

"You must and you will. I know you will," the Green Lama said with a somber smile. The enhanced radioactive salts were already beginning to take effect, giving his eyes an unearthly green hue, electricity crackled from his fingertips. "You all might want to hold onto something." He pressed a button on the side of the cabin and the hatchway hissed open. Air rushed out as the cabin depressurized.

"I…" Jean's voice became hushed as the air escaped, barely a whisper. "Jethro, I—"

"And I, you," the Green Lama said over the roar of wind, a warm smile that sent shivers down Jean's spine. "I will see you soon, Ne-tso-hbum… I'm counting on it." The Green Lama pulled the hood over his head, leaned back, and fell into the sky.

Chapter 17
AT THE GATES OF R'LYEH

*B*lood covered the cave floor, the walls and his hands. The fight—No, *Jethro corrected himself, it had been a slaughter—had lasted only seconds, a blur of motion and gore that left every member of the gang dead at his feet.*

"Om! Om! Vajra Guru Padme Siddhi Hum Hri!" Jethro murmured as he fell to knees, the blood running down his arms, staining his sleeves. He stared at the ring on his finger, finally understanding what it truly was. So this was power unlimited, the power of the gods, coursing through his veins? This was the price that came with it, the ability to kill without so much as a thought? A flick of his finger to break a man's neck, a twist of the wrist to snap a man in half. He could topple cities in a day, countries in a week, and the world in a month. He was a man of unbridled strength. Was this what he was chosen to do?

His entire body shook, less from the cold than his own terror. Bile rose from his stomach. He forced himself back to his feet and stumbled over the mess of bodies out of the cave into the unrelenting sunlight. He dug his hands into the snow and began scouring his hands, but the blood wouldn't come off, it just didn't come off. Shivering, he began pulling at the ring's threads with his fingernails, but no matter how many times he tried, the ring wouldn't unravel.

"Gotama Çãkyamuni! O Wisdom that is gone, gone, gone to the beyond and beyond the beyond: Svâhâ*...!" He looked toward the sky and screamed, "What have I done?"*

As he fell through the air, the Green Lama watched the multitude of flying horrors draw closer, each creature more monstrous than the last. Closing his eyes, he began to whisper, *"Gate gate paragate parasamgate bodhi svaha!"*

He felt the wind whip around him, fluttering his cloak; sensed gravity tugging him toward the cold waters below. He could hear the whistling sound of the approaching monsters, could smell the salt of the sea air. He saw the clouds, the plane flying above; saw Jean standing at the hatchway. Chanting the Threefold Refuge, the Green Lama let the energy flow through his body and push down against the ground, shooting him past the plane, and toward the onslaught. A sonic boom shattered as he broke the sound barrier, the air vibrating around him. Green electricity crackled from his hands, energy sizzled from his eyes. He had the power of the gods flowing through him now and all he needed to do was aim it. But as before, this came at a cost, pushing his all too human frame well beyond its natural limits, and with each passing second he could feel the power quickly draining. He remembered the Rabbi's prophecy. If he were to die today, let it be now, fighting to protect Jean, for it was within her, not the radioactive salts, that he found his strength.

As the first dragon descended upon him, its claws reaching for his skull, the Green Lama threw a fist forward and shouted, "*Om! Ma-ni Pad-me Hum!*"

And the sky erupted in green light.

"Jesus Christ," Rick exclaimed, covering his eyes from the light. He looked to Jean. "Did you know he could do that?"

"Buddy," she said, patting him on the shoulder, "you don't know the half of it."

Rick nodded somberly. "Well, let's see if we can help him out," he said returning to the controls with renewed vigor. "John, Ken. There are two turrets just past the cabin and I'm assuming that means there are a couple of very big machine guns attached to them. You two think you can shoot some of those things out of the sky?"

"Think I can handle it," Caraway said before racing out of the cockpit.

Rick and Jean turned to Ken, who silently shook his head, his face turning puce.

"Fine," Rick said, tossing a thumb back toward the cabin. "Jean, you think you can—"

"Way ahead of you, bucko," she said following after Caraway.

Rick pursed his lips in surprise and looked to Ken. "This is gonna get real rocky, real quick. Try not to throw up."

Ken crawled into the copilot's chair. "Can't promise anything."

"Wonderful," Rick sighed.

The Green Lama ripped apart the dragon's jaw, blood and bone splattering out. The creature howled in pain and fell limp from shock. Grabbing it by the throat, he spun it around and threw it toward three oncoming creatures, knocking them down toward the ocean. Something screeched in attack. Grimacing, the Green Lama wheeled toward an insect-like bat, its translucent wings beating madly. Clenching his fists, he sent out an incredible blast of energy, evaporating the beast's abdomen.

From behind him he heard the familiar whistling sound approach. Spinning around he found only sky. Suddenly, he felt something twist around him, squeezing tight, testing the strength of his bones. "*Om! Vajra Sattva!*" he cried, letting loose a massive bolt of energy from his body, instantly revealing a cancerous black snake wrapped around him.

"It is no use to fight," the flying polyp said telepathically as it continued to crush him. "We have conquered Yaksh and Tond, we have defeated the Great Race of Yith, and Earth too will fall and the Great Old Ones will rule again! What are you to try and stop Nyarlathotep? What are you to fight the will of the gods?"

Gritting his teeth, the Green Lama tensed his muscles, focusing all his energy on his strength. "I am the Green Lama!" he screamed as he threw his arms out, ripping the polyp in half.

As the creature's carcass tumbled to the blue below, a massive talon grabbed the Green Lama by the head. The claws dug into his neck and shoulders, and dragged him through the air.

"Come on, you big ugly bastards," Jean said, as she strapped herself into the ventral turret and aimed the machine gun at two giant insects. "Let's play." She squeezed down on the twin triggers and the gun erupted to life, filling the air with bullets and tearing the bugs apart until there was nothing more than black scraps floating down like a cloud of black snow. "Woo!" she shouted. "That's how we play in Montana!" She looked up toward Caraway in the dorsal turret. "Hey, Caraway. I've already got two! What's your count?"

"That's great, kid," Caraway shouted back, giving her a thumbs up. "Don't get cocky."

"Still haven't popped your cherry?" she called back as she shot down a leathery dragon. "Don't worry, your time will come!"

Caraway bit back a smile as he fired after a flying polyp. "Sweetheart, trust me, you couldn't handle me!"

Jean laughed. "Like to see ya prove it!"

Gunfire rang out around him, ripping through the air. Blood and pieces of flesh rained down as the bullets tore through the dragon's body. The creature screamed as it tumbled down to Earth, its talons refusing to release him. With the ocean rapidly approaching, the Green Lama focused all the power of the radioactive salts through his eyes, sending out two powerful beams of energy, disintegrating the dragon's claws. Tearing out a talon still gouged into his chest, the Green Lama watched in muted amazement as the wound instantly healed. A blast of energy struck him from behind, sending him reeling into the plane's wing. Rolling across the metallic surface, the Green Lama came to a sudden, painful stop against the side of the plane. Smoke emanated out of the wound on his back, his skin sizzling as it quickly healed, but nothing stopped the pain. Driving his fingers into the metal, he pulled himself up, the sound of the propeller engine and wind nearly deafening.

"*Om! Namah Shivaya!*" the Green Lama groaned. "Buddha make me stronger."

"I see you have unlocked the full potential of the Tibetan Tablet."

Whirling around, the Green Lama found a tall, tanned man hovering above him. The man smiled pleasantly as he crossed his arms. "It is humans like you that make me wonder if I have underestimated your species."

The Green Lama recognized the voice. "Alexei?"

"Come now, we know each other well enough now, Jethro," the man laughed. "Call me Nyarlathotep." He extended a hand and flames rushed out.

"Holy shit!" Ken howled as something rocked the plane, tossing him from his seat.

"Goddammit!" Rick shouted as he fought to level the plane. "Jesus, Mary and Joseph, what in fuck's name was that?"

Straining his neck to look out the window toward the left wing, Ken's mouth fell open. Clutching his chest, he turned to Rick as he collapsed into his chair. "It's the Green Lama! He's on fire!"

Rick's eyes narrowed as he swallowed the lump in his throat. "Oh, this is not good."

Blocking the flames with his *kava*, the Green Lama wordlessly let it go to the wind. Then, raising the Jade Tablet, he shot a blast of energy from his fist at Nyarlathotep, which the unholy creature easily avoided.

Nyarlathotep frowned. "Is that how you greet a god?"

"You are no god!"

"Aren't I? Hm. Then what would you like me to be? A corrupt sheriff?" Nyarlathotep's face cracked open, his skin rattling in waves as black bone and flesh rearranged into the familiar visage. "No, no... That's too recent. It lacks the impact one would desire... What about a possessed young girl?" A thousand hairline fractures laced Alexei's face as it transformed into the distinct, ravaged form of Desdemona Georgas, who had lost her life to the demons aboard the *Bartlett*. "Or does that failure sting too much, the wound too fresh? Why don't we go with something a bit more comforting then?" Desdemona's countenance broke open. "Why not the woman you love?" Jean Farrell said with a wicked smile.

The Green Lama growled wordlessly as he launched forward, but Nyarlathotep was faster. He caught the Green Lama by the throat and punched him in the face, a strike that sent shockwaves through the sky. Blood trickled out of the corner of the Green Lama's mouth, his eyes rolling back in their sockets while he struggled to remain conscious. "It has been so long since I have faced a worthy adversary, Jethro," Nyarlathotep said, letting the Green Lama go as he shifted back to Egyptian form. "Let us make this an even fight."

Without hesitation, the Green Lama swung a powerful roundhouse kick, hitting Nyarlathotep square in the jaw. Turning with the blow, Nyarlathotep seemed aroused by the sensation. "My, that almost hurt." Then, with a wolfish grin, "Hit me again."

When the Green Lama refused, Nyarlathotep grabbed the Green Lama's left wrist. "I said, 'Hit me again!'"

Striking Nyarlathotep with his right fist, the Green Lama sent the demon staggering back, a deep black crack scouring the side of his tan face. Nyarlathotep touched the wound, in shock.

"What's the matter, Nyarlathotep?" the Green Lama asked cordially, smoke wafting off the Jade Tablet. "Can't take a punch?"

Nyarlathotep's face twisted in anger. His fingers extended out into obsidian blades. Hissing, he leapt forward, swinging wildly.

Anticipating the attack, the Green Lama flew up into the air. "Or, is it the Jade Tablet that you can't handle?" he asked as he blasted Nyarlathotep with a ball of energy before swinging down and punching the ancient evil in the gut with his ringed fist. Nyarlathotep crumpled over, cursing in a forgotten tongue. "Tell me, Nyarlathotep, if you are truly a god as you claim, then why can a human bear the Jade Tablet while it cripples you?"

"Insolence!" Nyarlathotep screeched.

"You talk of prophecy," the Green Lama said as he continued to strike Nyarlathotep with the Jade Tablet. "You kill innocents in the name of 'god.' Align yourself with the cancer of this era. You have hunted me and mine for so long, you, more than anyone, should know that I will fight to the death to stop you."

"Honestly, Jethro," Nyarlathotep said, his body lined with black cracks, "that is exactly what I was hoping for." He caught the Green Lama's next attack and violently twisted his arm out of its socket. The Green Lama screamed in pain and collapsed onto the wing. Grabbing him by the hair, Nyarlathotep lifted him up until they were eye to eye. "No more speeches, Jethro. No more games. We have a prophecy to catch," he said, slamming the Green Lama's head into the propeller. The blades shattered against his skull, metallic shards bursting out into the wind.

An explosion sounded off the right wing, shaking the plane's very frame. A painful metallic screech and whine of a dying whale echoed through the ship.

"Did you feel that?" Ken asked, his voice cracking as he struggled to tighten the safety belts.

Rick bared his teeth in pain as he read over the dials. His hands wrapped around the controls, his knuckles bone white. "We just lost our right propeller," he rumbled as beads of sweat began bubbling on his forehead.

What little color remained in Ken's face quickly drained. "What?!" he shrieked.

Rick picked up the intercom. "All right boys and girls, play time's over. Better come inside quick. This is gonna get real rough, real fast."

"What just happened?" Jean asked moments later when she and Caraway ran into the cockpit.

Rick raised his eyebrows and scoffed. "Your *boyfriend* happened."

"We're crashing," Ken added weakly.

"We're crashing?!" Jean exclaimed.

"We're gonna crash?!" Caraway shouted.

"What is it with this crew? Can't seem to grasp the basic concept of gravity," Rick grumbled as he fought with the controls. "I'm going to try and glide her in for a water landing, but won't make any promises."

"Wait, what about Jethro?" Jean asked, her voice wavering.

"Green Sleeves can handle himself," Rick replied, though he sounded less than certain. He thumbed back toward the cabin. "Best thing you can do right now is strap your asses in and pray to whatever god you believe in. After we land—if we're still alive—there should be an inflatable raft stored at the front of the passenger's cabin. We'll use that to get us over to Rye Land, or whatever the hell it's called. Got it?"

"Yeah," Caraway said with a nod, turning toward the cabin.

"They got him," Jean whispered.

They followed her gaze, watching as a tall, tanned man dragged an unconscious Green Lama by his hood across the sky.

Caraway lightly placed a hand on Jean's shoulder. "Come on, Jean. Let's worry about saving him after— *if* we survive this."

Jean shut her eyes and nodded. "Okay," she said walking out of the cockpit. Then, glancing back at the looming black island on the horizon, she whispered, "We're coming for you."

The wind buffeted the airplane and the ocean rapidly approached.

Creatures of indescribable horror began attacking from all angles, snapping the wings in half, shattering windows. Beaks and claws pierced through the hull, screeching alien voices echoing around them. Jean dug her nails into her armrest, her knuckles turning white as she watched the twisted, organic shape of R'lyeh tower above them.

"We're goin' down!" Rick screamed over the loudspeaker. "We're goin' down!"

"Hang on!" Caraway shouted.

Ken sealed his eyes shut. "God, I hate flying…"

"All right, Prometheus," Jean said. "Here we go." As the plane hit the water, she kept her eyes on R'lyeh, but all she could think about was Jethro Dumont.

The engines exploded and all was pain.

Chapter 18
ATTACK OF THE SHOGGOTH

Bodhisattva, *what are you doing?" Tsarong asked as Dumont hurriedly tore apart his room, packing what few possessions he owned into a small knapsack.*

"Don't *call me that!" Dumont shouted, throwing his bag to the ground.* "Don't ever *call me that again!"*

Taken aback, Tsarong stuttered. "I... Jethro, I don't understand."

"This!" Dumont exclaimed, indicating the Jade Tablet bound to his flesh. The skin around the rainbow ring of hair was ripped and bleeding, as if he had been trying to dig the ring out. "I never wanted this! Any of it! I just wanted to find peace!"

"But, Jethro... Destiny doesn't ask us if—"

Dumont threw a clay bowl to the ground, shattering it. "No! Do not speak to me of destiny! I don't want to hear it! I'm just some rich boy forced into the games of the gods and I'm through playing!"

Tsarong looked at his friend with pity. "Jethro, destiny does not give you a choice."

"That is where we disagree, Tsarong," Dumont said, shaking his head. *"And I have made mine."*

The ground reminded Gan of coral, covered in jumbled and intricate designs. Puddles of seawater and dying fish brought up from the darkest depths of oceans surrounded him, flopping mindlessly in the southern sun. A massive obsidian gate loomed over them; its surface etched with alien words and symbols, pictographs that put the human mind on edge. It was as awe inspiring as it was terrifying. The smell, however, was unbearable; it was all Gan could do not to wretch. A cacophony of maddening shrieks resounded high above them. Looking up, Gan shielded his eyes from the sun to find the sky filled with creatures attacking an approaching plane. A small green dot fell out of the plane before flying out to engage the unearthly creatures, ripping through them like tissue paper. A lump formed in his throat. It was Dumont, he was certain.

"Do not worry, Herr Oberführer," Heydrich said limping over, his wounded eye hanging loose in its socket. "Dumont might be a man of strength, but I can assure you, he is no match for the power of the Great Old Ones."

"If that is so, Heydrich, then how do you plan on controlling them?"

"It will not be a matter of control. Rather, it will be a matter of common goals."

"And what goals are those?"

"Conquer the world, of course," Heydrich said.

"With the Führer on the throne, of course."

Heydrich's smile thinned. "Of course."

"Ironic isn't it, then, that Hirsch wanted the same thing?"

The Nazi mystic eyed Gan suspiciously. "Yes. I suppose it is. It is unfortunate that he did not share our vision."

"*Mein Gott*," Gottschalk said moments later, watching the spectacle above. "We are living in a fantasy. This is not possible."

"Oh, it is quite possible, sir," Heydrich said. "Just because you do not see the seams in the world does not mean they do not exist."

An explosion sounded from the sky, and the silver plane lost its right propeller in a flash of fire. Two small dots flew away from the damaged plane. His heart racing, Gan knew what it meant.

Heydrich smiled broadly, black ooze leaking through his teeth. "It seems we won't have to worry about our friends much longer."

Smoke trailed out from the ship's engine as it dove toward the ocean. Creatures of all shapes and horrors came at it from every angle, ruining the once proud machine. Gan followed its descent until it fell behind the towers of R'lyeh, wincing at the explosion that echoed out seconds later.

A shadow fell over them. Looking up, they watched Nyarlathotep descend, tossing a pile of green cloths before them. "Gentlemen," the ancient creature said with relish, his new face cracked like old paint. "I present to you, Jethro Dumont, the Green Lama."

Gan knelt down and pulled aside the hood, his stomach dropping as he revealed Dumont's face.

"Is he alive?" Gottschalk asked.

"For now," Heydrich answered wickedly.

Pain. White, searing pain.

Someone was shouting. "Move, move, move!!"

"She's bleeding, she's bleeding!"

Water, knee deep and rising.

"Wake up, come on! Wake up!"

Someone grabbed her, lifted her out of her seat.

"Toss the raft out! Quickly!"

She could hear whispers, voices beneath the shouting, familiar, almost human.

"Caraway! Come on, dammit!"

"I ain't goin' in there unarmed!"

"You wait any longer you're gonna be stayin' here!"

Her vision was blurred and red. "What…?" she groaned.

"Ken! Ken, you got her?"

"I got her. Christmas, how does someone so thin weigh so much?"

"Prometheus," she murmured.

"Hang in there, Jean. We're almost out of here."

She was floating, the sun above her, the blue sky littered with black swarms. A sharp shadow fell over her. Tilting her head up she gazed up at the monolith and murmured, "R'lyeh."

"This thing just keeps going from bad to worse," Caraway said, as they paddled away from the crash. Bits of flaming wreckage floated by while the plane gurgled down to a watery grave.

Rick let out a gruff laugh as he paddled forward. "You think this is bad, you shoulda seen what me and Twin Eagle went through in India. The Thugee are no joke. How's our girl doing?" he asked Ken.

Her head resting in his lap, Ken cleaned the wound on Jean's forehead with a torn handkerchief. Frowning, he said: "In and out. I can hear her murmur something every so often, but other than that…" He shook his head.

"Jean's a tough girl. She'll pull through," Caraway said. He shielded his eyes as he looked up at the walled structure floating in front of them. "Hopefully, before we get inside the city."

"And how do we plan on doing that exactly?" Rick asked.

"The Gates," Jean groaned, her voice monotone. "Through the Gates, with the broken key."

"Oh, boy," Rick sighed. "She's talking crazy."

Her eyes fluttered open as she shook her head, tentatively placing a hand on the wound on her forehead. "You're all heart, Masters," she said groggily as she propped herself up on her elbows.

"You okay, Red?" Ken asked.

"Head's killing me," she said, rubbing her temples. "Not sure if it's the gash, the voices running around inside my skull, the Tablets, or all of the above." She leaned forward and brought out the two glowing Jade Tablets from their respective bags. Her brow furrowed as she lifted the Tablets and looked over their engraved surfaces. "I'm gonna vote all of the above."

Ken bit his lip nervously. "This like the time you heard the voices at the Rabbi's?"

Jean nodded slowly. "Kinda, except it's a bit more... refined. I can sorta understand them a bit better."

Rick raised an eyebrow. "You're hearing voices?"

"Something like that," Jean replied. "Call 'em visions."

"Because that's better?"

"Listen, buddy, I've been to the future and back. I've seen how bad things get if we screw the pooch. This precognition—or whatever you wanna call it—might be the only thing we have to win this," she shot back.

Rick rolled his eyes. "No offense, lady, I've been up and down this globe, but hokey religions and weird visions are no match for a good pistol at your side."

"You'd think, by now, you'd take a leap of faith," Ken said sharply. "Talk to us, Red, how do we get in?"

Jean shrugged. "How do you think? The front entrance."

By his count there were a little over a hundred Nazis on the narrow coral platform before the immense black gates; a U-Boat docked nearby. Nyarlathotep and Heydrich stood closest to the entrance, the Green Lama unconscious at their feet. Moving back around the corner, Ken related this to the others.

"Do you see Vasili?" Caraway asked.

Ken shook his head. "If he's there, they're hiding him pretty good."

"Probably in the U-boat," Jean observed. "Keeping him close to the vest, so to speak. What about Gan?"

"Looks like he's got a bad limp," Ken nodded. "But, other than that, he's seems okay."

Caraway huffed, his fingers finding his pistol. "Give me a clear shot and he won't be much longer."

Jean eyed Caraway. "John, if it weren't for him, none of us would have made it out of the ruins alive."

"Tell that to Sotiria," Caraway bit back.

"Let's see if we can get closer," Rick said. "Maybe we can do something to stop them before they get inside."

Jean shook her head. "We're outnumbered at least five to one, not counting the creatures up there," she said pointing her pistol to the sky. "We make any kinda fuss, we're dead. But some more reconnaissance won't hurt, that way if anything goes down we'll be ready for it."

"What do you think is gonna happen?" Ken asked Jean.

"Hopefully not the end of the world."

"The Gates of R'lyeh," Nyarlathotep breathed. He pressed his hand against the cold black coral. "How many millennia have passed since I last gazed upon you? So much power within, begging to be released." He half-turned to Heydrich and extended his other hand. "Karl, the Shard, if you will."

Heydrich removed the Shard from its scabbard. Bowing his head, he silently handed it to Nyarlathotep.

Looking at the Nazi forces, Nyarlathotep smiled. "My friends! In my previous form I promised you power unimaginable. I promised you the keys to the kingdom. I promised you the world. And though my face has changed, I fully intend to stand by my word." Nyarlathotep drove the Shard into a hidden keyhole, sliding the crystalline blade all the way in up to the hilt. A loud hum echoed through the air as the gateway began to open inwards and inhuman screams echoed out. Several Nazi soldiers inched back toward the U-boat, shooting into the shadowed innards of the city out of instinct. Gan could feel his heart hammer against his chest. His hands shook uncontrollably.

Nyarlathotep removed the Shard and handed it back to Heydrich. Throwing his arms out he turned to the Nazis. "Now, my friends, come and see the power that is Cthulhu."

"Plan," Ken whispered as they watched Nyarlathotep drag the Green Lama into the city, closely followed by Heydrich and a large contingent of Nazis. "Please tell me someone has a plan."

"Jean," Caraway said, chewing the inside of his cheek. "You're our local prophet, what do we do now?"

"What've we got to work with?" she asked, gesturing at the small stash of weaponry they had freed from the plane.

"Six pistols, some additional ammo, two grenades," Caraway enumerated. "Not enough to stop Armageddon, but enough to keep us fighting."

Nodding, Jean quickly devised a plan. "Okay. We'll do this in teams of two and split everything up evenly, three guns per pair, one grenade each. John, you and Rick take the raft and the Second Tablet around to get inside the U-boat, see if you can find Vasili," she said as she checked her pistols. "He's the last piece of the puzzle. We get him, we've got a shot at stopping this thing."

"What about you and Clayton?" Rick asked.

"Ken and I are taking the Third Tablet and going after Jethro," she replied.

"Flip that around," Rick said. "It'll be safer for you out here."

"'Fraid I can't handle it 'cause I'm a woman? That what you're trying to get at, Masters? Don't forget you're still new to this dance and you still don't know the steps. Follow my lead and you might make it out of this alive." Jean said quietly and evenly. "And the next time you even insinuate I can't handle something 'cause I'm a woman, you'll be two balls short. We clear?"

Rick blinked and quickly nodded in understanding.

"Good," Jean said before briskly turning away.

"Wow," Rick whispered. "Bit of a pistol, isn't she?"

Ken smiled. "That's why we love her."

"And where do we find you?" Caraway asked after Jean.

"Follow the sound of gunfire," she said without looking back. "We'll probably be at the center of it."

Jethro awoke in darkness. It wasn't just the absence of light—he couldn't open his eyes. Nor could he hear, smell, taste or even speak, as though his mind was cut off from most of his body. He could still feel, however, the one sense that refused to be dampened. Pain radiated out from his bones, his muscles rang in agony. This sensation, more than anything, assured him that he was, at least for the moment, still alive, which meant there was still time however brief. He was being dragged, that much he could determine, his body scraped against the jagged yet slimy ground, the harsh surface ripping into his skin.

The last thing he remembered was seeing the plane's propellers explode. Had the others survived? And if they had, what then? While he didn't doubt Rick's capabilities, what would they do once they landed? Discounting R'lyeh, they were near the Pacific pole of inaccessibility, over a thousand miles from the nearest landmass. They couldn't escape, which meant they had only one option.

They were going to try and save him.

Though it filled him with dread, he was admittedly unsurprised. He had allied himself with Caraway, Ken, Rick and especially Jean because of their heart and strength of will. All of them had chosen to risk their lives, despite all logic time and time again, simply to do what was *right*. He still recalled, with some amusement, watching Jean run into a room full of mobsters without hesitation, guns blazing. She would no doubt be leading the charge into R'lyeh.

In fact, she always would, Jethro realized. No matter what would happen, Jean Farrell would always be there, not just for him, but also for anyone who might need her. She was brash and bullheaded, but she always aimed true. It was in part why he loved her, her inherent selflessness, a trait many Buddhists spent decades working to achieve.

And yet… What would that mean should they survive this? What sort of life would they have together? What sort of sacrifices would they be forced to make?

Before his mind could go any further, he felt something suddenly dig into the skin of his right hand, trying to pry the Jade Tablet loose. As flesh was ripped from bone, even his thoughts were screams.

"Where do you think they're taking him?" Ken asked Jean as they moved through the city's dark, narrow, and ever curving streets. The streets and the towers around them were silent, seemingly devoid of any recognizable form of life, but Jean and Ken were no less wary.

"To the temple," Jean whispered. "Where Cthulhu sleeps."

"And where will that be?"

"If you were an ancient alien god and the leader of a million year old cult where would *you* want your house to be?"

"The center."

"Exactly. That way everything's leading to you," she said peeking around a corner. "Quick, head into that alleyway." She indicated the shadowed passage to their right, the walls of the surrounding buildings curling over like frozen waves.

"What is this place made of?" Ken asked once they were undercover. He peered closely at the strange material that made up the textured walls around them. He tentatively ran his fingers over the undulating surface, brining them back coated in slime. "It's like some kind of color out of space. It doesn't even look like this stuff was even *built*. More like it was *grown*. And crazy as it sounds, I think this city is bigger on the inside than it was from the outside. It took us, what, five minutes to circle it in the raft? We've been running through this maze for almost thirty minutes now. How can that be— "

Jean pressed her hand over his mouth. "Ken," she whispered. "As much I love your musings, I really need you to stop talking."

Ken nodded in understanding. Pointing their pistols at the entrance to the alleyway, they waited in silence as something large slithered closer. Sweat trickled down Ken's forehead while Jean carefully cocked her pistols.

A long, faintly luminescent protoplasmic tentacle rounded the corner, the end of which bubbled out and split open to reveal a hateful green and yellow eye.

"Aw hell," Ken groaned. "More monsters."

"Go go go!" Jean shouted, pulling Ken away from the entrance as a fifteen foot amorphous creature flowed into the alleyway, multiple eyes forming and un-forming as it rushed toward them. Two mandibles extended out from the gelatinous mass, striking at their heels, shattering the ground.

"I'm going back into acting," Ken screamed as they ran. "No more of this adventure shit ever again, I swear to God!"

"Ken," Jean shouted, vainly firing behind her. "*Shut up!*"

"*Wo ist der Bank, bitte?*" someone called from the entryway.

The soldier walked up to the ladder and looked up through the portal. "*Was hast Du gerade gesagt?*" A loud *pop!* echoed down as a bloody hole appeared in the soldier's forehead. He dropped to the ground, dead.

"What did you ask him?" Rick asked Caraway as they slid down the ladder.

"I wanted to know where I could find the bank. I think," Caraway replied as he stole a Lüger off the dead trooper. "One of my officers taught me a little German while I was working with Gan, but he didn't know that much."

"I know some French, but I doubt that'll be any help right now."

Caraway shrugged. "Eh, try it out. Might throw them into a tizzy."

"Heh," Rick chuckled. "Why the hell not? *Je pars chez les Boches me taper leurs putes!*" he shouted.

Instantly, two German soldiers appeared in the narrow hallway, both of whom Rick and Caraway quickly dispatched.

"That was easy," Caraway laughed. "What did you say?"

"It's not exactly a sentence if I clean it up," Rick smiled wickedly.

Caraway raised a quizzical eyebrow; then, when Rick translated, "Jeez, if I was them I would have wanted to kill you, too."

"Huh, yeah," Rick chuckled. "I get that a lot. Come on, let's find your boy."

"I don't care what you smell, just get in there!" Jean shouted as she kicked Ken into a large shaft.

Glancing back over her shoulder she saw the gelatinous creature slither around the corner, its glowing green eyes staring at her. A mouth formed, a gaping hole filled with garish, razor sharp teeth, chomping down. As it lunged toward her, it howled, "Shhhhoggggooooth!"

Without hesitating, Jean fired, one of its eyes exploding in a mess of greenish-black goo. She jumped down the shaft backwards, her pistol trained on the opening as she slid into darkness. Seconds later, the creature burst into the narrow tube after her. Shooting the beast had proven futile, and with her bullets running low, her options were limited. Eyeing a small crack running down the ceiling of the pipe's coral-like structure, Jean fired a single shot at the fracture. The break quickly spread, crumbling up before ultimately crashing down onto the amorphous monster.

"Woo!" she exclaimed with a cocked grin as the creature exploded beneath shattered rock. Her expression quickly changed as the ceiling continued to crumble, huge chunks of coral tumbling down after her. "Aw, shit."

"Come on, wake up," Caraway said, lightly slapping Vasili on the cheeks while Rick undid his bindings.

"John?" Vasili groaned. "John, is that you?"

Caraway smiled sadly, remembering how much this man had recently lost. "Yup, it's me, in the flesh."

"My head…" Vasili squeezed his eyes shut, visibly in pain. "…Where am I?"

Caraway glanced up at the low ceiling. "A German U-Boat. Submarine, as we Yanks like to call 'em."

"All right, he's good," Rick said as he removed the last of the bindings before moving to guard the exit.

"Here, let me help you up," Caraway said, bracing Vasili as he stumbled off his cot.

His knees buckling, Vasili asked, "How did I get here?"

Caraway's face was unreadable. "Long story."

"I hear a voice…" Vasili mumbled. "It's telling me to wait, that my time is almost at hand. It sounds like Alexei's."

"Just bad dreams," Caraway reassured him.

Vasili looked toward Caraway like a scared child. "What about Sotiria? Where is she?"

Caraway's gaze fell to the floor. "I'll explain later," he said. He handed Rick the satchel containing the stone Jade Tablet, then put an arm under Vasili to help him carry his weight as they took a tentative step forward. "First things first, Armageddon."

"Armageddon?"

"Yeah, real bad news, like a rash that won't go away," Caraway said briskly as they moved past Rick toward the exit.

Vasili furrowed his brow at Rick. "Who are you?"

"Rick Masters. Pilot, hero, supporting character," Rick replied. Then, to Caraway, "This boy always asks so many questions?"

"He's usually the strong silent type, but he's been through a lot recently."

"I can only imagine," Rick grumbled to himself.

Ken splashed face first into the murky black pool, rolling end over end, losing all sense of direction. His lungs burning, he swam furiously until his head broke through the surface. Gasping, he wiped the opaque liquid from his eyes only to find himself in darkness. Seconds later, he heard Jean tumble down the pipeline, screaming several choice expletives before hitting the water. Turning toward the sound, he hollered, "Jean! Jean? Where are you?"

"Ken!" she coughed. "Ken, get clear!"

"What?"

"Get clear!" she shouted as the avalanche fell upon them.

"Jesus H. Christ, this place is a goddamn maze," Rick grumbled as he and Caraway carried the semiconscious Vasili through the curving streets. They had been moving through the city for the better part of a half hour and were no closer to finding Jean and Ken. "How the hell are we supposed to know where to go?"

Caraway shook his head. "Jean said to listen for gunfire. Not that we could hear it if we tried."

"Go to the center, to the temple," Vasili mumbled. "Follow the path, left, right, right, left, straight, right, right, left…"

Rick grimaced in befuddlement as Vasili rambled on. "What the hell is he sayin'?"

Caraway listened intently, trying to remember the order of the words the best he could. "He's tellin' us where to go."

A boot hit him in the face, cracking a tooth.

"Wake up, Dumont," Heydrich shouted. He kicked again, breaking Jethro's nose. "Wake up, you damn *Amerikanisch*!"

"Calm down, Heydrich," Nyarlathotep said. "He's coming around."

Jethro's swollen eyes peeled open. He was in a small domed room, curled in a fetal position in a narrow pillar of sunlight. The cylindrical walls were covered in algae and barnacles. Heydrich and Nyarlathotep stood above him. The former was dressed in a black ceremonial robe, a dark shadow of Jethro's own. The latter was adorned with vestments similar to those seen in the ancient hieroglyphics of Egypt, the *Necronomicon* in his hands. Both men—if they could be called that anymore—appeared to be in an advance state of decay.

"Where are the others?" he weakly asked as he painfully pushed himself up onto his knees.

Heydrich raised a torn eyebrow. "Your friends in the airplane? They are, I believe the expression is, 'in Davey Jones' Locker.'"

Jethro struggled to swallow the lump in his throat. "I do not believe you."

"Believe it or not, I could care less, Dumont," Heydrich said with a shrug. He began to circle around Jethro. "The fact of the matter is you and I have reached the point where our paths finally diverge. And whereas you once left me to rot in the snows of Tibet, I will leave you to bleed at Cthulhu's feet."

"Do not get ahead of yourself, Heydrich," Nyarlathotep scolded. "There is still the matter of the ring."

Jethro stole a glance at the Jade Tablet around his finger; the skin around the ring was raw but healing, flecks of blood covering the rainbow fiber. A rueful smile curled his lips. "Tried to take it off did you?" He looked at Nyarlathotep. "I figured you would have learned better."

With a vacant expression, Nyarlathotep backhanded Jethro. Blood spurted out of his mouth. Wiping the blood away with his sleeve, Jethro chuckled. "Are you going to beat me until I tell you how to remove the Tablet? I would have thought *gods* would have much more powerful means of persuasion."

"I've *seen* you take it off, Dumont!" Heydrich shrieked, grabbing Jethro's right arm and twisting it until the shoulder snapped free. Jethro grunted, but refused to give Heydrich the satisfaction of a scream. He felt something weigh down the edge of his sleeve, hitting against his arm, rattling quietly like a saltshaker.

"There are rules, Heydrich," Jethro said through gritted teeth. "Laws by which we must abide. The Tablet has will all its own, revealing its truths only to those who have earned them!"

Heydrich unsheathed the Shard and pressed its serrated point against the soft spot under Jethro's chin. "Perhaps we kill you? We have read that is one way to free the Tablet from its perch."

Jethro chuckled. "That is true, but if that were ever your plan you would have already done so."

Heydrich hesitated, stealing a glance at Nyarlathotep. "Perhaps, I wanted the pleasure of—"

Jethro started to laugh hysterically.

"Stop laughing!" Heydrich hissed. "I *will* kill you!"

"I have no doubt you will," Jethro said through the laughter. "But you and I both know that you need me alive to raise Cthulhu. Save your *phurba* for the actual sacrifice and leave the theatrics for those with talent."

Heydrich let go of Jethro's arm as Nyarlathotep snatched the crystalline blade away from him.

"You called it *phurba*," Nyarlathotep said, examining the blade. "I suppose you might consider it that; a ritualistic blade. And yes, in many ways, you'd be right. But it is so much more than that."

"It's a piece of the Third Jade Tablet, the 'Fire from Olympus,'" Jethro said. "And it's the same blade you used to kill that poor woman at Samothrace."

"You've been paying attention." Nyarlathotep smiled. "Tell me, Jethro, have you ever wondered why you of *all* the people in the world were chosen to bear the Sacred Colors?" He cocked his head. "Never once asked your former Tulku, Tsarong, or any of the other lamas why *you* became the Green Lama? No, of course you did. You probably asked every day, but they never gave a *real* answer, did they? Do you know the secret Tsarong kept hidden from you? What they had been training you for since the day you took on the Jade Tablet?" Nyarlathotep leaned forward so his cracked lips almost touched Jethro's ear. "Well, then, let me tell you," he whispered as he opened the *Necronomicon*, showing Jethro an image of a man dressed in green robes being brutally sacrificed before a squid-faced dragon "You are the Promised One, the Scion, heralded millennia ago for one single purpose: You were born to raise Cthulhu."

Chapter 19
CTHULHU RISES

*D*umont paced the cabin like a caged tiger, his hands firmly placed in his pockets, every so often glancing out the porthole as Bombay disappeared over the horizon. The ship's horns sounded. He was heading home. He chewed his lower lip, unable to quell the war within his mind. He had convinced himself he wasn't running away; he was simply taking the next step in his path. He had discovered all he could in Tibet, he had become a Bodhisattva, one who dedicated his life to the wellbeing of others, and now he would bring the Dharma to America and help all those who were lost.

And the ring on his finger, glowing subtly in the sunlight? It was nothing more than a trinket given by the natives. It was better to think of it that way. Safer.

He risked a glance at the ancient Tibetan man meditating on the cabin floor, now looking older more than ever. "I never asked you to come with me."

"No, you did not," Tsarong replied without opening his eyes.

Dumont nodded silently and returned to gazing out the window.

An hour passed before Tsarong spoke again. "We are but pebbles on the shore."

"Hm?" Dumont sounded, puzzled.

Tsarong smiled. "Oh, it is just that you and I have been sitting here in silence for so long I thought it best that I should say something that sounded profound."

Dumont laughed. "Pebbles on the shore. Yes, I remember…" He paused for a moment and then said quietly: "You belong at the Temple of the Clouds."

Tsarong tilted his head and gave Dumont a small smile. "Do I? You are my Tulku and my friend. I could not let you leave alone."

"You were my Tulku first," Dumont reminded him.

Tsarong's smile broadened. "Then ever more the reason I stay with you."

"New York is no place for men like you. It is a dangerous city, full of arrogance and greed."

"Is that why you so wish to return?"

Dumont placed his hands behind his back. "It is a city I understand," he said reluctantly. *"I speak its language, know its rhythms. I can navigate its canyons, its rivers. It is my home."*

"Truly? And so sure are you that you know it so well after ten years abroad?" Tsarong retorted. *Opening his eyes, he gazed at Dumont who looked so much like the young boy who had once walked through the mountains in search of his destiny. "We shall both be strangers in a strange land, Tulku. Would it not be preferable to take this new journey in tandem? Though if you feel otherwise,"* he said with slight bow of his head, *"then our paths shall diverge once we make the port of New York City."*

Dumont chuckled at that. "Fair enough, Tsarong. But don't say I never warned you."

Jean hacked out water as she brought her head above the surface, finding only darkness. "Ken!" she coughed, treading water. "Ken, you still with me?"

"Yeah," he said weakly nearby. "Yeah, I'm still here… If I knew where 'here' was…"

She tried to peer through the darkness when she noticed a faint green light emanating from the water. "Hold on a second." She reached into her satchel, brought out the Third Jade Tablet and raised it above her head, the room instantly filling with green light, revealing Ken wading inches in front of her.

"Look at that," Ken marveled. "It's also a night light."

"The wonders never cease," she said sardonically.

"Where the hell are we?" Ken asked, looking up at the black expanse above them, echoes of images hidden within the shadows of the ceiling.

"You got me," Jean voiced as she glanced around, noticing a long spiral stone staircase across the pool. "Looks like we can climb out over there."

"Do you think the Lama will ever get tired of this stuff?" Ken asked as they swam over.

"How do you mean?"

"This adventuring stuff, being a costumed vigilante, running around saving the day all the time. Do you think he'll, I dunno, *retire*?"

"Y'know, Ken," she said as pulled herself out of the water, "I never really thought about it."

"But if you two ever get hitched, how would that work?" he asked as Jean helped him on to the platform.

"Little soon for marrying us off don't you think?"

"Maybe I'm just traditional," he said with a shrug.

Jean screwed her face. "And I completely believe that."

"All right," he conceded. "But, even if you two just go steady, what sorta life would that be?"

"I don't know," she replied, her expression unreadable.

They began climbing the stones stairs, running two steps at a time until their legs became sore. The stairwell gradually became more and more illuminated as they made their way, enough so that they could begin to see shapes form around them.

"Hey, look at that," Ken said after several minutes, indicating the massive shadowed figure suspended high overhead. "What do you suppose that is?"

Jean risked a glance. A pit formed in her stomach as the green light shone off the thousands of man-sized scales. "To tell ya the truth, Ken, I'm not sure I wanna know."

"Okay, was it 'left, right, right' or 'right, left, left?'" Caraway asked as they reach a fork in the road.

Rick glanced back in the direction they came. "I thought we just did 'left, right, right."

"No, we just did 'left, left, right.'" Caraway looked at Vasili hoping he would have an answer, but the other man had slipped back into unconsciousness. "Come on, Vasili," he said under his breath. "Help us out here…"

"Who builds a city like this?" Rick grumbled. "No straight lines, everything made outta coral. Doesn't make any goddamn sense."

"Aliens," Caraway replied. "Really ancient aliens."

"Oh," Rick blinked with bewilderment. "Well, of course."

Jethro's whole body shook, sweat poured down his face. Could it be true? Was he really destined to bring about the end of the world? Everything he had done, all the injustice he had fought, was it all leading to this? Was his only true purpose in this realm to resurrect its greatest evil?

No, he refused to believe that. No matter prophecy or the words of demons, he would not succumb.

"Terrifying, isn't it?" Heydrich smiled. It was just the two of them now, alone in the small coral cell. "Being at death's door, knowing that in moments you will face the abyss and there is nothing you can do to stop it?"

Jethro glared at him. "I have no fear of death and no fear of you or your masters; the Führer or your false god. No matter what that creature says, I know the Dharma and my destiny."

"Buddhist fool!" Heydrich said. "So focused on your Dharma, you are blind to what is right in front you… You took away all that I was, for what? To save some native child? Look at what I've become!" he screamed, tearing a loose chunk of flesh from his face and holding it before Jethro. Black ooze spilled from the wound, down his neck, soaking his robes. "No more human than a vacant shell. This is on your head. Just as every single death that will come out of Cthulhu's rise. Every screaming child, every tormented woman, every crucified man. All the pain and agony that will be born into the world will all share one father: Jethro Dumont."

"This is all about *vengeance*?" Jethro gasped. He forced himself to his feet and grabbed Heydrich by the collar. "You've been conspiring with the greatest evils in existence, murdering innocents, bringing about the end of the world… *all to punish me*?"

"They say revenge is a dish best served cold, no?" Heydrich said, brushing Jethro's hands aside. "For me, it shall be a banquet."

Jethro stumbled back, lost for words.

"Make peace with your gods, Buddhist," Heydrich said as he exited the cell, "because in a few moments, you shall meet mine."

As the sphincter-like door sealed shut, Jethro fell down to his hands and knees, lost. Something in his right cuff *clinked* against the ground. Curious, he pulled at the torn seam and a small glass vial fell into his hand.

He chuckled softly as a smile broke his lips.

"Thank you, Tulku."

They found themselves on a large balcony overlooking an enormous hollowed out cavern, one side completely bathed in shadow. There was no singular source of light; it was the walls themselves that were glowing. A wide plateau of coral sat a hundred feet below them, the sharp cliff edge cut by the darkness. A narrow peninsula extended out from the center, like a dagger in the night; a small mound sat at the precipice. Jean could just make out the human handprint pressed into the coral. Two small terraces could be seen on either end of the horseshoe balcony, both in line with the mound at the center below. Intricate carvings lined every surface, done with such impossible detail that they seemed to move.

"What is this?" Ken asked Jean.

She swallowed the lump in her throat. "The Temple of Cthulhu."

Ken shot her a panicked expression. "Please tell me you're joking."

Jean shook her head. "No, this is it. This is where it all ends. Win or lose, the fate of the world gets decided here."

"Well. No pressure."

"Believe me, Ken, we don't wanna mess this up." She walked to the parapet and looked over the Temple. She pressed her tongue against her cheek in thought. "That's where the Tablets go," she said, pointing at the two terraces and the mound below. "We put 'em in place, we can stop Cthulhu. One to rise, three to—"

"Do you hear that?" Ken asked.

Jean cocked her head and listened for a moment when she heard the sound of hundreds of footsteps approaching, marching in time.

Caraway pressed his hand against the circular membrane, the spongy material holding his handprint for several seconds before retracting. "What in baby Jesus is this?"

"It's a door," Vasili said as he freed himself from Caraway's grip and stumbled forward.

"Well," Caraway grumbled, "how the hell do you open it?"

Vasili ran his hands across the door's gooey, spongy surface, stroking it like a pet. "You have to ask it," he said. Seconds later the membrane pulled open, revealing a long stairway leading upward.

"Oh, great," Rick groaned. "Stairs."

The door membrane contracted open as Heydrich and Nyarlathotep returned with Gan and Gottschalk. They found Dumont standing calmly in the center of the cell, his hands placed behind his back.

"*Guten Tag, Meine Herren,*" Dumont said warmly. "*Schade, dass wir uns treffen müssen unter solchen Umständen.*"

"Herr Dumont," Gan said with a slight bow of his head, his tone mournful. His friend Caraway was dead, as were Farrell and Clayton, killed during their approach to R'lyeh. Now only minutes remained for Dumont. Years of planning, of fighting the enemy from within, all of it was for nothing. "Indeed, it is a pity."

"It is time, Dumont," Heydrich said with a horrific grin.

"Yes," Dumont nodded without emotion. "Yes, I suppose it is."

Nyarlathotep silently walked around Dumont and placed a hand on each wrist. Black ooze grew out from Nyarlathotep's fingertips, binding Dumont's arms together.

As they led Dumont out, only Gan noticed the small pile of shattered glass and flecks of salt. A hallow smile formed on his lips and hope sparked his eyes.

"Look down there," Ken said as a steady stream of Nazi soldiers flowed in through a large doorway at the back of the Temple. They were soon joined by a medley of creatures, from Deep Ones to shoggoths, flying polyps to nightmarish dragons, marching in unison until they filled the plateau, leaving a narrow aisle leading toward the peninsula.

Jean's face silently steeled over. Her knuckles turned white as the Third Tablet rattled in her hands.

"Another sacrifice?" Gan whispered to Gottschalk as they marched into the Temple. "Sir, what have we allied ourselves with?"

Gottschalk glanced around nervously at the incalculable creatures surrounding them. "I no longer know."

"We must not let these monsters go through with this horror," Gan pleaded, gripping Gottschalk's arm.

"We do as the Führer commands," Gottschalk said, his voice cracking.

"Even at the cost of our souls?" Gan asked sharply.

Gottschalk sighed and looked to Gan with a glassy gaze. "Is it such a large price to pay for the safety of Germany?"

Caraway, Rick, and Vasili found themselves on a large horseshoe terrace overlooking the Temple floor as Jethro was being dragged before the mound. Glancing across the way Caraway caught sight of Jean, who waved silently and pointed toward the far end the horseshoe balcony.

"Well, looks like the gang's all here," Caraway whispered as he waved back in understanding; that was where they needed to place their Tablet.

"What's going on?" Rick asked, looking down at the throng of Nazis and monsters.

Caraway risked a glance down and swallowed the lump in his throat, remembering those horrible moments before Sotiria was killed. He felt a familiar scratching at the base of his spine, the thousand whispers of demons echoed in the back of his skull. He pitched his eyes shut and pushed the sensation away. He was stronger than them, he told himself. They wouldn't take him again. He pushed them away, down back into the depths of hell. He was immune to their touch, he realized, like chickenpox. Then he heard the laughter come from behind him. He forced open his eyes and glanced over at Vasili, whose eyes had suddenly gone black.

"Armageddon," Vasili whispered. A lascivious grin spread across his face as he grabbed Rick and tossed him across the balcony. Rick's head smacked hard against the wall and he dropped unconscious to the ground. Vasili then spun around to Caraway and laughed, "*Iä Iä Cthulhu fhtagn!*"

Silence fell over the temple as Jethro headed the small, final procession into the Temple, followed closely by Nyarlathotep and Heydrich. He could feel a thousand eyes follow him as he made his way toward the end of the coral peninsula. He gazed out into the darkness as a loud buzzing began to echo out from the back of his mind, a thousand mad, screaming voices. The shadows moved and broke open, forming two red, green, and yellow slits. Tentacles slithered out into the light, grasping for him. Reaching the mound, Nyarlathotep forced Jethro to his knees as the black bindings on his arms evaporated. Heydrich then grabbed his right arm and pressed his ringed hand into the imprint. Bright green light erupted from the Jade Tablet, throwing a deathly hue over the massive creature in the darkness. Jethro felt his graze drift away, unable to look at the monstrosity without feeling his mind begin to unhinge.

Nyarlathotep turned to the crowd on the plateau. He raised the *Necronomicon* and screamed. "Now begins the new dawn of Cthulhu!"

Ken braced himself against the parapet. "Oh, God. Jethro…"

Jean's heart hammered against her chest as she watched helplessly, the crystalline egg glowing bright. Everything she had seen, everything she had learned, it was going to be all for naught. She was going to watch the man she loved murdered before her eyes.

And there was nothing she could do.

On the coral peninsula below, Heydrich gripped Jethro by the hair, pulled back his head, and turned his face to the ceiling. Heydrich's eyes burned with madness. A wild grin stretched across his broken and deformed face, a living, breathing nightmare. He held the Shard's glowing serrated edge against Jethro's neck, drawing blood. He leaned in close, his breath like brimstone. "You have no idea how long I've waited for this day, Dumont," he whispered, black ooze dripping down his ruined face. "Truly, I feel as though my whole life has been leading to this day."

"This isn't over, Karl," Jethro said through gritted teeth.

"Oh no, Dumont. I am afraid it is." Heydrich thrust the Shard over his head. "To the end of an era! To the beginning of the next! In the name of the Führer! In the name of the Old Ones! I awaken the Sleeper! *Iä Iä Cthulhu fhtagn!*"

"*Iä Iä Cthulhu fhtagn! Iä Iä Cthulhu fhtagn!*" the Temple thundered in unison.

Jethro's eyes rolled back in his head and he began to whisper: "Salutation to the Buddha. In the language of the gods and in that of the *lus*, in the language of the demons and that of the men, in all the languages that exist, I proclaim the Doctrine..."

"Cthulhu rises!" Heydrich shrieked as he plunged the Shard into Jethro's throat, breaking off a piece of the blade's tip against the spine. He sliced to the side and ripped open the jugular, taking pleasure in the distinct wet sound of shredding tissue. Blood poured down the Green Lama's throat onto the altar, turning his robes a deep maroon. The Temple fell silent as a green beam of light shot out from the mound into the shadows. Then, from all around them, they heard the roar of Cthulhu. Heydrich's heart raced, lusting in the sound. He had done it; he had killed the Green Lama. He raised the Shard over his head once more, the Green Lama's blood dripping down the crystalline blade and onto his arm, staining his sleeve.

"*Iä Iä Cthulhu fhtagn!*" he screamed, feeling the great wizard's hot, sulfurous breath flow over him.

"*Iä Iä Cthulhu fhtagn!*" Nyarlathotep repeated with satisfaction as they both fell to their knees in unison, bowing their heads before their master.

Gan fell a step back, his mind nearing the breaking point as he stared at the hideous god, his hand instinctively reaching for his Lüger. "*Hashem*, no," he whispered.

Beside him, Gottschalk fell to his knees, his face twisted with madness as he screamed, "*Für das Vaterland! Für den Führer!*"

Above on the balcony, Jean covered her mouth and fought back a scream as she slid down the parapet and collapsed to the floor. She sobbed silently as tears streamed down her face. She had failed. It was all over, everything and everyone. This was the end.

Ken crumpled. "Oh, God no," he whispered. "Oh, please God, no."

In the shadows below two broad, leathery wings extended out, eliciting a sound like of breaking bones ripping through skin. The Temple rumbled as bits of stone and coral rained down, punctuated by screams of ecstasy and terror. An immense clawed reptilian hand struck out from the darkness and hooked onto the coral cliff, then the other, the fifteen foot long nails driving into the coral with a deafening crack. Elephantine muscles flexed as the beast pulled itself forward. A pulpy octopus head surmounting a grotesque scaly dragon-like body appeared out of the darkness and roared with a thousand voices.

The Green Lama was dead.

Cthulhu had risen

Chapter 20
THE GREEN LAMA, UNBOUND

*W*ell, Tsarong," Dumont said as the S.S. Heki *approached the Brooklyn Navy Yards, the sun shining brightly on Manhattan's brick and glass mountains. He had forgotten how beautiful they could be, a reminder that people could still accomplish wonders. "We'll soon be landing in New York! I confess I have waited ten years for this!"*

Tsarong firmed his lips, unable to look Dumont in the eye. "Waiting and studying hard, Tulku!" he said without much emotion.

Dumont nodded. "But all that time I was studying, Tsarong, it was with the idea that someday I would return and teach America the peaceful ideas of the Dharma."

Tsarong placed a cordial hand on Dumont's shoulder. "A most worthy reason, my friend."

Dumont smiled somberly. "A most humble reason," he added softly.

The ship's horn blared. They had docked. For the first time in a decade, Jethro Dumont was home. Collecting their meager possessions, they exited their cabin into the sea of disembarking passengers.

"Mommy!" a little blonde girl cried pleasantly as she walked past them with two other children, tugging at her mother's skirt. "Mommy, look, a real *live Oriental man!"*

"Meredith!" the mother scolded. "That's very rude!" She turned to Dumont and Tsarong, smiling bashfully. "Sorry, she didn't mean anything by that. You know how children can be."

"No offense taken, young miss." Tsarong bowed his head warmly. "May your children always be filled with such wonder."

The mother's smile broadened with bewilderment. "Huh, yeah. Hopefully, right?" she said as she was pulled away.

"You'll get a lot of that," Dumont said as they made their way through the ship's hallways toward the gangplank. "Though most of it won't be so

innocent. They like to say New York's a melting pot, but discrimination and hatred still run rampant. It is worse in other parts of the country where men in white sheets slaughter their fellow man for the color of their skin."

"Perhaps it is an injustice you can correct, Tulku."

Dumont nodded. *"I hope so, Tsarong, though I don't think it will be an easy task. But, we will do our best to teach my countrymen, no matter how long it takes," he said as they disembarked.*

Ahead of them, the young mother struggled with her baggage as her three children continued to drag her forward, all three rattling off all the stories they were going to tell their friends once they returned to school. Dumont smiled faintly. The excitement of children; he had forgotten how intoxicating their laughter was, how much he missed it. Maybe, now that he was home, perhaps, one day—

"Outta the way!

A sweaty, gruff looking man in tweed pushed his way down the gangway, knocking past Jethro and Tsarong, before shoving aside the young mother and children. The mother shouted after him, but the man in tweed ignored her as he stumbled toward the dock holding his suitcases shoulder high in a vain effort to quicken his pace. As the man reached the dock, Dumont heard the once familiar sound of squealing tires as a car came speeding down the shipyard, knocking over luggage and machinery as it raced toward the ship.

"There's that dirty rat now!" Dumont heard the driver shout. "He did come on that ship! Let him have it!"

"No! No! They found me! How did they find me?!" the man in tweed screamed. He stumbled backwards up the gangplank as the car drove up. A machine gun appeared in the passenger window.

"Get down!" Dumont shouted, throwing himself over Tsarong and the young mother as the machine gun sang its song of death.

As they tumbled down, Tsarong heard something whisper by his ear, quickly followed by an odd, hollow thunk! *as something warm splattered across his face.*

"That got him! Step on it, Slug!" the shooter said as the car peeled away.

"Is everyone okay?!" Dumont said as he stood up, flecks of blood covering his white safari suit. He moved to help the woman back to her feet

when he saw the bullet hole in her temple, and the brain matter spilling out the other side. Dumont's hand jerked away in shock, his fingers shaking uncontrollably. The man in tweed lay on his back in a growing pool of blood, his eyes stared vacantly up into the sky, a black and red bullet hole between them. Then Dumont saw the three children, facedown on the ground.

"Tulku..." Tsarong breathed as Dumont stumbled over to the little girl's limp form, blood staining her golden locks. "They have killed the little ones!"

"What manner of men are these who make war upon children?" Dumont asked mournfully as he carefully cradled the girl's body in his arms, when he caught something in the corner of his eye. Shifting his gaze he saw the Jade Tablet glowing subtly in the sunlight, and Jethro Dumont at last realized his destiny.

Jethro was standing in a seamless white room. There was no singular source of light; it was as if he were in the center of a cold sun. He took a tentative step forward and realized he was barefoot. He felt he should be cold, but he was warm, content and at peace. He glanced down and found himself dressed in familiar green robes; the chest stained a sickening maroon, though he was at a loss as to how they had come to be like that. He had no shadow. He instinctually looked at his right hand and found a glowing red scar where the Jade Tablet had once been. He blinked. He didn't remember taking it off.

"*Tashi shog,* Tulku," a familiar voice said.

Jethro turned to find a being of pure green flames standing behind him, its face constantly shifting, always beautiful and serene, but never human. Even so, Jethro recognize her instantly.

"Hello, O Magga," Jethro said with a calm smile, bowing his head in reverence. "I was wondering when I would see you again."

Magga bowed her luminescent head. She held a lotus flower in her hand. "But now you see me as I truly am. Do you understand?"

"Yes. And no." He looked over Magga's glowing form, finally piecing together all the mysteries surrounding her. "Are you an angel?"

Magga smiled. "Oh, Jethro... After all your time in Tibet, after all your studies, you still cling to so many Western notions." She held up the lotus flower in her hand, which shimmered into a jewel. Jethro peered into the center of the gem and thought he could see the swirl of galaxies. "Once, I was Yeshe Dawa, though I have been given many names since, some remembered, some forgotten, some truer than others. I am a Bodhisattva, much like you, but I am not of your realm. You may consider me a guardian, a guide, and, as always, the Revealer of the Secret Paths."

"Is this Nirvana?" he asked, gazing over the white expanse.

"It is…" she hesitated, searching for the word, "a gateway, a bridge between worlds."

Jethro blinked, he could feel his memories slowly reform, like a fog burning up in the sun. His hand went unconsciously to his neck. "Heydrich."

Magga nodded.

"And where are Jean and the others?"

She tilted her head to the side, trying to read his expression. "They are still in R'lyeh. Cthulhu has risen."

Jethro's face fell. "Then I have failed. Heydrich has won," he said mournfully. He looked to Magga. "Was that truly my destiny? To bring about the rebirth of Cthulhu?"

Magga smiled and shook her head. "No. *Your* destiny is far greater."

"But what of the Tablets?"

"The Tablets give access to one of the greatest powers in the universe. When the Great Old Ones came to this world they thought they could pervert it and use it for their own purposes. And for a time they did. But they quickly came to realize that even *they* could not control the Tablets, going so far as to try and break the Third Tablet in hopes of finding a way to mitigate their power."

"That was how Prometheus and his kind first obtained it," Jethro said. "And how they were able to defeat the Great Old Ones."

Magga nodded. "The Fire from Olympus. The Tablets were the source of the Great Old Ones' power, as well as their downfall."

He glanced down at the scar on his right middle finger. The Jade Tablet was still there, just not in this realm, he could still feel its echo across the divide. "Nyarlathotep said that Tsarong knew this day would come," he said; this was not a question. "That he has been training me for this…"

"Nyarlathotep is the Father of Lies, but in this instance," Magga added mournfully, she had hoped to avoid this conversation, "he speaks the truth."

Jethro scowled, biting back his anger. "Why didn't Tsarong tell me? There was so much we could have done to prevent this."

"To know one's destiny is to void it. Tsarong knew, as I knew, that were you conscious of the path laid before you, you would do all you could to prevent it, allowing you to fall prey to those hoping to alter your decisions, leading, ultimately, to this world's destruction." She took a step toward Jethro as bright light appeared beside them. "But now, Tulku, it is time for you to make one final choice, between this life and the next."

Jethro looked toward the light, then at Magga. "I need to go back," he said simply.

Magga touched his face. "So brave. Even now, you turn down Nirvana for Earth."

"I can't leave her there."

She smiled sadly. "I always knew you two would work out."

Jethro smiled.

"Go, Tulku, back to one you love. Be prepared, for the final battle has only just begun," Magga said as the light began to fade. "And remember to thank Tsarong for stacking the deck."

"Om! Ma-ni Pad-me Hum!"

Heydrich's eyes went wide. "No," he whispered. He turned toward the voice to find the Green Lama forcing himself to his feet, the gaping hole in his neck healing before Heydrich's eyes. "No! No! No! It's not possible!" Heydrich screeched. "You're dead! You're dead!"

"Jean!" Ken screamed, tugging at her sleeve. "Jean, look!"

Jean struggled to stand. Her vision blurred with tears, she looked down at the Temple floor in amazement as the Green Lama stood.

"Jethro!" Her eyes shot to Ken. "We don't have much time!"

Flashing forward, the Green Lama grabbed Heydrich by the throat and lifted him off the ground. "I've already killed you once, Karl," the Green Lama said quietly; "hopefully *the Dharma* will forgive me for repeating the offense. *Om! Vajrasattva Hum!*" He raised his ringed hand to Heydrich's jaw and wordlessly unleashed a torrent of energy, disintegrating most of Heydrich's head in a tremendous flash. The Green Lama dropped the partially decapitated body, along with the Shard, into the abyss. Black ooze poured out from the wound as it tumbled down.

His eyes a luminescent green, the Green Lama turned to Nyarlathotep. The creature's face had completely shattered, revealing the obsidian horror beneath. "You have not won, Green Lama." The tongue-like cranium wagged as it spoke. "Like you, I had a card up *my* sleeve." It pointed a gnarled finger toward the balcony above them, where the Green Lama saw a possessed Vasili viciously attacking Caraway. "One to rise. Three to sleep. Unfortunately for you, the count is still in my favor."

The Green Lama grimaced angrily. He held his hands out, a ball of energy forming between them. "No matter the measure, Nyarlathotep, you shall not succeed."

"I believe there is a deity who would disagree with you," Nyarlathotep laughed, bowing slightly. "He is all yours, my Lord."

The Green Lama's robes rippled as the air shifted around him, the beating of tremendous wing drumming in his ears.

"I SEE YOU, JETHRO DUMONT," Cthulhu roared, its voice echoing into the Green Lama's very core. "I SEE YOU, GREEN LAMA."

"And I see you, Cthulhu," the Green Lama said as he turned to face the towering alien god. "*Om! Ma-ni Pad-me Hum!*" he shouted, letting loose a powerful beam of electricity, filling the temple with an explosion of green light.

Gottschalk grabbed at Gan's uniform, pleading, his mind no longer his own. "We have to stop them!" he howled, spit flying form his mouth. "We cannot let them defeat the great Cthulhu! The time of darkness is at hand!"

"No, sir," Gan said, "it is not." He pressed his Lüger against Gottschalk's stomach and fired two quick shots, dropping the Obergruppenführer to the ground. "Not if I have anything to say about it."

Gazing up at the balcony, Gan wiped the sweat off his brow with the back of his sleeve. It was time to face his fate.

"Ewetwjk gx lzw yjwwf dses uomt—ywl slgesf!" Vasili hissed, his Cheshire grin threatening to rip apart his face. His eyes were black as coal; inky tears ran down his cheeks as he clawed at Caraway's throat.

"Get off me!" Caraway growled, punching Vasili in the face. But the blows did nothing to deter him. Even when Caraway shattered Vasili's jaw, it only seemed to goad him on. Reaching for his pistol, Caraway hoped to incapacitate Vasili long enough to get him to put the stone Tablet in place, though it was doubtful a bullet would be enough to stop him. "I'm sorry, boy-o, I know it ain't you doin' this," he said as he shot Vasili in the thigh.

Vasili grunted in pain, but was undeterred. Attacking Caraway with renewed ferocity, he struck him with a powerful backhand. Caraway flew back, his pistol falling from his hand. Before Caraway could find his way to his feet, Vasili was on him again, pinning him the ground.

"Yog-Soggoth! Hast'r! Ph'nglui mglw'nafh Cthulhu R'lyeh wgah'nagl fhtagn," Vasili laughed, placing a hand on either side of Caraway's head.

Caraway screamed as his eyes pushed out against his skull as Vasili began to squeeze.

"Go! Go! Go!" Jean exclaimed as they tried to make their way toward the Third Tablet's shrine. Deep Ones began to pour in all around them, appearing out of every shadow.

"Where the hell are they coming from?" Ken shouted as he shot down two fish men.

"Doesn't really matter right now!" she said as she kicked out a Deep One's knees. Out of bullets, she had no option but to fight the creatures hand-to-hand. "Come on, this is just like the factory, just keep shootin' them 'til they stop! Just don't get bitten like last time!"

Ken glanced at her quizzically. "What factory? What are you talking about?" he asked, shooting another creature in the eye.

Jean's stomach twisted. "Just don't stop shooting!"

"YOU ARE NOTHING, GREEN LAMA!" Cthulhu shrieked telepathically.

The Green Lama screamed, clutching his head as Cthulhu's

metaphysical voice threatened to shatter his human mind. He felt knives slice beneath his skin and tear it away from his muscles, endured the torment of having every bone broken, swallowing hot coals, and experienced the agony of drowning all with the blink of an eye.

He plunged to the ground and was caught mid-air in Cthulhu's colossal hand. Bringing the Green Lama close to its tentacled face, the Great Old One laughed. "WE RULED THIS WORLD FOR A MILLENNIA, BILLIONS OF YEARS BEFORE YOUR KIND EVEN DARED CRAWL OUT FROM THE MUCK. YOU THINK YOU CAN WIELD THE POWER OF THE GODS? YOU ARE A BUG." It slammed the Green Lama into the side of the Temple, giant chunks of coral crashing down onto the assemblage below. "AND YOU ARE CRUSHED LIKE ONE," Cthulhu scoffed when the Green Lama didn't resurface.

Seconds later, a boulder flew up from the ground, hitting Cthulhu's red, green, and yellow eye. "*Om! Ma-ni Pad-me Hum!*" The Green Lama burst out from the rubble, his fists and eyes glowing brightly from within. He struck Cthulhu's bulbous head with a tremendous right hook, sending the Great Old One sprawling back. Cthulhu spread his wings and soared up toward the high ceiling, the Green Lama followed close behind. Shadows overtook them and Cthulhu disappeared.

"WHAT DO YOU AIM TO ACHIEVE?" Cthulhu asked telepathically, hidden within the darkness. "DO YOU TRULY BELIEVE YOU CAN DEFEAT A GOD?"

"You are no god!" the Green Lama shouted back. He spun around, searching, unable to find his nemesis.

"SO CERTAIN ARE YOU?" The Great Old One's voice echoed in the Green Lama's mind. "BUT HOW CAN A MORTAL TRULY UNDERSTAND THAT WHICH IS GREATER THAN HIM?"

The Green Lama gritted his teeth in anger. "I may be mortal, Cthulhu, but I fight for a force far greater than you."

"THEN PROVE IT, HUMAN!" Cthulhu roared, launching out of the shadows.

Blinding pain echoed through Caraway's skull. Grabbing Vasili's wrists, he tried to pry himself free. "Please, Vasili," Caraway groaned, struggling not to lose consciousness. "It's John… Fight… This…"

CRACK!

Vasili's grip slackened.

Prying open his eyes, Caraway watched Vasili topple unconscious onto the ground to reveal Gan standing over them, the stone Tablet in hand.

"Gan?!"

"Didn't I tell you, John?" Gan said with a broad smile. "When the time came, we would be fighting for the same s—" There was a soft *pop* of gunfire and a small spot of blood began to form in the center of Gan's chest. He glanced down, baffled. "Oh," he said quietly.

"NO!!!" Caraway screamed as he ran toward his wounded friend.

Gan slowly turned to find a bruised Rick Masters holding up a smoking pistol. "Goddamn Nazi," Rick cursed.

Gan looked back at Caraway, his eyes wide in shock. The two men stared at each other before Gan let out a bloody cough and his knees buckled.

"Aw, hell. Aw, hell," Caraway moaned as he caught the Oberführer in his arms.

Gan gripped at Caraway's collar, his eyes glassy. "My family!" he croaked. "John. My family. You have to get them—You have to get them out of Germany."

"No, no, no," Caraway said, shaking his head. "Don't you worry, boy-o, you're gonna see them real soon—"

Gan pulled him closer. "John, listen to me. There is something terrible… Something *terrible* is about to happen in Germany. You have to—You *have* to get them *out*!"

"I..." Caraway stuttered, noticing the innate fear in Gan's eyes. "Okay. Okay."

"Promise me!" Gan hissed, forcefully tugging at Caraway's collar.

"I promise! I'll get your family out of Germany," he said with a nod. "I promise you."

Gan's voice grew weaker. "I am sorry—sorry, John, that I couldn't save the girl…"

Caraway grimaced, but remained silent.

"You must believe me… Had I been able, I would have—"

"You know, you never told me how you stopped that elephant," Caraway said quietly.

Gan let out a wheezing laugh and gave him a waning smile. "Because

I knew he would."

"That's not much of an answer, Gan," Caraway said with a sad laugh.

Gan shook his head, coughing while he weakly laughed. "'Gan.' That is… not… That's not my name," he struggled to say. "Hahn. My name. It's really Hahn."

"Hahn," Caraway repeated.

"I'm dying, John. Call me Heinrich."

"Heinwreck," Caraway struggled, fighting back tears.

Gan let out another coughing laugh. "*Amerikaner*… Harry. Just call me Harry."

"Harry," Caraway said with a somber smile. "Harry Hahn."

Gan's eyes drooped closed. "*Zu Befehl, Herr Leutnant…*"

And then he was gone.

The Deep Ones were closing in, surrounding Jean and Ken on all sides and pinning them against the wall. Jean had given up trying to count them, having lost track at thirty. She and Ken were standing back-to-back, trading off the last remaining gun, shooting any Deep One that dared approach.

"So, you're telling me you went to a *possible* future, met a *possible* future version of myself, and then watched him die," Ken complained as he fired at an approaching Deep One. "When were you going to tell me about this?"

"I figured it was better you didn't know," she admitted, taking the gun from him and shooting down another Deep One. "Besides, even if I had, would you have even believed me?"

Ken scowled in silent admission. Even now, with all the nightmares around them, it seem implausible. "I still reserve the right to mad be at you," he said eventually. Jean passed over the pistol and he immediately began to reload. "We're down to two."

"We've still got the grenade," she replied. She grabbed back the gun and took out another Deep One, turning one of its bulbous eyes concave. "And, fine, be mad at me, but this is the *worst* time for us to be discussing it!"

"Like we're going to get another?" Ken scoffed, glancing back at her. "Face it, Red, this is a one way trip."

Jean's heart raced, she had heard that before. "Let's try not to think that way."

"I'll do my best," Ken mused. He looked out at the crowd of creatures encircling them. "Hey, you ever go skeet shooting out in Montana?" he asked, a tongue pressed thoughtfully against his cheek.

"Couple of times, yeah," she replied, a little confused.

Ken reached into her satchel and brought out the grenade.

Jean cocked an eyebrow, instantly understanding. "Oh, this should be fun."

"Come on, let's end this," he said with a smile, tossing the grenade into the air.

Tentacles shot out and wound around him, squeezing the Green Lama's frame until his insides threatened to burst out. Cthulhu towered over him, its eyes blazing with unparalleled anger.

"DO YOU REALLY THINK YOU CAN STOP ME?" its voice screamed in the Green Lama's mind. "I HAVE RIPPED GODS IN HALF, IMPLODED SUNS, EXTINGUISHED GALAXIES WITH THE WAVE OF MY HAND. I FACED THE ARMIES OF EONS, THE CONQUERORS OF AGES, AND I HAVE DESTROYED THEM ALL!"

"But you've never faced me!" the Green Lama roared. He grabbed the tentacles wrapped around his arms and ripped them off Cthulhu's face, putrid black blood spilling out of the disembodied appendages.

Cthulhu howled in pain, unleashing a torrent of psychic energy that flooded the Green Lama's thoughts. Images poured before his mind's eye, horrible images of death and destruction, wars and famine; thousands of galaxies filled with creatures of both unimaginable beauty and maddening horror. Visions of nameless nightmares exploded behind his eyes. He witnessed the death of millions at the hands of Old Ones, sliced open neck to groin, their innards torn out with slow, diligent care. He watched the world burn with madness, saw the sea evaporate and fire rain from the sky. But, the Green Lama could also see there was something Cthulhu was hiding, a blinding green light from beyond, the light that was burning within him, burning within Jean and Vasili.

An explosion tore through the left balcony, sending chunks of coral and dismembered body parts raining down upon them. Something struck the Green Lama's head. Pain ripped through his body as he and Cthulhu fell to the ground.

"*Om! Ma-ni Pad-me Hum!*" he gasped. Looking up toward the source of the explosion he saw Jean and Ken standing by a gaping hole in the balcony. "Jean!" he shouted with elation.

"We'll chat later, *Smug*," Jean called down to him. "Right now, we've gotta save the world!"

A grin spread across the Green Lama's face as he watched her and Ken hop over the crater toward the far end of the mezzanine. Turning toward the wounded Cthulhu, the Green Lama's hands glowed with energy.

"Let's finish this."

The strangest thing about the sanctum was how *normal* it looked, like something out of a Roman history book. It was only the edges of the pillared shrine glowing in the dimly lit room that hinted at its otherworldliness. Intricate designs covered the coral, reminding Caraway of the images that laced the illuminated Bibles his preacher grandfather used to carry around, back when everything was fire and brimstone and the thought of alien gods something kept to penny dreadfuls. At the center of the shrine was a small rectangular gap in the stone—almost as if the Tablet had been cut directly from it.

"Creepy," Rick whispered as he and Caraway carried Vasili in. They could still hear the battle raging outside the partially enclosed area. The walls rattled, threatening to crack. Flashes of lights and silhouettes danced before a small window overlooking the Temple floor.

"Because *that's* the creepiest thing we've seen so far," Caraway said, biting. He looked to Vasili. "Come on, boy-o," he begged, slapping their unconscious passenger across the face. "Wake up."

"You sure you really wanna do that?" Rick asked nervously, raising his pistol. "Last time he tried to kill us both and tossed me around like a rag doll."

Caraway failed to hide his scowl. "Gonna be honest with you, Rick, you're not my favorite person at the moment, so keep your comments to yourself."

"Hey, I saved your life," Rick protested.

"Yeah, we'll *chat* about that later, but right now we need to get Vasili to put the Tablet in place or we're screwed." He looked to Vasili. "Open your eyes, buddy, come on…"

"Why him?" Rick asked, scratching the back of his head. "I've never really been clear on that."

"He's a scion, or something. He was chosen for this."

"Like that makes a lotta sense," Rick scoffed. He took out the Second Tablet from the satchel and walked toward the shrine. "Look, there ain't nothing to it, it's just like makin' love," he said raising the Tablet to the cut. "You put your thing into the hole and—" A small electric explosion popped out of the shrine throwing Rick and the Tablet several feet back.

"You all right?" Caraway asked in muted concern as Rick stumbled to his feet.

"Uh," Rick shakily replied, his steaming hair standing on end. "Yeah. I think. Feels like I stuck my tongue in an electrical socket."

"None but a scion can place the Tablet," they heard Vasili say.

Caraway looked down to Vasili, the Greek's eyes had returned to normal. "You with us again, Vasili?"

"Yes. I am now." Vasili nodded slowly. His expression downcast, he added, "I remember everything. It is all painfully clear now."

"What is?" Caraway asked nervously.

An angry scowl pierced Vasili's face. "It was Nyarlathotep. All of it, hiding in plain sight for so long. Playing me, and so many others, like a puppet on a string. He made me…" he trailed off, tears streaming down his cheeks. "My poor Sotiria."

Caraway looked away, blinking away his own tears.

"I used to dream he was chasing me," Vasili continued. He stood up, favoring his unwounded leg. "Had I only known the nightmares were real, perhaps then I would have tried to wake up and seen what was right in front of me. But I am awake now." He looked over to the Jade Tablet on the ground beside Rick. Lifting it up, he weighed it in his hands. Hobbling over toward the shrine, he raised the Tablet to the gap in the stone. "Let us end this."

"Whoa," Ken breathed as they approached the glowing crystalline shrine, a short stanchion in the center. Outside the partially enclosed sanctum they could still hear the sounds of battle. "That's... that's a 'whoa.'" He ran a hand over it, feeling for the seams in the crystal. He looked over at Jean. "My God, Red. This whole thing is one giant crystal."

"It's a real beauty," Jean said, uninterested as she approached the stanchion. Tracing her fingers over the top of the platform, she detected the faint hints of carvings in the crystal—the Tablet had been cut from here. Removing the Third Tablet from her satchel she raised it over the stanchion, and closed her eyes. "Here goes nothing..."

She held her breath and placed the crystalline Tablet down, turning it ever so slightly to fit perfectly with the cut. Her heart pounded in her throat. Jean risked opening her eyes and looked down at the crystalline egg. "Nothing happened."

Ken furrowed his brow. "Wait, what about the blood sacrifice?"

Nyarlathotep fell back into the panicked crowd. Everything was going wrong. The prophecies, the thousands of years of waiting, it was all being upended so quickly. He felt his control over Vasili shatter, could sense the Tablets being set in place, and most horrifically, watched as his god was struck again by the Green Lama—a human—green lightning filling the chamber.

No, he decided, this will not end well. No matter what had been prophesied, no matter the planning, the tides of fate were drifting away from them, and he refused to be pulled out to sea. Backing into the shadows, Nyarlathotep drew open a doorway and disappeared into the darkness.

"What happened?" Caraway asked, when nothing did.

Vasili looked over the silent stone. "The blood sacrifice," he murmured. Reaching down, he pressed his fingers deep into his bullet wound, coating them with blood. "Ο Χριστός ο Θεός μας..." he began to pray as he smeared his blood along the stone Tablet, "ποιοι σε αυτό όλος-τέλειο και τη γιορτή αποταμίευσης, είναι ευγενικά ευτυχείς να αποδεχθούν τις εξευμενιστικές προσευχές για εκείνους που φυλακίζονται στην κόλαση..."

There was the soft sound of stone scratching against stone as the Tablet, glowing with green light, *grew* into the surrounding shrine, illuminating the room. Falling to his knees, Vasili closed his eyes and smiled mournfully. "Rest in peace, my love."

Jean winced as she pressed the palm of her hand against the sharp edge of the crystal Tablet's crack, drawing blood. "So long, Cthulhu," she whispered as the blood dripped down over the intricate engravings. A sound like falling glass reverberated up as the Tablet's base reattached itself to the crystal stanchion, the already glowing shrine now becoming a blinding source of emerald light.

Ken thrust his hands into the air triumphantly. "Yes!"

Jean smiled and looked out on the Temple floor. "Your turn, Tulku."

Avoiding another powerful blast of energy from the Green Lama, Cthulhu flew up into the air, its massive wings flapping to keep it afloat. Black blood oozed over his scaly grey-green body in long streams. All around there were the screams of a thousand inhuman creatures crying out as their god bled.

"YOU WILL NOT DEFEAT ME, DUMONT!" it said defiantly.

The Green Lama replied with a small smile, blood dripping down his chin. Wiping it away with the back of his hand, the crimson fluid ran over the Jade Tablet, seeping into the threads.

"OM! MA-NI PAD-ME HUM!" he shouted, racing toward the peninsula's edge. He pressed his hand into the imprint and the mound erupted with light. At that moment, two beams of energy shot out from both ends of the horseshoe balcony, striking the center Tablet. The Green Lama screamed as the Temple filled with light. Small bolts of electricity ignited off the Tablet and began racing up his arm, illuminating his body from within. His eyes rolled back in his head as he rose into the air, energy seething through him.

For a moment he could see through the walls of the world, through the windows of time. He saw the darkness ahead—a bloody triangle within a circle—the victories and the defeats. He looked into the many universes that sat alongside his and understood, for a brief instant, that the Tablets were more than a simple gateway to power—upon them rested the very bonds of this and all realties. There were other, more powerful objects throughout the galaxy, but without the Tablets, all life would cease to exist. And for this instance, for this one moment, all the power in all the universes, in all the realms, was flowing through him.

He was the Scion. He was the Green Lama.

He opened his eyes and all was Jade.

Chapter 21
THE SINKING CITY

A deafening explosion threw Jean and Ken to the floor. The ground began to vibrate, threatening to crack. Small chunks of coral began to rain down from the ceiling. Below, a thousand screams echoed up like unending death.

Jean looked out onto the Temple floor. Her jaw dropped as her eyes fell upon the floating emerald man that had been the Green Lama. Cthulhu screamed, a sound of unparalleled pain that radiated out through her mind. Clutching her head, she watched as the winged monstrosity fell away from the Green Lama's impenetrable light, back into the darkness, back to his eternal sleep. The Green Lama wasn't killing Cthulhu, Jean realized. Cthulhu was more than simple flesh and blood; he was something *between* this realm and the next. Nothing, not even the Green Lama, could ever destroy him.

The Nazis and monsters on the Temple floor did not fare as well as their tentacled god, however; they were all evaporated by the Green Lama's power in an instant.

"Holy Christ!" Ken exclaimed, falling over himself as he tried to stand after another tremor. "What in God's name is happening?"

Jean pried her gaze away from the Green Lama's emerald form. "The city is sinking."

"Aw, crap," Caraway growled as a chunk of the ceiling collapsed beside them. "This can't be good."

"It never gets easy, does it?" Rick mused.

"Nope, never does," Caraway agreed. "Come on, Vasili, time to make our exit."

"Leave me," Vasili said, shaking his head. "There is nothing left for me. Let me die here."

Shaking his head, Caraway forced Vasili to his feet. "Not an option, buddy. Like it or not, you're coming with us."

"John!" Jean exclaimed when they met Caraway and the others at the end of the balcony. "You're all right!" She caught sight of Vasili's wounded leg. "Jesus, is he okay?"

"He's fine," Rick indignantly answered for him.

"He shot me," Vasili replied, indicating Caraway.

"*After* he knocked me out," Rick added angrily.

Caraway sighed. "It's not a fun story to tell."

The walls rumbled and hairline cracks began to spread across the floor.

"We'll do story time later," Ken said, trying to hide the panic in his voice. "Right now, let's get the hell out of here before we go Atlantis."

Jean nodded in agreement. "Follow me."

Wading through the rising water, they made their way through the city's curving streets following Jean's lead. All around them, buildings cracked and shattered, massive chunks of coral tumbling down.

"How much further?" Rick shouted over the destruction.

"We're almost there," Jean called back. "Just don't stop moving!"

As they neared the gates, a low rumble reverberated around them and the floor broke open beneath Jean's feet. Screaming, she slid down the coral toward the pit below when someone caught her by the hand. Gazing up at her savior, she saw Vasili's grim face looking back, water pouring down around him.

"Do not let go, Miss Farrell," he said calmly. "It is a very big drop."

She gave him a panicked nod. "Wasn't really planning on it," she said as Ken and Caraway appeared at Vasili's sides, grabbing her other arm.

"Hang on there, girl. We got you," Caraway grunted as they began to pull her up.

"Where do we go now?" Ken asked once Jean was safe, looking over the small canyon standing between them and their escape.

Rick silently looked over the crater, measuring the distance in his head.

"We jump."

"Okay, we're all doin' this at once," Rick reminded them as they stepped back from the edge of the crater, their arms laced together. The water was beginning to rise faster, the buildings crumbling in rapid succession. "No hesitating, we only got one shot at this."

"You gonna be all right to jump, Vasili?" Ken asked, indicating the bleeding bullet wound.

"I will be fine," he replied, his expression like stone.

"*Om! Ma-ni Pad-me Hum!*" Jean whispered.

Caraway gave her a sidelong glance. "*Om! Ma-ni Pad-me Hum!*" he softly repeated with a small nod.

"On three." Rick licked his lips. He was taking a vacation after this he had decided. "One, two… Three!"

The sunlight was blinding, drawing harsh shadows along the narrow coral platform outside the gates of R'lyeh. Explosions sounded from within and the coral city began to list and tilt as it slid back into the ocean.

"How the hell are we gonna get off this rock?" Caraway shouted as they ran up the platform's rapidly increasing incline.

"We'll take the U-boat!" Jean said, pointing at the silent submarine.

Caraway looked to Rick. "You think you can drive that thing?"

"Do we have a choice?" he replied with a shrug.

"Look!" Ken exclaimed. "The gates are closing!"

Jean stopped short, her heart hammering as she watched the black gates slowly close, a soft green glow peeking through. "What about Jethro?" she breathed.

"Emerald boy can take care of himself, Jean," Caraway growled, unsure if he believed it himself. He grabbed her by the arm and pulled her toward the U-boat. "We don't get off the rock now, we're gonna have to swim home."

"Don't worry about him," Ken said calmly. "He's *the Green Lama*."

But even then, her throat dry with fear, Jean couldn't remove her gaze from the gates, hoping against hope she would see the man she loved walk through before it was too late, and knowing that she wouldn't.

"Everything's in German!" Rick complained as he sat down at the U-boat's controls.

"Surprise, surprise," Caraway said sardonically, grabbing the seat beside Rick. "Don't worry. Next time we steal a submarine I'll make sure to get you an American one."

"You know, I'm not sure what worries me more, John," Rick said as he brought the engines to life. "The fact that you just said you'd steal an American submarine, or that I fully believe it will actually happen."

Jean tightened the impromptu tourniquet around Vasili's leg. "You lost a lot of blood, but I think you're going to be fine. Ken, look after him."

"Wait, where are you going?"

"Up," she replied as she climbed the ladder out to the hull.

Jean stood on the bow of the submarine, her arms wrapped around her body as she watched R'lyeh collapse in on itself and slowly descend into the water. Her gaze unwavering, she didn't see Ken climb out onto the hull and walk up beside her; didn't respond when he put a comforting hand on her shoulder.

Ken softly cleared his throat. "Jean, you should come back—"

"He isn't dead," she said sharply. Jethro—the Green Lama couldn't, wouldn't die. She refused to even consider the possibility. She had just seen him survive being stabbed in the throat, surely he could survive something as simple as a sinking city.

Ken firmed his lips and nodded slowly as he turned back toward the conning tower.

"Look over there!" Jean cried.

Ken spun around to see a glowing green ball of light shoot out from the remains of R'lyeh into the sky. The luminescent orb circled through the sky before turning toward them. Shielding his eyes from the light, Ken watched as the orb approached the U-boat, quickly taking on a human form.

"*Tashi shog*, Ne-tso-hbum!'"" the Green Lama said jovially as he floated down before them, the light dissipating as his feet touched the hull. "Greetings to you as well, Mr. Clayton."

A broad smile spread across Jean's face as she stepped toward him. "You had us worried there for a second, *Smug*. Not me, though," she added defiantly. "Ken, he was worried sick."

Ken scoffed at that, biting back a smile.

The Green Lama removed his hood, revealing the smiling face of Jethro Dumont. "My apologies. I never meant to worry you," he said to Jean.

Tears rolled down her cheeks as she looked into his blue-grey eyes. She placed her hands on his chest, tiny electric shocks tingling her fingertips. "Cthulhu?" she asked quietly.

Jethro lovingly touched her face, wiping away her tears with his thumb. "Gone. For now. The Tablets as well."

She closed her eyes in relief. "Good," she whispered.

"Hate to break you two lovebirds up," Ken said, stepping in. "But we better get inside before Rick and Caraway decide they're Captain Nemo."

Hours passed. Jethro, Jean, Ken, Caraway, Rick, and Vasili all stood in silence in the dimly lit, cramped space of the U-boat's bridge as they headed toward San Antonio, Chile.

Staring at the ground, Caraway was the first to speak up. "Who was Gan, really?" he asked.

"A member of the Jewish Underground," Jethro replied. "A double agent working within the Nazi Party in hopes of stopping Hitler."

Rick sank into his chair, crestfallen. "I didn't know," he whispered, nervously running his hands through his hair. "God help me, I didn't know…"

Caraway angrily kicked the side of the hull. "That stupid bastard! He should've told me."

"And if he had, would you've believed him?" Jethro asked.

Caraway laughed mournfully. "Probably not. Guess that explains a lot, though…" He hesitantly looked up at Jethro. "He said there was something bad coming to Germany…"

"Mass murder. A holocaust," Jethro said bitterly. "Hitler aims to wipe the Jews from the face of the Earth."

"That's insane," Caraway said in disbelief.

"Yes, it is," Jethro agreed.

Caraway rubbed his mustache. "Then I guess I'm going to Germany," he decided.

"I know some people in San Antonio," Rick offered. "They can get you into Germany while I get everyone else back to the States."

Jethro gave Rick a somber smile of thanks and then looked to Vasili. "What about you? Do you want to go back to Kamariotissa?"

Vasili shook his head, his face pale. "No. I… It would be too much. My whole life I have been a monster's puppet, but now I am without strings…"

"You're always welcome to come back to the States with us," Ken volunteered.

"Why? I would no more belong there than I do in Kamariotissa."

"Perhaps," Jethro allowed. "But I believe there is a man you should meet…"

The sun was rising as they approached San Antonio. Jean and Jethro once again stood on the submarine's hull, their arms wrapped around each other.

"Do you know when I fell for you?" he asked. "Havana, when you saved Ken and I from Zamora."

Jean laughed softly. "I was just looking for a mystery is all."

"And you found me."

"Ain't that the truth?" she breathed. "Tell me, Mr. Dumont," Jean said as she leaned her forehead against his. "I've heard tell that lamas are celibate. Any truth to that?"

Jethro smiled. "Well, in Tibetan Buddhism there are two main sects: the Gelugpas, or Yellow Hats, who are celibate, and the Nyingmapas, or Red Hats, who are not." He bit his lip as he pulled her closer. "And I wear no yellow hat."

Jean chuckled at that, her heart racing.

"There's an old proverb," Jethro said quietly, his voice just barely above a whisper, "that 'the man in love has eyes only in his heart.'"

"Yeah? And what do they see?"

"They only see you."

As they kissed neither chose to mention that the Jade Tablet, the rainbow ring of hair that had been bonded to his finger for more than a decade, had disappeared.

Epilogue
THE DARKNESS AHEAD

The soft roar of midtown traffic echoed up to the Park Avenue apartment, filling the massive study. Hundreds of thousands of books lined the walls, though if you were to ask their owner if he had read any of them he would say that reading was his *father's* hobby, when in fact he had read them all—and several thousand more. A small statue of the Buddha sat at the far end of the room, surrounded by a small group of butter candles, their light giving the idol an unearthly quality.

In the center of the room, Jethro Dumont and Geshe Tsarong sat cross-legged across from each other, the silence between them louder than the sounds of the city.

Tsarong sighed as he laced his fingers together. "Well… I suppose we have a lot to talk about, don't we, Tulku?"

"Yes," Jethro replied somberly. "I suppose we do."

"Are you sure about this?" Jean asked as they approached the idling plane's gangway, passengers streaming by.

"Yeah," Ken said with a nod, moving his heavy suitcase to the other hand. "I need a vacation from all this… *hero* stuff. My agent says they're casting the *Wizard of Oz*, of all things, and they want me to try out for the Tin Man. Or the Scarecrow. I can't remember which. Besides… you two need your space."

Jean smiled, touching his cheek. "Aw, Ken…"

He waved this away. "No, no. As much as I would *love* to sit around and watch you two necking, I'm just no good at being a third wheel."

"You better write," she said, firmly tapping his chest.

"Now, I can't promise that!" he said nonchalantly. "What with all the parties… and women."

Jean burst out laughing. "Yeah, like I'd believe *that*."

Ken laughed with her. "What about you, what are you gonna do?"

She shrugged. "I don't know… What do you do after you save the world?"

Arkham, Massachusetts sat just north of Salem and just west of the small port town of Innsmouth. The city was laid out like grid work, sliced in half by the Miskatonic River and the Boston & Maine Railroad. Between Church and College streets sat Miskatonic University, once a center of culture in New England, now known solely for its specialization in the occult. A small, rundown house sat at the corner of Pickman and Parsonage, the drawn windows and black door giving the house the appearance of a man screaming. Despite this, the tall, bearded traveler limped up to the entrance and knocked. Several moments passed before a gentleman, leaning heavily on a wooden cane, answered the door. He appeared to be in no more than his early forties, but his hair was shocked white.

"Excuse me…" the bearded traveler began, his accent untraceable. "Are you Professor Randolph Carter?"

The older gentleman tilted his head. "I am," he replied, his voice strong yet quivery. "And you are, my good man?"

The bearded traveler took off his cap. "My name is Vasili…" he introduced himself apprehensively. "I think we have a mutual… *acquaintance*."

Professor Carter narrowed his eyes as he silently scrutinized his disheveled visitor. His face slackened as the truth dawned on him. "Nyarlathotep."

Vasili nodded silently.

"A name I hoped to never hear again," Professor Carter said mournfully. "But then again… Zkauba *did* warn me." He placed an arm around Vasili's shoulders. "Come inside, my friend. We have much to discuss."

The beer hall in Berlin smelt of tobacco and liquor. A dank mist seemed to hover in the air as the uniformed patrons enjoyed their thunderous celebration. They fell suddenly silent when the stranger burst in, the twin pistols at his waist reminding most of the cowboys of American serials. The stranger silently walked over to the bar, mindful of the hundreds of eyes following. Sitting down, he waved the bartender over.

"*Was darf es sein?*" the bartender asked.

The stranger leaned forward. "I'm looking for a family," he said in English. "A Jewish family, name of Hahn."

The bartender let out an angry laugh before spitting a wad of phlegm on the stranger's shirt. "We do not like *Jüden* here," he said in English, loud enough so that the other patrons could hear.

The stranger grinned with menace. "I was hoping you'd say something like that," he said, swiftly grabbing the bartender by the hair and slamming his head against the bar. As the drunken Nazi stormtroopers closed in, Caraway drew his pistols and began to open fire.

They spotted the bodies halfway between New Zealand and Chile, scattered across the ocean like toys after Christmas. Smoking his Lucky Strikes as they brought the first of them aboard the *U.S.S. North Carolina*, Dr. Franklin Murdoch watched as they laid them across the deck, three hundred and sixty five *pieces* of dead Nazis, as many days in a year.

"That's a lotta dead Nazis," Crewman Elisha Pond said, wiping his brow with the bottom of his shirt.

Murdoch nodded as he took a drag. "Tell me about it," he said in a cloud of smoke. "Lot of dead Nazis and a *long* way away from the Fatherland."

"Whaddya think brought 'em out here, Doc?" Pond asked as Murdoch handed him a cigarette.

Murdoch closed his eyes and tilted his head toward the sun, soaking in the warmth. "My guess, Pond? They weren't out for a swim."

"Hey, Doc!" Crewman Reynolds shouted up to him, a robed torso at his feet. "Hey, Doc! You gotta take a look at this one!"

"Jeez-us!" Pond exclaimed as he and Murdoch ran up to the mutilated remains. "Look at his head! Looks like half 'is skull was blown off!"

Murdoch began to kneel down beside the torso, tentatively placing a hand on the chest when he quickly jumped back.

"What is it?" Pond asked.

Murdoch's eyebrows pinched together but he didn't reply. Looking over the torso, he noticed an oil-like ooze dripping out from the shattered skull. Rummaging through his pockets, he brought out a small pencil and dipped it into the goo.

"What the hell is that stuff?" Reynolds asked as Murdoch watched the black ooze move across his pencil.

Pond leaned in closer, his brow furrowed in thought. "Have you ever seen anything like this, Doc?" his voice momentarily taking on a slightly more educated accent.

Murdoch shook his head. "No, Pond, I can't say I have."

"What do you think it is?"

"I don't know," he said, his knees popping as he stood. "Wrap him up and take him down below. Try and make sure you put him in something waterproof, if you can. Don't want this stuff dripping all over the place. When we get back to New York I'll do an autopsy, see what's going on here."

"Will do, Doc," the crewmen said in tandem.

As Murdoch watched them slide the carcass into the body bag, he silently wondered if he had really felt a heartbeat.

The End

THE GREEN LAMA CHRONOLOGY
Bold indicates Moonstone Publication

1923 – 1933
- "The Case of the Final Column" by Adam Lance Garcia (Flashbacks)
- *The Green Lama: Unbound* **by Adam Lance Garcia (Flashbacks)**

1935
- **The Green Lama / Black Bat: "Homecoming" by Adam Lance Garcia**
- **The Green Lama / Secret Agent X-11: "Eye of the Beholder" by Adam Lance Garcia**
- "Case of the Crimson Hand" by Kendell Foster Crossen
- "Croesus of Murder" by Kendell Foster Crossen

1936
- "Babies for Sale" by Kendell Foster Crossen
- "Wave of Death" by Kendell Foster Crossen

1937
- "The Man Who Wasn't There" by Kendell Foster Crossen
- "Death's Head Face" by Kendell Foster Crossen

1938
- *The Green Lama: Horror in Clay* **by Adam Lance Garcia**
- "The Case of the Clown Who Laughed" by Kendell Foster Crossen
- "The Case of the Invisible Enemy" by Kendell Foster Crossen
- "The Case of the Mad Magi" by Kendell Foster Crossen
- "The Case of the Vanishing Ships" by Kendell Foster Crossen
- "The Case of the Fugitive Fingerprints" by Kendell Foster Crossen
- *The Green Lama: Scions* **by Adam Lance Garcia**
- "The Case of the Crooked Cane" by Kendell Foster Crossen
- "The Case of the Hollywood Ghost" by Kendell Foster Crossen

1939

- "The Case of the Beardless Corpse" by Kendell Foster Crossen
- "The Case of the Final Column" by Adam Lance Garcia (Altus Press)
- *The Green Lama: Unbound* by Adam Lance Garcia
- The Green Lama: "Dæmon's Kiss" by Adam Lance Garcia
- *The Green Lama: Crimson Circle* by Adam Lance Garcia

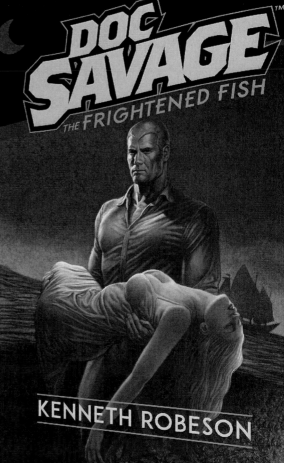